John Deane of Nottingham
Historic Adventures by Land and Sea

by

William Henry Giles Kingston

Double 9
BOOKS

John Deane of Nottingham
Historic Adventures by Land and Sea
by William Henry Giles Kingston

ISBN: 978-93-62764-46-1

Published by

DOUBLE 9 BOOKS

2/13-B, Ansari Road
Daryaganj, New Delhi – 110002
info@double9books.com
www.double9books.com
Tel. 011-40042856

ABOUT THE AUTHOR

William Henry Giles Kingston, also known as W. H. G. Kingston, was an English writer of boys' adventure stories. William Henry Giles Kingston was born in Harley Street, London, on February 28, 1814. He was Lucy Henry Kingston's eldest son, and he married Frances Sophia Rooke, the daughter of Sir Giles Rooke, a Court of Common Pleas Judge. Kingston's paternal grandfather, John Kingston (1736-1820), was a Member of Parliament who fought for the abolition of slavery while owning a plantation in Demerara. His father Lucy established a wine business in Oporto, and Kingston spent several years there, making regular trips to England and establishing a lifelong love of the water. He attended Trinity College, Cambridge, and then joined his father's wine business, but he quickly developed a passion for writing. His newspaper writings about Portugal were translated into Portuguese, and he aided in the signing of the commercial pact with Portugal in 1842, when Donna Maria da Gloria bestowed upon him an order of Portuguese knighthood and a pension. His debut novel, The Circassian Chief, was released in 1844. While still living in Oporto, he published The Prime Minister, a historical book partially based on the life of Sebastiao Jose de Carvalho e Melo, 1st Marquis of Pombal, and Lusitanian Sketches, a travelogue of Portugal.

CONTENTS

Preface

John Deane was a real person, and I hope that the readers of this my book about him will be as much pleased with it as I was with the history of his adventures, placed in my hands by a friend who long resided at Nottingham. He was born at that town A.D. 1679. Though of gentle parentage, in his early days he followed the occupation of a drover. He then went to sea, and became a Captain in the Navy; after that he was a Merchant Adventurer. He next took service under Peter the Great, and commanded a Russian ship-of-war. On leaving Russia, he obtained the post of British Consul at Ostend, held by him for many years. Returning home, he was made a Burgess of his native town, and took up his abode at the neighbouring village of Wilford, where, in 1760, he died. In the quiet churchyard of that sweet spot, his tomb and that of his beloved wife Elizabeth are to be seen:—

"His age, fourscore years and one."

"After life's fitful fever, he sleeps well."

The Author.

Chapter One
Mr Harwood and Alethea in Sherwood Forest, and Jack Deane's First Adventure

Romantic Sherwood! Its pristine glories since the days when bold Robin Hood and his merrie men held sway within its borders, and levied taxes from the passers-by, had sadly dwindled even in the year 1696, when our history commences. The woodman's axe had been busy and the plough had gone over the land, and mansions and homesteads had arisen where once flourished the monarchs of the forest, and the huntsman's horn had been wont to sound amid sequestered glades; still many a wide stretch of woodland and moorland remained, over which the fallow deer roamed at freedom, and rows of far-spreading trees overhung various by-paths green and narrow winding in all directions, and shaded the king's highway which ran north to York and south to the ancient and pleasant town of Nottingham. And there were likewise majestic avenues leading to the abodes of nobles and squires, and thick copses and scattered groves, above which rose the hoary giants of ancient days; and by the borders of the streams and rivulets which find their way into the Trent numberless trees had been allowed to stand. Wide strips also of grass-land were to be found running even with the road or between different estates, extending sometimes in an unbroken line for several miles together, with oaks and elms and beeches stretching out their umbrageous branches to meet from either side, and preserving by their shade the soft velvet of the turf even during the heats of summer.

Thus the old forest trees, if marshalled in close order, would have formed a wood of no inconsiderable magnitude.

The noon-day sun of the warm summer was shining down on the branches of the wide-spreading trees shading a long woodland glade, such as has been described running from the north towards Nottingham, the walls of whose siege-battered castle could be seen in the far distance, where on a slight eminence the trees opening out afforded a momentary glance of the country in front.

Just at that spot a gentleman of middle age, mounted on a strong, active horse, accompanied by a young lady on a graceful palfrey, was riding at a leisurely pace along the glade in the direction of the town. The gold lace with which his long, loose riding-coat was trimmed, his embroidered waistcoat, the gold ornament which secured the turned-up flaps of his beaver, and more than all, the jewel-hilted sword by his side, bespoke a person of position. He wore also leather breeches and buff-leather boots, the usual horseman's dress of the period.

The fair girl by his side sat her horse with that perfect ease which habit alone can give. Her blue riding-coat was turned up with white, with broad flaps and pockets, the petticoat below being of the same colour; her waistcoat was elegantly embroidered, and the small three-cornered hat with a jewel in front which she wore on the top of her light auburn hair, undisfigured by powder, completed her unassuming yet most becoming costume. Her figure was tall and slight, and her fair and brilliant complexion increased the beauty of her well-formed features, expressive of wit and humour, at the same time indicating thought and feeling.

Such at sixteen was Alethea Harwood, the only child of the Worshipful Mr Rupert Harwood, of Harwood Grange, the gentleman on the tall horse by whose side she rode.

"I have no great affection for yonder town," observed Squire Harwood, pointing southward with his hand. "I cannot forget my father's account of the times when Red-nosed Noll ruled the roost, and that arch-traitor Hutchinson held the castle, and insulted all the Cavaliers in the town and neighbourhood by his preaching, and his cant, and his strict rules and regulations; and now, forsooth, every man and woman in the place thinks fit to stand up for the usurper William, and not an expression of sympathy do I hear for the cruel fate of our lawful Sovereign King James."

"Poor king! it was treacherous in his ministers and officers to desert him; but what could be expected of men brought up in the days of the Commonwealth?" observed Alethea, with a slight tone of scorn in her sweet voice. "However, perhaps, when they get tired of the Prince of Orange, our king will have his own again."

"Pray Heaven he may!" ejaculated the Jacobite squire. "And now, daughter, let me counsel you to deport yourself with becoming dignity and reserve during our visit to the Deane family. Mr Deane is, I own, a man of credit and honour, and would never desire to injure a human being. I am, moreover, indebted to him for certain sums advanced on my estate, and of dire necessity only accepted; so that I wish he should be treated with all courtesy and respect. But he is an obstinate supporter of this vile government, and with him and one or two other exceptions, as I feel is my duty to my order and party, I hate them all, root and branch; they are a money-making, mean-spirited, trading set. It surprises me that any of the nobility and old families of the country can adhere to them. What, however, can be expected from stocking-weavers and such like? Well, well! I was speaking of that worthy man Deane. There is his wife, a good dame and a careful mother, and his two daughters. You know them better than I do—passable girls though, they seem to me; not exactly such as I might have chosen as your companions; but *tempora mutantur*, as we used to say at college! I'faith, most of my Latin has slipped out of my memory. And then there are those two sons. The eldest, Jasper, seems a quiet, proper-behaved young man enough. College has polished him up a little, but of the other I know but little; a broad-shouldered lad he seemed, not ill fitted to fight his way through life, as far as outward figure goes. And Master Jasper, what is to be his course in life? Will his father bring him up as a gentleman?"

"His sister Polly told me that Master Jasper is to become a physician, to follow in the footsteps of their esteemed cousin, Dr Nathaniel Deane," answered Alethea. "I suppose that might be considered the calling of a gentleman."

"Humph!" ejaculated the Squire, as if he had not quite made up his mind on the subject. "That, according to my notions, depends on the original position of a person. It is better than that of some others, my lord's chaplain, or the reverend vicar's curate, as was the lot of some of my college chums; however, I dare say, with so renowned a guide, Master Jasper will prove an honour to the profession. But the breeze feels cool beneath these trees; we will canter on, or you will not have time to change your habit, and be in readiness for Mistress Deane's entertainment."

At a touch of Alethea's whip, her palfrey broke into an easy canter, and her father's steed moving on at a trot, they soon reached Parliament Street on the confines of Nottingham, and passing Saint Anne's Well, they entered through Bridlesmith's Gate the broad market-place. This was, then as now, the widest open space in the town, and had many fine mansions standing round it. On their left was that long thoroughfare called the Pavement, with the grim old castle walls at the farther end, and the sparkling Trent on the other side; while close to them were butchers' and other shops, as well as those of the handicraftsmen, from which the different entrances on that side of the once fortified town took their names.

As Mr Harwood and his daughter emerged from the somewhat ill-paved and narrow street into the broad market-place, their ears were assailed by loud cries and shouts of men and boys, numbers of whom were issuing from the narrow passages which led out of Parliament Street, while from doors and windows appeared eager faces of spectators bending forward to ascertain the cause of the disturbance. The shouts, mingled with the barking of dogs, grew louder and louder, till they approached the Squire and his daughter. Now the mob was seen to move in one direction, and now in another.

"It is nothing, I believe, but some apprentice-lads baiting an ox," observed Mr Harwood as they moved forward.

Just at that moment the crowd, with a pack of barking dogs, came rushing on helter-skelter in hot pursuit of a brindled cow—so it seemed— whose heels its canine tormentors were ever and anon attacking, making it start forward with the pain they inflicted. At the same time a youth with his coat off and a stick in his hand was endeavouring to drive off the dogs, and shouting to the mob of rough-looking apprentices who were urging them on, to desist from the pursuit. His orders were, however, treated with but little attention, for the mob of lads and boys extending for some distance on either side continued their shouts and cries, with peals of laughter at the frantic movements of the unhappy animal. So completely was the road blocked up that Mr Harwood and his daughter were compelled to turn back to avoid them. Just, however, as they were about to do so, the maddened cow dashed forward, and before Alethea could turn her horse, its horns had struck the animal's side, and caught the skirt of her riding-dress. Dashing on, it would have dragged her from her seat, had not the young man who had been attempting to save the creature from its tormentors at that moment sprang forward and disentangled her dress, preventing her from falling from her palfrey.

"Stand back, you young ruffians!" shouted Mr Harwood to the mob. "Understand that I am a justice of the peace, and that I will summon you one and all before the magistrates of the town for this uproar."

The mob of apprentices, seeing the harm which their frolic might have produced, hung back, many of them taking to their heels, while others called off the dogs, which they had before been inciting to pursue the cow, which continued its course through Bridlesmith's Gate, glad to escape its pursuers.

"I have to thank you, young man, for the service you have rendered my daughter and me, and should be glad to reward you to the best of my ability," said Mr Harwood, turning to the youth who was holding Alethea's bridle whilst she recovered her seat in the saddle. "I must have these scapegraces brought up for punishment before the magistrates to-morrow; such proceedings ought not to take place in a well-ordered town."

The young man thus addressed drew himself up with a somewhat haughty air, as he replied, "I am glad to have rendered the young lady a service, sir, and require no reward for doing so; and as for punishing those fellows, I would rather have the opportunity of drubbing a few of them with my fists for worrying poor old Dame Pitt's lame cow, than see them sent to prison for their freak. It may be all very well for them to bait their cattle when they want tender meat, but they had no business to treat that poor animal in the way they did; and I told them so when they began, and promised them I would put a stop to it."

"You are a brave lad," said Mr Harwood, looking at the speaker approvingly. "May I ask your name?"

"I am called Jack Deane, sir," answered the young man, "at your service. I belong to Nottingham, and know every one of those apprentice-lads, and do not wish to bring them into trouble; but I will give the ringleaders as sound a thrashing as they ever had in their lives before long, for their conduct this day."

"Well, well! I suppose we must leave you to settle the matter in your own way," said Mr Harwood; "but if your name is Jack Deane, I conclude that you are the younger son of my friend Mr Jasper Deane, to whose house my daughter and I are now bending our way."

"Yes, sir, the house of my father, Mr Deane, is situated to the south there, on the farther side of the market-place, and with your leave, sir, I will accompany you and your daughter thither, after which I must be allowed to go in search of Widow Pitt's cow, and carry the animal back to her. I shall have time to do that and give a few of the apprentices a drubbing before dinner-time."

Saying this, Jack Deane, putting his arms again into the sleeves of his coat, adjusted his dress, which had been somewhat disordered by the scuffle; then placing his hand on the reins of Miss Harwood's palfrey, he walked by her side towards the house at which he had pointed.

"Well, well! I must leave you to keep order in the town, Master Deane," said Mr Harwood, laughing; "when there is so good a guardian of the peace as you appear to be, it would be useless for me to interfere; and I would not stop you from restoring the cow to the poor widow. At the same time, I may suggest that it might be as well to let alone the drubbing of the apprentices till a more convenient season, or you may get somewhat overheated and fatigued before your appearance at the dinner-table."

"Oh, that will be nothing, sir!" answered Jack, clutching his stout cudgel; "though to be sure the chances are that they will keep out of my way. When they get cool they will think better of it, before they will wish to encounter me. I only hope Miss Harwood's palfrey has not suffered, or her habit either; I am sure the poor animal did not wish to do her harm."

"Oh, no! thanks to you, Mr Deane, both my horse and I have escaped harm," said Alethea, looking at the young man with a kind smile.

On reaching the door of Mr Deane's house, Jack held the young lady's bridle while she dismounted, and then insisted on taking her horse and her father's round to the stables while they entered the house. Having unsaddled the steeds, and given them some corn and hay, he hurried off to fulfil his intention of restoring Dame Pitt's cow to her; but he was less successful in executing his purpose of thrashing the apprentices, in consequence, as he expected would be the case, of their judiciously keeping out of his way; when, failing in his efforts to discover them, he returned home, feeling that he might defer the execution of his purpose to another opportunity, should he on further consideration deem it necessary.

Chapter Two
Dinner at Mr Deane's in Nottingham—
Jack Deane announces the
Profession he has chosen

As the hour of dinner approached, the expected guests began to arrive at the hall-door of Mr Deane's substantial mansion in the market-place. With the exception of Mr Harwood and one or two others, they were relations of the family, or connected in some way or other. Mrs Deane received them in a cordial and hearty manner, showing, however, that she entertained a becoming sense of her own importance. The Squire and Alethea were evidently, from the style of their reception, amongst the most honoured. The lady of the mansion wore a tower of fine Flemish lace on her head, to which that on her gown, of handsome paduasoy, exactly corresponded; and her general appearance was matronly and dignified. Behind her, courtesying and smiling to the guests as they approached, stood two well-grown unmistakably English girls, their dresses ornamented with cherry-coloured ribbons, just then in fashion: the eldest, Catherine, or Kate, as she was called, a brunette, tall and slight, with a somewhat grave and retiring manner, and far more refined than her rosy-cheeked, merry-looking younger sister Polly, who gave promise of some day growing into the goodly proportions of her mother. Mr Deane, with full wig, lace coat, and sword by his side, stood in the old oak hall, accompanied by his son Jasper, ready to hand the ladies from their sedan-chairs as they were brought into the hall. The last to arrive, who was received with all due honour, was a Dr Nathaniel Deane, a cousin of Mr Deane's, the only physician, and one of the greatest men, in Nottingham. Jack was the last to enter the house, and had but little time to slip into his room, and put on his grey dress suit, before dinner was announced. For a few minutes he was seen standing behind the door, unwilling to enter and go through the ordeal of paying his respects to the assembled guests, little more of him being observable besides a broad shoulder and a well-turned leg, with a red clock to his grey stocking. Cousin Nat—for so Mr Nathaniel Deane was called by his relatives—soon however spied him out, and though at that moment tapping his jewelled snuff-box preparatory to offering it to Mrs Bethia Harcourt, Mrs Deane's maiden aunt, he contrived directly afterwards to find himself close to Jack, and to shake hands cordially with the young man, for whom he evidently had an especial regard.

"Well, Jack, what scrape have you last got into, or out of rather, I should say?" said Cousin Nat, "for I am told it is seldom you have not something of the sort on hand. However, you do not look the worse for that or for your studies either, boy, though I should be glad to hear that you had determined to follow some steady pursuit, instead of running your head into other people's quarrels, without any benefit to yourself."

"That is the very thing I have been thinking of," answered Jack, as he returned his respected cousin's greeting, "but I have no fancy for sitting at a desk, nor for any other indoor work. Jasper is more suited for that than I am."

He glanced as he spoke towards the slight figure of his brother, who presented a considerable contrast to himself. The elder had handsome features, with a somewhat sickly hue in his countenance, such as is often produced by study and thought. His manner was refined, and the expression of his countenance denoted an amiable and gentle disposition.

"We will not attempt to make an M.D. of you, at all events," answered Cousin Nat. "Perhaps you would rather take to breaking men's bones than attempting to cure them of their ailments, as I try to do, and as your brother Jasper hopes to do also."

"Not especially," answered Jack: "I should like to see the world, but I have not a fancy for knocking men on the head, and could never understand the amusement some people find in it; but I have no objection to stand up and defend my own if I am attacked, or to draw my sword in the defence of a friend or a right cause."

Dr Nathaniel smiled at his young kinsman's remark. "You will not have to wait long then, lad, before you find sufficient excuse for drawing your sword, and fighting away with as hearty good-will as any of old Noll's Ironsides ever did."

Just at this juncture dinner was announced, and the guests being marshalled according to the strictest rules of precedence, took their places round the well-covered table, on which the summer's sun, flaring through the three tall windows, lighted up the goodly array of silver tankards and pewter dishes, and a great store of blue oriental china. Mrs Deane's duties were of no ordinary kind, every joint being placed before her in succession, that she might employ her well-skilled hands in carving it, the duty of passing the bottles in quick succession being left to the host at the foot of the table.

The quiet, though far from retiring-mannered Jasper had enjoyed the honour of handing down the fair Alethea, and had dexterously managed to place himself by her side. Jack, who sat opposite, observed that she listened attentively to his conversation, which, although he could not catch the substance of it, he saw was of an interesting character. Dr Nathaniel Deane, however, took upon himself the entertainment of a larger portion of the guests, Mrs Deane occasionally keeping up the ball of conversation by a hearty joke and a jovial laugh, while Mr Deane, with more gravity of manner than his spouse, threw in a remark here and there as occasion required.

Nottingham was at this time, as its inhabitants asserted, the most genteel town in the midland counties, a distinction it owed in some measure to the noble palace, built by the Duke of Newcastle as his family residence, on the site of the old fortified castle that had been identified with nearly all the chief periods of English history, from the time of Isabella and Mortimer, who made it their stronghold, to that when Cromwell, riding back towards London, the Civil War being over, saw the greater part of the walls pulled down. On that occasion he told Colonel Hutchinson, who had so bravely defended those stout walls for the Parliament, that he was heartily vexed at it. The Colonel replied that he had procured it to be done, and believed it to be his duty to ease the people of charge when there was no more need for it. Some of the tower? and walls, however, still stood conspicuous among the newer parts of the edifice with which they had been incorporated by the architect. In the market-place, as has been observed, there were a number of fine old mansions belonging to the country families who were accustomed to spend their winters in the town. There were also a good many other handsome places in the immediate neighbourhood. None, however, could be compared for beauty of situation with the castle which crowns the rock rising abruptly from the Trent valley, with its stream at the bottom, which, after coming down from the Yorkshire moors, finds its way through the midst of that vast forest district, with its heaths and leafy alleys, which was once all included under the name of Sherwood Forest.

"Well, Neighbour Deane, what news do you bring from the big city of London?" inquired Mr Samuel Pinkstone, a most respected burgess of Nottingham, during a pause in the conversation. "I am glad to see that you and Master Jasper have escaped all the dangers you had to encounter there and on your way back. They say that housebreakers are as thick there as gooseberries on a gooseberry-bush; and as for highwaymen, I wonder any stage escapes being robbed from the number of them, I am told, who throng the roads."

"Thank you, Master Pinkstone, we met with no accident of any sort or kind," answered Mr Deane. "I did not set eyes on the muzzle of a pistol either in London or on our way from it. Some of the young rakes, who have not forgotten the pranks they played in the last king's reign, occasionally had a scuffle with the watch, and a few heads were broken now and then, but no brains were let out—for the best of reasons, that there were none within. It is proposed, however, to light the city, if our Greenland whalers would but bring us oil enough; but unless they have a fortunate fishing season, there is but little chance of their doing that. I saw some odd sights in the city, I must say; and unless the ladies of quality mend their manners, I am afraid things will come to a pretty pass before long."

"But as to public matters, neighbour," said Mr Pinkstone, "what about them? We do not hear much about them down here. What is our fleet about?"

"We have as fine a fleet as ever sailed, under Mr Russell," answered Mr Deane. "All the year he has managed to keep master of the Mediterranean, and has had the French fleet shut up within their ports, though contrary winds have prevented him making a descent on Marseilles or at Toulon, though he has had regiments of soldiers on board for that purpose. Then we have another fleet in our Channel, ready to bombard the French coast. They have destroyed Gronville, and have made an attack upon Dunkirk, but they failed in that, I am sorry to say. But the worst matter, however, is, that the Marquis of Carmarthen, with a squadron under him, which lay off the islands of Scilly to protect our trade, fancying that a superior French fleet was coming out to attack him, when it was only a fleet of merchant-ships, left his station and retired into Milford Haven. This mistake has caused a great blow to our trade. Many of the Barbados ships have been taken by French cruisers, and two rich ships coming from the East Indies have also been captured, besides which three other large ships have fallen into the hands of French privateers off the Irish coast. All the city of London therefore complains that neither the Admiralty nor the Government take proper care to preserve the wealth of of the nation."

"Nor are they likely to do so," observed Mr Harwood in an under-tone to his next neighbour, "while we have men of the present stamp at the head of affairs. Old England is going to rack and ruin, I see that very clearly, with all her new-fangled schemes and arrangements. They are yielding to the cry of the manufacturers, and are about to pass a law to put a stop to our free trade in wool and corn; and they will soon shut us up to our home markets, and not allow us to sell where we can get the best price abroad."

Mr Harwood among country gentlemen was not singular in his opinions on that subject.

The first course being removed, Mrs Deane folded her arms, to recover after the fatigue of carving for so many guests; no slight labour, considering the size of the joints which had been placed before her. Now, the cloth being removed, and the dessert spread on the shining mahogany table, came the usual accompaniment of pipes and tobacco, which Kate and Polly Deane had to prepare with their own pretty fingers for the use of the gentlemen. This being done, and small pieces of lighted charcoal being brought from the kitchen, wreaths of smoke began to ascend round the table.

"There is an important toast to be proposed, Neighbour Deane, is there not?" said the Worshipful Mr Pinkstone, turning to the host; "but that should be Dr Nathaniel's task, I opine, should it not?"

"To be sure, certainly," said Cousin Nat, "I will gladly undertake the honour. Our friends are generally aware of the object which has called us together this day. I have, then, the pleasure to announce that my kinsman, Mr Jasper Deane, is about to enter into the profession of which I have, for so many years, been an unworthy member, and I trust that by devoting his mind to science, and his energies to the care of those who are placed under him, he may be the means of largely benefiting his fellow-creatures, which all will agree is the great object a physician should have in view. I have infinite satisfaction, therefore, in proposing the health of the future M.D., my young kinsman aforesaid, Mr Jasper Deane."

At the conclusion of Dr Nathaniel's short speech the guests rose to their feet, and all turned towards the young Mr Jasper, wishing him in succession health, happiness, and success in his proposed profession. He received the compliments paid to him with due modesty. His voice slightly trembling from nervousness, he returned thanks in a very neat and proper speech, which it is not necessary here to repeat.

Mr Deane then rose, and filling his glass, did the same in his own name, and in that of his dame, for the honour paid to their son, and then drank to the health of all the guests present, beginning with the ladies, and taking Mr Harwood first among the gentlemen, expressing at the same time his gratitude to Dr Nathaniel for having undertaken to introduce his son into the noble profession to which he himself was so great an ornament.

Alethea watched the countenance of Mr Jasper as he was addressing his guests, and she probably remarked that it lighted up with far more expression and animation than a stranger who saw him under ordinary circumstances would have supposed it capable of exhibiting.

"Well, Mr Jack, and what profession do you intend following?" asked Mr Harwood across the table.

"That depends upon circumstances, sir," said Jack. "I have no fancy for sitting indoors all day, and driving a pen, nor any other pursuit that would keep me out of the fresh air. To say the truth, if I had a free choice, I would follow some calling which would let me see the world at large, and our own country in particular. Last year, during the vacation, I took a trip with Will Brinsmead, Mr Strelley's head drover, as far as Stourbridge, to the fair, and I never enjoyed any thing more in my life. I thought then, and I think now, that for a young man who likes being on horseback, and enjoys the free air of heaven, galloping across country, there is not a pleasanter sort of life. And it is not unprofitable either, if a man knows any thing about beasts, and where are the best pastures on which to put flesh on their bones. If my father and mother, therefore, have no objection, I have made up my mind to turn drover."

Most of the company expressed their surprise at this announcement, by their looks if not by their remarks. Mr Deane was evidently somewhat annoyed at the announcement his younger son had made. Alethea especially looked at him across the table with surprise, while the colour mounted into his sister Polly's cheeks, for though she had heard him express the same resolution, she little dreamed that he was in earnest in the matter, thinking that it was only a way of talking in which lads of his age were apt to indulge.

"I should think, my lad, that you are fit for a higher walk in life than the one you have mentioned," said Mr Harwood across the table. "With a trusty sword by your side, and a hundred men at your orders, you would be more in your place, I suspect. There is plenty of work for gentlemen in these days, if not in Old England, at all events out of it. There are many wrongs to be righted, and many good causes to be sustained. There are many I could tell you of who would willingly accept the offer of your sword."

Mrs Deane looked highly pleased at the compliment Mr Harwood was paying her son, and thanked him with one of her beaming smiles, although Cousin Nat screwed up his lips in a peculiar manner and gave a significant look at Jack.

"Thank you, sir," said Jack, "but I have no fancy for offering my sword to any one out of the country, however high he may bid for it, or in using it, indeed, except in my own defence, or in that of my country. I do not see what is amiss in the life of a drover, such as I hope to be one of these days. It is no easy task, I should say, to drive three hundred head of cattle from the

Yorkshire hills down South, and I hope in time to deal on a large scale, like Mr Strelley, and other friends I know of."

"Well, well, Master Jack, you must take your own way," answered Mr Harwood, "or be guided by your honoured parents: we will have a talk another time about these matters."

Mr Deane's lips had become considerably compressed while his son was speaking, and there was an hysterical cry from Aunt Bethia, whose great wish had always been to see her favourite Jack figure in what she called good society.

"You may quit the society of your equals, for which you have so little respect, Jack," said his father in somewhat stern accents; "those you do not value will take little pains to keep you among them; but let me hear no more of this matter. Now, friends," he continued, making an effort to recover his usual tone of voice, "fill the ladies' glasses, and keep the bottles moving among you. Lads often talk nonsense when they fancy they are talking sense, and so may I beg you to forget what my son Jack has just said? He will think better on the subject another day."

"Don't be too hard on the lad, cousin," said Dr Nathaniel, turning to the host. "It is a great thing, in my opinion, to get a young man to choose a profession for himself. There are too many men like Jack who are not content unless they can mount a helmet and jackboots, and go about the world slaughtering their fellow-creatures without rhyme or reason, should they not find a good cause to fight for. So, Jack, here's to your health, my boy, and success to you in whatever honest calling you determine to follow!"

Dr Nathaniel's word was law in Mr Deane's family, as it was in several others in the town, and he therefore quickly succeeded in smoothing down the somewhat ruffled temper of different members of the family.

Other toasts and speeches followed, but the songs which were generally sung on such occasions were reserved for the supper, of which all the guests present were expected to partake, at a later hour of the day.

The ladies then rising, gracefully sailed out of the room, while the gentlemen continued to pass the battle round for some time longer. It was still broad daylight, though the fresh air of evening was already blowing through the windows. Mrs Deane therefore proposed to her female guests that they should enjoy the breeze for a while on the Castle Terrace, which was the usual promenade of the gay world of Nottingham, and there was a general call for hoods and gloves. The party of ladies, as they glided out of the house, precedence being given to the more elderly dames, took their way towards the castle, and passing through the grand gateway which had stood so many attacks, soon ascended the broad stone steps with massive balustrades which led in two flights to the noble terrace in front of the building. It was well paved with large flat stones, and with a breastwork of stone, and on the south side of the castle a convenient arcade, where in rainy or hot weather the gentry of the town could walk under shelter. On that beautiful summer's evening, however, the ladies required only their green fans to protect their eyes from the almost level rays of the setting sun, which fans the young ones occasionally found useful for other purposes—either to hide their faces from an unwelcome admirer, or to beckon a too timid one, perchance. The park with its three long avenues lay before them, and the steep declivities which ran down from it to the river Leen were covered with woods, broken here by some old tower which had withstood all attempts at its demolition, and there by a jutting mass of grey rock, looking scarcely more solid than the rock-like masonry of the tower. The new building had only been finished the year Jack was born, as Mrs Deane was in the habit of telling any friends who came to visit her for the first time at Nottingham. It was built in the Italian style of architecture, with a fine double flight of steps to the principal entrance, over which was an equestrian alto-relievo of Charles the Second. The flat roofs were surrounded by balustrades, and the spaces between the long terrace of windows were filled up with architraves and entablatures, which produced a rich and picturesque though somewhat heavy effect. On one side the view ranged over the town, with its fine churches, and the distant sweeps of Sherwood Forest, and the nearer woods of Colwick Park. On the other side lay a rich and varied expanse of country, with the silvery Trent winding through the valley, and round many a bold and thickly wooded promontory; while the hills of Derbyshire and Leicestershire formed a beautiful background to the peaceful and smiling landscape.

Kate and Polly Deane, with Alethea Harwood, after taking a turn or two, sat down on one of the stone benches on the terrace. This was the first moment that they had had the opportunity of speaking together on the subject of Jack's determination to leave home, though neither Alethea nor Kate could believe he really purposed following the calling of a drover. Polly, who knew him better, was not so sure on the subject. He had often described to her in glowing language the life which he proposed to lead, and she could not help sympathising with him in that as in most other matters in which he took an interest.

"But surely he is formed for better things than that," observed Alethea, and Polly thought she saw a slight blush rise on the cheek of her friend.

"He would never consent to associate with the rude, rough men which drovers surely must be, even though he might meet occasionally with the adventures you describe," she exclaimed.

"Oh! but he intends not only to be a drover, but a grazier; and that, he tells me, is a sure road to wealth and independence," observed Polly.

"Here he comes to answer for himself," said Kate, and the young ladies, looking up, saw Jack advancing towards them, and presenting a very becoming appearance in his grey suit, with his hair brushed as smoothly back from his smooth open forehead as its curly nature would admit of, and his hat in his hand, a fashion he gladly adopted, to avoid the necessity of constantly removing it as he passed his numerous acquaintances.

Polly's affectionate little heart bounded at seeing many friendly glances thrown at him, and she whispered to Kate, in a tone which Alethea overheard, "He does not look as if we need ever be ashamed of him, after all."

"If he follows the life he proposes, he will never wear a sword like a gentleman," observed Kate.

"He is tolerably well able, I should say, to defend himself without one," observed Alethea, "from the specimen he gave us of his prowess this afternoon," and she described the scene which had occurred on their entering the town, when Jack had so bravely taken the part of the poor widow's cow.

While she was speaking, Jack himself came up to them. The sisters immediately attacked him on the subject, and Alethea inquired whether he had driven back the animal to Widow Pitt's paddock.

"Oh, yes!" he answered; "but I should have had a far better appetite for dinner, had I been able to find the fellows who had been so cruelly baiting her. However, they will not manage to escape me altogether, I'll warrant; but, as you know, I do not expect to remain here much longer, now that I have finished my course at the Grammar School. They will be for sending me to college if I do, and that I could never brook. But before I go, I must come and pay you a visit at Harwood Grange, Mistress Alethea."

"We shall always be glad to see you," said the young lady, looking up with a bright glance at Jack's honest countenance. "Here comes my father to say the same."

"Yes, indeed we shall, Jack," said Mr Harwood, who came up at that moment. "I may be able to give you some useful introductions, when I hear where you are going. I have many friends scattered about the country, north and south."

"And you will not mind introducing me," asked Jack with kindling eye, "though I follow the calling of what Kate calls a poor, miserable drover?"

"Oh, no, no!" answered the Squire, "not if you always show the spirit you did this afternoon, and that I am sure you will wherever you go, or whatever calling you follow."

Here he took Jack's hand, and pressed it kindly in presence of the various people of fashion who were walking up and down the terrace. Mrs Deane observed the action, and seemed well pleased with the attention paid her younger son. Taking somewhat after herself, he was, it must be confessed, her favourite.

The sun was now sinking over the distant hills, and as the mist began to rise from the river below, the parties on the terrace gradually dispersed, the Deane family and their friends returning to their mansion, where they assembled once more round their well-spread board, at eight o'clock precisely, the fashionable hour for supper. Jack, in better spirits than he had been in the afternoon, joined the family party. Songs were sung, and numerous stories told by Dr Nathaniel, Mr Pinkstone, and other acknowledged wits of the party. Ere ten o'clock had struck, the whole party retired to their chambers, our forefathers being of opinion that early to bed and early rising was far more conducive to health than the late hours adopted by the present generation.

Chapter Three
A Poaching Expedition to Colwick Park—Jack forms an Acquaintance who leads him into Difficulties

As soon as the party broke up, Jack hurried to his room, and very contrary to his usual custom threw himself into a chair, and unconsciously pressing his hand on his brow, rested his elbow on the little oak table which stood by his bedside. The way in which the walls were adorned showed the tastes of the occupant of the chamber. The most honoured ornament was a fowling-piece with a curious lock lately invented, the gift of Cousin Nat, and which had superseded the stout cross-bow hanging beneath it. One wall was devoted to fishing-rods, tackle, and nets. Among them was a rod of which Izaak Walton, that great professor of the gentle art, had himself spoken approvingly when once, while fishing in the silvery Trent, he had seen it flourished in Cousin Nat's hands. There were two sets of foils with masks and gloves, and several cudgels with strange knots and devices, cut from ancient trees in Sherwood Forest, beneath whose once wide-spreading boughs certain feats of the renowned Robin Hood were said to have been performed. In one and all the tales relating to the exploits of the bold outlaw, it is scarcely necessary to say that Jack put the most implicit faith, and would have been highly indignant had any one ventured to doubt their authenticity or correctness. In one corner of the room stood a book-case, a very unpretending piece of furniture in itself, but it contained every ballad Jack believed to have been written, or at all events on which he could lay hold, connected with Robin Hood. It contained however other tomes: besides several schoolbooks, their dark covers sadly battered, and their leaves inked, dog's-eared, and torn, there were kind Izaak Walton's "Complete Angler," highly prized by Jack; Foxe's "Book of Martyrs," presented to him by Aunt Bethia; and a work he valued more than all the others—Purchas's "Travels:" and often and often as he conned these pages he longed to be able to visit the strange countries and to go through the wonderful adventures therein described.

The fact was that Jack had a very good head on his shoulders, and had he broken his leg, or met with any other accident which would have confined him to the house, he would have taken very readily to reading. In his case his physical powers demanded more exercise than his mental, whereas in the case of his brother Jasper his mental activity preponderated over his mere animal spirits. Jack required a tether to keep him within bounds, Jasper a spur to make him move fast enough to keep up with the times. Yet in most respects the elder was superior to the younger brother—cast in a finer mould, with keener sensibilities, a gentler heart, and more moral if not physical courage. Jack had, however, many good qualities, but many of his doings were not such as deserved imitation. Such book knowledge as he possessed he had obtained at the Nottingham Grammar School, where, as was the case at other places of education of the same character, boys were allowed to pick up what they chose, and if not inclined to learn, no great effort was made to instruct them. Jack had therefore run wild, and had done many things for which he had cause to be sorry, and had sometimes even got into trouble about them. He had not, however, even yet learned wisdom. His character was, however, to be developed, and may probably be so in the following pages.

"I would do any thing to please her," he said to himself. "I do not think she would like to know the work I have promised to engage in to-night, and yet how am I to be off it? I know myself it is not right, but I gave my word to those fellows, and ought I to break it? I do not like the forest laws, but they are laws notwithstanding, and it behoves honest men to obey them—there's the rub. How I did not come to think of that before, I don't know. Perhaps Alethea put it into my head; and yet she did not speak very approvingly of the king and the Parliament, so I suppose she would not much object to my breaking the laws which they have formed. Still she would not like to see me placed in the pillory, and that would be my fate if I was caught poaching—there's no use mincing the matter, that's the word. But I was never frightened at any thing, and I am not going to be frightened at that. I gave my word, and I must stick to my word."

Saying this, Jack started up, and began to throw aside his holiday suit. Instead, he donned his roughest clothes, took down the fishing-boots from the wall, filled his pockets with tackle, and threw a landing-net over his shoulder. Thus prepared, with a slouched hat that concealed his features, he gently opened the window, and by means of a leaden water-spout, and a pear-tree growing up the wall under his window, slipped noiselessly to the ground. He quickly scaled the garden wall, and took his way down a narrow lane winding between tall and irregular houses, till he reached the side of the narrow river Leen, which, sweeping by the foot of the castle hill, ultimately falls into the Trent. He was soon clear of all the buildings, when, stopping under a tall hedge-row which ran down to the stream, a low whistle reached his ears.

"That is Smedley," he said to himself. "Well, I will fulfil my promise, and then break with these fellows for good."

He whistled in return, in the same manner, and immediately a youth of about his own age stepped out from the shelter of a hedge.

"Well, Jack, I am glad you have come at last," said Smedley; "it's growing late, and the other fellows will be waiting for us down the stream."

"Where is the boat?" asked Jack. "I promised to go with you to-night, and I am not the man to break my word; but just let me tell you, Tom, once for all, I am determined that this shall be the last time."

"Don't say that, Jack," answered Smedley: "we cannot afford to lose you. We want a good leader in all our work, and you are just the man for us. As for the boat, she is down by the edge of Colwick Causeway, under the bushes; and Ned Bligh has got mufflers for the oars, and all ready; so come with us now, and don't be bothering your head about the future."

The young men were soon walking along the sward of Colwick Park, with the great trees throwing their shadows across it, when the moon, often hidden by clouds, came out, and cast its light upon them. Sometimes also it showed groups of cattle lying down sleeping, or lazily chewing the cud, among the sweet herbage of the river's side. No other living creature was in sight, so that Jack and his companion were not afraid of talking in their usual tone of voice. They kept, however, well under the shade of the trees.

"Those are some of Mr Strelley's beasts, I believe," said Jack: "a fine lot they are, too; they will soon be off towards Cambridge, and bring a good round sum at Stourbridge Fair. I wish I had the driving of them; and I should not mind the selling, either!"

"Are they the highland cattle which Will Brinsmead bought for him at Saint Faith's?" asked a voice, so close to the two speakers that they both started.

"Come out into the moonlight, friend," said Jack, boldly; "I don't answer questions to a man that keeps out of sight."

The stranger stepped out from beneath the shadow of a row of beech-trees which grew on the bank close to the path which Jack and his companion were following. He was a broad-set countryman in appearance, habited in a well-worn but strong riding-suit, with leather leggings, a horseman's jackboots, and a broad leathern belt, in which Jack's quick eye caught sight of a pistol-barrel. He seemed considerably entertained by Jack's challenge, and repeated his question with great good-humour, in an unmistakable Yorkshire accent.

"You perhaps know as much as I do about the beasts," answered Jack. "Some of them are Scotch, and well fed on these rich water-meadows, till they are nearly as valuable as the Leicestershire breed. I see a few down there which are real Herefordshire, too. And now may I ask who you are?"

"Well, a fair answer deserves another in return. I am a Yorkshire cattle-dealer, at your service, just passing through Nottingham, and I walked out here to see if there was any thing likely to suit me, in case I chose to make a bargain to-morrow morning. I must be early on the road to Derby. I hope you are satisfied, young man. And now let me ask you what game you are after?"

"To be honest with you, we came out to catch a salmon or two," answered Jack. "There are some fine ones now and then down the stream a little way, though it is not often salmon come so far up the river. We shall have a boat here, which will carry us close up to the weir."

"Ah! I like that sort of thing!" said the Yorkshireman; "I have seen a good bit of such sport in my time. What now if I were to lend you a hand? With the leister we would soon have a fine one that way, and if we had a lantern ready, we might take a few by 'sunning' besides."

"Oh, yes! we shall be glad for you to come," answered Smedley, before Jack could say any thing. "I should like above all things to see fish sunned."

"Well, then," answered the Yorkshireman, "you and your friend here must give me your word to forget, if ever you should see me again, that you met me this night. On that condition I will show you some north-country sport—on that alone, mind. You," he added, turning to Jack, "for I can trust you by the tone of your voice, must answer for your friends in the boat."

"Oh, yes! I will answer for them as I would for myself," said Jack, who, forgetting his former good resolutions, was almost as eager as Smedley to witness the new style of sport which the stranger promised them.

Just then the boat of which they had been talking came stealthily in sight, rowed by two other lads, much of the same age as Jack and his friend. The latter with the Yorkshireman quickly stepped into her, when without loss of time the boat glided again down the stream.

"This is a friend we have picked up, who is going to show us some sport, Bligh," said Smedley in a low tone of voice. "We can trust him, and he knows that he can trust us; so it is all right."

In a short time they entered the Trent, and quickly arrived at the weir, which was formed by large stones roughly laid together, so as to throw the water into a broad cascade, as it came tumbling over it to the lower reach of the river. Smedley was more inclined to be talkative than Jack or the other lads in the boat.

"What are we to call you, master?" he asked of the stranger.

"Call me Master Pearson; that is a good midland-county name enough," he said with a low laugh. "You have not got a leister in the boat, have you? I have an idea, from the look of the place, that if I had one, I could catch you a salmon quicker than by any other way."

The leister of which Master Pearson spoke is a three-pronged fork used for spearing fish.

"No," answered Smedley; "none of us are good hands at using such a thing."

"Well, just pull in here to the bank, and I will see if I cannot get a stick which will answer the purpose," answered Master Pearson.

Without having to search long, he found a stake which had been driven into the stream to prevent drawing nets across it. The stick apparently suiting his fancy, with a piece of wire, with great dexterity, he in a short time manufactured a pronged harpoon. Balancing it in his hand, he seemed satisfied with his performance. Sitting down in the boat, he next took off his boots and long-skirted great coat, which he deposited on the seat, and then, tucking up his ample trousers, waded up to the weir, while the boat was still rocking some distance from it. Jack followed close behind him, and with delight saw a noble salmon glistening now and then in the straggling moonlight, and playing securely in the shallow water, but ready to dart out into the deeper part of the stream at the slightest sound. In another instant a crimson bubble came up to the surface of the water, showing with how unerring a hand the clumsy-looking weapon manufactured by Master Pearson had been struck home. At a signal the rest of the party came up to him to carry off their prize, while he continued looking about for another. They felt inclined to be rather annoyed at the ease with which the stranger had captured a fish which they would have thought it impossible to kill in the same way. Smedley at that moment declared that he heard sounds in the distance, which made him fear that the keepers were coming through the wood. "If we are not off we shall be getting into trouble," he sung out.

"Hoot, mon!" cried Master Pearson, loud enough to be heard through the brawling of the weir; "you have time enough to learn how to strike a 'sawmon;' but come, I will show you another trick, since we have joined company for the night."

Saying this, he returned to the boat, and, putting on his coat and boots, produced a small lantern from his capacious horseman's pocket. With a flint and steel it was lighted, when, leaning over the side of the boat, he slowly moved the light along the surface of the water.

"Now stand by with your nets," he answered, "and you will soon pull up enough fish for your suppers."

As he spoke, the lads saw a number of small fish attracted by the light to the surface of the water; and, following his advice, in a short time a considerable quantity were caught.

The Poachers disturbed.

"This is not proper sunning," he observed: "if I had had such a lantern as we use in the north, we should have caught far larger fish. It should be made watertight, and then, when lowered down close to the net, the fish are so eager to come and see the cause of the brightness, thinking, maybe, that the sun has come down to pay them a visit, that they swim right against the net, and are caught in great numbers. That is what we call sunning in the north."

"I heard a voice!" exclaimed Smedley, as Master Pearson ceased speaking. "There!—there again! It's the keepers as sure as we are living men!"

"Hold your tongue!" exclaimed Master Pearson somewhat sharply. "Here, give me the oars; we will soon distance the keepers, if so be that they are coming this way. You're right, I believe, though."

Taking the oars in his hands, he sent the boat through the water at a rate she had seldom moved before. The noise of the oars attracted the keepers, who rushed down to the water just in time to see the boat turning a reach of the river. They hurried along the bank for some distance, shouting to those in her to stop—an order not very likely to be obeyed. So vigorously did Pearson ply the oars, that there seemed every probability of the boat escaping its pursuers. Still the latter continued to chase along the banks.

"You must take the consequences, then," exclaimed a voice, and directly afterwards a shot whistled over their heads.

The lads crouched down in the boat, with the exception of Jack, who followed Pearson's example in sitting still.

"A miss is as good as a mile," observed the latter coolly. "They must be good marksmen to hit us at the rate we are going in this uncertain light. Now, if I was minded, I might return the compliment with one of my long pistols, and maybe they would wish I was farther off."

"What do you carry pistols for?" asked Jack in a tone of surprise.

"Never you mind, young man," replied Pearson, in a different style of voice to that which he had hitherto spoken. "If I spoke of pistols, maybe I was joking: you understand me?"

All this time he was vigorously rowing away, edging the boat off to the other side of the bank to that on which the keepers were following. In a short time they reached the shade of some tall trees which overhung the stream, and here the boat was completely hid from sight.

"A few more strokes, and there is little danger of their finding us," observed the stranger; and now once more they entered the mouth of the little river Leen, up which he turned the boat's head. "We have now to pull against the current," he observed, "and my advice is to land and leave the boat to look after herself."

"The best thing we can do," answered Jack, and a few strokes brought the boat to a spot where they could easily leap on shore.

"Don't leave your fish behind you, lads, or your tackle either. If you leave one, you will lose your suppers; and if you leave the other, you will be very likely to be discovered. Now, lads, you take your way, and I'll take mine, only just remember your promise. I consider it as good as an oath, and any man who breaks his oath to me will have cause to repent it. Now, good night to you all."

Having bid the stranger farewell, Smedley and the other two lads took their way along the banks of the river, in the direction of some dilapidated sheds, where they had arranged to meet and enjoy, according to their own fashion, their hard-won supper. The stranger lounged away across the bridge at some little distance from the sheds, while Jack, anxious to get home, hurried off in the direction of the market-place.

"I was wrong to go," said Jack to himself. "Suppose one of us had been shot, it would have been paying very dear for our night's sport. Such doings might be easily overlooked in a boy, but I am one no longer. I feel that. I claim to be a man, and as a man I must act. I hope there is work for me to do in the world of some sort, and the sooner I begin it the better, and put aside all my boyish pranks."

"A good resolution," said a voice behind him.

Jack was not aware he had been speaking aloud.

"I followed you, because I want to have a word more with you," said the speaker, in whom Jack at once recognised his late companion, Master Pearson. "There's mettle in you of the right sort," continued the stranger. "What say you? Would you like to join a band of brave fellows who have a right good cause to fight for?" he whispered in a low voice. "There's honour and distinction to be gained, and a name, maybe, and wealth in the end. It is what most men fight for, and I take it that you would not be less ready than others to use your sword for such an object."

"I am much obliged to you for the compliment you pay me," answered Jack, "and for the good opinion you have formed of my courage; but I have no great fancy for undertaking what I know nothing about. Men do not always agree as to the goodness of a cause, and what you may consider a good cause, you will pardon me for saying it, I may consider a bad one."

"A very discreet answer," observed Master Pearson, "and I think all the better of you for making it. Well, I will not press you just now. I have no doubt we shall meet again before long, and though I cannot tell you where to find me, I have a fancy that I shall have no great difficulty in putting my finger upon you at any time. So farewell, Master John Deane: you see I know you, and moreover I wish you well."

Saying this, the stranger wrung Jack's hand cordially. Still he lingered, rather unwilling perhaps to let the young man go without making a more favourable impression.

"It is a good cause and a right cause which I invite you to join. I must not explain it more to you just now, but just think the matter over; and stay, it's just possible I shall remain in Nottingham all to-morrow. Will you meet me in the evening as soon as it is dusk, down by the bank of the river, where you fell in with me just now? I will explain matters more fully to you then."

Jack did not answer for a minute or more. "I must think of it," he said at last. "You may be a very honest man, Mr Pearson, and your intentions towards me perhaps are fair, but I tell you again, I have no fancy to take a leap in the dark. I have a plan in view myself, and I would rather carry that out than try any other. You have wished me farewell to-night already, and now I will wish you the same, and leave you."

Saying this, Jack took the stranger's proffered hand, and shaking it, hurried off in the direction in which he was previously going. Master Pearson looked after him for an instant, and nodding his head, said to himself, "He is an honest lad as well as a brave one, and may be made of use if I can get a bridle into his mouth."

Chapter Four
Fire near Mr Strelley's Warehouse—Jack Deane shows that he is a lad of Courage

Jack soon again scaled the garden wall, and stood under his bedroom window. He had left it wide open; it was now almost closed. The old pear-tree nailed against the wall enabled him to climb up a considerable distance, so as to reach the window-sill, by which he could haul himself up, and get into his room.

"Probably the wind has blown it to," he said to himself. "I hope no one has found out my absence."

Climbing up, he gently pushed back the window. On looking in, what was his dismay to see his father seated in the chair by the table, with a candle now almost burned out, and a book, from which he had evidently been reading, before him! His eyes were however closed, and he was nodding, fast asleep. Jack was a man of action, and always more ready to face a danger than to avoid it. He crawled in, therefore, as noiselessly as he could, and sat himself down on a chest at the farther end of the room, waiting for his father to awake. Jack did not trouble himself much as to what he should say, planning, and inventing, and twisting, and turning the truth in all sorts of ways, or inventing all sorts of falsehoods, but, like an honest man, he determined to tell the whole truth openly and frankly at once, and so brave the worst, and take the consequences of what he had done, whatever they might be. In fact, so little agitated was he at the thoughts of what he had to go through, and being moreover excessively tired, for he had been up and actively engaged all day, that he soon became drowsy, and imitating his respected father, began to nod much in the fashion he was doing. In a short time Jack was fast asleep. He was not very comfortable though, for he had an unpleasant sort of feeling, which was carried into his dreams, that all was not right, and that something very disagreeable was about to occur. How long he had slept he could not tell, but suddenly he was awoke by a bright glare which passed across his face, and starting up he saw flames issuing from the sheds by the side of the river, in which his late companions had proposed to enjoy their supper. He started to his feet, and remembering that Mr Strelley's great wool warehouse was near the sheds, as well as a number of cottages thatched with straw, belonging to the people employed on the river, he dreaded that a very considerable conflagration might be the consequence. Jack sprang to the window.

"I beg your pardon, sir," he exclaimed in a voice loud enough to awake his father; "I am sorry to rouse you up, but there's a fire near Mr Strelley's warehouse, and I must be off to try and get it put out. I hope it has not caught any of the premises yet; but pray call up some of our neighbours, there's not a moment to be lost!"

"Where! where! what's the matter?" exclaimed Mr Deane, starting. "Why, Jack, what have you been about?"

Jack repeated what he had just said; and before his father had time to make any answer, he had leaped out of the window and across the garden, and down the lane by which he had previously gone. As he ran through the narrow streets, he every now and then shouted, "Fire! fire!" By the time he had reached the sheds, they were blazing furiously. The wind had also carried some sparks to an outhouse nearer the cottages, and already the people were running to and fro; women with babies in their arms, roused out of their sleep, rushing from the doors, and boys hallooing and men shouting, and yet none doing any thing to stop the progress of the flames. Jack, seeing that unless some one took the lead all the neighbouring buildings might catch fire, shouted out, "Form a line, my lads, down to the river, and you women bring your 'pancheons,' pails, kettles, any thing that will hold water; and now, lads, pass them along, and we will soon put out this fire. Now, you lads, tear away the burning dry thatch from the tops of those cottages; never mind a little singeing. You won't have a house standing in the place if you don't look sharp about it!"

Jack, as he spoke, set an example, by doing himself as he directed others to do. As soon as the people saw what was necessary to be done to stop the progress of the flames, they worked willingly enough. Jack leaped up to the top of a wall, and having buckets passed to him, threw the water over the burning roof. Several of the most active of the men did the same, while the women and children passed the buckets along with considerable rapidity. It was very doubtful, however, whether their efforts would avail in checking the progress of the fire. Jack continued to encourage them with shouts and cheers, and by this time many more people having arrived with buckets, he began to hope that his efforts would not be without success. The shed in which the fire had originated, and two or three hovels, had already been burned down, while the outbuilding which communicated with the warehouse was already in flames: on this, therefore, Jack now directed the people to bestow all their efforts. A loud cheer at length announced to those who were arriving on the spot, the owner of the warehouse among them, that Jack's efforts had been crowned with success, and that the fire was extinguished. Jack, with his hands blackened and burned, and his clothes and hair singed, was now called for by the crowd, and before he was well aware what they were about to do, he found himself seated in a chair, and carried home in triumph, just at the break of the early summer morning. Jack, however, was more burned and injured than he had at first supposed; so much so, that his father forbore making any remark on his absence during the night. On awaking a few hours afterwards—for he had been immediately put into his bed, and doctored by the careful hands of his mother and sister Kate—he found Dr Nathaniel Deane seated by his side. The latter having felt his pulse, and complimented him on his achievements, "No, no, Cousin Nat," he answered; "if you knew all, you would not praise me. I have acted like an idiot, or worse than an idiot."

"I am glad to find that no great harm has been done except to your poor hands, my lad. It will be a fortnight, or nearly so, before you will be able to use them," answered the doctor. "You will have time to stay quiet and get wisdom, if that is what you want."

One of Jack's first visitors was Mr Strelley.

"I have come to thank you, Mr John Deane, for saving my property," he said, as he took his seat by his side. "You have not only benefited me very greatly, but I can scarcely tell you how many poor families would have been thrown out of work if my factory had been destroyed."

Jack of course made a suitable answer.

"I just did what I saw ought to be done," said Jack. "Really, Mr Strelley, I do not think you have anything to thank me for."

"There may be two opinions even on a matter of that sort," answered the manufacturer; "and, at all events, I wish you would tell me how I can best serve you. I wish to do it for your father's sake, as well as for your own. We are old friends, you know; so do not stand on ceremony, at all events."

The occurrence of the night had made Jack more than ever anxious to leave home for a time; for he felt that even should his father not question him as to the cause of his absence during it, he was bound to tell him. He therefore explained fully to Mr Strelley what were his wishes with regard to becoming a cattle-dealer and drover.

"If you really have made up your mind on the subject, I will most gladly forward your views," said Mr Strelley. "You know my trusty old head drover, Will Brinsmead, as you took an excursion with him last year, I rather think. He will start in a few days in charge of a large drove now grazing in Colwick Park and adjoining meadows, and dispose of them at Stourbridge Fair. With the price he obtains he is to buy Scotch cattle at Saint Faith's, near Norwich; for, as you know, the Highland drovers bring their lean beasts to that place. I have a correspondent at Norwich, my old friend Mr Gournay, the manufacturer, and several merchants; and Brinsmead will have to transact some business with them. Now you could not do better than serve your apprenticeship under him, and act as his clerk. You will learn in that way how to do business on a large scale, and that, I take it, will be your aim as a young man of spirit. You would not be long content to follow at the tails of oxen, and keep them moving on the straight road."

"The very thing above all things I should like," exclaimed Jack. "I hope my Cousin Nat will get my hands all to rights in a few days; and however my father might have objected to my starting with strangers, I am nearly sure he will agree to the plan you so kindly propose."

Mr Strelley's offer was duly placed before Mr Deane.

"If Jack remains much longer idle at home, he will be getting into mischief, if he has not got into it already," he thought to himself. "I have no reason to be ashamed of my boy, and perhaps it will be my own fault if I have cause to be at any future time. Cousin Nat is a man of judgment, and he asserts always that there is more in Jack than any of us suppose; and that if we allow him to follow the bent of his own inclinations, he will be sure to work his way up in the world, even though we let him begin at the bottom of the ladder. Some people want help, and don't get on well without it; others are all the better for being left alone, and help only makes them idle."

The assurance which Jack received that he would be allowed at length to carry out his much-cherished plan, contributed not a little to his restoration, and the burns on his hands and legs healed more rapidly than Cousin Nat had predicted.

Squire Harwood and his daughter had returned to the Grange the day after the occurrence which has been narrated; and as soon as Jack was able to leave the house, although not fit for a journey, he expressed his intention of riding over to pay a farewell visit to his friends. Often when left in solitude he had conjured up a vision of the sweet countenance of Alethea, and he could not help longing once more to see the reality. His proposal met with every encouragement from his family.

"If any body can civilise our boy Jack, Miss Harwood can," observed Mrs Deane to her husband.

"I doubt whether she will think it worth while to make the attempt," observed Mr Deane. "Jack is in no way suited to her, whatever he may flatter himself is the case. However, let the lad go; he can come to no harm, at all events; and Mistress Alethea may give him a taste for better society than he seems to have a fancy for."

Chapter Five
Jack's Visit to Harwood Grange—Is urged to assist in the Jacobite Plot

Jack accordingly donned his best suit, and his sister Polly put his hair, which had been considerably singed by the fire, in as good order as it was capable of. His left hand was still in a sling, but he had no difficulty in mounting his horse with the aid of his right, and managing him as well as most people could with two hands at liberty. With a note from his father on business, and numerous messages from his mother and sisters, he set out on his expedition. He rode merrily along through the green wood, often indulging in daydreams, which, had he known more of the world, he might have suspected that there was little probability of being realised. The fair Alethea formed a prominent feature in most of them. Cousin Nat had charged him not to heat his blood by galloping, lest it might retard his recovery; but when he came to the commencement of a fine open glade, it was hard to restrain either the horse or his own feelings, and more than once he found himself flying over the ground as fast as he would have done had a pack of hounds been before him in full chase of a deer. In a shorter time than he had calculated on, therefore, he arrived at the front of Harwood Grange. It was a mansion built in the time of Elizabeth, with high roof and pointed gables, richly ornamented with the arms of the family, deeply carved in stone, over the principal entrance. It had no moat nor other means of defence having originally been a hunting-lodge. It was also out of the highway, and had thus escaped being turned into a fortress, and suffering the fate of many mansions throughout England during the wars between the "Cavaliers" and the "Roundheads." It was of considerable size, the outbuildings affording ample accommodation for horses and dogs.

Both the Squire and his daughter were at home, and had seen him approach as he rode up the avenue. He received a cordial welcome from the Squire in the old hall, into which the entrance-door opened. It was hung round with the usual trophies of the chase, hunting-poles, boar-spears, deer-horns, old cross-bows, and modern fire-arms, as well as curious pieces of ancient armour, which had done good service when worn by his father and his retainers in the time of the first Charles, under whose banner the family had ranged themselves. In the corner stood whole suits of armour, placed on lay figures, while on a table at the farther end lay hawk's jesses, and hoods, and bells, and other apparatus of the gentle sport of heronry. A long massive oak table, with a side board of the same wood and style of construction, and numerous high-backed chairs, completed the furniture of the room, while at the inner end was a huge fire-place, with a mantel-piece high above it, and carved oak seats on either side. The hall was used generally for banquets and other entertainments; smaller rooms leading off it were more usually occupied by the family.

Alethea had followed her father into the hall to welcome Jack, which she did in as cordial a manner as he could have desired, though the perfect self-possession she exhibited, and the total want of timidity, might have created some uncomfortable doubts in the mind of a person better acquainted with the female heart than Jack could have been. The Squire insisted on Jack's remaining to dine with them at the usual hour of noon, telling him that he had a good deal to talk about, and if he still proposed setting off on the journey he had spoken of, he would entrust him with several letters to be delivered on the road.

While the Squire went to write his letters—a task which, although they were not very long, took him a considerable time—Jack was left to the society of Alethea. He was more inclined to be sentimental than he had ever been before in his life; but she seemed in such good spirits, and laughed so heartily at some of the remarks he made, that he very soon returned to his natural manners. She seemed, indeed, more anxious to persuade him that the Jacobite cause was the right one, than to attempt to induce him to give up his proposed journey. Now she praised the late king, and his energy, and the numerous good qualities which she declared he possessed; and now she did her best to lower William in Jack's opinion.

"Such a king as he is!" she exclaimed: "his manners are positively repulsive, and he has no love for the fine arts: why they say that he hates 'bainting and boetry,' as he calls them; and when they have brought him poor diseased children to be touched for the king's evil, as used to be done by the royal Stuarts, he absolutely refused to put his hand upon them. Now, you know, if he really had been a king, his touch would most certainly have cured them."

"That never struck me before," answered Jack; "but I know when I have read accounts of his various actions, I have often thought that he was like a great hero: I am sure he was at the battle of the Boyne. Have you never read an account of it? I found one only the other day in an old 'News-letter,' I think it was, or it might have been in the 'post-boy,' or the 'Flying Post' The tide was running fast in the river, and the king's charger had been forced to swim, and then was almost lost in the mud. As soon, however, as the king reached firm ground, taking his sword in his left hand—for his right arm was still stiff with a wound and the bandage round it—he led his men to the spot where the fight was the hottest. The Irish horse retired, fighting obstinately. In the midst of the tumult of pistols flashing and swords cutting in all directions, William rode up to the gallant Enniskilleners.

"'What will you do for me?' he cried out; but not being immediately recognised, a trooper, taking him for an enemy, was about to fire.

"'What!' said he, 'do you not know your friends?'

"'It's his Majesty!' exclaimed the colonel of the regiment.

"On hearing this, a loud shout of joy burst from the men, who were all Protestant yeomen.

"'Gentlemen!' said William, 'you shall be my guards to-day. I have heard much of you; let us now see something of each other, and what we can do.'

"With this he led them forward against the enemy, who at length took to flight, and in a short time there was no doubt that the battle was won.

"Since I have read that account, I have always looked upon the king as a real hero."

"As a mere fighter or a leader of men in battle, he may not be contemptible," answered the young lady, not quite liking Jack's remarks; "but, for my part, I should prefer acknowledging the sovereign 'who is every inch a king,' as William Shakspeare says."

"I have never read any of Shakspeare's plays, or seen them acted either; but of one thing I am very sure, that King William would not allow such doings as have been long taking place in France, and which James Stuart would ere long have imitated. Just think, Miss Harwood, of the way the poor Protestants are treated there. If they refuse to turn Romanists, they are persecuted in every possible manner. The roughest soldiers are quartered in their houses, and allowed to treat them as they think fit. The ministers are driven from the country, and if any Huguenot gentlemen are captured attempting to make their escape, they are sent to the galleys, and have there to row on board those vessels, chained to the oar like slaves. Had King James remained in the country, there is no saying whether he might not have treated us Protestants in the same way."

Alethea was a little disconcerted at Jack's matter-of-fact view of the Stuart cause.

"But then, you know," she exclaimed, "James was the rightful sovereign; you cannot deny that."

"My father says that both his father, King Charles the First, and he broke their vows; and that, had they proved faithful to the people, the people would have proved faithful to them. We none of us believe it was right to cut off King Charles's head; but when it was very evident that James wished to make himself a despot, and to introduce the Romish faith again, we all think it was quite right that he should have been dismissed from the country."

"Oh, you are a dreadful Roundhead!" answered Alethea, in a half-vexed tone, though she laughed at the same time. "I am afraid we shall never convert you to our principles; and yet, if you come to view the matter in the light we do, you may see that King James has right on his side."

Alethea then entered into arguments in favour of King James, more fully than is necessary here, and which it might weary the reader to repeat. Sometimes, indeed, so well did she argue her cause, that Jack was inclined to agree with her. Then again remembering the opinions which he had heard his father and Cousin Nat express, he thought the present state of things was satisfactory. However, in the end Alethea contrived to leave him very much in doubt about the matter, and certainly at that moment, if she had put a sword in his hand, and told him that King James was coming back, and that he must go and fight under his banner, he would very probably have obeyed her orders.

The dinner hour at length arrived, when Mr Harwood returned with several letters in his hand. The Squire treated him with every kindness and attention, as the son of an old friend, and did not in any way allude to the subject on which his daughter had been so energetically expatiating. A stranger coming in would not have heard any thing to make him suppose that the owner of Harwood Grange was one of the greatest Jacobites in that part of the country.

"Remember," said Alethea, as Jack's horse was brought round to the front door, and he was about to mount, "I shall expect to hear that my arguments have had due effect, and that you will be ready to drink the health of the king over the water, whenever you hear it proposed."

He gallantly kissed the fair hand held out to him; and receiving a hearty shake from that of the Squire, he mounted his horse and took his way towards Nottingham. He returned at a much slower pace than he had come. A variety of thoughts and feelings troubled his head and his heart. He thought Alethea the most beautiful creature he had ever set eyes on. He wished to please her in every way in his power. If she had desired him to give up his intention of accompanying Will Brinsmead, he would have done so, or he would even have gone to college, and tried to study like his brother, if she had desired it; but she had not intimated a wish on either of these subjects, and seemed perfectly content that he should follow out his own inclinations. And yet she evidently desired to influence him in some way, and that was what most puzzled him. He had always heard William spoken of as the best king for England, and James as a man likely to prove an opponent of religious liberty and of the advancement and prosperity of the country.

He was even more than usually silent when he reached home, and Polly had to stir him up before he would give any account of his visit to the Grange. He, however, said nothing on the subject which Alethea had discussed with him.

A few days after this, having been declared perfectly convalescent, Jack set off to pay his respects to Mr Strelley, and to receive that gentleman's last orders. As he approached the door, he saw Cousin Nat's scarlet cloak a little ahead of him. He soon overtook the worthy doctor.

"Well, Jack, I am glad to find you," said his cousin: "I want to have a few words with you before you start, and there's no opportunity like the present. Let me advise you, as you have entered into this business, to stick to it, and you will find it as lucrative, at all events, as any you could well engage in. You will pass in your journeys many a fine park and noble palace going to decay through the fines and alienations which have fallen upon them, and you will thus see for yourself how truly it has been lately written, that 'an estate is but a pond, but trade a spring;' for you will also come upon fair houses, whose owners' names were unknown before the late Civil Wars, and you will find them flourishing by means of trade, honourably carried on from father to son, whereby not only wealth, but titles too have been won for this generation, and which promise to last for many yet to come."

Mr Strelley received Jack pleasantly, not the less so, perhaps, that he was accompanied by the doctor, who told him of the advice he had been giving his young kinsman.

"Ah, indeed!" observed the worthy manufacturer, "the wool trade is the great staple, and next to it I place the cattle trade. I will not detain you now to give you an account of these two great sources of wealth; you shall see them another time in my study: and take heart, my young friend; you have your foot on the ladder, and will climb some day to the top, if you gain all the knowledge your honoured kinsman is ready to give you, and are guided by his advice."

"And by your own good sense, Jack," added Cousin Nat. "Don't wish to be master before you have learned to be man, and don't trust every one you may meet, however civil they may be and pleasant in their manners; and above all things, my boy, do not forget that there is a God in heaven who watches over you, and sees and knows every thing you do. Do not fear to displease man, but dread greatly displeasing God. Remember that He is your friend, and that you can go to Him on all occasions. If you go boldly and frankly, as He has told you to do, trusting in His Son who died for you, He will never turn aside from your petitions."

Mr Strelley enforced what Cousin Nat had said with further arguments, and then having given Jack various directions for his conduct on the road, and for the commissions he was to perform for him, shook him cordially by the hand, and wished him every prosperity on the journey which was to commence the following morning.

Chapter Six
Pearson's Visit to Squire Harwood—
Plan to entrap Jack

On the day Jack had paid his visit to Harwood Grange, while the Squire was walking up and down the terrace, enjoying the cool of the evening, he saw a horseman riding along the avenue towards him. He was a strongly-built, active-looking man, with somewhat coarse features and a bold expression of countenance. He dismounted as he approached Mr Harwood, and presented a letter which he drew from his bosom.

"That will tell you who I am," said the horseman, as the Squire opened the epistle and glanced at its contents.

"Ah, yes!" he said, looking up at the stranger, "we have met before. I remember you now. Come along here, down this walk; we shall be out of ear-shot. Well, what success have you had?"

"Not so much as I should have expected," answered the stranger. "There's no spirit in the young men now-a-days; they all seem to be finding employment either at home, or at sea, or in the plantations, and there are few worth having, or who can be trusted at all events, who seem disposed to draw a sword for King James."

"I am afraid you are right," answered the Squire. "Most of those I have spoken to seem perfectly contented with this Dutch William we have got over us, and do not show any wish to have back their rightful king. But still we must not despair, Master Pearson."

"I am the last man to do that either," answered the stranger; "and if we cannot find them on this side of the border, there will be no lack on the other. It will not cost much labour to arouse the Highlanders, while some of the best soldiers in the country, though they refuse to join us, will stand neutral, not for love of the Stuarts, just the contrary, but because William did not treat King James as Cromwell and his party treated his father."

"What say you, Master Pearson? Do you think you could arouse the people in the fen-country? You might raise and drill an army in those wilds without the Government knowing any thing about the matter."

"If the people had any spirit, it could be done," said Master Pearson; "but they are too dull and stupid, I fear, to be aroused by any motive, and I suspect they care little what king sits on the throne."

"I am afraid, then, we must be content with small beginnings," said the Squire. "A good time will come if we wait for it; and if William dies, though I would have no hand in hastening his death, there would be no doubt that the people would be glad enough to get King James back again."

"As to that, his life is as good as James's," observed Pearson; "and if we have not a strong party in readiness to take advantage of any thing that may occur, I fear the Puritan Nonconformists generally will still be too powerful in the country to allow the return of a Catholic sovereign. We must go on recruiting, Squire, and work away among gentles and simples till we have increased the strength of our party, and then will be the time to strike a blow, which may set things to rights again."

"Perhaps it may be so," observed the Squire musingly; "but we must be cautious, Master Pearson; too many honest men have lost their heads for want of that quality, and I have no desire to lose mine or my estate either, which a plot of this sort, if discovered, would seriously imperil. Mind, all I say is, that we must be cautious, and wait patiently till we can gain strength; and by-the-bye there is a young man I wish to win over, a fine, spirited lad, and I'm sure if we can gain him he will prove valuable to the cause. Should you fall in with him, Master Pearson, I must commend him to your care. We have pressed him here pretty hard, and though he seemed stubborn, I think if right arguments coming from another source were to be used, he might yet be gained over. He is the younger son of Mr Jasper Deane of Nottingham. You are very likely in your rambles to come across him."

"I have done so already," answered Master Pearson, "and formed the same opinion of the youth as you have expressed. I hoped, indeed, to have gained him over by this time; but though he promised to meet me again, I missed him. Having, however, now received your further recommendation, I will be on the watch for him, and I dare say I shall come across him before long."

"Do so, good Master Pearson. I wish we could find a few hundreds such as he is, and the king would not long be kept out of his own. And now come into the house: we will send your horse round to the stable, and probably you and he will not be the worse for some refreshment."

"As to that, Squire, I have not ridden far to-day, but I know not how many leagues I may have to cover before to-morrow morning, and I make it a rule to keep my horse and myself in readiness for a gallop north or south, as I find necessary."

"Well, come in, Master Pearson; you can rest here as long as you like. My people are faithful, so that even if they suspected any thing, you need have no fear of their betraying you."

At a summons from the Squire the groom appeared, and was about to take Master Pearson's horse round to the stable, when he interposed.

"Stay," he said; "my beast is a sorry-looking jade, but I have a regard for the animal, and always make a rule of seeing her fed; so you will excuse me, Squire, while I go round, and I will join you presently. Take care of her heels, lad," he added, as the groom led the mare into the stable: "she has a trick of kicking, if she is not handled as she is accustomed to, for I always look after her myself. I will not unsaddle her, but just loosen the girths. There, that will do. There's as much corn there as she will require, and a few handfuls of hay will serve her for supper besides. You understand me now? You will be wise not to come into the stall unless I am here."

As he spoke, he crossed the groom's hand with a piece of silver, and having removed from the holsters a brace of pistols, which he deposited in the ample pockets of his riding-coat, he left the stable.

"You will keep an eye on the stables, and let me know if any one comes near them in my absence," he said, in a tone which made the groom feel that he was not a man to be trifled with.

With an unconstrained, independent air, Master Pearson entered the house, where the Squire stood ready to receive him. Alethea came into the supper-room for a few moments, but not liking the manner or appearance of their guest, asked leave of her father to withdraw, guessing indeed that the Squire would not require her presence during the meal.

About the hour at which the family generally retired to rest, Master Pearson rose from his seat, declaring it was time for him to take his departure.

"I must be twenty miles from hence before midnight," he observed, laughing. "I make it a rule if possible to put about that distance between the place where I am last seen, and the spot I sleep at, on most nights of the week. It is seldom I should thus fail to prove an *alibi* if necessary, while it would be difficult for any one, however sharp, to catch me."

The Squire accompanied his guest to the stable, where Master Pearson carefully examined his horse's hoofs, as well as the girths of his saddle, threw himself into it, and shaking hands with his host, started off at a quick trot down the avenue.

"A hard life he must have of it," thought the Squire, who was beginning to be fonder of his ease than of physical exertion. "I hope that he is trustworthy, for he has my life, and that of a good many other worthy gentlemen, in his power."

Chapter Seven
Jack's Journey to Stourbridge, and Adventures on the Road

Jack, when he placed his head on his pillow the last night before leaving home, fully expected to awake of his own accord the following morning; but for several hours sleep did not visit his eyelids; and when at length he opened them, he saw his eldest sister Kate leaning over him. She had been watching for some time his youthful face, which even in sleep bore so determined an expression, while the brown, strong hand outside the counterpane looked well fitted for any work he might undertake.

"Jack," she said, "you did not answer, dear brother, when I knocked at the door, and I was afraid you would over-sleep yourself: besides, I want to have a few words with you which I had no opportunity of speaking last night. Brother, you are going into a world where, although there is some good, I am afraid there is a great deal of evil, and treachery, and deceit. Though you have done wild and thoughtless things, still you know what is right, and I am sure you wish to follow it. But, dear Jack, I know you better than perhaps you know yourself. Do not trust to your own good intentions. You may think now that nothing will tempt you to do what is wrong, but remember that Satan is always going about to lead us away from the right course; therefore, Jack, I want you to look to your Bible to learn how you ought to walk, and then to pray to God that He will, by His Holy Spirit, enable you to walk aright. Here is a Bible, Jack, and I hope you will take it with you; but I must not preach more. I see you have a letter from Mr Strelley to Mr Gournay at Norwich. You know that our friend Giles Dainsforth is staying with him, and I must tell you, Jack, what I have never told you before, that I have promised to become his wife, if our father and mother will give their consent. He has not as yet much worldly wealth, but he is steady and industrious, and that will come in good time; only I want you to speak to him, and hear what he has got to say to you. It will not be time lost to you: of that I am sure. You will tell him all about us, and should he not be at home, you will make a point of trying to find him, will you not, Jack?"

As she spoke, she imprinted a kiss on her brother's brow.

"And now I will go down-stairs and get your breakfast ready. May God ever be with you, my dear brother!"

While Jack was dressing, he received a visit from his brother Jasper, who had some kind words and good advice also to give him. Although the brothers were on the best of terms, they associated very little with each other, their habits and amusements being very different. Still, Jack admired and respected Jasper for his talents, his amiable disposition, and his refined manners, though he felt little disposed to imitate the latter. Jasper had been away at the time Jack paid his farewell visit to Harwood Grange, and whether he admired Alethea or not, he at all events showed no jealousy of his brother, or annoyance at his having been there without him.

Polly's farewell was even more hearty than that of her brother and sister. Her parting salute was a slap on the back, in return for some words which he whispered in her ear, and a glance of pride, perhaps, as she saw the good figure he cut, equipped in his horseman's suit and thoroughly prepared for the road.

His parents gave him their blessing, but the manner of his father especially was somewhat cold, and showed him that the old gentleman had not altogether got over his dislike to the calling he had resolved to follow.

In a few minutes more, mounted on a stout cob, with a serviceable pair of pistols in his holsters, he was jogging along the road to Cambridge by the side of Master Brinsmead, accompanied by an ample number of drovers in charge of one of the largest droves of cattle which had for some time past left the Trent valley. It may easily be imagined that such a journey, begun in summer time, continued at short stages, with frequent delays at towns, and lonely inns, and farm-houses, was full of interest to Jack, who had only made one short trip of the sort before. The long droves of cattle went slowly along the roads, which in most places were little better than causeways roughly raised from the mud that lay on either side in bad weather. Even the best highways were allowed to fall into a miserable condition, so that carriages could with difficulty traverse them, except in the immediate neighbourhood of London and some of the larger cities. The hedge-rows every where afforded ample shade, and the wide green margins of the lanes gave space for the herd to lie down during the heat of the day. At such times Jack would pursue his beloved sport of angling—for he was never willing to be idle—and many a delicious repast of trout, and chub, and barbel did he broil over the drovers' gipsy fire. On such occasions Will Brinsmead seldom failed to bring forth his well-worn Bible, or his beloved Bunyan's "Pilgrim's Progress," from which, lying down with his elbow on the grass, he would read half aloud to himself, raising his voice if he saw any one approaching near enough to listen. Jack was frequently among Brinsmead's auditors.

These quiet rests were generally succeeded by the bustle which was to be found in the various towns and markets through which they passed; but though for the moment the impressions received appear to have worn off, in after-years Jack remembered his old friend's quaint remarks with no small amount of satisfaction and profit.

Brinsmead's droves were often joined by others belonging to different masters. They usually travelled as far as possible in the earliest morning hours, to secure the freedom of the roads. On all occasions the drovers were armed with various weapons to defend their charge from the cattle-stealers who were too often apt to hang upon their skirts, ready to carry off any stray beast they could find, though the gibbet was the penalty if they were captured. Trains of pack-horses also would bear them company as they approached Cambridge, carrying all kinds of stores and goods for Stourbridge Fair.

Jack, following the advice of his friend, resolved to obtain as much information as he could, and therefore often fell out from his own party, and jogged along by the side of the merchant or pedlar who seemed most ready for his society. Jack had also occasionally to ride on before the drovers, to make arrangements for the feeding and rest of the cattle with some farmer or grazier a little off the high-road. In most instances the worthy farmer was so well pleased with his honest countenance and pleasant manners, that he invited him with Master Brinsmead, who was well-known all along the road, to partake of his family supper. If good old Will found a fitting opportunity, he would on such occasions suggest reading a chapter in the Bible, which he expounded in his own peculiar phraseology, in a clear and edifying manner, never failing to offer up a fervent prayer that a blessing might rest on the house of his entertainers, that his honoured master might prosper, and that he and his companions might be preserved from the dangers of the road, and obtain a satisfactory price for their cattle. Seldom indeed did his hosts refuse his offer, or fail to be sensible that besides his fair payment for keep of man and beast, he had left a blessing behind him.

At many of these midland farms great bargaining took place, for Mr Strelley's droves supplied them with store cattle, as agriculture was beginning to be better understood than it had ever before been in England. Whole carcases were still salted down for winter consumption at the great country-houses. At these also Brinsmead and John Deane were welcome visitors, and chaffering in the steward's room, or with his honour the squire, or even with my lord or my lady herself, would frequently take up many hours of the day. They had also to buy as well as to sell, for the larger the supply they could take to Stourbridge Fair, the better would it be for their speculation.

One day Jack had been riding by the side of a travelling merchant, the owner of a train of pack-horses, when, as he was dropping behind to join his own party, he felt a hand pressed on his shoulder, and heard a voice which he thought he recognised exclaiming, "What cheer, lad? Glad to see that thou hast kept to thy intention, and taken up the honest calling of a drover. Better than cutting weasands any day for the sake of keeping a Dutch usurper on the throne," he added in a lower tone.

Jack looked at the speaker once or twice, unable to recognise him. At length it occurred to him that he was the very man who had joined him on their poaching expedition.

"I think I know you," he said, looking at him again.

"You ought to do so, for we have met before; and it was not my fault that we did not meet again," answered the stranger.

"What! Master Pearson?" said Jack, examining his countenance more narrowly, and looking down on the somewhat clumsy, ill-groomed horse which the speaker bestrode.

The animal was, however, he saw at a second glance, not destitute of bone and muscle; while the rider's expression of countenance and general appearance made it difficult to believe that he was of the pacific character his words would imply. A pair of substantial saddle-bags hung across the saddle, and Jack observed that the butts of two pistols projected from the holsters on either side.

"Why, Master Pearson, you have made good despatch with your business in the north," said Jack; "for I think I am not wrong in calling you by that name. I hope that it has been successful."

"As things generally go with me," answered Pearson carelessly. "I am now on my way south again to Cambridge and other places; for I also have some interest in the wool trade, and hope to be at Stourbridge Fair: that beats every other mart in the world, in my opinion."

"I have heard that it was far above our Goose Fair," said Jack, "though we are not ashamed of that either."

"That is a right curious name you give your fair, Master Deane," observed Pearson. "There must be a great sight of geese sold there, I'm thinking."

"Not exactly," answered Jack. "I do not know that more geese are sold then than at any other time."

"Then come, tell me why it is called Goose Fair: there must be a reason for it," said Pearson. "If you know it, out with the truth, lad."

"The reason why our Nottingham Fair is called Goose Fair? Well, if you needs must know the story, I'll out with it," said Jack, thus pressed by his companion. "Of course, having been born and bred in Nottingham, I believe all about it. You must know that some time, since bold Robin Hood ranged through Sherwood Forest, at all events between his days and ours, there dwelt within it, some ten miles away, a worthy knight and his dame. The better half of the knight was a shrew, and led him a wretched life. He had a son, on whom he bestowed all the affection which his wife might have shared. At length death relieved him of his tormentor. The dame died and was buried. He had a wonderfully heavy stone put on the top of her grave, lest she should come to life again; and then he gave all his thoughts to the education of his son. He resolved, moreover, that he should not make the mistake of which he had been guilty by marrying too early. He therefore kept the boy closely confined within the precincts of his own domain, within which not a female of any age, old or young, was allowed to enter. They were all alike, he declared. The oldest might inveigle his boy as well as the youngest. At length the lad having approached the age of twenty-one, and being perfectly contented with his lot, his father thought that he might with safety take him to Nottingham Fair where he had business. Scarcely had they dismounted from their steeds than a damsel with black eyes and rosy cheeks came tripping by. The lad regarded her with eyes of astonishment and admiration.

"'Oh, father, father, what is that curious animal?' he asked, seeming about to run after her.

"'Why, my boy, that is but a goose—a silly, weak, worthless goose,' answered the knight, greatly alarmed at the effect the sight of the damsel had had on his son. Nevertheless they entered the fair, where not one but hundreds of damsels presented themselves to the astonished gaze of the young man.

"'Ah, this must be Goose Fair!' he kept saying to himself; but being well brought up, he kept steadily by his father's side. This so well pleased the knight, that he promised to give him any fairing he might ask for.

"'Oh, thank you, dear father!' he exclaimed instantly. 'Oh, buy me a goose—by all means buy me a goose!'

"From that day to this our fair has been called Goose Fair; and really, Master Pearson, I think you'll allow that there are some very pretty geese to be seen there."

Master Pearson laughed at Jack's account, and at his notion of its importance.

"Well, there are some fairs abroad which I have visited almost on as grand a scale. There is Leipsic in Saxony, Neuremberg, and Augsburg, all great in their way, but not to be compared to Stourbridge as to the value and amount of property sold."

"What! have you ever been to those places?" asked Jack with surprise, glancing at the rough-looking drover, "or do you only speak from having heard of them?"

"Oh, I have attended the fairs held there myself!" answered Master Pearson. "I have been to many others too, such as that of Frankfort-on-the-Maine; and I tell you, my lad, the great corn-field near Casterton shows a more wonderful sight than any of them. You are lucky in having to make your first business trip there, instead of northward."

"I do not care greatly which way I ride," answered Jack cheerily; "all the world is new to me, and I want to see as much of it as I can."

"You will see a specimen of a good deal of what I call the world in a few days," said Master Pearson. "We have had such splendid weather, that the corn has been got off the fields, otherwise it would be a bad look out for the farmers. The fair-keepers have a right, you must know, to trample it under foot, and to lay out their streets, and set up their booths on the ground, whether it is standing or not. However, you'll know all about the fair when you have been there. You'll have extensive dealings in one way or another for your employer, I doubt not."

"Yes, probably," observed Jack. "We shall have a good sum to lay out, I know; for we have done very well with beasts. They say that the drovers from the north have had great losses from the attacks of Ben Nevis and his gang, who have been bolder than ever this year. It is a pity a fellow of that sort cannot be caught and hung. I have no fancy for allowing rogues to disturb honest men in their proper trade. For my part, I should like to organise a bold band of fellows and hunt down the robber. I have learned one thing—that black is black, and white is white; and though, maybe, he is a bold fellow, that is no reason he is not a rogue, and richly deserves hanging."

Master Pearson laughed as Jack spoke.

"You must catch your hare before you cook him; remember that, lad," he observed.

"There is the difficulty," answered Jack. "They say that no one has caught sight of him except at a great distance; and I am told his horse flies like a meteor, and is as light as the wind. He can follow his master up-stairs as easily as a cat, and up a tree for that matter, I verily believe, and will leap down precipices high enough to break the bones of any ordinary man or horse. Thus there is scarcely a chance of coming up with him, although the country has been scoured again and again, and even some of his rogues have been caught and hung."

"A valuable animal that you speak of," observed Master Pearson coolly. "I dare say his master is as proud of him as I am of my poor beast, who, though he has no great speed, is a trusty friend on the road, and has carried me many a long mile. 'Slow and sure' is his motto."

"I do not fancy that you always ride at a slow pace though, Master Pearson," observed Jack, laughing carelessly. "Your legs cling too tightly to your horse's sides, and you have too easy a seat in your saddle to care much for a slow beast, sure as he may be."

"I was bred in Yorkshire, Master Jack Deane," answered Pearson with a peculiar glance at Jack. "Every boy there knows how to bestride a horse as soon as he can run; though, to be sure, I won't deny that I have taken a gallop now and then in my day. And now I think we understand each other. You remember our meeting down by the river-side: I took a fancy to you on that night, and I told you I had something to talk to you about. Are you willing to hear it now? But I have no fancy that any passer should hear the chance words we may let drop: so speak low when you reply my ears are sharp enough; and you will give me your word of honour that you will not repeat what you hear of me, unless I give you leave."

Jack, whose curiosity had been aroused by what Master Pearson had said, gave the required promise, and without further circumlocution his companion proposed to him a scheme which Jack would have been the wiser had he at the first refused to listen to.

Master Pearson showed himself to be an able diplomatist, and Mr Harwood would have been thoroughly satisfied had he heard the way in which his wishes were carried out.

"Think of what I have been saying, my lad," he continued. "You have got the right qualities in you, depend upon that, and it's your own fault if you don't rise in the world in the way I have pointed out. And now, farewell;

we shall meet again before long, I doubt not; but I have some business to settle a short distance off the road, and I must get free of this crowd."

Saying this, Pearson shook Jack by the hand, and trotted past him at a quick rate. A wide ditch and hedge divided the road from a large field, along which the way was free and open. A few drovers only were in sight, urging on their cattle. Jack, who had kept his eye on his late companion, was somewhat surprised to see his seemingly sorry jade take a spring which cleared both hedge and ditch, and then to observe him cantering along the field at a rate which would have distanced many horses at a gallop.

"He is a strange person," thought Jack, "but he seems good-natured and well-intentioned. I cannot make him out, but as to doing what he advises, I must take time to consider about that."

Chapter Eight
Attacked by Cattle-lifters

Jack, drawing up by the side of the road, waited till Brinsmead again overtook him, and then jogged on as before quietly by his side.

"Well, Master Deane, I hope you have not been engaged in any idle conversation with the varlets you have fallen in with along the road," said the old man. "There are some good men and true among them, but not a few rogues too, depend on that. For my part, I think it's generally wiser to keep myself to myself, unless one meets a godly man who can discourse discreetly on spiritual matters."

Jack was afraid that his good old friend was about to commence one of his long discourses. He therefore, to put a stop to it, and feeling that it was right to do so, mentioned his encounter with the stranger, though he was compelled by his promise not to say he had met him before, or to repeat the main subject of his conversation. He could not help remarking the contrast between the expression of honest Brinsmead's countenance, as he jogged along on his steady old grey horse, and that of Master Pearson: the one free and open, with a kind smile generally playing over it, and the other strongly marked and coarse, with a cunning look in the eyes, and a constant tendency to a sneer on the lips.

"After all, I had better not trust that man," he said to himself. "His words are seemingly fair, but I don't altogether like him."

Brinsmead and Jack continued along the road for some way, with high banks and thick-set hedges on either side, till they reached a flat at the bottom of a dip, extending for a considerable distance, along which the water lay pretty deep, having long overflowed its proper banks, and wandered lazily for miles over meadows on either side of the road. Here they were stopped by a cart greatly overloaded with wood, the two heavy wheels of one side having sunk deep in the mud. An old man in smock-frock, and five or six other carters in the same dress were working hard, apparently to extricate the waggon.

"Why don't the fellows unload the cart?" exclaimed Jack; "they will never get it out otherwise."

The pack-horses and the other herds must have passed before the accident had occurred; for there was scarcely room to allow the animals to get by between the cart and the ditch. Just as Mr Strelley's herd arrived at the waggon, over it went, completely blocking up the road.

"Had we not better try and help them?" exclaimed Jack to Brinsmead; "they will never do it of themselves, and we should soon get the wood off the waggon."

Jack and the Cattle-lifters.

"Let us see how they manage for themselves first," answered Brinsmead. "I don't see what business they have to upset their waggon just at this moment. It is my belief that they could have prevented the accident had they chosen, from the way it went over."

Meantime the drovers with shouts and blows were turning back the herd, to prevent them rushing into the water, which they were about to do when they found they could pass no other way.

"Shall we help you?" cried Jack to the carters. "We should soon with a few ropes be able to get your wheels on dry ground, if you take the weight off the top."

"Mind your own business, young man!" exclaimed a voice from the neighbourhood of the cart. "We know what we're about, and that's more than you do, I'm thinking."

"I do not like the look of things," said Brinsmead to Jack. "I will stay here, and you go back and see after the cattle; I don't know what may be happening otherwise."

Jack accordingly, whip in hand, rode back, the herd being much more separated than usual. As he went on, he saw a considerable number of stragglers in the rear; and as he approached them, what was his astonishment to find that they were being driven away by a dozen fellows or more across the country! He instantly put spurs to his horse and galloped after them, drawing a pistol, and holding it in his hand as he advanced. The cattle-lifters, however,—for such there could be no doubt they really were,—took no notice of his approach, only urging on the beasts the faster. As he came up to the nearest man, he pulled the trigger, but the pistol flashed in the pan; while the man at whom he aimed uttered a scornful laugh in return. His second pistol behaved in the same manner; and on putting his hand in his pocket for his powder-flask, he found that that had gone.

"You will get the worst of it," cried the man, "if you attempt to approach," drawing, as he spoke, a pistol from under his smock-frock. "You had better go back and look after the rest of the beasts, and think yourself fortunate we have not taken the whole of them."

Jack had lifted his heavy stock-whip, intending to dash in at the man; but at that instant the report of fire-arms from the direction of the cart which had been upset reached his ears. It was too evident that Brinsmead and the rest of the men had been attacked, and Jack felt he could be of most use by riding back to assist them. As he was hastening on, approaching the rear of the frightened herd, a horseman who had just come along the road approached him. The stranger, from the pistols in his belt and his general appearance, was, he had no doubt, one of the gang of cattle-lifters. Jack, however, was not inclined to yield without a struggle. Drawing therefore a long knife, or rather dagger, which he carried in a sheath in his belt, he dashed at the horseman.

"Halloo there, my lad, sheathe your blade, if you have not a fancy for having your brains blown out!" exclaimed the other, quietly at the same time drawing a pistol from his belt.

Jack saw that he was covered by the weapon, and restraining his anger exclaimed, "These beasts are under my charge, and I want to know by what right you and your people dare to drive them off the road?"

"By the right of might," answered the robber, for such he seemed to be. "Just calm yourself, my lad; perhaps we may settle matters more easily than you now fancy. You will understand that we could manage to carry off every one of your drove if we chose, but we do not wish to do that. Will you listen to my terms?"

"I will listen to them, but will not undertake to agree to them," answered Jack. "What are they?"

"We will take ten shillings sterling a head for every one of the cattle in the drove. If you agree to that, those which have been driven off shall be returned; if not, we shall take the liberty of helping ourselves to as many as we fancy."

"I will mention the terms you propose to our head drover," answered Jack: "if he agrees to them, I have not a word to say to the contrary."

"Well, be smart about it, my lad. Will Brinsmead is a man of sense, so I have no doubt he will listen to reason on this occasion. Hasten down, therefore, to your friends in the swamp there; they and our men have played long enough at quarter-staff; and mark you, if Brinsmead does not like my offer, remind him I have the power to settle the business in another way."

Jack looked doubtfully at the horseman, fearing that when he went up to the front, more of the cattle would be driven off.

"You need not be afraid, Mr Deane; your cattle are safe enough, I give you my word for it: none shall be taken till you come back," said the robber, observing Jack's hesitation.

Jack found Brinsmead looking very disconsolate at the turn affairs had taken.

"We have fallen among the Philistines, Jack, and it's not likely they will let us go till they have fleeced us completely."

"Cheer up, Master Brinsmead!" said Jack. "I will speak to them, and see what can be done."

On this Jack called a parley with their opponents, who seemed prepared for the proposal; but not without much grief and many doubts did Will Brinsmead listen to the terms. Seeing, however, that his chance of escape was hopeless, he at length consented to pay the levier of black-mail his iniquitous dues. On this Jack rode back to the top of the rise where he had left the horseman, and told him that the arrangement was agreed to.

"Well, then, send your people to look after the beasts, and I will come down and settle with worthy Master Brinsmead. You will not find it silver thrown away, let me tell you; for we shall take care that not a crown more will you have to pay till you get safe back to your master with the profits of your journey."

With many a groan and sigh Brinsmead produced his leathern purse from a side-pocket carefully secured round him, and counted out the pieces into the broad palm of the cattle-lifter, who coolly deposited them in his pouch, as if he had been receiving the result of an honest bargain. Meantime the waggon without much difficulty was lifted up from its position, and dragged on one side to allow the beeves to pass by.

"I will give you an acknowledgment if you like, friend," said the robber with a laugh. "If you will write out the paper, I will sign it with my mark; for as to writing, it's an art I never learned."

"How came you to know my name?" asked Jack. "I don't remember you."

"We know every body who travels along this road, and maybe we have met before, though you don't recollect me," answered the robber. "And now farewell to you, and may you find a good market for your beasts, and success in all your dealings."

Saying this, the robber turned his horse, and rode up the hill, while the rest of the band withdrew quickly out of sight. The poor fellows who had been hurt were placed on horseback, and Brinsmead and Jack Deane trudged along by their side, considerably downcast by the adventure. Brinsmead had never appeared so much put out.

"This comes of the way you have of talking to all the people you meet, Mr Deane," he observed, in a tone very unlike that he usually used. "I have a belief that the man you were riding so long by the side of has had something to do with this day's business. I marked him when he passed me, and I told you then that I did not like his looks."

"You mean Master Pearson, I suppose," answered Jack. "I cannot make out how he can have had any thing to do with the thieves. He told me all about himself; and if he was not an honest man, he would not have done that. He is a Yorkshireman, a dealer in wool and drapery, and is on his way to Stourbridge Fair and Newmarket. If he had had any sinister motive, he would not have spoken as frankly as he did."

"Then who stole your powder-flask, and drew the bullets out of your pistols?" asked Brinsmead.

"Not the man you speak of, certainly," said Jack. "I looked at the priming of my pistols this morning, and they were all right, though to be sure, not thinking that they might have been tampered with, I did not examine the charges. However, he could not have done it while riding alongside of me. In what state did you find your pistols, Brinsmead?"

"I must own, Jack, they would not go off either; and yet I did this morning what I always do, examine them before starting, when I have my master's property to defend upon the road."

"But did you never lose sight of them after you had examined them?" asked Deane.

Brinsmead thought a few moments.

"Yes, I remember now, for once I did; and now I think of it, I remember seeing a man, very like the fellow who has just left us, watching me as I went out. That's it, depend on it."

While Brinsmead was speaking, he pulled out his pistols and examined them with his ramrod. The charge of both had been withdrawn. He put them back into his holsters with a look of annoyance.

"Ah! these are old tricks, and more shame to me I was not up to them; but now, for the sake of the poor fellows we have got here, we must push on as fast as we can get the drove over this mud and these mortally bad roads. There's a house called Winn's Farm about three miles off from here, where we shall be able to get good pasturage, and the men will be well looked after."

Pushing on, in the course of another hour the drove approached Winn's Farm which had been spoken of, when Deane walked on before that he might explain to the farmer what had happened, and make arrangements for remaining there during the night. The names of Mr Strelley of Nottingham and his old drover were well-known along the road, and accordingly a kindly welcome was given to the whole party. The kine were turned into some good grazing-ground, and the wounded drovers were carefully placed on a bed, and their hurts looked to by Dame Winn, the farmer's wife. The good woman prided herself on her surgical knowledge, having received instructions from her mother, who in her younger days had had unhappily, during the Civil Wars, too much opportunity of gaining experience in the art of attending to gunshot wounds.

"We must have better laws, Master Brinsmead; these sort of things cannot be allowed in the country," observed Farmer Winn, when his guests were seated round his hospitable board, at which all his family, as well as the drovers and his old farm-servants, were also assembled. "I have suffered from some of these caterans from the north, so I have a fellow-feeling with you, I can tell you."

"The laws are not so bad," answered Brinsmead, "but we want people to carry them out. The king is willing enough, but it is hard to get people to assist him. However, things are improving in many respects, and depend upon it these gentlemen have not a much longer course to run."

Will Brinsmead had no objection to the good things of life, and while enjoying the substantial fare set before him by Farmer Winn and his good dame, soon forgot the annoyance he had suffered.

Chapter Nine
Stourbridge Fair—Adventures at Cambridge

As Will Brinsmead and John Deane with their charge approached Cambridge, they found the roads, always far from good, becoming worse and worse, in consequence of the vast amount of traffic which had passed over them; while crowds of other small dealers and purchasers from all parts of the country would account for the vast concourse of people who were to be seen both in the town of Cambridge, along the banks of the river, and thickly scattered over the meadows. From all directions were seen moving on carts, waggons, caravans, and vehicles of all sorts, from London and elsewhere, as well as innumerable trains of pack-horses laden with Yorkshire goods from Leeds, Halifax, and other towns in an apparently endless succession, bound for the Duddery, the great mart for wholesale dealers in woollen manufactures, which was to occupy a considerable portion of the meadow in which the fair was held. In the vehicles from London were conveyed milliners, toy-sellers, goldsmiths, turners, haberdashers, mercers, drapers, hatters, and in fact representatives of all the trades of the metropolis.

At a short distance from Cambridge the drove came fairly to a stop, when, as it chanced, Brinsmead and Jack found close to them, mounted on a tall pack-horse, a personage who by the peculiar cut of his somewhat threadbare garments they took to be a humble student of divinity. He wore a shabby cassock and a shovel hat, sitting the animal on which he journeyed sideways with a book in his hand, making a reading-desk occasionally of a bale of some sort which towered above the horse's neck. Old Will at once entered into conversation with him, and confided afterwards to Jack that he had been highly edified by his correct and judicious remarks. Jack had, however, remarked a peculiar twinkle in the student's eye when talking to the old man, which made him suspect his sincerity. He appeared, however, to be very well informed on many subjects, and still further won Master Brinsmead's heart by showing that he possessed some knowledge of the art of breeding cattle, and of healing their diseases, but little understood in those days. They were, however, again separated, and no more was seen of the divinity student.

At length the towers and spires of Cambridge, rising from the groves and gardens of the classic Cam, came in sight.

When Jack Deane rode up to the far-famed meadow, he might well be astonished at the scene he beheld. The sun shone brilliantly on a vast expanse of canvas, with bright-coloured streamers flying over it, and appropriate sign-boards, gilt weathercocks, and other painted ornaments, forming regular streets, and reaching from the high-road which runs between Cambridge and Newmarket to the river.

The "Duddery" was separated from the rest of the fair, and contained larger and more substantial buildings for the display of its valuable bales and its vast pockets of wool, one of which was sufficient to load a waggon. Here, too, great quantities of Yorkshire clothing were exhibited for sale, as well as the produce of the hosiery towns, such as Nottingham, Leicester, and Derby. The sale of wool, however, did not begin till the lighter goods had been disposed of, so that Brinsmead and Deane had ample time to execute the various commissions with which they had been entrusted, and to wander about and to enjoy the wonders of the fair, which Jack did to his heart's content.

One whole street was devoted to hardware of all sorts, from excellent Dutch delf to the coarse pottery furnished by Staffordshire, with occasional luxuries in the form of Chelsea tea-services, or costly jars of grotesque shapes from Pekin, sent by the London china-shops. All sorts of toys and fancy articles were to be found. Painted mirrors, which were then greatly in fashion, fans, long leathern gloves, jewelled snuff-boxes, wooden balls, and whirligigs might be seen, to satisfy the fancy of those who came rather for amusement than business. The great characteristic of the fair, however, lay in the enormous quantity of merchandise of the best quality that was accumulated there from all parts of England. The price of hops was fixed in Kent and Herefordshire by their value at Stourbridge Fair, and the horse-market and the cattle-market were the largest of the year any where. Nearly a thousand horse-packs of Yorkshire cloths, such as kerseys, fustians, and pennistons, together with Manchester goods, took up one side and a half of the Duddery, and it was not uncommon to hear that 100,000 pounds worth of woollen manufactures had been sold there in less than one week's time.

Among the tents and sheds were eating-houses and innumerable places of refreshment, and coarse entertainment to suit the lowest tastes, with the customary sights and shows popular at such gatherings. Dwarfs and giants, jugglers and ballet-dancers and rope-dancers with their painted booths were more common than wonders from foreign lands. Mountebanks attracted also great attention, and so also did some curious clocks from Neuremberg, and Dutch figures made to move by concealed machinery. Play-actors and mummers also were to be found, some of their troupe in front of their large booths drumming and piping and shouting, and inviting the passers-by to enter and behold the wonders they had to exhibit. There were tumblers also, and fat pigs, and learned pigs, and dancing bears, indeed sufficient exhibitions of all sorts to captivate and amuse every description of taste.

Brinsmead, as he walked through the fair, kept Jack close to him. The play-actors especially excited his indignation.

"Don't look that way, lad," he observed; "they are seducing follies, just invented by Satan to lead the young astray, and no good ever came to those who have frequented such places. I would I were the chief magistrate, to put them all down; but the Evil One must have his way, I'm afraid, though it will be a happy day when he is driven out of the world."

The magistrates' booth held an important position in the array of lath and canvas, which had been erected as soon as the harvest had been got off the ground. Here a regular court of justice was held as long as the fair lasted. The magistrates wore their gowns and gold chains of office, and arrived every day in some considerable state by water from Cambridge, when they were generally followed by a crowd of gaily-painted barges and passenger-wherries, which had, as has been said, been brought from London. All disputes arising out of the traffic of the fair were settled at the magistrates' booth, which was also duly attended by constables and several officials, to preserve order and bring up culprits.

The liveliness and brilliancy of the scene were greatly increased by the dresses of the many-coloured crowd: the gay cloth jackets and gold and silver lace, the bright ribbons in the head-dresses of the women, and the feathers in those of the men. These were the days when stockings of the brightest hue were worn by the women, with silver and variously coloured clocks, and high-heeled shoes; while the habits of the men were varied and many-coloured. No one seemed at rest. Men, women, and children were moving about in all directions; now stopping before the mercers' shops, or the sempsters from Cheapside, or looking into those of the goldsmiths: while the vintners were never without a crowd inside or out of their booths. Here was a quack doctor selling his infallible specifics from his cart, promising an unfailing cure for all manner of diseases. There was a mountebank conjurer seated on a table, performing all sorts of wonders before a gaping crowd. Here stood a seeming orator on a barrel, vociferating at the top of his voice, generally, however, inviting purchasers for some article of which his partner, who sat below him, had to dispose. The venerable town itself was of course overflowing with visitors of every degree, and one-half the guests at the inns were accommodated in the stables or lofts, where travellers of higher degree than Brinsmead and Deane were thankful to sleep on straw.

Their first business was very soon accomplished, as the butchers, to whom Mr Strelley's beasts were well-known, looked forward to supply themselves regularly from those which were brought to them by his drovers. The sums obtained for the cattle were to be spent in wool and hops; and besides this more important business, Brinsmead and Deane, with their men, had a great variety of private purchases to make for their families and friends.

Chapter Ten
Jack encounters Master Pearson,
and goes to Norwich

"Vanity Fair! Vanity Fair all over!" exclaimed Brinsmead to Jack, as they worked their way amidst the gaily-clad talking, higgling, laughing, shouting throng. "It's many a day since I came to this part of the meadow. It becometh me more to keep to the Duddery, where staple wares are to be found, than to be wandering about in this fool's paradise; but I wished you, my young friend, to see what is to be seen, that I may point out its folly, and that you might not be fancying you had missed some great delight. See yonder shouting fool, with bells and cap and painted face, grimacing away to the gaping crowd, who think him the merriest fellow they have ever set eyes on. Look into the poor wretch's heart, and, take my word for it, it's well-nigh breaking. Maybe he has a sickly wife and ten small children at home, who will starve if he ceases to grimace: so grimace he must to the end of the chapter. But who is this? An old friend, I verily believe!"

"Yea, and a trusty one, friend Brinsmead," said a person who at that moment confronted Will, and took him cordially by the hand. "But what can have brought you into this hurly-burly of folly and wickedness?"

"And what has brought you into the midst of the same hurly-burly, Job Hodgkinson?" asked Will.

"I desired to make a short cut from the Duddery, and took my way across it," answered the stranger.

Jack did not hear more of what was said; for Will having let go his arm, and the crowd pressing on them, they were speedily separated from each other. Jack looked about for his friend, but old Brinsmead's low-crowned hat was completely concealed by the higher beavers of more pretentious and taller persons. He pushed on as well as he could among the crowd, hoping to overtake Brinsmead, but probably passed him. Suddenly he caught sight, as he thought, of the worthy drover's broad-built figure, moving in a different direction to what he had expected at a pretty quick rate. This made Jack exert himself to overtake him. By the time he came up with the chase, he found that he had been following a stranger. At last, after wandering about in all directions, he gave up the search as hopeless, and determined to amuse himself as best he could, and then to try and find his way back to their quarters in Cambridge.

Jack, not quite entering into Brinsmead's opinions with regard to the wrongfulness of watching the tricks of the mummers and mountebanks and other similar performers, had stopped before the booth of a conjurer, who was by his amusing tricks producing a succession of broad grins on the countenances of a crowd of rustics standing round him, and occasional loud shouts of laughter. As the hubbub for a moment ceased, Jack heard his name pronounced; and turning round, he saw two persons of a class superior to the generality of the crowd standing close to him. The eyes of one of them especially were fixed on him. The other he recognised as the humble college student who had passed him and Brinsmead on their entrance into Cambridge. A second glance showed him that the student's companion was no other than his quondam acquaintance Master Pearson, though no longer habited as a drover, but as a substantial merchant, with a long coat of fine broadcloth, a broad-brimmed beaver on the top of his periwig, a long neckcloth, and high-heeled shoes with huge buckles.

"Ah, you are surprised to see me, Master Deane!" he observed with a laugh, putting out his hand. "I told you that I was a dealer in woollen goods, so that it is but fit I should appear in the proper guise of a decent merchant, instead of in the habit of a common rough-rider, in which you have before seen me. We have well met, for I have been hunting for you through the fair; and my reverend friend here told me he thought he had seen you, and would assist me in the search. I have brought a despatch for you from a friend; for since we parted I have ridden to Nottingham and back again, and have a communication of importance to make to you. It must be in private though, for it will not do to have eaves-droppers, and we know not who standing round might hear us. Where is worthy Will Brinsmead?"

Jack in reply told Pearson how he had lost his friend in the crowd, and begged to be informed of the tenour of the communication.

"I told you that I cannot deliver it out here," answered Pearson; "so come along with me and my reverend friend, Master Simon Stirthesoul; for you have not a chance of meeting with Brinsmead again before nightfall; and I will see you afterwards to your lodgings, if you cannot find the way by yourself."

Jack instinctively gave a hopeless glance round once more for his friend, and then seeing no signs of him, agreed to accompany Pearson and the minister. Pearson seemed anxious not to let Jack escape him, for he took him by the arm, and held it fast while they were working their way through the crowd. This took some time, for the busy throng seemed in no way inclined to make room for them. At length, however, they reached the banks of the Cam, where Master Pearson hailed a wherry and bargained with the rowers to convey them to Cambridge. By this time the shades of evening were coming on, and Jack could not help feeling glad that he had fallen in with Master Pearson, rather than have to find his way by himself back to Cambridge. Never was the river more alive with boats passing and repassing, filled with all descriptions of people, from the magistrate with his chain and cloak of office, his gold-headed mace, and gaudily dressed officials, to small tradesmen and humble artisans with their wives and families. Many returning from the fair were shouting and singing, evidently having paid frequent visits to the vintners' shops, while the children blew their trumpets and sprung their rattles, as an accompaniment to the vocal music of their elders.

On disembarking from the wherry, Pearson, instead of entering the town, led the way to a distant part of the outskirts, stopping at the door of what appeared to be a small farm-house. A knock with his walking-stick gained him admittance, when exchanging a few words with the inmates, he desired his companions also to enter. A decent-looking woman placed a tankard of ale, with pipes and tobacco, before them, and then, without making any remark, withdrew to an inner room.

"They are trustworthy," observed Pearson, as he closed the door; "and now, Master Deane, I will deliver my message. In the first place, you remember that evening I met you down by the water-meadows. It appears that in some way or other you have offended your companions on that evening, and one of them being taken up on suspicion of poaching with the hope of saving his own carcass a flogging, or the pillory, has informed against you and me. You will, therefore, find it somewhat dangerous to revisit your native town for the present. Your friend Mr Harwood hearing of this, and knowing that I had become acquainted with you, sent you this packet, which you will examine at your leisure. It contains a further supply of introductions to several people of importance which he wishes you particularly to deliver in person, and I promised him to invite you to accompany me in the journey I propose making shortly to the north. You will there enjoy a wilder sort of life than you will find in this part of the country, and meet with a variety of characters which will afford you a subject of amusement."

"How provoking!" exclaimed Jack; "I did not think Smedley and Bligh would have turned traitors; and—and—" he hesitated for some seconds.

"You mean to say, you would like to pay another visit to Harwood Grange," said Pearson, with a laugh. "Well, to my mind, you will serve your own purpose better if you carry out Mr Harwood's wishes. In a few months probably the matter will be forgotten, and in the mean time you can see something of the world. A trip over to the Continent would be of interest."

"But I have engaged to accompany Brinsmead to Norwich," observed Jack; "and I have several commissions of importance to execute there for Mr Strelley. I must not neglect them."

"No need for you to do so," answered Pearson. "Go on to Norwich, as you purpose, and I will meet you in a week's time at Saint Faith's. I have agreed to wait there for a party of Highland drovers, who are on their way south with some large herds of lean beasts, for the purpose of getting flesh put upon them in the Lincolnshire fens. What do you say to this plan?"

"I will think it over," said Jack. "I would rather go back to Nottingham and meet the charge like a man. If a fine would get me off, I would sell every thing I possess; though I have no fancy for the pillory, I will confess."

"You would run a great risk of the pillory, let me tell you," observed Pearson; "so I would advise you to carry out the plan I proposed; I think our reverend friend here will give you the same advice."

"Indeed would I, my son," observed the minister; "and though by it you have made yourself amenable to the laws, I cannot see that you are called upon of your own free will to expiate your offence by undergoing the punishment that would await you. I propose to accompany Master Pearson, and may be I shall be able to give you such counsel and advice as will keep you in future from committing such follies and transgressions. These are bad times we live in. Our ancient customs are being overthrown daily, and no man can say where it will all end."

"I thought that most people were pretty well contented now that King William is firmly seated on the throne, and that great improvements are taking place throughout the country in all directions," observed Jack, repeating the remarks he had often heard made by his father, Dr Deane, the Worshipful Mr Pinkstone, and others.

The minister sighed.

"What some call improvements others may look upon in a very different light," he observed; "but we will talk of these things by and by, my young friend; perhaps matters which you now see in one light, you may then see in another."

It is scarcely necessary to repeat the conversation which took place. Jack was excessively puzzled with many of the remarks made by his companions, especially by the divinity student, who seemed to have notions very different to those held in general by Puritan divines. He was evidently a shrewd man, with cunning, piercing eyes, and sharp features, professing to care very little for the good things of life. It appeared that he was to remain at the house where they then were, for Master Pearson wished him good night, and, telling him that he would return anon, invited Jack to accompany him into Cambridge, where he would endeavour to find out the Cat and Whistle, the sign of the hostelry at which Brinsmead and his drovers had put up.

"No necessity to tell old Will what we have been talking about," observed Pearson; "especially that poaching matter, for instance. Tell him that you have received instructions to part company with him at Saint Faith's; and if you render exact account of all your transactions, and give him up any money you may have received belonging to Mr Strelley, he can have no cause of complaint."

Pearson accompanied Deane to the entrance of the inn, where, shaking him warmly by the hand, he said, "Remember Saint Faith's; for your own sake keep to your present intention."

Jack followed Pearson's advice with regard to the account he gave of the cause of his absence. Old Will fixed his keen grey eyes upon him; and Jack could not help feeling that he looked at him with suspicion.

"It's always that Master Pearson!" observed old Will; "I should like to have a few words with him myself. I don't like these strangers who come dodging our steps and turning up in all manner of places. I have an idea, Master Jack, that he has been using you as a pump, to get up through you what information he can about our business. Now, Jack, if you have been communicative to him, you have acted like a fool, and, more than that, have done very wrong. A wise man should keep all his own affairs to himself; and still closer should he keep his master's affairs. They are not his property, remember; and he who talks about them is giving away what is not his own, and that no honest man will do."

"You are hard upon me, Master Brinsmead!" said Jack. "I am not conscious of having said any thing about Mr Strelley's affairs to Pearson, or to any one else. I have committed faults in my time, that I know, and am very likely to have to pay the penalty—I rather hope I may—but I have never acted dishonourably to any one who has trusted me."

Jack, though he spoke thus, was not altogether comfortable in his mind. That night's fishing expedition, and many others of a similar character, which he was conscious were unlawful, rose up before him. Besides, he felt he had spoken more freely to Master Pearson than he ought to have done, though he had not, that he was aware of, communicated any information which might prove detrimental to the interests of his employer. For the first time in his life, perhaps, he had little inclination for supper, while his dreams were far from being of a pleasant character.

The next day he and Brinsmead, with all their party, had an abundance of work to get through. One of the company of pack-horses had to be laden with wool and sent off to Nottingham, while another was got ready to proceed to Norwich. Brinsmead and Jack were to accompany the latter.

The wool for Norwich was to supply with material the worsted manufacture carried on in that town. It had long been noted for it, having been introduced by the Flemings as early as the twelfth century; and it was followed up in latter years by that of Sayes arras and bombasins. Gauzes and crapes had of late years been introduced by the French Huguenot refugees, to whom every encouragement was wisely afforded to set up their looms and other machines.

Chapter Eleven
Jack's Visit to Mr Gournay—The Story of Madame le Mertens

Evening was drawing on when Brinsmead and Jack saw the towers of the numerous churches which Norwich possessed, each situated on its own peculiar mound or hill. On entering the town, they proceeded through its narrow and winding streets to the Bear Inn, which Brinsmead usually frequented.

"There is time to present your letters this evening," he observed to Jack. "When there's business to be done there's nothing like doing it immediately. It's provoking to find when you have delayed that the person whom you wished to meet has left the town the morning after your arrival, when you might have found him had you gone to his abode immediately."

Jack, nothing loath, prepared himself to call upon Mr Gournay. He liked old Brinsmead very well in his way; but could not help sighing for more refined society than his late companions afforded. He therefore put on his Sunday suit, and made himself as presentable as possible. He had no difficulty in finding his way to Mr Gournay's handsome and substantial residence, it being one of the principal mansions in the place. The great merchant himself was out; but he was admitted into the presence of the mistress of the family, who received him with a sweet and matronly grace. She wore her soft brown hair without the addition of any false curls, a rich grey silk gown woven by the Huguenot weavers in Spitalfields, a Norwich-crape shawl, and fine Flemish cambric in her cap, neckerchief, and ruffles. Although it was the custom for ladies of rank to wear rouge as thick as paste, she wore none. She made many inquiries after her esteemed friends Mr and Mrs Strelley, as well as Jack's father and mother, and invited him to remain for their evening meal, which was to be served as soon as Mr Gournay and the other gentlemen inmates of their family returned. While they were speaking four young boys came into the room, whom Mrs Gournay introduced as her sons. They were followed by a tall and graceful lady in deep mourning, no longer young, but bearing traces of considerable beauty.

"I must make you known to my friend and inmate Madame de Mertens," said Mrs Gournay. "She speaks English perfectly, having resided with us for some years, since she was compelled by the Popish Government of France to quit her native country."

"Ah, yes; and I have found a happy and quiet home here," said the lady. "If those I have lost could be restored to me, I would willingly abandon all hopes of regaining thè fortune and estate I once enjoyed. Ah, Monsieur Deane," she exclaimed, after some further conversation had passed between them, "how can any English people regret their Popish king? I am told that even now among your noblest families there are some ready to risk life and fortune to bring him back! See what ours has done for us! Think of the atrocities of his barbarous dragoons in our Protestant districts—peaceful homes given up to pillage, to fire, and the sword. The best of our pastors flogged, and tortured in other ways, imprisoned in loathsome dungeons— what do I say? worse, oh, worse than all! the horrors of the galleys reserved for the noblest and best, for such as my own dear husband Eugene, who, if he still lives, may yet be labouring at the oar, among slaves and outcasts of all nations! Oh, may heaven in mercy rescue him from such an existence!"

She ceased, for her feeling, roused by the recollection of the terrible scenes she had gone through, overcame her power of speech. She hid her face for some moments in her hands!

"I should not have ventured to speak on this subject," she said, when she again looked up. "My husband was Dutch, of an old family; but when he married me he became naturalised as a Frenchman. For a few years after our marriage we lived a life of tranquillity and happiness in a chateau which I had inherited, removed from the turmoil of the world and political strife. We had one only child, a fair-haired, blue-eyed little damsel, with bright rosy cheeks and a happy, joyous smile on her countenance. At length, however, fearful troubles broke upon us on the revocation of the Edict of Nantes, just ten years ago. It was a time fatal to Protestants who ventured to remain in the country. Many of the best and noblest in the land fled from persecution. Some effected their escape, but many were overtaken, and were executed, or are still groaning in prisons, or, like my dear husband, in the galleys. My dear sister and her husband had come to reside with us, hoping that in our secluded abode they would escape observation. Her health was delicate, and on that fatal night when the dragoons burst into our house and carried off my brother-in-law, so greatly was she affected that her spirits gave way, and in a few days afterwards she sank to rest from this troubled world. My brother-in-law was heart-broken at the loss of his wife. He little knew how soon he was to follow her! My husband was absent from the house, when one evening I received notice that some officers of justice, as they were called, were approaching, in search of Protestants. I had just time to snatch up my little Elise, and to hurry off to the woods, where, in a hut which had been prepared by a faithful attendant, and known only to him, we were able to conceal ourselves. My dear husband, not aware of the personages who had possession of our house, returned late in the evening, having missed those who were on the watch to give him notice of what had occurred. He was instantly seized, and carried off for trial before the Government officials, who had been sent to the neighbourhood for that purpose. He, like a faithful servant of our blessed Master, refused to deny Him, or to acknowledge the truth of any of the dogmas of Rome. He was accordingly condemned to the galleys, a fearful fate! He was immediately marched off with many others, condemned for the same crime, to one of the naval ports; but from that day to this I have had no tidings of him, and if he has survived the hardships he has had to undergo, he is still labouring at the oar in one of those dreadful ships, enduring the worst kind of slavery, for life alone will terminate it. My poor brother-in-law was also captured, and refusing to recant, he was treated, being a Frenchman, even more severely than my husband, for he was first tortured; still holding out, the barbarians placed him on the cruel wheel, where, while still alive, his bones were broken, and he, as did many other faithful Protestants, expired, though in fearful torments, still crying to their Lord and Master, and acknowledging His love and the efficacy of the perfect sacrifice He offered for them. Our faithful Pierre, the steward of our estate, having collected all the jewels and other property which he could find, brought them to me and urged me on no account to return to the chateau, being sure that both Elise and I should be sacrificed to the fury of our enemies. Having friends in England, I resolved forthwith to escape to this country. I will not trouble you with my various adventures as I endeavoured to make my way with little Elise in my arms to the sea-coast. The poor people in the villages through which I passed, compassionating me and my little girl, gave us all the assistance in their power. Often some honest farmer, though at considerable risk to himself, would drive me some distance, concealed in his waggon, in the direction I wished to go. Thus I at length reached the neighbourhood of the north coast, where I hoped to find a vessel which would convey me to the shores of England. I had already gained the beach, when in consequence of the waves breaking on the shore, there was great difficulty in embarking. Fearing that Elise might receive some harm should I attempt to hold her while getting into the boat, I committed her to the charge of a seaman, an officer he seemed of some sort, who told me he was going off with us. A considerable number of other people were about to embark in the same vessel, and were crowding down to the edge of the water, when there was a cry that the dragoons were advancing towards us. I in vain attempted to reach the boat. Other people were crowding in, and the seamen, afraid that some accident would happen from her being overloaded, shoved her off into deep water. In vain I entreated that Elise might be restored to me, or that I might be taken on board.

"'The dragoons! the dragoons!' shouted the people all around me.

"'Come, madame, this is no place for you!' I heard a person say close to me. He seized my arm, and almost dragged me along the beach. 'I know of a place near here where you can be concealed,' he said. 'I will conduct you to it; there is no time to lose.'

"Again I entreated him to look for Elise.

"'That will be useless,' he answered: 'she is in God's hands, and He will preserve her! You can do nothing now.'

"He forced me on; and I could not indeed help feeling the justice of his remarks.

"Assisted on by him we reached some rocks, amid which he worked his way, even though it was dark, showing that he was well acquainted with the spot. After going on for some time longer, I found that we were in front of a small cave.

"'Go in there,' he said, in a low voice. 'It is large enough to contain many people; and I have stored it with food for such an emergency as this.'

"The stranger then told me that he was the Protestant pastor of the neighbouring district, and that, though compelled to quit his church, he still ministered in secret among his former flock, who supplied him with food, and warned him of the approach of danger. He had devoted himself to assisting those Protestants who, less fortunate than himself, came to that part of the coast.

"'I am aware,' he said, 'that at any moment I may be discovered; and yet I feel that I am called to this work. God in His mercy has thought fit to preserve me from the hands of my persecutors!'

"Supplied with food and other necessaries by this brave and good man, I remained for several days in the cave. He had a sad account to give me of the fate of most of the fugitives who had been unable to get on board the vessel. Some were cruelly sabred by the dragoons, even though crying for quarter. Others—men, women (young and old), and children—were lifted up on their horses, and carried off at full speed to the neighbouring town, where they were thrown into the dungeons already crowded with prisoners.

"At length the good pastor considered it safe to conduct me to a lonely farm-house, where he told me I must remain till he could arrange for my passage to England. I longed to go, in the hopes of recovering my dear little Elise. Nearly a month passed before he was able to make the desired arrangements. I wished to pay the good people with whom I had lived, but they would receive no remuneration, and insisted on carrying me in a cart to the beach, where the boat was ready to receive me. A gale came on soon after we were at sea, and we were driven up the Channel till we were off the town of Yarmouth, where at length I landed. Some co-religionists of the good Mr Gournay, living in that town, hearing of my arrival, received me in their house; and from thence I came on to Norwich, where I have ever since resided. In vain I have made inquiries for my dear little Elise, greatly helped by my kind friends in this house, but no news have I received of her. You, I am told, Monsieur Deane, are likely to be constantly moving about the country, and it is possible that you may thus hear of the little girl, should she have escaped."

"But she must have greatly grown since the time you speak of," observed Deane: "it was fully ten years ago, was it not?"

"Ah, yes—yes!" answered Madame de Mertens; "but she cannot be so changed that I should not know her; and you may hear, among the Huguenot families, of a little orphan girl, though, I fear, alas! that there are many, many such. I will show her picture to you as I conceive her to be, and that perhaps may help you. I have drawn it often and often; for my great delight is to think of the little girl, and of my dear husband also. You would not know him though, I fear, if he survives, so greatly changed must he be by the hardships and barbarities he has gone through. Compared to his, my own fate has been fortunate, thanks to the generosity of my kind friends in this house, and to others. I have also been able to support myself by teaching, and have even had it in my power to help others of my countrymen who required assistance; but still the picture of my dear husband, in that dreadful slave-ship, is constantly coming before me; and often and often I think of my beloved child, thrown among strangers, who may too probably be of an inferior class, unable to give her instruction, or perhaps Papists, who will bring her up in a faith so contrary to that for which her father died, and those who love her suffered!"

Jack, much interested in what he heard, promised faithfully to lose no opportunity of making inquiries for the little Elise, who, however, by that time must have been fifteen years of age—a fact which her mother, when first describing her, seemed to have overlooked.

When Jack afterwards told Brinsmead of the commission he had undertaken, the old man smiled somewhat grimly, as was his wont when he smiled at all, saying, "I am afraid it will be something like looking for a needle in a stack of hay, but at the same time the needle may be found, so I do not tell you not to do your best to execute the poor lady's wishes."

Madame de Mertens had just brought her history to a conclusion when Mr Gournay, accompanied by Giles Dainsforth, entered the room.

"Friend Deane, I am truly glad to see thee," he said, taking Deane by the hand. "I have heard of thee from friend Dainsforth here, and of thy family, and I trust that anon we shall become better acquainted. Thou hast an honest face, and if thou art diligent in business, thou art sure to gain the competency which is all that a man need desire in this life, and albeit its wealth flows in on some, by God's providence; remember, shouldst thou ever possess it, that wealth may prove a snare and temptation to thee, even as great as want and poverty is to some men. Thou wilt have need of prayer for guidance, even as much as thou hast at present, for the devil is ever going about like a roaring lion, seeking whom he may devour; and the rich man may prove as dainty a morsel to him as the poor one—but above all does he delight in feeding upon those who have a name to lose, those who are ensigns and leaders in their church, elders and deacons, and such like. However, thou hast been journeying all day, and I will not speak to thee more of this subject at present, so come with us that thou mayst recruit thine inner man."

Saying this, the hospitable and generous Quaker led the way to his handsome parlour. Though his own dress was simple—for he had abjured ruffles and periwig, and wore neither sword, nor lace on his cloak, nor clocks to his stockings—yet it was of the best material, and in no way different in form from that of other wealthy merchants and commoners, while the apartment into which he ushered his guest was richly furnished, and the table was covered with a handsome service of plate and china.

Giles Dainsforth, who, though not a Quaker, was dressed with Puritan simplicity, was a tall, strongly-built young man, with intelligent, though not refined features. He welcomed Jack warmly, as the brother of one to whom he was engaged. Mr Gournay treated him with a respect and consideration which showed that he had confidence in his integrity. Jack thus at once made himself at home, and he could not help contrasting his present position to the life he had been leading for so many days.

His host, John Gournay, who was born in 1655, was the founder of the family, who have since become known for their wealth and liberality. At an early day he had joined the Society of Friends, or Quakers, as they were called, and established himself as a merchant at Norwich, where he became the owner of several manufactories. It was greatly in consequence of the encouragement and support which he gave to the French Protestant refugees that he was enabled to lay the foundation of the vast wealth of the family in trade, which their industry supplied. His generosity, liberality, and industry being thus speedily rewarded by the hand of Providence. His silk and wool mills were the best then in England for the usual Norwich manufactures, as also for other delicate productions, such as crape shawls and dress-fabrics. Although somewhat grave and formal in his discourse to strangers, at his genial board his formality soon disappeared, and Jack Deane, as has been said, passed a pleasanter evening than he had enjoyed for some time. Although profane music was not indulged in, Mistress Gournay and Madame de Mertens sang some very sweet and touching hymns, which went more to Jack's heart than any music he had ever heard.

Giles Dainsforth insisted on accompanying Jack back to his inn, to which he wished to return, though hospitably pressed to remain by Mr Gournay. Dainsforth of course had many inquiries to make about Jack's family, and especially about Kate. He confided to Jack his intention of seeking his fortune in the new colony in America, established by Master William Penn, the son of the celebrated Admiral.

"As to worldly wealth, dear Jack," he said, "I might gain that in England, but of freedom of conscience and freedom of worship, we may at any time be deprived, I fear. Our present king—may Heaven preserve him!—is liberal, but there are many malignants yet in the country who are striving for place and power, and we know not what another reign may bring forth. Other Acts of Conformity may be passed; and I cannot forget the cruel way in which our divines were treated in the last reign, when they were cast out on the cold world to gain their livelihood, as best they could, by those who sought to obtain only the loaves and fishes which their livings afforded."

"But will my father agree to let sister Kate cross the ocean, and leave him for ever?" asked Jack.

"Thy father is a man of sense," answered Dainsforth. "In most things he agrees with me; albeit he is more inclined to associate with malignants than I approve of, yet he, too, sees how the wind blows, and if he thinks it is for the happiness of thy sister Kate, he will not prevent her following the bent of her inclinations. Often has she said to me, 'Where thou goest I will go,' and therefore, without undue presumption, I may hope that she will consent to accompany me across the wide ocean to the land of promise. It is a beautiful and rich country, Jack; I would that thou wouldst make up thy mind to come with us! We might there, in a new England, enjoy that peace and prosperity and liberty of conscience, and freedom to worship God as we list, which may be denied us in this old country."

The idea was quite a new one to Jack. It had never occurred to him to seek his fortune abroad, simply, probably, because he had not been thrown in the way of persons who spoke on the subject. He promised Dainsforth, however, to consider the matter.

"I will talk to thee anon more about it, Jack," said Dainsforth, as they parted. "For a young man enjoying the health and strength that thou doest, I cannot picture a finer calling than that of subduing the wilderness, of turning a desert into a garden, and producing fruitful corn-fields out of wild land. The vine and the olive, and the orange flourish, they say, out there; and that corn which they call maize, with its golden head, so rich and prolific; and there are deer in the woods, and quail innumerable, and fish in the rivers and in the sea which washes its coasts. Indeed all the wants of man can there be amply supplied."

Dainsforth having given a description of the New World to Jack sufficient to keep him awake all the night with thinking of it, took his departure at length from the inn, promising to call for him on the morrow, and to assist him in transacting the business he had undertaken for Mr Strelley and other friends in Nottingham. Dainsforth expressed his hope of meeting him ere long at Nottingham, to which place he expected to be sent in the course of the autumn on some business for Mr Gournay. Jack was sorry when his visit to Norwich came to an end.

Chapter Twelve
Jack meets Pearson at Saint Faith's and accompanies him to the North

John Deane's stay at Saint Faith's was to be very short, and then he and Brinsmead were to take their way back to Nottingham.

Will Brinsmead seemed somewhat out of temper as Jack rode alongside him on their journey to the former place. He seemed unreasonably jealous of the attention which Jack had received from Mr Gournay. He had also, it appeared, not got over some suspicion of Jack, in consequence of his apparent intimacy with the stranger who called himself Master Pearson.

"He may be Master Pearson, or he may not be Master Pearson," observed Will, sententiously: "and he may be an honest man, or he may not be an honest man. There are many rogues going about the world, and he may be one, or he may not be one; but I do not like a man who turns up here and turns up there, and dodges one's footsteps, and does not give a reasonable and proper account of himself. Now, it appears to me, Master Deane, that you have talked to this Master Pearson, supposing he is Master Pearson, a great deal too much. If you had held your tongue, he would have gained no information out of you. When you are among strangers, it's my opinion, that, if you are wise, you will say nothing. If you hold your tongue, those you are with will think you wise; but if you talk, ten chances to one they will think you a fool!"

"Thank you, Master Brinsmead, for the compliment," said Jack. "I told you before that I did not think I had said any thing to this man Pearson in any way detrimental to our interests, or to those of our employer, Mr Strelley. If I did, I am heartily sorry for it: but even if I did, it must be proved that he is a rogue before you should say that any harm could have happened from what I talked about."

Brinsmead, however, was not to be brought back into good-humour; and Jack was very glad when the tall, square tower of Saint Faith's church rose up in sight above the dead flat of marshy country over which they were travelling, which, however, was relieved by occasional groups of tall beech and birch-trees, and lines of weeping ash, amid which in spring and summer were happy birds singing all day, and some too even during the night.

Saint Faith's, although but a small village, was just now crowded with visitors, albeit rather of a rough description, being chiefly highland drovers in plaid and kilt, or trowes, with daggers stuck in their belts, carrying, however, long goads or staves in the place of broadsword and targets. There were purchasers also of the cattle they came to dispose of from all parts of the country, mostly as rough in their way as the Scotchmen they came to meet. The accommodation which the inn afforded was suitable to such characters as the visitors who frequented it. Fortunately for Jack, their stay was to be short, as Brinsmead had merely to make arrangements with certain drovers he expected to meet to purchase cattle, which, instead of coming so far south, were to be driven to Nottingham. Jack heard Brinsmead making inquiries about the person he expected to meet, and seemed rather disappointed at not finding him at the hostelry where he had arranged to come. On a second visit, however, to the Black Bull, the landlord informed Brinsmead that a Highlander had been inquiring for him, and was even now in the public room awaiting his coming.

"There he is, Master Brinsmead!" said the landlord, pointing to a strongly-built man in Highland dress, who was seated at a table, with a huge tankard of ale before him. By his side, in rather incongruous company, it appeared to Jack, was the reverend minister he had met at Cambridge. The Scotchman rose as Brinsmead, conducted by the landlord, approached him.

"If you are Master Brinsmead, as I have ne'er doobt is the case," he said, "I have to tell you of a sad accident which occurred to our respected friend, Jock McKillock, whom you expected to meet here: and, seeing that he could not come himself, he deputed me to transact the proposed business with you."

On saying this the speaker presented a letter to Brinsmead, which the latter handed to Jack to read, observing, "You're a better scholar than I am, Mr Deane, and I'll beg you just to see what friend McKillock has to say."

Jack took the epistle, which was somewhat dirty, the superscription being in a large though not over-legible hand. He saw, however, that it was addressed to Master Brinsmead, drover, at Saint Faith's. On opening it, Jack saw that it purported to be signed by Jock McKillock, introducing his trusted friend Mr Allan Sanderson, who would make all the arrangements for the sale of the cattle they had spoken of at their meeting on the previous year. The price had risen somewhat, he observed, in consequence of the demand for salt-beef for the fleet, and the licence-fees, which, against all right and justice, they were compelled to pay to King William, who, worthy as he had been in other respects, had committed the same grievous sin of which the King of Israel had been guilty when he neglected to hue Agag in pieces, in not taking away the life of the Popish monarch when he was delivered into his hands, as also in favouring the prelatic priests of the Church of England.

These remarks had a considerable effect with Brinsmead, who agreed with the principles of his correspondent, though he did not object to his master paying the licence-fees, considering they did not come out of his own pocket.

Jack on delivering the letter to Brinsmead, examined more narrowly the countenance of the person who had brought it, and felt immediately convinced that it was no other than Master Pearson. He could not help giving a glance which showed that he recognised him; but the other returned his look with so calm and unmoved an expression of countenance, that he was almost staggered for a moment in his belief. Still, when he recollected that Pearson might have some cause why he should not wish to let Brinsmead know of their previous intercourse, he determined—wisely or not, it may be a matter of opinion—not to address him as an acquaintance. The minister in the same way stared at him as if they had never met before. Jack was exceedingly puzzled, not being able to understand for what reason he did not wish to be recognised. He had time, however, to think over the matter while Brinsmead and the Highland drover were making their arrangements, in accordance with the suggestions contained in the letter. The minister also pulled a volume out of his pocket, and appeared to be completely absorbed in it.

"But who is this young man with you, Master Brinsmead?" asked Sanderson, turning an inquisitive eye, as it seemed, towards Jack. "Though you are unable to travel so far north to inspect the beasts, if he understands cattle, and is intelligent and trustworthy, would it not be well to let him come in your place? My respected friend, Jock McKillock, would rather you looked at the cattle before they are driven south."

"The lad is trustworthy enough," answered Brinsmead, in a low voice, so that Jack should not be supposed to hear it. "He understands, too, the points of a beast better than most lads of his age. Though his shoulders are young, he has got an old head on the top of them; but it's a long way to send him all alone, and he has yet to learn something more of the world than he knows at present. An old bird like me is not to be caught by chaff. He must be a sharp blade to deceive me, you may suppose, Master Sanderson, whereas he might easily be led in the toils of the many sharpers and impostors going about in all directions. It would be wiser not to trust him alone."

"Do not fear that, Master Brinsmead," answered Sanderson, "I am returning north, and will look after the lad, and guard him from all dangers such as you hint at. I cannot side with him when he is making his bargain, and help to beat down Jock McKillock, but I will give him all the advice in the general way I can, and Jock's an honest chield, and would not take advantage of him when he puts his trust in his honour."

Jack all this time could not help overhearing the conversation, and became more puzzled than ever how to act. A journey to the north for the purpose of purchasing cattle was exactly after his own taste, but he could not understand the deception which was being practised upon his companion. If Pearson was honest, why did he now assume a different name from that by which he had before been known? Which, also, was his right name? The minister too, who was his companion, had heard him called Pearson, and he now announced himself as Allan Sanderson in his presence, and yet the reverend gentleman made no remark on the subject.

Sanderson continued to urge his point with Brinsmead, and used many arguments to induce him to allow Jack Deane to proceed north. At last, not a little to Jack's satisfaction, Brinsmead yielded his consent, provided Jack would wish to accept the offer.

"What say you, Mr Deane, will you take a trip into the land o' cakes, and make a purchase of three hundred head of cattle for Mr Strelley? You will have the driving of the beasts south, and have the pleasure of seeing good honest meat and fat put on their bones in our rich water-meadows before many months have passed away after their arrival."

Jack had had time to consider the matter, and without hesitation accepted the offer, believing that in a short conversation with Pearson he could soon clear up the mystery.

"I should be on my guard," he thought to himself, "more than would Brinsmead, who does not suspect him, and thus I think I shall better be able to look after the interests of my master Mr Strelley."

When a person desires to do a thing, it is very easy to find excuses, and as easy to lull the conscience asleep, and hide the consequences which may be the result.

It was finally arranged that Jack should start the next morning in company with the respectable Mr Allan Sanderson, Brinsmead purposing to follow at a slower pace in the course of the day.

Jack was aroused next morning by the sound of his quondam acquaintance calling him to "boot and saddle," and to be off. Slipping on his clothes, he went to the bedside of Will Brinsmead, who was still sleeping soundly, to tell him that he was summoned to be off.

"Ah, lad, the Scotchmen keep early hours," said Will, sitting up and rubbing his eyes. "The dawn has scarcely broke, surely. He is right, though, thou hast a long ride before thee, and it's as well to be off by times, though it would have been prudent to lay in a store of provender before you depart; however, two or three hours' ride before breakfast will do thee no harm, lad. And now, Master Deane, I have a word to say before you leave me. Thou hast a fair opening, lad, and an important commission to execute. Take this advice from an old man. Keep your own counsel on all occasions. Judge which is best for your master's interests, and let nothing turn you aside from following that out. Avoid quarrelling with any one, and let no one pick a quarrel with thee. Mr Sanderson seems a fair-spoken man, but there's one thing I would have you remember, that he is not Jock McKillock himself. Jock I have known well-nigh a score of years, and an honest and fair dealer, as I doubt not thou wilt find, if he is afoot and well again when you get to the north. And now, fare-thee-well, John Deane, an old man's blessing go with thee! Thou hast shown thyself to be ready-witted and brave, and if thou rememberest always that it is better to please God than man, thou wilt not fail to succeed in thy undertakings."

With these words the old man put on his clothes, and accompanying Jack down-stairs, assisted him in getting his horse ready for his journey.

"Weel, weel, laddy, you're o'er long in mounting your nag!" shouted Master Sanderson.

"I am ready for you now, at all events," answered Jack, as he threw himself into his saddle, and once more shook hands with Brinsmead.

"Stop, stop, Mr Sanderson, you be off without your stirrup-cup!" exclaimed the landlord, who at that moment appeared at the door with a tankard in his hand. "Such doings are never allowed at my house, however early in the morning my guests depart. It will do thee good, man, and help to keep the cold mists of our fen-country out of thy throat this morning; and thou, lad, must not break through our rules, either," he said, turning to Jack, who, it must be confessed, took the proffered tankard and drained its contents, then touching the flank of his horse with his spur, and giving a farewell wave of the hand to honest old Brinsmead, rode after his new acquaintance nothing loath.

Chapter Thirteen
Jack and Pearson's Journey to the North, and how Jack was employed on the Road

The sky was clear overhead, and a damp mist was swept by a south-east wind over the face of the country. Jack and the Scotchman rode on till they were clear of the village without speaking.

"I am glad to have you in my company, Master Deane," said the latter, now for the first time throwing off all disguise.

"I am obliged to you," said Jack. "I knew you, Master Pearson, the moment I saw you."

"So I thought," was the answer. "When we parted at Cambridge, I was not certain in which character I should come to Saint Faith's. However, you might have found it difficult to come north without me, and I therefore have made arrangements to accompany you."

"But why this masquerading, Master Pearson?" asked Jack. "Mr Harwood's recommendation makes me place confidence in you, but I tell you frankly, I would rather know more about you than I do!"

"Very sensibly spoken," said Pearson, laughing. "The state of the times makes 'masquerading,' as you call it, necessary; but of one thing you may be sure, that I mean you fair; I will treat you honourably. Had I not given you warning, you would have returned to Nottingham, and have been clapped probably into the stocks; for depend upon it some of the country gentlemen round would have been too glad to get hold of your father's son, and by punishing him, keep in awe others of less degree."

"I am sure you mean me well," said Jack, whose disposition made him unsuspicious of others. "But we shall pass within a short distance of Nottingham, and I should like to go and pay them a visit during the evening, when the darkness will prevent me being recognised, just to tell them where I am going, and what I propose doing."

"Oh, Master Brinsmead will do that in a few days!" answered the northern drover; "depend upon it there are some on the watch for you, and you would run a considerable risk in returning home, even for a short time."

Jack thought this very likely, and did not press the point, but suddenly another idea occurred to him.

"I might surely visit Harwood Grange?" he observed; "no one would be looking for me there, and I should like to see Mr Harwood and gain some information respecting the persons to whom I am to deliver these letters."

"I will think about that, my lad, as we ride on," answered Pearson. "Our direct road will take us a good deal to the east of Sherwood Forest, and your visit to the Grange would cause considerable delay. I do not at present see that this is necessary, though, to be sure, you may have some attraction there with which I am not acquainted."

He gave a peculiar glance as he spoke, which drew the colour into his companion's cheeks.

Jack was mounted on a strong, active nag, but he soon found that it was very inferior in speed to the one Pearson bestrode, and frequently he had to use whip and spur to keep up with him.

"We must get you another beast," observed the latter; "it will make the difference of two or three days to us in our journey, and I always like to know that my friend is mounted on as good a steed as I am when we ride together. We know not the moment when we may have to try the metal of them both."

"If that's the animal you were riding when I met you between Nottingham and Cambridge, it's a good one," observed Jack, remembering the leap he had seen Pearson take, and the speed with which he had afterwards gone over the ground.

"Ay, the very same," answered Pearson; "Black Bess and I seldom part company. I would have no other person bestride her; and I doubt whether she would allow it, if any one were to make the attempt."

"But this horse belongs to Mr Strelley," said Jack; "I have no business to change it for another."

"Oh, I will settle that matter," answered Pearson; "you will accept the loan of one from me, and I will send your nag to meet old Will as he comes west. In a couple of hours we will stop to breakfast at the house of an old friend of mine, and I have no doubt that we shall find a steed in his stables just suited for you."

At the time Master Pearson specified, they drew up before a farm-house a little off the high-road. A sign, however, swinging over the door showed that occasional entertainment was afforded there also to man and beast. The landlord, who had very few of the characteristics of a Boniface, being a tall, thin, hard-featured man, received Pearson as an old acquaintance, and, the horses being sent to the stables, ushered them into a small oak parlour, intended for the accommodation of his private guests.

"We may here rest without the risk of being observed," said Pearson to Deane, as he threw himself into a chair. "A wise man will not make more confidants than are necessary, and will not let the rest of the world know what he is about or where he is going. We will have some refreshment, and then I will go and search for a better steed than yours, which shall be returned in due course to your employer."

Pearson having intimated to the host that refreshment would be required, it was quickly placed on the table; and, like a man who knew not when he might have another opportunity of feeding, he applied himself to the viands, advising his companion to do the same. This Jack did with right good will; and the meal being despatched, Pearson advised him to amuse himself as best he could in the room, while he went out to look for a horse fit, as he said, for Jack to ride.

Deane could not help feeling puzzled at times at the caution his companion considered necessary to use. Still, so little accustomed was he to the world, that it did not occur to him that he was otherwise than a respectable character, with whom he was perfectly safe in consorting. He paced the room without finding any thing to amuse himself with. Not a book on a shelf, nor a picture on the wall. A sanded floor, a dark oak table, several benches, a chair of large proportions, used probably for the president at clubs of convivial meetings; with a few of smaller size, completed the furniture of the oak-wainscoted room. He was not, however, kept very long before Pearson returned, telling him that he had procured a horse on which his saddle was to be placed; and Jack, going out into the stable-yard, found a man leading up and down a fine, strongly-built steed, which, if not possessing all the points of which Pearson's own horse could boast, was evidently an animal well capable of performing a rapid and long journey at a stretch.

"The account is settled; and now let us mount and be off," said Pearson, throwing himself into his saddle, and, having whispered a few words into the ears of their ill-favoured host, he put spurs to his horse, and with Jack by his side quickly left the village behind. Jack was highly pleased with the paces of his new acquisition, and soon saw that he should be able to push on over the ground at far greater speed than when he had his own steady-going nag under him. In a short time, coming to a fine open, grassy piece of land, he could not resist the temptation of putting spurs to the animal's side, and starting off for a gallop. Pearson shouted after him to stop; but Jack found it no easy matter to rein in his steed. On turning his head, he found that the drover was following him; and, though he fancied that he himself was going at full gallop, his companion was quickly alongside him.

"That is very like a young man, but not the act of a wise one!" said Pearson. "You should always keep your horse's strength for an emergency on a long journey. His limbs are supple enough, I'll warrant; there was no necessity for trying them just now."

"I could not help it," said Jack, tugging at the same time at the rein. "The animal has mettle enough for any thing, I should think."

"I see that I must help you," said Pearson, "or you will not bring that animal up in a hurry, till you have well-nigh sawn his mouth in two. So-ho! Rover!" he cried out, adding a few cabalistical-sounding words.

In an instant the animal threw himself on his haunches, so suddenly indeed, as nearly to unseat his rider. He was too good a horseman though to be played such a trick.

"The beast is no stranger to you, Master Pearson," he observed.

"No; he has carried me over many a mile," was the answer. "I would not wish to put you on an animal I had not tried. And now we will make play over this ground, though at more moderate speed than you were going at just now."

They found accommodation for the night in a small roadside inn. On the next day, when passing through Grantham, as the travellers were approaching the open square of the market-place, they observed a large crowd collected round a person elevated above their heads on the top of a huge cask or table, so it appeared. He was throwing out his arms in every direction. Now pressing his hands together, now lifting them towards heaven in the attitude of prayer. Most of his auditors seemed to be listening to him with rapt attention. As they drew nearer, Jack, on looking at the countenance of the speaker, was convinced that it was no other than the Independent preacher whom he had met in company with Master Pearson. From the words which fell from his mouth it was difficult to ascertain what principles he was inculcating. He was speaking at the moment of some wonderful dream with which he had been favoured by Heaven. He was warning the people of the dreadful calamities which he knew, in consequence of what he had seen in his vision, were about to fall upon the land. He seemed, however, to be dealing out tolerably even-handed justice towards all other denominations. He had nothing in its favour to say of Protestant Episcopacy, and as little of Romanism. He was hurling abuse at Presbyterianism, and warning the Independents that their day of grace had passed, that they were no longer holding up a standard in Israel, while he condemned the Baptists for maintaining unscriptural doctrines.

"Woe! woe! woe!" he shouted, "woe to this country! woe to this people! Listen, ye stiff-necked and stubborn generation! A new revelation is about to be vouchsafed to you; will you receive it, or will you refuse it? Those who are ready to receive it will hold up their hands, and shout with joy at the thoughts of their emancipation from the slavery under which ye have hitherto groaned in the bonds of bitterness and the darkness of despair! Those who have made up their minds not to receive it must take their departure from among us, and go back to the place whence they came, there to await till summoned to go down into the pit full of fire and brimstone, already boiling up to welcome them!"

No one moved from among the crowd, the greater number of whom held up their hands, as invited by the speaker, and gave way to a shrill cry, which swelled by degrees into a loud ringing shout, which was repeated again and again.

Jack, to satisfy himself, asked Pearson if he knew the name of the speaker.

"I know his name, Master Deane," answered his companion: "you must ask the bystanders if they know it. They will probably tell you that it's the Reverend Simon Stirthesoul, one of the newest of new lights who have appeared in the kingdom in this favoured reign. There are many such; and of great advantage will they prove to the spiritual welfare of the people. They have an especial work, it seems to me, to show that all the old forms of worship are wrong, and invent as many new ones as their imaginations can devise. Wherever they spring from, they're serving the Pope of Rome well, for the more the Protestants are divided, the better will it be for his faithful children in this realm of England."

Jack wished to stop and hear more of the remarks made by the preacher, but to this Pearson objected, observing that he did not wish to delay, and that they would bait their steeds a few miles beyond the town, at a roadside inn.

Pearson expressed a more important truth than he himself was aware of at the time. From the time of Elizabeth up to that period, a number of Popish priests, chiefly Jesuits, had been introduced into the country under various disguises, having received dispensations from the Pope to act any part they might consider most advisable for the establishment of new and strange doctrines; thus dividing Protestant interests. There is undoubted evidence of this. Most of these men, well trained in foreign universities, accustomed to the ways of the world, were admirably fitted for the part they were destined to perform. Some pretended to be Episcopalians, others Presbyterians, and others Nonconformists of all denominations. Many exerted their talents in the invention of new sects, and they were certain to gain proselytes, being well versed in the study of human nature. They knew thoroughly how to adapt the principles they advocated, and the tenets they taught, to the tastes of their hearers, and there can be no doubt that the rise of the many strange sects which appeared at different times, from the accession of Elizabeth, was owing to the efforts of these Popish emissaries. A considerable number were from time to time apprehended, and found possessed of treasonable documents, proving that they were Papists in disguise. Some indeed were executed in consequence of having been found guilty of treasonable practices, while others narrowly escaped the same fate. It seemed but probable, from his connexion with the Jacobites, that the Reverend Simon Stirthesoul was one of these disguised plotters.

"I gave you a packet of letters from Mr Harwood," observed Pearson, as they were standing in the evening at their inn. "If you look over them, I shall be able to tell you the best route to take in order to call on the persons to whom they are directed. Your friend made it a great point that you should deliver them in person, and I am sure that he is a gentleman you would wish to oblige." He fixed his keen glance at Jack as he spoke. "The greater number are, I see, directed to gentlemen in Yorkshire. You may well consider it an honour to be so employed. Sir Herbert Willington, I see; Colonel Slingsby, Joe Hovingham of Hovingham Hall, Master Haxby of Haxby Grange, are all good men and true. In Northumberland too, I see you have a few to Oxminston, and Widdrington. It will take you some time to get through them all, for they're not men who let you come to their door and ride away again without showing you hospitality. It will give more time to Jock McKillock to get the herd together."

Deane made many inquiries of his companion with regard to the character of the people on whom he was to call, and he was somewhat surprised to find that they were all strong Jacobites, the greater number indeed being Romanists. Still, his suspicions were not sufficiently aroused to make him refuse to deliver them. This would of course have been the wisest thing to have done. He was, in truth, anxious in every way to please Mr Harwood. He still continued to indulge in dreams of some day winning the fair Alethea. He very naturally thought that if he could please her father, he would have less difficulty in so doing.

The horse Pearson had selected for Deane showed wonderful speed and bottom, and seemed scarcely fatigued when, between sunrise and sunset, he had gone over the best part of a hundred miles. When once in Yorkshire they proceeded at a somewhat slower pace, having somewhat longer time to rest at the houses at which they called. On these occasions, Pearson assumed the character of Jack's servant, and invariably accompanied the horses to the stables, and stayed during the visit with the grooms and other servants. He was not idle, however, though he might have appeared to be so. He lost no opportunity of making inquiries as to what was going on in the neighbourhood, as well as informing himself of the proceedings of their masters.

Jack had no cause to complain of any want of hospitality on the part of those to whom he delivered Mr Harwood's letters, but in several instances he was received with an air of stiffness and formality which showed that full confidence was not placed in him. Indeed, when on one or two occasions he was cross-questioned, having really no information to give, he was speedily again dismissed. He received, however, several letters in return, which he was especially directed to deliver in person to Mr Harwood. On looking at the covers, he was surprised to find that no superscription was placed on them.

"Never mind," was the answer, "you know for whom they are intended. Keep them securely, and the object we have in view will be attained."

He mentioned, at length, the circumstance to Pearson.

"It's all right," he replied; "a letter without an address, provided the bearer knows to whom he is to deliver it, is safer in these perilous times than a letter with one. Keep them carefully, Master Deane, and Mr Harwood will be duly grateful to you when you deliver them."

As they advanced north, Pearson invariably left the high-road to seek for quarters at some distance from it during the night. Before lying down to sleep on these occasions, he never failed to visit the stables. Jack observed also that he remained booted and spurred during the night. Generally before daybreak they were again in the saddle, and proceeding at a rapid rate on their road. The Cheviots were already in sight, when one morning Pearson roused up Jack.

"To horse, my lad, to horse!" he exclaimed. "If you wish to retain your liberty, or your life indeed, you will put a hundred miles between you and the Cheviots before sundown. I have just had the information brought me, that you have been accused of delivering letters to disaffected persons, and that a plot has been discovered for dethroning the present king and bringing back King James. As I did not see the letters which you had to deliver, I cannot say how far the accusation is just, but to you it will come to the same thing. I have so far led you into the scrape by giving you the letters, and I have resolved to bear you company; for I doubt, without me, that you would manage to escape."

"This is bad news indeed," exclaimed Jack, sitting up in bed, and beginning to dress as rapidly as he could.

"But if I go south, how shall I be able to execute Mr Strelley's commission? What will Jock McKillock do with the cattle he has brought thus far on the way? and what am I to do with the money with which I was to pay for them?"

"I have thought of all that, my friend," answered Pearson. "Give me the money, and I will settle the matter with Jock McKillock, and the cattle shall be driven south as safely as if you were at their tails."

Jack could not help feeling considerable hesitation as to the propriety of yielding to Pearson's proposal. Honest and unsuspicious as he was himself, great doubt had crossed his mind as to the character of his companion. To be sure, if he persisted in continuing his journey, and endeavouring to meet Jock McKillock, he very likely might be apprehended, and in that case he would certainly lose the money in his possession; but then if Pearson was not honest, it would equally be lost. The latter saw by the working of his countenance, the doubts that were crossing his mind.

"You hesitate to give me the cash," he observed. "You are perfectly right; at the same time, I promise you that it shall be properly spent for the advantage of your employer. Oaths are like pie-crusts, too often only made to be broken, therefore I will not swear what I will do: but accept the promise of a man who wishes you well, and you will have no cause to regret having trusted me."

Jack at length, seeing that there was no help for it, agreed to Pearson's proposal, and, though not without some reluctance, handed him over the money for the proposed purchase of cattle.

"It is safer in my pocket than in yours, let me tell you, Master Deane," said Pearson, as he stowed it away in his leathern pouch. "There breathes not the man on either side of the border who would attempt to take it from me."

Chapter Fourteen
Adventures at the Hagg

"There is ne'er use fashing yourself, my young friend, about the matter," observed Pearson, in his usual unconcerned manner, "many as pretty a man as yourself has been in a far worse difficulty, and my advice now to you is to make the best of it. I could hide you away among the mountains in the north, where, should every man in Dutch William's army be sent out on the search, they could not find you; but, I'm thinking, a lad of your spirit would not be altogether satisfied with that sort of life. Better far come with me south. There will soon be work for you to do in that quarter, such as will be more suitable to your taste, I'm thinking, than following at the heels of a drove of bullocks. I own a dairy-farm in the fens of Lincolnshire, where I have a wife and daughter, and am known as a steady, quiet-going farmer, who, may be, has a little better notion about horse-flesh than his neighbours, and bestrides occasionally a fleeter steed than most of them. No one would think of looking for me there, nor will they for you, or, if they did, it would be no easy job to find us. For that matter, indeed (your vanity will not be offended, I hope, when I say it), your countenance has so little remarkable about it, and so few people know you, that you might safely go to London without the slightest risk of detection. You should understand that some friends of ours may ask you to undertake a commission of importance in the metropolis, and I would advise you not to refuse it. All your expenses will be paid; and if you prove trustworthy and discreet, it will lead to your further advantage."

"You have proposed so much to me, Master Pearson, that I am rather confused, and must think a little before I reply," answered Jack. "You tell me that information has been laid against me for delivering treasonable letters between persons desirous of overturning the present order of things and of restoring King James to the throne, and that if I am not very careful I shall be taken and imprisoned, and perhaps hung. Now, even though I have really been accused, as you have heard, of treason, I am sure that I can have no difficulty in proving my innocence. I was not aware of the contents of the letters I delivered, and have certainly no wish to overturn the present Government."

"Very possibly, my young friend," remarked Pearson; "but it will avail you nothing to say that you did not know the contents of the letters, or that you did not do this or that. You must confess to having delivered the letters, and you cannot prove that you did not know their contents and are not anxious to support the cause they advocate. Judges and juries require proofs of a man's innocence. Can you give proofs of yours? that is the question, Master Deane. Besides, let me ask you, suppose a certain young lady, who shall be nameless, were to promise you the best reward she can bestow, if you will join heart and hand in the cause her father supports, what reply would you make—eh, my lad?"

"You seem to know every thing, Master Pearson!" exclaimed Jack, somewhat annoyed at his companion's familiarity, and not wishing to give a direct answer. "With regard to the probability of my being unable to prove my innocence of the accusations which may be brought against me, I acknowledge that you are right; but with respect to other matters, it is no man's business to interfere."

"Of course, Master John Deane, you are the best judge in your own affairs. I gave you but the advice of a friend," answered Pearson: "what motive can I have to speak otherwise? But again let me remind you, that if you venture within the lion's jaws it will be no easy matter to get you out again. Be wise, then, put yourself under my guidance, and you will be safe. Go your own gait, and you will find yourself shut up in prison, or, maybe, run your head into the noose. However, an obstinate man is not to be persuaded."

"But I am not an obstinate man," said Jack; "I believe that your advice is kindly intended, and I beg that you will understand I do not reject it. I only ask time to think over the matter, that I may decide what course I should pursue."

It was not without a considerable amount of vexation and disappointment that Deane found himself galloping away to the south, instead of proceeding, as he had hoped, over the border into Scotland. He felt some doubt, also, as to whether he had acted wisely in confiding so completely to Pearson; and he also regretted having allowed himself to be made a tool, as it appeared too evident that he had been, of the Jacobite party. Still he did not blame Mr Harwood, and thought that probably some of the other gentlemen whom he had visited were the cause of the accusation being brought against him. Though Pearson pressed him to proceed south, he did not object to the proposal Jack made of visiting Harwood Grange on his way.

"It is the best thing you can do," he observed. "You can then in person deliver the letters you have received, and he may better be able to explain matters to you than I am, and he will also advise what steps to take that you may clear yourself from the accusation which has been brought against you."

Jack's heart beat at the thought of the proposed visit. The inconvenience and disappointment which he had gone through, seemed as nothing when he contemplated again seeing Alethea. It did not occur to him that he was rushing into a trap in which he was very likely to lose his liberty altogether. They had proceeded about forty or fifty miles to the south, when a horseman was seen approaching them. He drew up as he reached Pearson, and exchanged greetings with him. He then turning round, and allowing Jack to go on out of ear-shot, the two rode alongside each other. In the course of ten minutes or so they again overtook Jack.

"Mr Deane," said Pearson, "I have fortunately met a friend who knows the country well, and will prove a good guide to you. He is willing to return south, that I may ride to the north and make the arrangements which you were to have done with our friend Jock McKillock, for the purchase of the cattle. There is no time to be lost, and I assure you that you may trust my friend as you would me."

Without any further remark, Pearson shook Jack by the hand, and, wheeling round his horse, galloped away to the north, while the stranger rode on alongside Jack. As Jack glanced at his companion, it struck him that he had seen him before, but where, or under what circumstances, he in vain attempted to discover. He was a strongly-built, active-looking man, considerably younger than Pearson, with a determined look and expression in his countenance which Jack did not altogether like. He did not seem either much inclined for conversation, and answered briefly all the questions which Deane put to him.

"I think we have met before," said Jack.

"It's very likely," was the reply; "but you have the advantage of me, if you know where it was, for I see so many people in the course of a day, that it would be a difficult matter for me to recollect those I have met once in a way. I will give you a useful piece of advice, however: remember, the fewer questions you ask, the less likely you will be to have falsehoods told you. You have a long ride before you, and you will be wiser if you save your breath, instead of wasting it in talking."

It is hopeless to enter into conversation with one who is determined not to speak. Jack found this to be the case, his companion generally only answering in monosyllables to all the remarks he made.

When, at length, they stopped at nightfall at a farm-house, similar to those which Pearson had selected on their way north, his companion pursued the same system, exchanging only a few words with the people of the house, and scarcely speaking to him all the evening. As Pearson had done, he visited the stables several times to see that the horses were well cared for, evidently considering it as important as did his friend, that they should be in a fit condition for a hard gallop. They travelled, indeed, a couple of days before Jack discovered the name of his companion. He at length heard him spoken to as Master Burdale.

"Yes, that's my name," he said, when Jack addressed him as such; "I am known here and elsewhere as Ned Burdale, at your service."

Jack at last became heartily tired of his companion's society: at the same time he had to confess to himself that there was nothing particularly with which he could find fault about the man, except his sulky silence. With great satisfaction Deane at length caught sight of the well-remembered patches of woodland scenery by which he knew that he was once more within the ancient boundaries of Sherwood Forest. He now, for the first time, told Ned Burdale of his intention of visiting Harwood Grange.

"My directions were to conduct you to Master Pearson's farm in the fens," said his companion. "I cannot be answerable for your safety if you part company from me."

"I have no desire to do so," said Jack; "but if you will accompany me to the Grange, as soon as I have delivered my message to Mr Harwood, I shall be ready to set forward to the place you speak of."

"Remember, then, it's at your own risk," said his companion. "I have my reasons for not wishing to go there myself, but I will wait for you at a farm which we shall reach in a couple of hours, and from thence you can ride over to the Grange. I would advise you to go there in the evening, to avoid being seen by the people in the neighbourhood. We can send a messenger on before to the Squire, that he may be on the watch for you. Take my advice: don't allow a bright eye and a rosy cheek to detain you there longer than is necessary."

Jack, being unable to suggest any better arrangement, was compelled to be contented with his companion's proposal.

Putting spurs to their horses, they galloped on through the forest. Now they had to pass several miles of cleared country; then again they came to more forest-land. Now they passed over a wild piece of heath; then through dingle and dale, and thick copses, and along the banks of a stream, avoiding the high-road as much as possible, and making their way wherever they could across the country. At length they entered a thicker part of the forest than any they had hitherto passed through.

"We shall soon be at the farm," observed Burdale. "We will take a day's rest then for the sake of our steeds; for though at a push they would have gone twice as far without knocking up, it's as well to give them a holiday where it can be done."

At length a grey-stone tower, with a building attached to it, round which ran a broad balcony, appeared in sight. It had evidently been a hunting-lodge in olden times, and from the balcony ladies fair used to shoot with cross-bow, or, perhaps, in later times with fire-arms, at the deer as they were driven past. An old man and woman, apparently as old as the building itself, came forth at the sound of the horses' hoofs. They looked somewhat askance at Jack, but welcomed Burdale as an acquaintance.

"You can give us shelter for the night, Master Rymer, I hope," he said, jumping from his horse. "Here, I will help look after the steeds, while your dame shows my companion the way into your house."

The old couple continued to cast somewhat doubtful glances at Jack.

"Have no fear," said Burdale; "he is of the right sort, and no risk of his peaching, even if he did find out any thing he should not know."

With this assurance, as soon as Jack dismounted, the old man took his horse, and accompanied Burdale round the tower to the stables. The dame, meantime, beckoned to Jack to follow her. A flight of dilapidated stone steps led them up to the entrance-hall, which occupied the whole of one floor of the tower. A rough stair led to another floor above it; and Jack observed the top of a flight of steps of more pretensions, descending apparently to chambers below.

"Sit down, young sir," said the dame, pointing to an old oak chair. "Thou wilt be hungry after thy long ride; and I will prepare a steak for you and Ned Burdale."

The view from the window of the tower was confined on all sides by the forest, through which, however, here and there glades opened out for some distance, up which, in former days, the deer were accustomed to sweep by, and afford an opportunity to fair dames and lords to exercise their skill with their fowling-pieces. Already the sun was sinking beneath the tops of the trees; and Jack began to fear that he should not have time to reach Harwood Grange before the night altogether closed in. He waited impatiently, therefore, for the return of Burdale, purposing to set off immediately his horse should have had its food and enjoyed a short rest. His companion, however, was longer than he expected, and by the time he arrived the meal prepared by the old dame was almost ready.

"Take my advice," said Burdale: "remain here quietly to-night, and to-morrow you will be able to visit the Grange, and give our horses sufficient time to rest, that we may continue our journey into Lincolnshire. The distance from this to the Grange is far greater than you suppose: you could not reach it till an hour or more after dark, and you would scarcely be able to find your way back through the forest by yourself."

Unwilling as Jack was to give up his purpose of paying a visit to his friends that evening, he was compelled to comply with his companion's wishes, for Burdale gave him to understand very clearly that he had no intention of accompanying him. A substantial meal of venison-steaks, wheaten bread, and oaten cakes, to which Jack was nothing loath to do ample justice, was soon placed on the table.

"Come, Master Rymer, you can find us a flagon of wine, too, and of the best, I know that," said Burdale. "Come, man, rummage out your stores, you used not to be niggard of your liquor."

The old man, after some hesitation, pretended or real, took a bunch of keys, and descended the stairs to the chamber beneath the hall. He soon returned with a flagon of wine, which his guests pronounced to be excellent. Burdale drank freely himself, and pressed Jack to imitate his example. Being generally temperate, Jack found at length that he had taken more wine than was his wont, and began to feel an unusual drowsiness stealing over him. The old couple kept up a conversation with Ned Burdale, seemingly somewhat indifferent of Jack's presence. Now and then they addressed him.

"You belong to these parts, do you?" asked the old man, fixing his keen glance on Jack.

"I was born and bred in Nottingham," answered Jack.

"And never been out here at the Hagg before?"

"No," said Jack, "I never heard of the place before."

"Well, to be sure it's a good long distance from the town, and away from all high-roads. You would have a hard job to find it, even if you were looking for it, I suspect."

"You have a bold heart, I hope," said the old woman, "for those who spend a night in this house require one."

"I am not much given to be afraid," answered Jack, laughing; "but what makes you say that?"

"Why, for a good reason: because the old tower is haunted. We didn't like it when we first came here, but we've got accustomed to it. There was an old family lived here in the time of Charles, the king whose head was cut off, when all the men of the family lost their lives in the Civil Wars, and the ladies died of broken hearts, or something of that sort. At all events, the old tower was left deserted, and for many years no one came to live in it. At length, one family came to try and see how it would suit them, but they very soon gave up; and then another and another rented the farm, and tried to stop in the tower, but they could not stand the sights they saw, or the sounds they heard, and threw it up, one after the other. At last my good man and I came here. We were told before what we were to expect, and so we made up our minds for the worst. Well, the very first night we came, as we were sitting here at supper, just as we may be now, we heard the ghosts of the family to whom the tower had belonged all talking away below us. Sometimes it was an old man's voice, then a young girl's, and then the voice of a strong man of middle age, and then a youth, maybe, like yourself, and young children. It was curious to hear them go on in that way. We could not make out what they said exactly, but there was a change in the tone of their voices, just as clearly as if they had been in the room with us. As to sights, I cannot say that we saw any thing; and I'm not ashamed to confess it, neither my good man nor I felt inclined to go into the chamber below, to have a look at the ghosts. They went on talking for some hours, till we heard them scuffling off to bed, so it seemed, and we therefore followed their example. This went on, as I say, night after night. I need not tell you what we saw when we did see any thing, but I will just advise you to be prepared, should you hear any strange noises; and provided you don't go and interfere with the ghosts, depend upon it they will let you alone."

"Thank you," answered Jack, "for the advice. I never yet have met a ghost, though maybe I shall some day, and if I do I intend to treat it with all due respect."

"You had better treat the ghosts here in that way," observed Burdale, with a peculiar glance at Jack; "I have heard of them before, and I am sure they would not like any one to interfere with them."

"Oh, yes," said the old woman, "we have ghosts inside the house and out of it too. Did you mark that big old oak, as you rode up to the door? They say there's a ghost lives inside it, of some man who was murdered under its branches years gone by. How he do groan at night sometimes!

It has been the same ever since we came here. At first I could not sleep for listening to him, and thinking what a pain he was in: just like the pains of souls in purgatory." This remark made Jack suspect that his hosts were Romanists.

He could hear very little more about the ghost in the old oak, but he promised next morning to examine the tree, and ascertain in which part of it the spirit resided.

"You had better let he alone," observed the old man; "these sort of gentry don't like anybody to come and pry after them. That's what I think; and so I have let them alone, and he has never come to do me any harm."

The guide and the two old people talked on for a considerable time; but gradually to Jack's ears their voices grew less and less distinct, till his head dropped on the table, and he fell fast asleep. How long he had been asleep he could not tell, but when he awoke he found himself stretched on a pile of straw in a corner of the great hall, so it appeared to him, but no light was burning, and it was with difficulty he could distinguish objects by means of the streaks of moonlight which came through the chinks of the shutters. He had not been many minutes awake before he heard voices. They were certainly not those of the old people or of Burdale, and they appeared to come from below him. He listened attentively. He had no doubt that they were human voices he heard; in earnest conversation, too. Now high, now low; now the voice was that of a strong, hale man; now that of one shaking with age; now of a bold, eager youth; now several seemed to be speaking together. The tales he had heard that night recurred to his mind. Could it be possible that these were the spirits of the departed owners of the Hagg? Again he listened, to assure himself that he had not been misled by fancy. He sat up and rubbed his eyes—still the voices reached his ears. He was constitutionally brave.

"I will not be mocked by real ghosts or pretended spirits," he said to himself, springing to his feet.

He felt for his weapons. His pistols were in his belt and his knife was by his side. He looked about him, and ascertained the position of the doors in the room.

"I can find my way to the top of the stairs which I saw led down into the vaults below," he said to himself, "and I can easily grope my way down-stairs, and find out what these ghosts really are."

To think was to act with him. The moonlight enabled him to find his way with greater ease even than he had expected, and on reaching the top of the stairs he was more sure than ever that people were talking below. Holding a pistol in one hand, he felt his way with the other, descending the stone steps, careful to make his footing sure before he advanced again. He thus, without breaking his neck, reached the bottom, when not only did he hear the voices more distinctly and catch many of the words which were spoken, but he saw a bright light shining through a chink of a door before him. He approached the door in the hope of being able to see through the chink, but this he found was impossible. As, however, he was pressing against the door, it flew open, and what was his amazement to see between two and three dozen people, either sitting or standing round a long table, with many others, strongly armed, scattered about the vault! The noise made by the door as it flew open was heard by the assembly, and several men sprang forward and seized him ere he could make his retreat.

"An eavesdropper!" exclaimed one.

"We are betrayed!" cried another.

"His mouth must be stopped," muttered a third.

"It would be safer to kill him at once," growled another.

"What has brought you here?" asked a fine, dignified looking man, in a handsome costume of somewhat antique fashion.

"I am a traveller, and put up here on my way to the fens," answered Jack. "I do not wish to injure any one, but hearing voices, and having been told that the house was haunted, I came to see whence they could proceed, not believing that ghosts could make such a racket as disturbed my rest."

"The lad is no spy, or he would not speak as frankly as he does," observed the gentleman.

"I can answer for his honesty," said another person, whom Jack had not hitherto noticed, rising from his seat and advancing towards him. "He is ready to serve in a right cause and be of use to his country."

Jack on looking towards the speaker discovered that he was no other than Mr Harwood.

"Thank you, sir," he said, "for your good opinion of me. I was, in truth, on my way to visit you, to give an account of the mode in which I have executed your commissions, and I'm sure that you will bear witness that I am not addicted to telling falsehoods."

"A brave lad, and worth winning for a good cause!" exclaimed the gentleman who had first spoken. "Mr Harwood having answered for your fidelity, you will be put to no inconvenience about this matter, but as we have affairs of importance to discuss, and the night is drawing on apace, you must go back to your bed, and try to persuade yourself that what you have seen is merely a dream which you are not at liberty to mention to any one."

"Though we have met here, Mr Deane, I shall be glad to see you at the Grange, to speak to you more at large than I can now," said Mr Harwood, as he shook Jack by the hand.

Accompanied by two of the persons present, Jack returned once more to the room above, where, having advised him to go to sleep instead of listening to the voices of the ghosts, they left him. He wisely endeavoured to follow their advice.

Chapter Fifteen
Jack again visits Harwood Grange

The next morning when the old couple and Burdale made their appearance, they did not in any way allude to what had taken place during the night, as if they had been totally ignorant of it. Breakfast was got ready by the aged dame; and afterwards Jack stole about the building, and found his way without difficulty into the vault below. Not a trace of any of the occupants of the previous evening was to be seen, but how they had gone he could not discover. Certainly they had not come up by the steps by which he had descended, and passed through the hall.

As the afternoon approached, Jack became more impatient than ever to pay his proposed visit to Harwood Grange. Mr Harwood had spoken so kindly to him, that he could not help hoping he would not reject him as a son-in-law. At length the hour fixed by Burdale for starting arrived, and Jack eagerly threw himself into the saddle.

"Why, your horse partakes of your spirit," observed his companion, as, clapping his spurs in the horse's side, Jack galloped over the greensward at a rate which put his guide's steed on his mettle.

He would willingly have gone by himself, but unacquainted with that part of the forest, he would scarcely alone have found his way in the dark. A couple of hours' hard riding, sometimes across cultivated ground, and at others over what remained in a state of nature, brought him to the neighbourhood of the Grange. Leaving the horses with Burdale, who promised to remain concealed with them under a thick clump of trees, he went towards the house on foot. Jack found the Squire waiting for him in a sheltered walk at a short distance from the house, and having delivered the messages and letters he had received from the various persons he had visited, gave him a full account of his adventures.

"You have indeed managed admirably, my young friend," said Mr Harwood. "You would make a first-rate diplomatist, and I shall have very great satisfaction in recommending you to a good appointment for which your talents peculiarly fit you. You will find Pearson thoroughly trustworthy, and as he advises you to stay for a short time with him in his farm in the fens, I would advise you to accept his invitation. You will meet persons there who will be able to forward your interests, and you will besides find ample amusement of various sorts during your stay. You will come in now, and take some refreshment," he observed; "and my daughter Alethea will be happy to welcome you. We may possibly have some visitors at supper, who are engaged in a certain important undertaking, but do not mention to them, and especially to my daughter, having met me last night. I know that I can trust you, but I am unwilling to implicate others in the matter I have in hand."

As Jack, in company with the Squire, was about to enter the house, he saw a horseman ride out of the courtyard, and kissing his hand to Alethea, who stood at a window overlooking the avenue, take the way towards Nottingham. A second glance at the horseman, though already at some distance, convinced Jack that he was his brother Jasper. He loved his brother. His first impulse was to shout out to him, and to call him back, that he might make inquiries about home, but then, recollecting the accusations brought against him, he dreaded Jasper's rebukes in the presence of the Squire; and next, for the first time in his life, a feeling of jealousy stole over him. Had Jasper—the quiet, studious unassuming Jasper—been paying court to the fair heiress of Harwood Grange? And how had Alethea received him?

The Squire having stepped on in front to open a door, prevented him from asking any questions, and he presently found himself ushered into the hall. A shout from Mr Harwood brought Alethea into the open gallery at one end of it; and seeing Jack, she at once came down-stairs. She greeted him in a friendly way, and then, not without some embarrassment, told him that he had narrowly missed seeing his brother.

"Had I known of your coming, I would have begged him to stop and meet you," she said, looking, however, down on the floor as she spoke. "You will, however, probably overtake him if you go on to Nottingham to-night, or you will see him with the rest of your family to-morrow."

Jack replied that circumstances would prevent him returning home. He naturally felt disinclined to tell Alethea more of the truth than was necessary. They had little time for conversation before the servant announced that supper was ready, when two other persons were seen crossing the hall in the direction of the supper-room.

"Some friends I told you that you might possibly meet," observed the Squire to Jack, as they took their seats at the table.

From the dress of the strangers, Jack at once came to the conclusion that they were ecclesiastics or ministers of some denomination. When he glanced at the countenance of the man opposite to him, he had little doubt that he at least was a priest of the Church of Rome. The person had a somewhat pale face and hollow cheeks, with bright intelligent eyes, and thin, undemonstrative lips. His was one of those countenances formed rather to conceal than express the thoughts of the mind. The first words uttered by the other man, who sat by his side, made Jack turn round to examine his features, for in the tones of his voice he recognised those of the Reverend Simon Stirthesoul. He looked at him again and again. The form of the features was the same, but their expression was now very different. Once Jack caught him eyeing him, as he was bending down over his plate, and he felt sure, by the cunning expression of the man's face, that he was not mistaken. Still Master Simon gave no other sign of recognition. His dress, though different from that which he had before worn, did not stamp him positively as a priest of Rome, though its cut and colour were such as were generally worn by clericals in those days. Each time the man spoke Jack was more and more convinced that he was Master Simon Stirthesoul. At the same time, so earnest was his application to the viands placed before him, that he did not indulge himself much in entering into conversation. That was chiefly kept up by Alethea and Jack's opposite neighbour, who devoted himself to her. His conversation indeed was agreeable, for he had visited many countries, and had shrewd remarks to make on all he had seen. Jack at length heard him describing Rome, and picturing the glories of the Eternal City.

"Ah, Miss Harwood," he exclaimed, "there we have the blessing of pure religion, sanctioned by the authority of the ancient Fathers, by the great Apostle Peter, and by Councils, and by the infallible head of the Church—the Pope himself! What a blessing to have no dissent, no difference of opinion; all united in one brotherhood, under one loving father, and to be relieved of all care and responsibility, and to know that whatever the Church decides is a right thing for us to believe!"

From what the person said, Jack had now no longer any doubt that he was a priest of Rome; but the more he listened the less inclined he became to acknowledge the correctness of his assertion. Jack watched Alethea's countenance, and he could not help hoping that neither did she altogether agree with him. They seemed, however, to have more effect upon Mr Harwood, for whom, in all probability, they were equally intended. His fathers had been Romanists, and he himself, though belonging to the Church of England, had never very perfectly imbibed Protestant truth. Master Stirthesoul made no remark, which surprised Jack, as the doctrines put forth by the priest were diametrically opposed to those which that worthy had himself been a short time ago enunciating to the public. There was a twinkle occasionally in his eye, but that might have arisen from the pleasure with which he was discussing the viands placed before him, and Jack could not discover whether he approved or not of the doctrines which were being laid down. Still it was curious to find two persons of apparently different opinions so closely associated with each other, as it was evident was the case.

Jack all the time was longing to have some private conversation with Alethea; but the other guests showed no inclination to take their departure; and he felt that he could not remain much longer, as his companion, Burdale, would naturally be becoming impatient. He himself could not agree with the priest's remarks, plausible as they were. Though he had not seen much of Romanists, he had heard a good deal of what took place at Rome, and believed truly that the union spoken of was very far from being real. He had heard, too, of a Spanish army of Roman Catholics attacking Rome, and of its being given up to them to pillage, they having treated the dignitaries of the Church and the Pope himself with even less respect than did their Protestant brothers-in-arms. He had heard, too, that it was not proved that Peter had ever been at Rome, much less that he was a Bishop of that city; and he was not altogether ignorant of the existence of the Inquisition, and of the mode by which that institution endeavoured to support the Church of Rome and the dogmas it inculcated.

The more the priest praised Rome and its system, the more anxious Jack became to speak to Alethea on the subject, and to do away with any impression he might have made. He had a clear, straightforward way of looking at things, the characteristic of the best type of Englishmen. He had been led into scrapes, he had done things for which he was sorry, and he was even now suffering the consequences of doing what was wrong, but instead of attempting to get out of the difficulty by twisting and turning and prevarication and falsehood, he always endeavoured to escape by going straightforward, boldly telling the truth, and, if needs be, doubling his fist, or drawing his sword and fighting his way out. Thus the sophistries and arguments which he heard brought forward by the Romish priest, far from having any effect upon him, made him more than ever inclined to oppose the system which Rome endeavours to spread over the world. He still waited on in the hope that the two guests would take their departure, but they seemed in no way disposed to do so, and at length Mr Harwood remarked that the shades of evening were approaching, and that he would have some difficulty in finding his way through the forest, if he delayed much longer. This hint was too clear not to be taken, and, very reluctantly, he at length rose to pay his adieus to Alethea. She wished him good-bye, expressing a hope to see him on his return to Nottingham, in a friendly tone, but gave him no opportunity of saying any thing to her alone. He bowed to the two other guests, and Mr Harwood accompanied him to the door, pointing out to him the way he was to take to reach the spot where he had left his horse. "Can she be aware of the character of those people," thought Jack to himself, as he walked on through the wood, "or the plots which, it seems, are hatching? I wish Mr Harwood had nothing to do with them! I wonder how that he, a Protestant gentleman, can engage in such a matter. I hope that I shall hear nothing of them where I am going; and I heartily wish I had not helped the enemies of our good Protestant king by conveying those letters! Still, what has been done cannot be undone; and having been trusted by Mr Harwood, I cannot attempt to give information of what, I fear, is taking place, even though I might enable him to escape. I suspect those two men I met just now are engaged in it. I like neither of them, least of all that hypocritical-looking Master Stirthesoul, as he called himself. I wish Pearson had nothing to do with him. Indeed, Master Pearson evidently knows a good deal about the plot; and I should be thankful if I was free of him also. But what can I now do? I am in his power; and if I were to go back to Nottingham, I should be in difficulty about that poaching affair; while, if I offend him, he can at any moment inform against me for delivering those letters. Well, I must go through with it, and wait patiently for the result."

Such thoughts occupied his mind till he reached the clump of trees within which he expected to find Burdale and the horses. The shades of evening were already approaching, and a thick mass of brushwood, which grew outside, prevented him from seeing into the interior of the wood. He had to walk round some distance indeed before he could find an entrance. More than once he gave a whistle, the sign agreed on, without receiving any answer. The idea occurred to him that Burdale had turned traitor, or, weary of waiting for him, had gone back with the horses. At length he shouted, "Master Burdale! Master Burdale! where are you?"

He was at last relieved by seeing the man leading the horses towards him.

"Why, Mr Deane, you shouted loud enough to wake up Robin Hood and his merry men from their graves!" said his guide, as he came up. "It's to be hoped no strangers were passing whom we should not like to meet! You forgot the side of the wood where you left me. However, let us mount now and be off, for the night promises to be dark, and I should like to get into a part of the forest I know better than this while we have a little twilight to guide us."

A ride through a forest in the dusk is a difficult matter, and dangerous withal, from the outstretched boughs overhead, and slippery roots, and holes beneath. Fully three hours were occupied in reaching the Hagg.

"Go in!" said Burdale to Jack, as they came in front of the old building. "I will take the horses round to the stables; and you will be welcome there."

"I hope I may not see any more of the ghosts!" said Jack: "I had enough of them last night."

"As to that, I don't know," answered Burdale; "but do you follow the old people's example, and let them alone, and they will let you alone, depend upon that!"

Some loud groans were heard above Jack's head as he spoke, and he could not help starting, so melancholy and deep sounding were they. The next instant, however, he recollected the old woman's description of the haunted oak, and, looking round at the venerable tree, he had little doubt that the noise was produced by some branches moved by the wind, or else the passage of air through its hollow trunk.

Jack slept too soundly during the night to hear the conversation of the ghosts; but, on the following morning at his early breakfast, ere he and his guide took their departure, the old woman assured him that they had been talking as usual, making, if possible, even more uproar than she had ever before heard.

"But what was it all about?" asked Jack; "could not you hear that?"

"No, no," she answered; "maybe they spoke in a tongue I cannot understand, for, though often and often I've listened, not one word could I ever make out!"

Chapter Sixteen
Residence in the Fens of Lincolnshire

The raw wind from the fens was driving the mist before it, and bending masses of willows, bulrushes, and tall sedges all one way—and that way right against the faces of Deane and his guide, when they commenced their devious course across the marshes, within which Master Pearson's farm was situated. A dead level was before them, broken here and there only by a group of willows, or occasionally a few small trees which had taken root on patches of firmer ground than that with which they were surrounded, otherwise the horizon was as clear as that of the ocean. The whole country had a raw, cold, damp, and agueish look about it. It was any thing but tempting.

"Where is the farm?" asked Jack, as he pulled up for an instant to survey the unpromising country before him.

"Some miles on," answered Burdale. "It's lucky you have a man with you who knows the country, or you would have a bad job to get over it. If you were to ride straight on now, you would be up to your horse's ears in slush, with very little chance of ever getting out again alive. Come, I'll show you the way; follow me. Don't turn either to the right hand or to the left, or you will get into trouble!"

Saying this, Burdale spurred on his somewhat unwilling horse, who seemed to understand the difficulties of the way before him. Here and there, and scattered thickly on every side, were large patches of water, sometimes expanding into the size of lakes, while others were mere pools and puddles. Now a patch of reeds was to be seen. In some places soft velvety grass, growing over, however, the most treacherous spots; now a group of low willows, scarcely six feet high; now a bed of osiers, barely three feet above the surface. There was scarcely a spot which offered any promise of ground sufficiently hard to enable the travellers to move out of the snail's pace at which they had hitherto been obliged to proceed.

"Well, this is about the worst country I ever rode over!" Jack could not help exclaiming.

"Now, don't be grumbling, Mr Deane; if it affords you shelter, you may be grateful for it: and the country's not so bad after all. You should just see the pike which are caught in the rivers! they are larger than any you will see in the Trent, I have a notion. There are sheep too here: larger and bigger animals, though somewhat awkward in their gait, than you will see throughout England; but they yield very lusty wool, let me tell you. And though, perhaps, you don't think much of the willows, of which you have passed a goodly number, they're very useful to the people who live here. There is an old proverb they have got—'A willow will buy a horse before an oak will buy a saddle.'"

Burdale, indeed, seemed to have a good deal of information to give about the fens; and Jack could not help thinking that he must belong to the country, or, at all events, have lived a considerable time in it. Indeed, no one but a person thoroughly acquainted with the nature of the ground could have managed to find his way across it. The water was soon over the horses' fetlocks, and here and there up to their knees. More than once Jack could not help fearing that his guide had made a mistake, and that he was leading him into dangerous country; but he did not wish to show any suspicion of his judgment, and made no remark. Again the horses rose up out of the slough across which they had been wading and enjoyed for a short time some hard ground; but they soon had to leave it, to wade on as before. On every side was heard the loud croaking of frogs; their heads poked up in all the shallower marshes, with the object, it seemed, of observing the travellers, and then their croaking became louder than ever, as if they were amusing themselves by talking about them.

"We call those animals 'Holland-waits,'" observed Burdale. "Their king must look upon himself as fortunate, for he has got a large number of subjects; but they're not so bad as the midges. If you were to cross where we are on a hot day, with the sun broiling down on your head, you would wish you had a thick net over your face, for they do bite mortal hard!"

Burdale's horse seemed better accustomed to the country than was Jack's. After having gone a considerable distance, he left Jack some way behind. The marks of the horse's feet had immediately been lost, by the spongy ground returning to its former state. Jack, however, thought there could be no difficulty in pushing on directly behind him. He had not, however, gone far before he found that, instead of following Burdale's direction to turn neither to the right nor left, he had by some means got off the track. His horse began to flounder, and the more he floundered the more difficult it was to extricate himself. Deeper and deeper he sank into the mire, till Jack, fearing that he might lose him altogether, shouted out to Burdale. Burdale heard his voice at length, and hurried back to his assistance. Jack had already got off his horse into the mud, hoping in that way to relieve the poor animal, but it did but little good, and he himself was also sticking fast!

"Here, catch hold of the end of this rope!" exclaimed Burdale, as he threw one which was secured to his saddlebow. "I will haul you out; and then, maybe, we will get the horse free. You could not have followed my advice, or this would never have happened."

Happily, Jack soon reached firm ground, and then he and Burdale together managed to get out the unfortunate horse.

"I must not in future let you get a foot behind me, Master Deane," said Burdale. "You see that a man can as easily be lost in this fen-country as he could in a big forest, and now we must make the best of our way onward; the evening is advancing, and the night is growing desperately cold. It will require some good liquor to warm up our veins again."

As soon as they got on dry ground, Burdale, with a whisp of dry hay and grass, wiped down the horse's legs, and made him look in a more respectable condition than the mud of the marsh had left him in. Burdale, standing up in his stirrups, looked round in every direction to ascertain that no one was approaching.

"We're getting near Master Pearson's country," he observed, "and, as there are some sharp eyes on the look-out for him, we must take care not to betray his abode."

Hour after hour passed by, and still they seemed to have made but little progress across this inhospitable-looking country. Now again a few mounds were seen just rising above the ground, which, Burdale told his companion, were the huts of the inhabitants.

"Well, what sort of people can live here?" asked Jack.

"An odd sort, I must own; something between fish and geese. They must be waders, at all events. In some places they have boats in which they can get about: however, every place has its uses, and so has this, you will find out, before you have been here long!"

Jack and Bardale arrive at Parson's farm.

At length, as the sun was about to sink beneath the long straight line behind their backs, Jack saw before them what looked like a clump or two of trees which stood on a piece of ground a few feet above the dead level which surrounded it. Objects, too, seemed to be moving about it, which he at length discovered to be horses and cattle. A more perfect Rosamond's labyrinth could scarcely have been contrived than that to which the path they now followed led. Before, however, they came in sight of the bower, they heard the lowing of cows and the barking of watch-dogs, and Jack, who by this time was very hungry, even thought that he sniffed a savoury odour of cooking in the damp air, that mightily urged him forward. At length, they saw before them a large rambling cottage, with dairy-buildings adjoining it, standing on a firm piece of pasture-land that formed a green peninsula rising above the black fens they had just been traversing. A row of poplars behind it, and a plantation on either side, shut it in from any one passing at a short distance. There was also a kitchen and flower-garden in front, and considerable care had evidently been taken to keep the ground around clean and fit for walking.

"You go in, and give your letter to Dame Pearson, while I take the horses to the stables," said Burdale. "You will find it all right, for she will know well that no one could find his way here without a trustworthy guide."

Jack had expected to find a somewhat rough, and perhaps ill-favoured, dame the wife of Master Pearson. Greatly surprised was he, therefore, when, on opening the door, he was received by a remarkably attractive, neatly-dressed woman, with a pleasant smile on her countenance, and agreeable manners, superior even to those of many ladies he had met.

"You are welcome here, Mr Deane, as a friend of my husband!" she said. "We live a secluded life, but shall be glad to see you as long as you can remain. And perhaps you will find some amusement in the sports of our fen-country. Ned Burdale will be able to show them to you as well as most people; but we are not likely to be alone, for my husband tells me that several persons are coming here, and I have been making the best preparation in my power to receive them. My little girl Elizabeth and I will soon get supper ready for you, and make you as welcome as we can. After your hard day's ride you will then be glad to go to bed, for it is a trying country to a stranger. We came here most of the way by water, but it was bad enough even then; and I am told that coming across from inland it's still worse."

On entering the sitting-room, Jack found a fair, pretty-looking little girl, of about fourteen or fifteen years of age, busily employed in spinning, so busy indeed that she did not stop even when she rose from her seat to make him a courtesy as he entered.

"Ah, yes, Elizabeth is always at work," said Dame Pearson; "it is one of the secrets of her happiness, never to be idle from morning till night. To be sure we have plenty to do, and not many people to do it out in this place, and so a good deal falls to our lot—but come, Elizabeth, we will go and prepare the supper for Mr Deane and Ned Burdale, who has come with him; and, perhaps before it is ready, others may make their appearance."

Saying this, she, followed by the little girl, glided from the room, leaving Jack to his own reflections. He had not been left alone long before a knock was heard at the door, and Dame Pearson hurried through the room to open it. As she did so, a tall dark man, in a rough riding-suit, with pistols in his belt and a sword by his side, entered the house with the air of a person accustomed to consider himself at home wherever he might be. After exchanging a few words with the dame, while she returned to the kitchen he entered the room, and, seating himself in a large arm-chair, stretched out his legs, without taking any notice of Jack, who sat before him, while he commenced tapping his boot with the end of his sword, as if lost in thought. At length he condescended to take a glance at his companion.

"Not long arrived in this part of the world, lad, I suppose?" he said, in a tone which showed he was very indifferent as to what answer he might receive. "It is possible that you may pass your time pleasantly enough here, if you are not troubled with the ague, and are fond of the music of frogs and wild-ducks. From what part of the world do you come, I ask?"

"I last came from the borders of Scotland; a pretty long ride too!"

"Ah!" exclaimed the stranger; "what matter brought you south?"

"My own good pleasure," answered Jack, not liking the tone of voice of the speaker. "You will excuse me if I do not explain the reason for my movements until we are further acquainted."

"Spoken like a sensible youth!" remarked the stranger. "I will ask no further questions then, though I suspect you have no cause to be ashamed of whatever you are about."

The conversation, if so it could be called, was cut short by the entrance of Dame Pearson and her young attendant, bearing the dishes for supper, which they placed on a table on which the cloth had already been spread. The tall stranger took his seat at it with the same self-confident air with which he had entered the room. At that moment Ned Burdale came in, and was about to take his seat at the board, when, seeing the stranger, he stopped short.

"I beg your pardon, sir! I did not know—"

"Never mind!" said the stranger; "sit down, Ned; say not a word about it, man!" and he gave him at the same time a significant glance.

Burdale obeyed; but he evidently stood greatly in awe of the person who had spoken to him. Very little conversation took place during the meal; and Jack had time to examine the countenance of the young girl who had assisted Dame Pearson in preparing the supper, and who now took her seat by her side at the head of the table. There was a bright, intelligent look about her, and a refinement of expression which Jack scarcely expected to find in a dwelling so remote from the civilised world. Her education also had evidently not been neglected, for she had apparently read a good deal, and her mind was well stored with information on various subjects. Jack did not find all this out at first; but he very soon began to suspect it. He discovered also that she had derived a good deal of her information from the dame herself, who, though apparently a mere farmer's wife, was evidently a person of superior education, equalled, indeed, by very few ladies in Nottingham or elsewhere at that period. The stranger also treated her with considerable respect; and though he spoke in a rough way to Jack and Burdale, whenever he deigned to address them, his manner was greatly softened as he turned to the dame or the young girl. She was acquainted with most of Jack's favourite authors; could recite many of the ballads about Robin Hood; and she was also especially well versed in Foxe's "Book of Martyrs," a copy of which she exhibited with no little satisfaction to him. He observed, when she brought it out, that the tall stranger looked at it askance.

"Ah," she observed, "what fearful accounts Master Foxe gives us of the persecutions which Protestants have suffered in all lands since the Reformation which Luther was the means of bringing about! In Germany, in Italy, in Spain, and France, and, oh, I tremble with horror when I read of the sufferings of the poor Protestants in the Netherlands, under that cruel Alva! In France also, how barbarously have the Reformed been treated! I have reason to know something about it; and I'll tell you some day, Mr Deane."

This was said after supper, as Jack was seated at a little distance from the rest of the party, while the fair Elizabeth was nimbly plying her distaff.

"Fictions or gross exaggerations!" muttered the stranger, who overheard some of the remarks uttered by the little damsel.

At length the dame, who had observed the rising anger of her guest, came over to Elizabeth, and whispered a few words in her ear; after which she did not again allude to the subject of which she had been speaking.

"When do you expect your good man?" asked the tall stranger. "I fancied that I should have met him here to-day."

"He has sent me word that he will be with us in two or three days, sir," answered the dame. "He has been longer absent than usual; but he has been busy buying cattle to send over to our farm; and we expect to have a considerable increase this year."

"Ah, yes! they thrive well on the rich grasses about here," observed the stranger. "Well, I must wait his arrival; though how to pass away the time till he comes I scarcely know."

"We can give you some sporting, sir," said Burdale. "We lack not a variety—as wild-duck shooting, and fishing; and we have a new decoy establishment not far off. You may be interested in seeing that work, for we sometimes catch a great number of wild-fowl in it."

Jack was not sorry to hear arrangements made for the sport next day, hoping that he might be allowed to join in it, though he thought to himself he would rather have gone in the company of any body else than in that of the tall stranger. That he was a person of some consequence he felt sure, from the way in which he was treated; and when the family prepared to retire to rest, he observed that the dame herself showed him up-stairs to what was called the best guest-chamber in the house. A shake-down was prepared for Jack in a corner of the hall; and Burdale made off to a room in one of the out-houses.

"We treat you now as we shall have to do while you stay here," said the dame, apologising for the homely entertainment she had given Jack. "Before long we are expecting several guests, who come here to transact business with my good man, either to buy cattle or horses, or about certain affairs abroad. He was a seaman in his younger days, and visited many strange countries, and even now is often hankering after the ocean. However, I hope he will settle down quietly soon, for I think he must be weary of riding about the country in the way he does; but he's a good, kind husband to me, and I have reason to be grateful. He saved my life in the time of the Civil War, and protected me from fearful dangers when all my family were killed, and I was left penniless; so I have reason, you see, to be grateful to him and love him. I should be glad if we could move back to the part of the country we came from, for this fen-district is trying to the health, though Elizabeth and I keep ours indeed wonderfully, considering the fogs which so often hang about us. But the inhabitants of Holland retain their health often to a green old age, and the country is very similar to this, only there drains have been cut in all directions, and it is only of late years that attempts have been made to drain our Lincolnshire fens. It would seem impossible to carry the water off from around us, and yet, looking to what has been done in Holland, perhaps too some day we shall see corn-fields and orchards where now we have only marshes and ponds."

Jack, taking courage from the disposition to talk the good dame exhibited, asked her the name of the tall stranger who had just arrived.

"That is more than I can tell you, young sir," she answered. "He calls himself Long Sam, or Sam Smart, and desires to be addressed by that name alone; but whether that is his real name or not, I leave you to judge. He is evidently a man who has seen the world, and courtly society too, though he can be rough enough when he pleases, as you will find if you offend him, and let me advise you not to do so on any account."

Jack, much interested with the information he had received, at length put his head upon his straw-stuffed pillow. As he lay there he heard heavy footsteps pacing up and down the room overhead, which he concluded to be the one occupied by the gentleman who chose to call himself Long Sam.

Chapter Seventeen
A Decoy described

The following morning, with Burdale as a guide, Long Sam and Jack set off to visit the decoy which had been spoken of, mounted on rough-looking fen horses, with broad feet which enabled them to get over the soft ground at a considerable rate, while, they kept the legs of their riders out of the water. The horses were left at a hut at a little distance from the decoy, under charge of one of the persons employed in attending it. It was situated in the midst of somewhat higher and firmer ground than any they had before passed over, and was surrounded also with willow, poplar, and other trees.

The decoy consisted of a pond of a hundred and fifty acres, or more perhaps. On the surface of it floated a number of water-lilies, the aquatic ranunculus, and the flowers of other water-plants, while at the edges for a considerable distance gulfs—or canals, they might be called—had been cut, about seven yards wide at the mouth, more or less, terminating in a sharp point. About ten or twelve yards from the entrance of each canal, an arch was formed over the water of about ten feet in height, a number of other arches succeeding it gradually, as they advanced towards the inner end decreasing in height and width, the innermost of all not being more than two feet in height, and about the same in width. Over these a strong net was thrown and pegged closely down to the ground, thus forming a complete cage, with a broad entrance opening on the pool, there being only at the inner end a small door, through which the fowler could insert his hand to draw out his captives.

"This is what we call a pipe," observed Burdale, as he exhibited the arrangement to Long Sam.

On either side of the pipe, commencing at the pond, and continuing to the farther end, was a screen formed of reeds, about five feet in height, built in a zig-zag form, and broken into lengths of about five or six feet, and at about a foot from the edge of the pipe. While the party were examining this pipe, the chief fowler, accompanied by a little dog, came up to them.

"This is our piper," he observed; "without him we could not manage to catch any fowls."

He was a little foxy-coloured animal, evidently very obedient and submissive to his master.

"You will see, sir," observed the man, "we have got ten pipes to our decoy, all branching off in different directions. The reason of this is that wild-fowl, when they get up from the water, always fly against the wind, and so, if we only had the pipes on one side, it would only be when the wind came from that quarter that we could catch any fowl; so you see we have them from all sides; and thus from whatever point the wind blows, we have the chance of catching birds. Now, you see those birds swimming out in the middle of the pond there? They're our decoy-ducks; without them we could not catch any wild ones either. I had a good job to train them. You see, the first thing I did was to shut them up by themselves, and pretty nigh starve them. I then carried them a little food; and did the same several times every day, till they knew me. At last they began to look out for me, and, instead of flying away, they were too glad to come up and take the food from my hand. Whenever also I fed them, I whistled just a faint whistle, like this. And so, at last, as soon as they heard my whistle, they knew that I was going to give them some food, and I kept on whistling all the time they were feeding in the same gentle tone. It took me, I suppose, three or four months before I could trust those birds out; and now, if I did not continue to feed them, and whistle all the time, they would soon be off with the rest. I had to train the dog, too; and that took me some time. You see, his business is to run along the edge of the pipe, show himself now and then, and then leap through those openings in the screen. Well, to make him do that, I taught him by giving him a piece of bread each time he came through; and if he would not jump, then he got no bread and no cheese, for he is fond of cheese, I can tell you.

"Now, you will understand, that if we are to catch any birds, you must not show yourself; and you, tall gentleman, if you please, will just keep stooping down all the time. No disrespect to you, master; if they caught sight of your face, not a bird would come up the pipe.

"Now there's another thing we shall have to do: we must just each of us carry a piece of lighted turf, for the birds can smell as well as see; and they don't mind the smoke, and that carries away any scent by which we might betray ourselves. Now, we will go round to the side from which the wind blows directly over the pond. Stoop down, master, if you please. I will first go and fasten the net over the end of the pipe, that the birds may fly into it, as I hope there will be many of them doing before long. Here we are, masters: just step softly over the turf, and keep bending down. That will do. Now don't speak any more, but just do as I do. You will see a sight of birds in a few minutes."

After going some little distance towards the edge of the decoy, the fowler drew aside a small shutter, it might be called, in the screen, through which he beckoned Jack and his companions to look. A number of birds, ducks, teal, widgeon, and others, were either floating lazily on the surface of the lake, or rising and circling round it, while others were bobbing their heads beneath the water, or diving in search of their prey which swam below. Again the shutter was closed, and the fowler threw a few handfuls of bruised barley into the centre of the pipe, which was soon blown down by the wind to the mouth. He now called the little piper, and sent him in, in front of the screen, at the same time whistling low—the well-known signal to the decoy-ducks. On hearing the sound, they instantly rose and flew towards the mouth of the pipe. Now the little dog ran along for a few feet in front of the screen, where the birds could see him, and then suddenly disappeared, by leaping through one of the openings. On came the wild-fowl, following the decoy-ducks and fearless of evil. Seeing the dog, the curiosity of the birds was excited, and up the pipe they began to swim. Again the dog was turned in, and again the birds followed him in his treacherous course up the pipe. The same trick was played over and over again, till the birds had been led well out of sight of the entrance of the pipe. The fowler then stepping forward in front of the screen, without making any noise which might frighten the birds still outside, waved his cap round and round. Frightened by this unexpected apparition, the birds rose from the water, and rushed at headlong speed towards the narrow end of the pipe. On they went, driven by the fowler, till they reached the very end; where, finding what they supposed to be an opening, they darted through, to discover, when too late, that they were hopeless captives within a strong net!

The scene was very exciting, especially to Jack, who had never seen it before, and full forty birds were captured together. The decoy-birds, as soon as the fowler ceased whistling, employed themselves quietly in picking up the grains of barley which floated on the water, instead of proceeding, like their brothers whom they had treacherously betrayed, up towards the end of the pipe.

"You see you have no risk of starving, Master Deane," observed Burdale, as he assisted in ringing the necks of the captive birds. "We live like princes here, as far as food is concerned; and when the weather allows it, and we can send across the fens, we could always get a good market for our game."

"We're not always so lucky as we have just been," observed the fowler; "we have a good many enemies who try to prevent our success. Sometimes I have seen a heron sit on the top of the outermost arch, just waiting to dive down and catch some fish he may see swimming below. Now as long as that heron sits there, not a bird will ever come up that pipe, not knowing what trick he will play them, and our only chance is to try another. There are some ducks, too, which nothing will tempt to come up the pipe. They are the *pochard*, or, as we call them here, pokers. Now they're the cunningest birds you ever saw! If ever they find themselves within the mouth, they will suddenly dive and swim out again, generally making the other birds follow them. At other times they will stop just at the mouth, where the barley is floating about, and swim backwards and forwards till they have eaten the whole of it up, and then off again they will go, laughing at the way they have deceived us. The worst of all, perhaps, is when an otter builds his house near the mouth. At first we could not find out what was the matter when no birds would ever come near, and it was not till I caught the gentleman one day, that I found out the reason why. No birds are more timid than these wild-fowl. All the work about the decoy we have to do at night, for if they hear any sounds they're not accustomed to, they will keep away from it. As few people ever come out here we are safe enough; but if strangers were to come, or any body was to fire a gun, we might not catch a bird for weeks afterwards. However, masters, the wind has shifted a little, and we will try another pipe; so come along."

The next pipe was worked in the same way as the first. The decoy-ducks performed their part to admiration; Toby, the little piper, doing his in a way to gain the applause of all who saw him. His reward was a piece of cheese at the end of his day's work, for although a number of ducks were piled up around him, not one of them would he touch.

"Oh, no, no!" said his master; "it's one of the chief things he has to be careful about. If he had a taste for duck's meat, he would never do for a piper."

With a large supply of ducks for the farm, the party returned by the way they had come, Jack promising to pay ere long another visit to the decoy.

Had it not been for Elizabeth, Jack would have found his time hang rather heavily on his hands, but as soon as her day's work was over, and she had resumed her distaff or spinning-wheel, he took his seat by her side, and either read to her, or talked to her about the books which she had read. Her quiet, gentle manner put him more in mind of his sister Kate, than of Polly or Alethea, with whom he could not help occasionally contrasting her. Not that he fancied he admired Alethea less than he had done; but, at the same time, he could scarcely help acknowledging to himself that he was greatly taken with Elizabeth's quiet and gentle manners. It is possible that the desire to be with Elizabeth induced him to offer his services to Dame Pearson as an assistant about the farm, as he assured her he was well able to perform most of the duties of a farm-servant; and he thus had ample employment in driving in the cows, assisting in milking them, leading the horses to water, churning the butter, of which the dame manufactured a considerable quantity, and performing many other similar duties. He was very glad, however, when on the third day after his arrival Master Pearson himself appeared at the farm. Jack was anxious to hear whether the arrangements regarding the purchase of cattle for Mr Strelley had been satisfactorily carried out.

"Oh, yes, my young friend," answered Master Pearson, "the money was honestly paid, and the cattle are now on their way south, and I will warrant they arrive as safely as if Will Brinsmead himself had been driving them. They will have no black-mail to pay, either to Master Nevis or to any other cateran who is in the habit of levying it on the road. I met a friend from Nottingham, and I've heard about your family; and I sent them word that you were all safe, and would come back among them some day,—so you need not make yourself unhappy on that score."

This information greatly relieved Jack's mind, and he was now far better able than before to enjoy his visit to the farm. Soon after the return of Master Pearson, much to Jack's satisfaction, Long Sam took his departure. There was something about the man he did not at all like, for in general he was overbearing and dictatorial, though he could be courteous when he chose, as he occasionally was when speaking to Dame Pearson or Elizabeth. With that young lady, as has been said, Jack spent a considerable portion of his time, whenever he was in the house; Dame Pearson made no objection to his so doing. Indeed, so quiet and sedate was the little girl, that she seemed to treat him more in the light of a brother than an admirer. From the remarks made by Dame Pearson, Jack had been anxious to learn more of her early history, but whenever he introduced the subject to Elizabeth, she invariably tried to turn him from it.

"Dear mamma and I are very happy now, and quiet and contented: but we have gone through some very painful scenes, and we desire not to recall them; so don't, I pray you, speak to me again of my early days."

Pearson seemed to be occupying himself very busily about farm matters, and wherever he went took Jack with him. On the various pasture-lands, some partially drained, others tolerably dry by nature, a considerable number of cattle were fed. They were of all breeds, though the greater number appeared to have come from the north. There were a good many horses also—some carefully sheltered in sheds, and others roaming at large. Pearson exhibited them to Jack with considerable pride.

"I have a number of valuable animals here," he observed, "which will fetch high prices in the London market, and I purpose early in the spring sending some up. If you will undertake to accompany them, it will give you an opportunity of seeing the big city. I may or may not go myself, but I wish to place them under charge of a trusty man who knows London well, so that you need have no responsibility in the matter. In the meantime, you shall try them by turns, so that you will be able to speak of their various qualities."

This last proposal was very much to Jack's taste, and from that day forward, he was constantly employed in exercising the horses. In this way he gained considerable knowledge of the fen-country, and was able to traverse it in most directions by himself, learning by degrees to distinguish even at a distance the soft and marshy places which were impassable, and to pick out the harder ground, even though covered with water. Frequently he was thus occupied from morning till night, often being sent considerable distances from the farm with messages to the surrounding towns. Though the life was a rough one, it was much to his taste; and he was recompensed for any extra fatigue by the kindly welcome he always received on his return from the dame and her young daughter. As the winter grew on, also, various guests arrived at the farm for the purpose, so they stated, of purchasing cattle or horses; but though some of them mentioned the subject in his presence, none of the cattle, at all events, were ever driven away. Jack concluded, therefore, that they would be sent in the spring to the purchasers. Now and then a valuable horse was, however, purchased; and sometimes fresh animals were brought and left there while the owners took their departure by some means towards the sea-shore, Jack supposed for the purpose of embarking and going abroad; while others proceeded towards London. Jack could not, however, help occasionally having suspicions with regard to the proceedings of the various persons who came to the farm. He himself was not trusted with their secrets, if secrets they had; nor did he wish to be so; but most of them were evidently far above the class of cattle-dealers. Some, indeed, from their conversation and manners, were undoubtedly men of rank and position in society. As the winter drew on, the number increased; and from the remarks which they occasionally let drop, Jack felt convinced that some undertaking of importance was about to be carried out. He one day hinted the subject to Elizabeth. She shook her head.

"Don't speak of it," she answered; "I don't like to think about the matter. I know, as you do, that these men who come here are not cattle-dealers, but I cannot believe that my father would undertake any thing wrong or dangerous. I should like to learn what it all means, but I dare not speak to him on the subject, for though he is very kind, he does not choose to be questioned about any of his proceedings, and neither my mother nor I ever venture to do so."

It did not occur to Jack that he might be made a tool of in any way, but yet he suspected that he might possibly be drawn into some undertaking against his better judgment. It therefore occurred to him that his wisest course would be to wish good-bye to Master Pearson and his family, and either to return to Nottingham and risk the possibility of a trial, or to throw himself upon the kindness of his future brother-in-law, Giles Dainsforth of Norwich. "He is so calm and right-thinking, that he will advise me what to do," he thought to himself.

But then, again, when he found himself by the side of Elizabeth, he came to the conclusion that a short time longer would make but little difference, and for that time, at all events, he would enjoy her society, while he might also take a few more gallops on Master Pearson's thoroughbred horses. He had not forgotten Alethea, however, and he nattered himself that he was as true in his allegiance to her as he had been before.

Chapter Eighteen
Journey to London with Long Sam

The month of February, 1696, had commenced, when one evening a rider was seen coming across the marsh from the direction of the sea. He threw himself from his horse, and called out loudly for Master Pearson. Jack recognised his voice as that of the tall stranger, Long Sam, whom he had met on his first arrival. He took Pearson, who went out to him, by the arm, and walked up and down in front of the house rapidly for some time, talking earnestly to him. Meantime, the dame and Elizabeth were preparing the evening meal. The new arrival, whose appearance was very different to what it had been formerly, now entered the house, and placed himself before the table, to partake of the food provided for him. While he was thus engaged, Pearson called Jack aside.

"Our friend here has business in London of importance, and requires a trustworthy attendant. Are you disposed to accompany him?" he asked. "You will find it, as I have before promised you, a good opportunity of seeing the great city, and all your expenses will besides be paid, while you will receive a handsome gratuity to boot. Take my advice: don't throw the chance away. As I told you before, you will be as safe there as you are in the middle of the fens, and you will, besides, very likely find an opportunity of pushing your fortune, which you certainly will not out here."

Jack thanked Pearson for the offer. The temptation was strong, and whatever might have been his suspicions of the tall stranger, he determined to accept it.

"You will set off to-morrow morning by daybreak, with eight horses. Each of you will take charge of three and bestride another, and you will be able to dispose of them in London or its neighbourhood for handsome prices. They will make fine chargers, and will very likely be purchased by officers of cavalry. Long Sam knows London well, and will make all the necessary arrangements for their sale."

Elizabeth's colour changed when Jack told her that he was about to take his departure for London.

"Going away!" she exclaimed; "I thought that you would remain here always and help my mother look after the farm when Mr Pearson is away. She much requires help. Oh, I wish that you were not going!"

"I hope to come back again soon, Elizabeth," he answered, taking the young girl's hand. "You have made my stay here very pleasant, far pleasanter than I expected, and I shall always remember you."

"And I, I am very sure, shall not forget you, Master Deane," replied Elizabeth, looking up in his face. "I have never felt sad or dull as I used sometimes to do before you came—and I have been very happy! My only fear is that you will not recollect me as I shall you; and I want to give you something to make you remember me. I have very few jewels or any thing of value of my own, besides this ring. Please, then, take it and wear it for my sake."

She took his hand, and put on his finger as she spoke a massive gold ring of a peculiar make, with a chameleon and a vessel under full sail engraved on it.

"It is all I have to give, but I entreat you to accept it, that you may be reminded how grateful I am for the kindness you have shown me since you came to live here!"

Jack did not like to refuse the gift, and yet he thought that he ought not to accept it.

"I should ever remember you without it," he answered. "But it is too valuable. Give me something of less cost, which I shall prize as much for your sake as this, for I shall value whatever you give me."

"Oh, no, keep it!" she murmured. "It is the only thing I possess suited for you. I have a locket and brooch and other jewels, but they are not such as you would care for."

Jack could no longer resist the gift. He kissed her brow and thanked her again and again, and promised never to forget her. He felt honestly what he said.

Jack slept very little all that night, thinking of what he was to see in London, and the adventures he might meet with on his journey there. Whatever suspicions might have arisen in his mind he shut out, anxious to have nothing to interfere with the pleasure he anticipated. The light of Pearson's lamp, as it gleamed in his eyes when he came to call him in the morning, aroused him from his sleep, and he found the horses already at the door prepared for starting. The dame and Elizabeth were on foot with breakfast prepared, and they gave him a friendly farewell, as, following Long Sam's example, he stepped out to mount his horse. A thick rime covered the ground, and a cold air blew across the fens, as the two riders with their charges took their way south. Jack, who by this time was well accustomed to the devious track across the fens, led the way at as rapid a pace as the horses could move, closely followed by Long Sam, who was now dressed as an ordinary jockey or rough-rider. They stopped to bait at various places: sometimes at the private residence of some gentleman who Long Sam said wished to look at their horses; at other times at a farm-house, and occasionally at inns, but these were generally avoided. While traversing an open country, Long Sam called Jack by his side.

"You will understand, Deane," he observed, "that you have a very simple part to play when you reach London; but I must have your promise that you will do nothing without my orders, and that you will make all the inquiries I may direct, and gain all the information you can on certain points which I will explain to you. You will thus be enabled to render great service to an important cause, and run no risk or danger yourself."

"As to that," answered Jack, "I am ready enough to run all sorts of risks where there is a good object to be attained; and I would rather be trusted than asked to act in the dark, as I am now doing!" Long Sam smiled grimly.

"Others may not be so willing to trust you as you suppose," he answered. "Indeed, it is better for all parties that you should not be acquainted with what is taking place. I wish you, however, to understand, that the men with whom I am engaged are persons of honour and character, and are not likely to do any act unworthy of their position."

"Then there *is* some plot or scheme afoot?" said Jack. "I have long thought so, but could gain no information about the matter."

"You are right in that respect," answered Long Sam: "there is an important scheme about to be carried out; and as soon as you have given proof of your fitness to engage in it, you shall be informed as to the particulars. In the meantime, all I require is simple obedience to my directions, and then all will be well."

After riding for some distance across somewhat hilly country, on reaching the summit of a height, he pulled up his horse, exclaiming, "Why, surely that must be London!"

Before him, spread out, and extending some way both to the east and west, were numberless streets of houses, with towers and spires rising above them in all directions, Before them, glittering white in the sunlight, rose the pinnacles of the magnificent fane of Saint Paul's, with its lofty dome—just then verging towards completion, to the satisfaction of its talented architect, Sir Christopher Wren—while beyond could be seen, winding on through meadows and green fields, and then amidst the houses and stores of London and Westminster, the city and the borough, the blue stream of the Thames, covered with numerous boats and barges. Keeping to the right, Long Sam led his companion round the outside of London, at the back of the palace at Kensington, to the village of Hammersmith.

"We shall there find proper stables, and a careful groom to look after our horses," he observed; "and purchasers will not object to ride down there to inspect them—they may deem them of more value than if they were brought to their doors."

The village then consisted chiefly of a single street, with here and there a few houses on either side of branch roads. Instead of selecting the chief inn, Long Sam rode up to the door of a small house, with the sign of "The Bear" swinging on poles before it. Some good-sized stables showed that he had selected it more on account of the accommodation it could afford the horses than that which they would find within its doors for themselves.

"We're pretty full, masters," said the landlord, as he eyed the two travellers; "but I'll manage to put you up as best I can, as it's cold weather to sleep out in the lofts. I've got a room for you," he said, looking at Long Sam, "where, by adding two or three feet to the bed, you will find room to stretch yourself; and you, my lad, will be content with a little closet we have got on the stairs. There's not much air or light comes in, but it's pretty warm, considering it's near the kitchen chimney; and as for light, you will do well enough without that at night."

Jack, who had been accustomed to rough lodgings since he started with Will Brinsmead, expressed himself perfectly satisfied with the accommodation which was promised him. Long Sam, taking a valise which he had before him, followed the landlord up to his room.

Jack soon found that his companion intended to make him act the part of the careful groom, the person he spoke of, for some reason or other, not being forthcoming.

"You must keep a watchful eye on the horses, Jack," he observed, when he came down-stairs. "I have business which calls me elsewhere, and I must entrust them to you. Take care that they are well fed, and that their shoes are in good order. See that no tricks are played with them; for in this city rogues of all sorts abound. Some, for instance, on pretence of looking at them, may come in and lame them, perchance to depreciate their value; you understand me? You must watch, too, that no one, pretending to try their paces, gallops off, and leaves you to follow if you list, and to find, when you come back, that the rest have been disposed of in the same way."

"When I engaged for a ride, Master Smart, my object was to see the big city," said Jack, in a tone of expostulation.

"Have patience, lad!" answered Long Sam; "you will see the city soon enough, and perhaps have more time to spend in it than you expect I have the means of rewarding you in a way that will suit your taste. So let me hear no more grumbling, I pray thee!"

Saying this, Long Sam, turning on his heel, walked away from the stables, leaving Jack to groom the tired horses. Jack was fortunately accustomed to make the best of every thing, and, therefore, though somewhat hungry and tired, he set to work with whisp and brush to get the dust and dirt of the roads off the animals, and to put them into a condition to enjoy their food.

Several days passed by, during which Jack found himself almost a prisoner in the stable-yard. Occasionally Long Sam appeared, accompanied by various persons who took a look at the horses; but, strange to say, although they were lavish in their praises of the animals, no purchasers were found. At all events, the horses remained in their stalls. Among two or three who one day came together, Jack observed a person whose countenance he thought he recognised. The man turned a cold, unmeaning glance towards him as he caught Jack's eye fixed on his countenance.

"I am sure that is Master Stirthesoul!" Jack said to himself. "He is the same man I met at Mr Harwood's, and the same who was in Master Pearson's company at Saint Faith's. What can he have to do here?"

Jack resolved to solve the doubt by addressing him. Just as he was about to open his lips, the man, giving him a somewhat menacing look, turned round and followed Long Sam out of the stable. Jack saw him whispering a few words into Long Sam's ears.

"Oh, he's all right and faithful!" he heard the latter say. "He knows nothing, and if he did, he's not the lad to betray us!"

Jack could not tell whether these words were intended for his ears or not. However, the visitors walked away without taking any further notice of him.

In spite of Smart's promises, Jack began to feel very weary of confinement in the precincts of the inn, and determine on insisting that Long Sam should take his place.

"He pretends to be a groom, and therefore I do not see that he should not act as one," said Jack to himself.

Just, however, as he was about to insist on this arrangement with his companion, Long Sam told him that he might go into the city and take a look round London, and see what he could of the sights.

"Only take care to find your way back again here before the evening," he observed. "Keep in the broader streets, and don't tell any strangers where you come from, or what has brought you to the city."

It was Sunday morning; and Jack, putting on his best garments which he had brought with him, started on his walk. He took his way along a very bad road leading to the Strand, with the fields and cabbage-gardens to the right, and Hyde Park to the left, which then extended nearly to the Palace of Kensington. Fortunately the weather was dry for the season of the year, or he would have been splashed over from head to foot. Besides Saint Paul's, a number of beautiful churches were already raising their heads by the genius of Wren in various parts of London. Seeing a number of people collecting before a church, and having never failed at home in attending Divine Service, he took courage, and followed the crowd within the building. Although he had been accustomed occasionally to see people take their eyes off their books to watch the entrance of a stranger, or to examine the dress of their neighbours, or perhaps to exchange glances with one another, he was little prepared for the style of behaviour in which the congregation of the church where he now found himself indulged. Here were collected many of the beauties, and a few of the fine gentlemen of the day. It may have been that they lost little by not attending to the preacher. So Jack thought from what he could catch of the discourse, little of which he could understand, so full of flowers of rhetoric was it. Most of his neighbours were, at all events, flirting and ogling all through the service, and as they entered and took their seats all courtesied and bowed to their acquaintance, as if they had been at a theatre. Jack could not help feeling thankful when the service was brought to a conclusion.

"If this is the way the great people worship God in this big city, I am afraid the citizens and poorer ones can pay very little attention to Him at all," he thought.

Jack found himself looked at askance by several persons of ordinary degree, among whom he stood at the farther end of the building. At length he made his way into the open air. He much admired, however, the coaches and sedan-chairs that came to fetch away all the grand people, with little negro boys from the Sugar Islands to hold up the trains of the ladies, and pages who sat on the steps of the gaily-painted coaches, drawn, some by four, and some by six horses.

In a walk along the Mall, where, of course, no one paid the least attention to the open-mouthed country lad, Jack saw a still greater number of fashionable people. Among them was a very stout lady, carried in a sedan-chair with painted panels, and he heard the passers-by remark that she was the Princess Ann. Her chair was followed by another sedan, which, he was told, contained the Lady Churchill, whose beautiful face looked, however, in any thing but a good-humour. He saw many other sights, some of them curious enough but altogether he was disappointed with this his first day in London.

"They say that the streets are paved with gold; but that is a mistake. They could only once have been gilt, and the fine gentlemen I have met must have rolled in them, and the gilding must have stuck to their clothes."

Jack had been looking out all the day in the hopes of seeing the king, of whose courage, wisdom, and remarkable clemency, he had often heard his father and cousin Nat speak. They looked upon him, indeed, as the bulwark of the Protestant faith in England, and notwithstanding all the efforts which Mr Harwood and his daughter, and Master Pearson and others had made to eradicate that notion from Jack's mind, it remained in reality as firm as ever. The very reason which the king's enemies brought forward to depreciate him, raised him more and more in his opinion. His desire was at length gratified, when, on the 8th of February, Long Sam told him, that if he would go and stand near the gates of the Palace of Kensington he would there very likely get a glimpse of the king.

"And hark you, my lad," he said, "you must observe carefully all that happens at the time, and bring me word. Take your stand, also, with your right foot before the left, and your hand in the breast of your coat. A person will then probably come and speak to you, and you will repeat to me all he says. If he does not speak, he will give you a note, which you are to bring immediately to me."

Jack, as directed, took up his post at the gates of the palace at Kensington. He had not long to wait, when the gates were thrown open, and some guards appeared, and then a coach with six horses, within which sat a gentleman with a long nose and prominent features, dressed in a rich riding-suit. On either side were more horsemen, who Jack heard were the King's Dutch guards. They were followed by several Dutch officers of the court, among whom was the faithful Duke of Portland, and others of high rank. Jack had a good view of that clear hawk's eye, and the large Roman nose and the serious countenance, which expressed little but acute penetration into the mind and motives of others, with all of which the coinage of the realm had made his subjects familiar. The sight of the great warrior and wisest statesman of the day, who knew himself to be surrounded by plots, and yet went his way with perfect coolness, had great effect upon Jack's somewhat excitable mind. He threw up his cap, and shouted, "Hurrah! long live the King!" in as good faith as any of the many bystanders; and his first impulse was to run off, following the coach, shouting, as youths and boys are used to do after any great personage. The king leaned forward over a paper which he held in his hand, so that nearly the whole of his figure was visible at the window of the coach, which took its way towards Richmond.

Suddenly Jack remembered the direction he had received from Long Sam. Going back to the place he had before occupied, he put himself in the position in which he had been standing. Looking round, he saw a person who had come out of the palace observing him narrowly. The person, who was dressed in the livery of the palace, at length passed close to him.

"Are you Long Sam's messenger?" he asked.

"At your service," answered Jack.

"Where does he lodge?" asked the stranger.

"At the Bear," was Jack's answer.

"Take this note, and deliver it quickly," said the stranger; "but do not move from where you now stand till I have re-entered the palace."

Saying this, the stranger slipped a sealed packet into Jack's hand. He immediately concealed it in his doublet, but as he did so a shade of doubt crossed his mind that all was not right. He waited, however, a few minutes till the person who had given him the packet had re-entered the gate, and then took his way back to the Bear. He could not, however, help occasionally looking round to observe whether his steps were followed. He felt that he was engaged in some secret transaction; and from some of the remarks which Long Sam had let drop, as well as the appearance of the concealed Jesuit in his society, he could not help fearing that the plot afoot was against the welfare of the king. He reached the inn, however, in safety, and described exactly to Long Sam all he had seen.

"But you must tell me honestly," he said, "whether this matter has any thing to do with any proceeding which may injure the king. As I watched him just now, I thought of the many brave actions which he has performed, and his calmness and courage at the present time, and could not help feeling that I would rather fight for him than against him."

"You are a foolish young man!" answered Long Sam, in a more angry tone than he had ever used towards Jack. "Follow my directions, and all will be right. I do not want to hurt your feelings," he added, seeing that Jack's colour came to his cheek. "And now I must leave you."

"As to that," answered Jack, "I have no wish to quarrel with you, or any other man; but it strikes me I have been made a 'cat's-paw' of, and I tell you frankly I should like to know our object in coming to London."

"Then as frankly I will tell you—I cannot give it," answered Long Sam. "If you don't know your own interests, it's your own fault; but remain here a few days longer, and I have no doubt you will learn all you wish to know, and probably much more than I know now."

Chapter Nineteen
The Conspiracy

Several days passed by after this conversation, during which Long Sam was constantly absent. Other circumstances had occurred which made Jack more suspicious than ever. He had been waiting all day for his companion, when, as Long Sam had not returned at ten o'clock at night, it being past the usual time of retiring, Jack went to his bedroom, into which, as the entrance was in rather a public position, he securely bolted himself. After he had been asleep for some time he awoke with a start, and was greatly surprised to hear voices close to him. At first, he thought himself transported back to the old house at the Hagg, and that the sounds he heard proceeded from the ghosts which were said to haunt it. However, on sitting up, and more perfectly recovering his senses, he perceived that the speakers were real personages in close proximity to him. Although a gleam or two of light came through a partition which separated him from the room where he supposed them to be, he was unable to find any chink or opening through which he could observe what the speakers were about. As he had not been placed there intentionally for the purpose of hearing the conversation, he did not feel that he was guilty of eavesdropping, or that it was his duty to refrain from listening to what was spoken. There appeared to be a number of persons collected together, two or three of whom took the lead among the others.

"My friends, I have to thank you for meeting me here to-night," were the first words Jack heard uttered. "We have an important object to carry out, and it requires all the nerve and courage we possess to ensure its success. We have a rightful cause, and that should strengthen our arms for any deed which may be necessary. Remember we are not acting for ourselves, but under the full authority and sanction of our lawful sovereign, King James. It becomes necessary for his interests, and for our own, and for that of all England, and moreover for that of the only true and pure faith, which we profess—the faith of Rome—that the Usurper should be removed. You perceive, then, that we lift the responsibility off our own shoulders upon those who give us authority to act. I should be myself ever far from advocating assassination, or any other unlawful way of getting rid of a rival, but in this instance it seems that no other mode presents itself. I hope, then, that you are prepared to go through with the plan I have to propose, by whatever way it is to be carried out, or whatever may be the consequences."

"Yes, yes, we are all prepared!" exclaimed several persons.

"Stay, friends!" cried another; "say not that all are prepared. We are all ready to draw our swords in a lawful quarrel and in an open manner, such as true soldiers may fight for, but there are other ways at which Sir George has hinted, and it may be that some of them are not such as honourable men would desire to engage in."

"What mean you, Captain?" exclaimed the first speaker. "Do you dare to affirm that I propose any scheme which is not honourable and lawful? Whatever I do, or whatever I say, I act under the authority of my true and only sovereign, King James. I acknowledge no other, and therefore I feel myself at liberty to draw my sword in opposition to any one who claims the title of my king."

"How are we to be sure that you have this authority, good sir?" asked the former speaker. "I have served under the banners of many leaders, and have always been faithful to those who trusted me; but before I draw my sword against the Prince of Orange I should like to know that it is according to the wish of James, late King of England, who by that means may recover his own."

"Here, then, incredulous men," exclaimed the person who had been addressed as 'Sir George;' "listen to the commission I have received from King James himself:—

"'Our will and pleasure is, and we do hereby fully authorise, strictly require, and expressly command, our loving subjects to rise in arms and make war upon the Prince of Orange, the usurper of our throne, and all his adherents, and to seize for our use all such forts, towns, and strongholds within our dominion of England as may serve to further our interest, and to do from time to time such other acts of hostility against the Prince of Orange and his adherents as may conduce most to our service. We judge this the properest, justest, and most effectual means of procuring the Restoration and their deliverance, and we do hereby indemnify them for what they shall act in pursuance of this our royal command, given at our court of Saint Germain-en-Laye, the 27th of December, 1695.'

"This will, I hope, satisfy you, gentlemen, that we are not acting without due authority; moreover, you should be aware that the Duke of Berwick came over to England a few months ago, and visited many of the principal adherents of King James, who are all ready, on the signal which we shall make them, to rise in arms, and raise the standard of our lawful king. He is also at the present moment prepared to put himself at the head of an army of 20,000 French soldiers, who are drawn out of the different garrisons of the neighbourhood of Calais. There is also a fleet ready to bring them across as soon as they receive the signal which we are preparing to give. The French king has promised to support King James, and will follow with another army, which will be as soon as possible collected."

"That appears a well-arranged, straightforward scheme, such as soldiers and men of honour can engage in," observed another speaker.

"I am glad you think so, Captain," observed Sir George; "and I feel very sure, that as soon as the signal I have spoken of is given, we shall have hundreds like yourselves flocking to the royal standard."

"But what is to be that signal, may I ask?" inquired another, who had not before spoken. "I am willing to draw my sword at the command of the King, but I never like to take a leap in the dark, and am better pleased when all matters are explained clearly beforehand."

"It is not usual for a general to give a sketch of his campaign to his subordinates," answered Sir George, in a haughty tone. "There are certain matters of which it is better that as few as possible should be informed. I trust that this reply will satisfy you."

"It must, by my faith!" mattered the old officer; "but, for my part, I have no taste for these secret plots; I would rather a band of brave fellows had been collected together, and that King James's standard had been raised, and that then we had marched through the country, gathering strength in our progress."

"To be cut to pieces by Dutch William's soldiers, or to be surrounded and strung up like foot-pads!" observed another speaker.

"There are difficulties in our way, but they are such as brave men will gladly encounter."

Such was the strain in which the conversation continued. As yet nothing was said which might lead Jack to suppose that any immediate outbreak was likely to occur. Yet his suspicions were aroused, and he could not help fancying that the voice of the speaker who was addressed as "Sir George" was very like that of Long Sam. If so, he felt that he himself would be in some way implicated in the plot.

At length the party appeared to be breaking up, and most of the persons who had formed it took their departure. Still some remained; and at length he heard the door bolted and barred behind those who had gone out. Those who remained poked up the fire and drew their chairs round it.

"All will go well!" exclaimed the person who had been addressed as "Sir George."

"And now let us see to the more important part of our work. While Dutch William lives, or at all events is at liberty, King James will not move from his present position, and even the King of France cannot beard the lion in his den. As long as the Protestants have a leader they will be united, and a rising of the adherents of King James will be hopeless; but once let the head of William be laid low, and before they have time to make arrangements to secure another Protestant sovereign, King James can be brought over, and the Catholic religion again be established in the land. The end sanctifies the means, as my excellent father-confessor assures me, and I therefore have no compunction as to that matter. King James has sent over a number of his 'gentlemen of the guard' and others, who have come as it were on their private concerns, but who are all prepared to unite, as soon as they receive directions from me, to carry out any scheme I may propose. To those who are squeamish I have suggested merely that we seize and bring away the Prince of Orange, carry him on board ship, and thence convey him over to France: but that will never do; before he could be got to the Thames he would be rescued, and our necks would have to answer for our folly. There is but one safe plan, and that is to set upon him armed with pistols and strong pushing-swords, and thus at once to put him to death. As soon as he is dead his own adherents even will be afraid to assault us, not knowing who may next be at the head of affairs, What say you, gentlemen?—I have spoken plainly to you."

"I have been advised on this matter before," was the answer. "With you, I feel that which you propose is the only way of proceeding, especially if by that means we can establish again our religion in the land. If once we can gain the upper hand, we may without difficulty so oppress and keep down these Protestant heretics that we may compel them to come over to the true faith, or drive them from the country."

"We are all agreed, then, my friends?" said the leader of the plot. "Listen, then, to the plan which I have arranged. The king, as you know, frequently drives out from his palace at Kensington for the purpose of hunting in Richmond Park, and takes boat near Turnham Green to cross the Thames to the Surrey side. I have arranged several leaders, each of whom has five men well mounted to act under him. They will be well-armed with blunderbusses, musketoons, pistols, and well-sharpened swords. There is a spot at Turnham Green where the road is narrow, with high hedges and ditches on each side, so that a coach and six horses cannot easily turn on a sudden. Just about there, also, there are some shrubs and bushes which will afford shelter to our men. We have spies in the palace who will give us exact information of the hours and days when the king goes forth in his coach; and as he has but a small body of guards with him, there will be little risk of a miscarriage. All we have now to do, is to fix the day for the carrying out of the scheme. It is well conceived, and cannot fail; and, moreover, if any of those engaged in it have qualms of conscience, I am able to promise them full absolution, should the king fall by their hands."

Jack was horrified at what he heard. What course was he to pursue? Should he at once make his way to the palace and give information of the atrocious plot? It was not at all likely, should he do so, that he would be believed. He lay on his bed in deep distress of mind. That his companion who had brought him to London was engaged in the plot, he had no doubt whatever; indeed, he fully believed that he was one of the leaders.

While he lay thus, considering what course to pursue, he heard some of those who had been in the room take their departure. One, however, remained, and he thought he recognised the heavy footsteps of the principal speaker. He kept walking up and down the room, occasionally muttering to himself. Jack was on the point of dropping off to sleep when again the door opened gently, and another person entered hurriedly.

"Ah, Ellis, what news do you bring?" asked the occupier of the room.

"Bad news indeed, Sir George," answered the other. "I was in the neighbourhood of the residence of the Earl of Portland two days back, when I saw Captain Fisher passing by. Although he was disguised I knew him, and, aware that he was acquainted with all our secrets, I followed him closely. I watched him till he entered the Earl's house, and, though Lord Portland himself was out, he remained there till the return of his lordship. This made me dread that his purpose was to denounce us. I was made sure of this, when, after waiting a considerable time, Lord Portland himself came forth, and drove at full speed to the palace. Still I had no certain information of what Fisher had been about, and I therefore kept the matter secret; watching only carefully the proceedings of all those who are acquainted with our plot. I kept a watch also at the Earl's door, and at length received notice that Captain Pendergrast had also visited the Earl; and only this very night I have obtained information that he and La Rue have both been at the palace. As you know, also, this morning the king gave orders that his coaches and guards should be made ready to go out hunting as usual, but suddenly, just at the moment they were to set forth, notice was sent to them that the king was unwell, and could not go abroad that day. Putting these things together, I am sure that the king has been warned of our plot, and that those who are in it will ere long be seized. He probably now only waits till he has learned the names of our party, and ascertained where each of us are to be found."

"Ellis, you deserve my gratitude!" exclaimed Long Sam. "It is time then that each of us should seek his safety in flight. I shall be off this moment; and I will leave the raw youth I have brought with me from the north to pay the score as best he can. He knows nothing; and if he is taken up and clapped into prison, he can do me no harm. Will you come with me? Here's a horse at your service."

"Thank you, Sir George," answered the other man, "I have business to do which must be done this night, in London, and I hope to get on board ship before daybreak and be off for France. I will not delay longer here."

Saying this, Ellis took a hurried departure, uttering but a short farewell to his companion. Long Sam immediately followed him out of the room. Jack sat up in bed and rubbed his eyes to be sure that he had not been dreaming.

"This, then, is the plot in which Mr Harwood has been engaged," he thought to himself. "I can serve him best by giving him information that it has been discovered. If I remain long here, I shall probably, as Long Sam observes is likely, be seized and sent to prison. Instead of paying the score, I will leave the horses to do that, and take the one which will most quickly carry me along the road to Sherwood Forest."

Jack, on this, quickly dressed himself in a rough riding-habit, and packed his other garments into his valise. Having loaded his pistols and seen to their priming, he stuck them in his belt, and, carrying his valise under his arm, with his boots in his hand, he silently stole down-stairs. Without difficulty he found his way into the room where the conspirators had met; then, putting on his boots, he made his way to the stables. He dared not strike a light, but, knowing well the positions of the horses, and the place where the saddles were hung up, he hoped to find no difficulty in getting off. He quickly opened the stable-door, and was about to enter, when a deep voice exclaimed, "Stand, or you're a dead man!"

He felt sure the person who spoke was Long Sam.

"Don't fire," he answered, calmly, "you will gain nothing by so doing!"

"Then tell me what you are about to do, youngster," exclaimed Long Sam, stepping forth, leading a horse by the bridle.

"I have as much right to take a midnight ride as you have," answered Jack. "I don't wish to stop you, but if you go your way, I claim a right to go mine."

"You are crowing loudly, my lad!" said Long Sam, with a curse.

"I have no wish to crow," answered Jack, "but if you have to ride to save your life, I wish to do the same to save my liberty. If you attempt to stop me I will give the alarm, and you well know what the consequences will be. You wish to make a tool of me—you will find that if you still attempt to do so, you will cut your own fingers."

"You are a sharp lad," answered Long Sam, or Sir George Barclay, for Jack before long had reason to know that such was the real name of his late companion. "You have found out a great deal more than I supposed. However, I believe you honest: and now make the best of your way out of this city. If you can give notice to any of our friends that they are in danger, you will be rendering them an important service, which, perhaps, some day or other they will be able to repay; and if not, you may rest satisfied that you have performed a kind action."

Saying this, Sir George led his horse through the gateway of the inn, which was left ajar, probably by pre-arrangement, and disappeared in the darkness. Jack quickly saddled the steed which had been bestowed on him by Master Pearson, and took his way northward by the road along which he had come to Hammersmith. As soon as he was at a distance from any houses, he clapped spurs to his horse and galloped over the ground at as fast a rate as the bad state of the roads would allow.

Chapter Twenty
A Ride for Liberty

While Jack is galloping towards Sherwood Forest, we will give a short description of the plot which had been designed for the overthrow of William of Orange and the restoration of James the Second to the throne of England, and the re-establishment of Romanism throughout the realm.

The adherents of James, who desired to retain him on the throne of England in spite of his attempts to establish a despotic government, and to restore the Roman Catholic religion in the country, were called by their opponents "Jacobites." A large number of them belonged themselves to the Church of Rome, and, instigated by their priests, many of whom, in consequence of the liberality of King William, were allowed to remain in the country, were with other discontented persons continually plotting for the restoration of King James. At length, the two plots which have been hinted at in the previous pages were concocted. One, in which Mr Harwood and a number of noblemen and gentlemen of honourable character were engaged, had for its object the rising of the Jacobites generally throughout England, while Louis the Fourteenth undertook to send an army of 20,000 men to their assistance. This was about the year 1693. At the same time, another plot of an atrocious character was either proposed to James or suggested by him. He had himself, by this time, become thoroughly imbued with Jesuit principles, being surrounded by priests of that order. At all events, there is no doubt that the plot met with his cordial sanction. The plan proposed was to assassinate William as he was on his way to hunt in Richmond Park. While the country by his death was thrown into a state of confusion, the Jacobites were to fly to arms and the French army was to cross the channel.

Towards the end of 1695, the Duke of Berwick, a natural son of Charles the Second, came over secretly to England to try the temper of the Jacobites, Louis having promised to send his troops across immediately that they should rise. The Duke landed in Romney Marsh, where he took up his abode at the house of a smuggler of the name of Robert Hunt. By means of this man he was enabled to transmit the information he received to France. It appears, however, that the Jacobites were unwilling to risk their lives by rising while William remained firmly seated on the throne, dreading the arm of that bold and sagacious monarch.

There is no doubt, that in consequence of the failure of the Duke of Berwick's attempt in England to induce his friends to rise in arms, James and Louis agreed to the plot which had before been suggested for the assassination of William. The king was to be murdered on the 15th of February, as he was leaving his palace at Kensington to hunt in Richmond Park. Now it appears that a few days before this, James left Paris, and journeyed to Calais, where he set himself at the head of an army of about 20,000 men, who were drawn out of the garrisons which lay near the frontier. A considerable fleet also assembled there from Dunkirk and other ports, while transports, and more men-of-war to convoy them over, were also brought together. Several regiments indeed were already embarked while James waited at Calais, and no one can doubt that he remained there to receive the first notice of the projected assassination. Louis had communicated to the various courts in which he had ministers, the facts that he had acknowledged James King of England, and that he purposed to invade that country to re-establish him on the throne. At this time William had a large fleet at Spithead, and an army attached to him, while the larger part of the nation were desirous that he should remain their king. With all of these facts Louis was well acquainted, and there can be no doubt that he was himself also aware of the intended assassination, as he had far too much sense to suppose that while William lived any invasion of England would have been successful.

The chief promoter of the scheme for the invasion of England was Sir John Fenwick, a baronet of good family, but it does not appear that he was in any way connected with the assassination plot. Sir John Friend, a city knight, was also implicated in this plot. The Earl of Aylesbury and Lord Montgomery, with many others, were also connected with it. Charnock, Sir William Parkyns, Rookwood, Lowick, Cranburn, Knightley were among the chief persons engaged in the assassination plot.

The conspirators were to be scattered about Turnham Green in taverns and ale-houses, and to be brought together upon a signal being given. Each body of them was under a leader, so as to give the proceeding the air of a military act. While some were to attack the king's guards, others had been especially selected to shoot at the king himself. James had sent over a number of his own body-guard to be in readiness to support the conspirators. It appears, however, that the military men engaged in the work were very unwilling to undertake it, unless they received a commission from James himself. This document was therefore drawn up and signed by the king, and on seeing it, some of them imagined that the undertaking in which they engaged, although of a somewhat desperate character, was as honourable as that of entering into a campaign in regular service. Some, however, felt great doubts about the matter, as they could not help viewing it in its true light. Among these were two captains, Pendergrast, an Irish officer, and Fisher, an Englishman, and a Frenchman named De la Rue, who without any agreement with each other, at different times gave information to the Earl of Portland of the contemplated assassination of the king.

William at first was very unwilling to believe in the plot, and it was not without difficulty that the Earl of Portland could persuade his Majesty not to go forth on his hunting expedition on that eventful 15th day of February.

The greater number of the conspirators not having received such early information as did Sir George Barclay, continued to meet, even on that very day, hoping still to carry out their plan on the following Saturday. They were nearly all seized, most of them in their beds, before they had received any notice of the discovery of the plot.

Charnock, who had been a Fellow of Magdalen College, Oxford, and had become its Popish vice-president, was an indefatigable agent of the Jacobites. So completely imbued had he become with Jesuitical principles, that he had persuaded himself that he had full right to murder the king, having as he supposed a commission from the person he considered the legal proprietor of the throne. He offered to disclose all he knew of the consultations and designs of the Jacobites, if his life were spared, and the reply of King William is worthy of note: "I desire not to know them," feeling assured probably, that many were in it whom he hoped still to win over by generosity and kindness.

Sir John Friend and Sir William Parkyns were next tried, and were executed, on being found guilty, at Tyburn, on which occasion three of the non-juring clergy attended them, and had the audacity at the place of execution to give them public absolution, with an imposition of hands in the view of all people, for the act in which they had been engaged.

Sir John Fenwick, was captured shortly after the discovery of the plot, while attempting to escape to France. His trial lasted for a considerable time. He was, however, clearly found guilty, and executed. He richly merited the fate he met, for although he did not propose to assassinate the king, his aim was to bring over an army of foreigners, and subjugate those of his countrymen who differed from him in opinion, and to re-establish the Romish faith in England.

The people had before this been grumbling at the British fleet being detained so long at Spithead by contrary winds, but it was the presence of this fleet which contributed greatly to prevent James from attempting to cross the channel with an army placed under his command by the French king. Immediately also on hearing of the plot, a number of seamen who had remained concealed for fear of the press-gangs, came forward and volunteered on board the various ships which had commenced fitting out. Indeed the discovery of this abominable Jacobite plot had such an effect upon the nation generally, that many who formerly pitied the condition of the exiled king, were now completely alienated from him, by this means producing a more perfect establishment of King William on the throne.

John Deane's residence in the fens, and the experience he there gained in finding his way across country, assisted him greatly in the ride he was now taking northward. He had carefully noted every spot as he came by with Long Sam, and he was thus able to ride forward without having to inquire the road. His nerves were well strung and he was constitutionally brave; but never before had he felt so uncomfortable as he now did. Every moment he expected to have Long Sam galloping after him; and he felt very sure that those who contemplated the assassination of the king would not hesitate to kill him, if they fancied it would conduce to their safety or interest to put him out of the way. He could not help expecting also to be stopped by adherents of King William who might have heard of the plot and would naturally inquire why he was thus spurring onward away from London. They might, he thought, suppose that he was one of the conspirators. It could be shown that he had been associating with those who had engaged in the plot. He might thus probably from being unable to prove his innocence, lose his life along with them.

He rode on through that long winter's night without stopping. His horse was well trained, having both spirit and bottom; and thus daylight found him still pressing onward. At length he was obliged to pull up at the sign of the Fox and Chickens, a small roadside inn some fifty miles or more from London. The landlord eyed him askance as he led his horse into the stable, and began carefully to rub down the animal, to prepare it for its food.

"Will it please you to take some breakfast, my master?" asked Boniface, with a peculiar expression. "You seem to have ridden pretty hard since sunrise?"

"Yes," answered Jack; "my poor beast has borne me well. He has a few more miles to go before I can stable him for the night; and he needs rest and refreshment more than I do after his gallop over these bad roads."

"I will go in and tell my dame to get breakfast for you," said the landlord, "while you are looking after your horse. I like to see a man treat his beast well, as you are doing; and you deserve the best rasher my dame can cook for you."

The landlord was as good as his word; and when shortly afterwards Jack entered the inn, he found a dish smoking on the board, and a tankard of good ale standing by its side. His anxiety had not deprived him of his appetite; and he resolved, if his horse could hold out, to push on till nightfall. He, however, was not perfectly satisfied with the manner of his host, and could not help fancying that he suspected him of being either a highwayman or a fugitive from justice; and every time the door opened, he expected to see a bailiff or a Government official of some sort enter, to interrogate him as to what he was about and where he was going. He fully experienced the truth of Shakspeare's saying, "Conscience does make cowards of us all"! As soon, therefore, as he thought his horse was in a condition again to take to the road, he started up, and paying his score, walked out to the stables. The landlord followed him, and touched him on the shoulder.

"I like your looks, young master," he said; "but still there are one or two things about you which might excite suspicion. I would advise you, therefore, not to stop at any large town, if you have again to put up before you reach your destination."

Jack, while he thanked the landlord for his kind intentions, put on an indifferent air, as if his advice was unnecessary, and springing into the saddle, wished him good-day, and trotted at an easy pace till he was out of sight of the inn. He then once again put spurs to his steed, and away he flew along the road Master Pearson had not over-praised his horse when he told him that at a push he could cover a long distance, for, bad as was the road in many places, the good steed never stumbled nor hesitated, but kept up his pace, as if well aware that much depended on the progress he could make.

The farther north Jack advanced the better he knew the country; and as he found that it would be impossible to get to the other side of Nottingham that night, he turned aside off the high-road, to put up at the house of a miller, where he had several times stopped when making holiday excursions from Nottingham. The man was hearty and good-natured, with a buxom, kind wife, and a pretty little daughter. He thought he might there possibly gain some information of what had taken place at home, and be guided accordingly. He might probably also, should his own good steed be unable to proceed, obtain another horse from the miller, on which to continue his journey to Harwood Grange. It was getting dark as Jack rode up to the mill, and he found the miller knocking off work and disconnecting his water-wheels.

"Don't you know me, Master Simpson?" said Jack, as the miller stared at him from beneath his well-powdered brows.

"Ay, in troth, that do I! Mr John Deane, if I mistake not," answered the honest miller. "Why, lad, you seem to have ridden hard this evening! What is your pleasure?"

"A night's rest, and some food for my horse and myself," answered Jack, dismounting. "You will give it me, like a kind man, and ask no questions. I have business of importance which takes me some distance from hence, and I'm afraid if I were to ride on through the night with my tired steed, that we both of us should roll in the mud before day dawns."

The miller made Jack welcome; and, having stabled his horse as usual, he was soon seated opposite pretty Margery Simpson, by the side of the kind dame. Jack had to confess that he had not been at home for some time, in order to make inquiries respecting his friends at Nottingham. He could, however, gain no information; but the miller told him that as soon as the roads dried up a little with the March winds, he purposed going there. It struck Jack, therefore, that by this means he might communicate with his family, and fortunately having some paper in his valise, he was able to write a few lines to his brother Jasper. He told him of his welfare, and that he purposed immediately going on board a man-of-war, and seeking his fortunes at sea.

"I will not enter into my reasons, brother Jasper," he wrote; "but I find the land not suited for me, and I wish to prove my loyalty to our brave King William, and to seek for adventures on the ocean, where, I have an idea, more gold, and as much honour is to be gained as on shore."

Jack sent his best love to his father and mother and sisters, and begged that they would not forget him, or condemn him, whatever they might hear to his discredit. He carefully sealed this letter, which Master Simpson promised faithfully to deliver either to Jasper, or to Polly, should the former be absent from home.

"Now, Master Simpson, I will ask you still another favour; the moon will be up in four or five hours: let me sleep till then, and allow me to rise and proceed on my way. I shall thus reach the end of my journey soon after daybreak, where I can get further rest for myself and horse."

Although the good miller at first objected to this, Jack induced him to agree to let him take his departure. The air was bitterly cold, for the wind was from the north and a sharp frost had set in, and Jack feared lest a snowstorm should come on and impede his progress. He was therefore thankful that he had started at that early hour, hoping without impediment to reach Harwood Grange. His good steed, after a few hours' rest, carried him as well as when he first started from Hammersmith, and the sun had only just risen as he rode up the avenue to the Grange. He was anxious to make as little disturbance as possible, and he therefore at once rode up to the stable, and begged the groom to attend to his horse while he went up to the house. The man, who did not know him, seemed indisposed at first to obey his orders.

"It is a matter of importance," said Jack; "and I may have but little time to rest my tired beast."

As the housemaid was just opening the front door, Jack entered, and learned that the Squire was already on foot, and that Mistress Alethea would soon be down to breakfast. Jack hurried into the Squire's own room, where he was examining several fire-arms, placed against the wall.

"Mr Harwood," he exclaimed, "I fear that you are in danger! If you have been connected with those engaged in the conspiracy to bring over a foreign army, and to dethrone King William, let me urge you to fly or to conceal yourself. The plot has been discovered!"

Mr Harwood turned deadly pale on hearing this, and trembled in every limb.

"I am deeply thankful to you for the warning you have given me," he answered. "But what am I to do? I cannot leave my daughter, and know not where to conceal myself."

"Mistress Alethea will surely find a welcome and shelter in the house of my father," answered Jack. "I will endeavour to assist you to escape to a place of safety. It may be that no one will search for you here; but if you think it more advisable to go abroad, I will accompany you either to Yarmouth or Harwich, where you may take ship and get across to France."

Mr Harwood overwhelmed Jack with thanks, and gladly accepted his offer. Their plans were scarcely arranged when Alethea entered the room. She showed far more courage than her father had done on hearing of the discovery of the plot, though anxious about his safety. She at once declared her intention of accompanying him.

"That cannot be, my child!" said Mr Harwood. "You know not the difficulties and dangers I may have to go through; and though you might be willing to share them, they must of necessity be greatly increased should you be with me. We have friends in this neighbourhood who will, I am sure, take charge of you. With them you will live happily and securely; and I trust that in a short time, when this matter has blown over, I may be able to return once more to England."

Jack's heart beat violently when he heard these remarks of Mr Harwood.

"Oh, yes!" he exclaimed; "I feel sure that my mother and sisters will gladly afford all the protection Miss Harwood requires. I wish that I could accompany her to Nottingham. Could I not do it, and rejoin you, Mr Harwood?"

"What, and run the risk of being apprehended yourself?" exclaimed the Squire. "No; I will send Alethea under the escort of two trusty grooms with her tirewoman, and will throw myself on the kindness of your family. Already I am deeply indebted to them, and shall but add to the obligation."

The Squire spoke with some hesitation. Even at that moment his aristocratic feelings influenced him, and he felt as if he was honouring the Deane family by thus confiding his daughter to their charge. Some time had thus passed when the Squire recollected that Jack must require food.

"It would never do to set forward without being prepared," he observed. "Take your breakfast with Alethea, while I go and put together such valuables as it may be prudent for me to carry; and you, my daughter, will take the remainder, for I know not, should I be informed against, what will be the fate of the old Grange and of the estate my fathers have held for so many centuries."

Jack, as he sat by the side of Alethea endeavouring to eat his breakfast, in vain tried to utter the sentiments with which his heart was full. Whenever he attempted to speak he hesitated and stammered, and his tongue stuck to the roof of his mouth. Alethea was more serious, naturally, than he had ever seen her before.

"I foresaw that it might come to this," she said, at last, to Jack. "But, do you know, I rather glory in suffering for what I believe to be a right cause!"

"But oh, Miss Harwood," exclaimed Jack, now able to speak, "surely no cause would justify the means by which the conspirators have attempted to carry out their project—to murder the great and brave king! Surely nothing can justify assassination!"

"Oh, no, no!" exclaimed Alethea. "But surely those with whom my father was associated have not attempted to commit so fearful a crime?"

"Most certainly the crime was contemplated," answered Jack. "I heard the whole plan discussed, but whether Mr Harwood's especial friends were acquainted with it or not, I cannot say; but of one thing I feel very sure, from what I heard, that James was well aware of the project, and sanctioned it by the countenance he gave to those who undertook to carry it out."

"If I were sure of that," exclaimed Alethea, with a tone of indignation, "my whole feelings towards King James would be changed! While I thought him an honourable and an injured man, and the rightful sovereign of these realms, my feelings were in his favour; but if his principles would allow him to act as you describe, then I cannot but feel that the nobles and commons of England were right in their dread of having such a man to reign over them."

"I wish Mr Harwood had seen matters in that light before he allowed himself to be drawn into the plot!" said Jack. "Perhaps, however, he may now be induced to do so. If so, when those who have principally engaged in it have suffered the penalty of their crimes, he will probably be allowed to return home, and live quietly as heretofore. For my own part, as I have been consorting with the king's enemies, though unknowingly, I have determined, from henceforth, to fight for him and his friends, and to try my fortune on the ocean. It will be more to my taste than being pinched up in breastplate and helmet, and having to fight on shore. I may there win a name and fame, Alethea; and perchance when I come back I may look forward to—"

Whatever Jack was going to say was interrupted by the entrance of Mr Harwood. As may be supposed, he had but a small appetite for breakfast, though pressed by his daughter, who in every way tried to keep up his spirits, to partake of it. The steward and head groom were ordered to accompany Miss Harwood into Nottingham, while his own fleetest hunter was to be got ready to start as soon as Jack's horse was sufficiently rested.

In vain Jack waited for an opportunity to finish the sentence he had begun, for having, as he thought, broken the ice, he hoped to get yet farther in, but just as the party were rising from breakfast, which had been put off to a later hour than usual, a visitor was announced, and Jasper Deane entered the room. His surprise at seeing Jack was very great. They greeted each other, however, as affectionate brothers, though Jasper refrained from asking Jack questions which it might have been disagreeable to him to answer in the presence of Alethea and Mr Harwood.

"I am sure, Jasper, you will answer for our parents being ready to receive Miss Harwood," said Jack, "during the temporary absence of her father. I have brought him some news, with which I need not trouble you, which requires him to leave home immediately."

"Why not trust me?" answered Jasper; "surely I would not betray Mr Harwood's secrets!"

"For your own sake it may be better for you not to know them," answered Jack. "It is time that we should be on our road. Bear my duty to my father and mother and my love to our sisters, and I will write to them of my proceedings as soon as I have an opportunity."

Jack saw that Mr Harwood was impatient to be off, while he himself knew the importance of losing no time in getting to a place of safety; he had no opportunity, therefore, of asking Jasper questions as to what had taken place at Nottingham, nor did he himself wish to tell him what he had been about. He merely mentioned his letter entrusted to the miller. "That will tell you more about my intentions," he observed. If a pang of jealousy crossed his heart when he saw his brother ride off by the side of Alethea, he quickly banished it, and immediately afterwards he and Mr Harwood, with their valises strapped to their saddles, were making their way through the forest to the east.

Chapter Twenty One
John Deane turns Sailor, and joins the "Weymouth," Captain Jumper

At no time for many years had there been greater activity in the chief naval ports of England than in February, 1696. All the ships in the service were ordered to be brought forward, and as many more as could be obtained were purchased for the Royal Navy. Officers and men eagerly offered their services; indeed the enthusiasm of all ranks and professions was very great. Numerous seamen from the merchant service joined the navy, and there was no lack of volunteers eager to be employed. A squadron lay in the Medway, fitting out as quickly as stores could be brought on board them and the men could be collected. Among them was the "Weymouth," a ship of forty guns, commanded by the well-known Captain Jumper. Her sails were bent, and she only waited for her powder to be brought on board to go to sea, as soon as she could fill up with her proper complement of men. A boat had just come alongside, and the first lieutenant reported that she contained a number of volunteers.

Among the first who stepped on board was a fine, active-looking young man, though, to the nautical eye, he had not much the look of a sailor.

"Where have you served before, my man?" asked Mr Cammock, the first lieutenant; "and what do you know of seamanship?"

"I have served nowhere, please you, sir," was the answer, "but I am ready to learn. And I know how to handle a cutlass, and shoot a partridge or pheasant flying."

"You are the lad for us then," answered the officer. "What is your name? We will enter you as a landsman; but you will soon make an able seaman."

"John Deane, at your service, sir," answered our friend; for he it was who, having put his purpose of joining the navy into execution, had volunteered for the "Weymouth."

It was the first time he had ever stood on the deck of a ship. No wonder then that he gazed about him with a look of astonishment, at the guns thickly ranged on either side; at the numerous brass swivels and other pieces which graced her quarters and forecastle, and the high lanterns of brass astern; at the numberless ropes which led here and there from the masts and spars, with their ends neatly coiled down on deck; at the seamen, in their loose dresses, shirts, and trousers, with belts round their waists, contrasting with the officers in their three-cornered hats and long coats, laced with gold or silver, large embroidered belts by which hung their rapiers—each dressed rather according to his fancy and means, than to any authorised uniform.

A number of other men were then called up. Among the first was one whose countenance Jack thought he knew. He looked at him several times, till at length it struck him that it must be the very man who had guided him to Pearson's farm in the fens—Ned Burdale. There was the same sturdy, independent look, bold eye, and manner. What, however, had induced him to enter on board a king's ship, Jack could not divine. At all events, he felt it would be wise in him not to claim acquaintance with a person of so doubtful a character.

He little expected to find any body else whom he had met before; but he had not been long on board, when a seaman came up to him, and, putting out his hand, exclaimed—

"What, Jack Deane, don't you know me?"

"Yes," said Jack, at last, wringing him by the hand; "but I should not have recognised you in that dress and with that ugly cut down your cheek, if I did not remember your voice."

"Yes; I have seen some service already," answered the seaman. "I have a bullet through my leg, and this pretty little remembrance on my cheek; but it's what we have to expect. We're paid for it, you know; and besides, we give as good as we take, and that's a consolation."

"But what made you come to sea?" asked Jack. "I had no idea you had any fancy that way."

"I may ask the same question of you, friend Deane," said Smedley, for it was Jack's old poaching acquaintance. "The honest truth is, I found Nottingham too hot to hold me, and so here I am come to serve his majesty. It is a pretty hard life, I will own; but I have brought myself into it, and so I have determined not to grumble."

"Well, I have my own reasons, too, Smedley, for coming to sea," said Jack, "but you will excuse me if I don't explain them. I hope we may both do our duty, and fight bravely for our country. That's what I have come to sea for, with the hope of seeing a little more of the world than I should if I had remained at Nottingham, or continued to drive oxen between Scotland and Stourbridge."

Smedley, who had already been some weeks at sea, was able to give Jack a good deal of instruction in his duties, and found him an apt scholar. Jack was determined to make himself a seaman as soon as he could. From morning till night he was employed in picking up information, and he soon gained some knowledge in the arts of knotting and splicing. He quickly, too, found his way aloft; and though at first he felt rather giddy at the mast-head, his eye soon got accustomed to look down on the deck below, and he could run out on the yards in a short time with any man on board. He soon, indeed, surpassed Smedley himself. The man he took to be Burdale, from the way he walked the deck, was evidently accustomed to a sailor's life.

So rapidly were the ships got ready for sea, that in a short time a large fleet was collected in the Downs under the command of Admiral Russell. He had under him Lord Berkeley, Admiral of the Blue, and Sir Cloudesley Shovel, Vice-Admiral of the Red; Mr Aylmer, Vice-Admiral of the Blue, with two Dutch squadrons under two rear-admirals.

As soon as the fleet was collected, they set sail for the coast of France, arriving shortly afterwards off Dunkirk. It was here that the celebrated French Admiral, Jean Bart, held the command of a French fleet. As the English fleet passed Calais, three or four hundred vessels of all sorts were seen with their sails bent ready for sea. As soon as the French saw the English fleet approaching Dunkirk, several of their men-of-war ran close up to the pier. Hopes were now entertained by the English crews that some fighting would take place. Sir Cloudesley Shovel, with several captains, stood in towards Dunkirk, to see if there was any possibility of burning the fleet. This, however, was declared to be impracticable, and Admiral Russell therefore sailed back to Dover, leaving a squadron under Sir Cloudesley Shovel, to watch the movements of the enemy. A short time after this, Sir Cloudesley Shovel, who had returned to the Downs, was ordered to take with him the bomb-vessels, and such small ships as he should think necessary; and attempt the burning of Calais with the transports, and other ships in that harbour.

Calais was soon in sight. The English could see the harbour crowded with vessels, which as they approached, however, ran close up under their batteries where the ships could not get at them. The wind was off shore, which gave them smooth water; and the squadron, in gallant style, beat up as near to the town as the water would allow. They now anchored, their men-of-war protecting the bomb-vessels, which instantly commenced throwing shells into the place. It was a fine sight to see them, like vast rockets, rising in the air and curling over, until they fell into the devoted town.

For several hours the fiery shower continued. Now flames were seen to burst out in one part of the town, now in another; and now the vessels in the harbour caught fire; several in succession exploded. As each of the enemy's vessels blew up, the English crews burst forth with loud cheers, and redoubled their efforts. The enemy were not idle, but the English ships were so placed that not many of the French shot did damage. The shipping in the harbour suffered most, as the chief aim of the English was to destroy them, and a large number of privateers were blown up or burned. A strong wind was blowing when the action began, and it continued increasing, till the squadron could with difficulty hold their position before the town. Still the English persevered. A large portion of the town was burnt down, and a considerable amount of shipping was destroyed. Such would have been the fate of the whole, had not the gale at length compelled Sir Cloudesley Shovel to throw out a signal for retiring. This was done in good order, and the squadron returned to the Downs.

Soon after this, a squadron of which the "Weymouth" formed one of the ships, was sent to cruise off Dunkirk, where it was understood that Jean Bart, with several ships of war, was still lying ready for sea. Rear-Admiral Benbow was placed in command of this squadron; but on his arrival before the place, he found the number of ships he had with him too small to guard both channels; the weather, also, proving extremely foggy, Du Bart slipped out, and, steering to the north-east, fell in with the Dutch Baltic fleet of about a hundred sail, escorted by five frigates, all of which he took, and above half the merchantmen. In the midst of Du Bart's victory, he was surprised by the appearance of the Dutch outward-bound Baltic fleet, under the convoy of thirteen men-of-war, which so closely pursued him that he was obliged to abandon most of his prizes. He burned four of the frigates, and putting their crews on board the fifth, turned her adrift, which, with thirty-five of the merchant-ships, were retaken. A fast galley brought this news to Admiral Benbow, who immediately steered in pursuit of the French squadron. The "Weymouth" was one of the leading ships.

Jack Deane, who was now rated as an able seaman, was constantly at the mast-head looking out for the enemy, eager as any on board to come up with them.

"Several sail ahead!" he shouted out one morning at daybreak.

There was no doubt that this was the enemy. The signal was thrown out accordingly, and the English crowded all sail in chase. The wind, however, which was in their favour, began to fall, and, greatly to their disappointment, it became almost a calm. The Frenchmen, however, retained the breeze, and were soon again out of sight.

In vain the English seamen whistled for a wind. Noon passed by, and still they remained becalmed. Whether it was their whistling or not produced the breeze, one sprung up towards evening, and the brave Benbow steered after the French. Again they were discovered, and again lost sight of. Once more their white canvas was seen ahead, and hopes were entertained that they would be overtaken before they could reach the shelter of Dunkirk, towards which they were steering. They, however, made good use of their heels, and before a shot could reach them they had run into Dunkirk.

The fleets of England were, however, enabled to punish the French severely for their audacious project of invading our "tight little island," and for their still more nefarious plan, which had been hatched under the sanction of their king, for assassinating the constitutional and Protestant monarch whom her people had chosen, and imposing on them in his stead a Papist and a tyrant.

Jack kept his eyes and ears open, and picked up all the information he could as to what was going forward in all directions. He had resolved when he joined to become an officer, and he knew very well that the only way of accomplishing his object was to attend strictly to his duties, to be obedient to his superiors, and to gain all the information in his power.

Among the novelties which had lately been introduced into the ships of the Royal Navy were brass box-compasses. These were placed in front of the steering-wheels, and were a great improvement upon the former contrivances for the same object. A large number of ships having been wrecked on the Eddystone Rock, off Plymouth, an application was made to the Trinity House to erect a lighthouse on it, which was begun that very year, and it was supposed that it would be completed in the course of the next three years. The masters and owners of ships agreed to pay a penny per ton outwards and inwards to assist in defraying the expense.

A register for thirty thousand seamen was established. They were to be in readiness at all times for supplying the Royal Navy, and were to receive a bounty of forty shillings yearly. On the 29th of January of that year, the "Royal Sovereign," built in the reign of Charles the First, and at that time the largest ship ever built in England, was by accident burned at her moorings in Gillingham Reach, in the river Medway.

"Well, Deane, and how do you like a sea life?" asked Smedley, after Jack had been some time on board.

"I will tell you when I've been longer afloat," answered Jack. "From what I have seen of it, I am ready to stick to it; that's what I've got to say. And how do you like it?"

"To confess the truth, I am getting rather tired of it," answered Smedley. "I thought it would be an easier life than I find it, but this cruising up and down the Channel and blockading the enemy's ports is trying work, and often I wish myself on shore again, taking a stroll or galloping through Sherwood Forest."

"That's because you have not a right object in view," answered Jack. "Now I have made up my mind to take the roughs and smooths as I find them. If I get shot or wounded, it is the fate of many a better man; and if I escape, I hope to fight my way up to wear a cocked hat and laced coat."

"That's very well for you, Deane, because you were born a gentleman," said Smedley. "I came to sea because I could not help it: all about that poaching affair, and the burning of the houses."

"I wish we had never engaged in it, I own," said Jack. "It has cost me dear; and what I regret most is the injury it did my character in the place, and the annoyance it must have caused my family when it was found out."

"What do you mean?" asked Smedley. "I do not understand you."

"Why, that the man who met us on that night, and showed us how to spear the salmon, told me that a warrant was out against me for poaching and firing the huts, and that if I went back to Nottingham I should be sent to prison," answered Jack.

"He told you a lie, then. Your name has never been mentioned in connexion with the affair; and to this day, unless you have told any body, I am very sure that no one in Nottingham knows any thing about it."

"Then what object could Pearson have had for saying so?" said Jack.

"I have an idea," said Smedley; "I may be right or I may be wrong; and from what you have told me of the man, he has just wanted to keep you from going back to Nottingham. Why he did so I cannot exactly say, except that he probably wanted to make use of you in some way or other."

The light at length burst on Jack's mind, and at once he saw the danger of getting into bad company. Had he refrained from joining in that fatal expedition, he would not have met Pearson; and if he had not met Pearson, he would never have been drawn into the plot which had so nearly cost him dear. Perhaps even his life might have been sacrificed in consequence! He did not say this to Smedley, because he had determined not to say any thing to him about the plot in which he had been unintentionally mixed up.

"It shall be a lesson to me through life," he thought. "If a person once associates with evil-disposed people, he knows not how soon he may be led to do as they're doing."

Often he thought of honest Will Brinsmead and his wise sayings, and the advice he had bestowed on him. Jack was every day becoming far more thoughtful than he had been hitherto. He was living among a wild, careless, rough set of men. Most of them were brave and honest; but there were rogues and cowards among them. The greater number lived only for the present moment, and were utterly thoughtless about the future. Now, John Deane felt that he must either be drawn in to act as they were acting, and to become like them, or he must keep himself as much as possible aloof from them. This, however difficult it might be, he determined to do.

In former days laws had been passed, not only to maintain a discipline in the navy, but for regulating the moral conduct of the men. There were regulations against profane swearing, or gambling, or fighting, or quarrelling; and orders were issued for the performance of Divine Service, not only on Sundays, but on weekdays, and on every occasion before going into action with an enemy. Unhappily, however, by this time this had become a dead-letter; and a general indulgence was allowed to the seamen in all the vices which have been mentioned. The men were also badly and tyrannically treated; and often their pay was kept back from them. The provisions were frequently very bad, and the greater number of men who were sent as surgeons on board the ships were grossly ignorant of their professional duties. Still the love of adventure existing in the breasts of English lads, the opportunities which seamen enjoyed of obtaining prize-money, and the efforts of the press-gangs, kept the Royal Navy tolerably supplied with men. A large number also joined, whatever can be said to the contrary, from patriotic motives, desirous of maintaining the honour of the British flag, protecting the commerce of the country, and guarding their native shores from foreign aggression. Such was the feeling which animated the breasts of thousands when Jack Deane joined the navy. Such is the feeling which has induced many thousands more on various occasions, when their country needed their services to assist in manning her fleets.

It was a great relief to Jack Deane to find that he still maintained an honourable name in his native town, and he at once wrote home in a strain he had not before ventured to use, telling his father, to whom he addressed his letter, that he had come to sea for the sake of fighting for the cause of King William, and that he hoped when he returned home to present himself in the rank of an officer.

Chapter Twenty Two
First Sea-Fight

John Deane had soon the opportunity he had long wished for, of engaging in a naval fight. As the "Weymouth" was cruising in the Channel, a sail was seen on the lee bow. Captain Jumper immediately ordered the ship to be kept away, and clapped on all the canvas she could carry in chase. The stranger, on seeing this, bore away, but the "Weymouth" was a fast ship, and rapidly came up with her. The drum beat to quarters, and the ship was prepared for action. Shot were brought up from below and placed in the racks ready for use. The powder-magazine was opened, and the powder-boys were sent up with their tubs and arranged in rows along the deck, ready to supply the seamen who fought the guns with powder. The slow-matches were got ready, and pistols, boarding-pikes, and hangers served out to the men. Jackets and shirts were discarded, and the crew stood ready, dressed alone in their trousers, with belts round their waists in which their pistols were stuck, and their hangers attached. There could be no doubt that the stranger was an enemy, though he had not yet shown his colours.

Few would have supposed that the crew who now stood at their guns were about in a short time to be engaged in deadly fight. Jokes of all sorts were passed along the decks, and peals of laughter were indulged in, till silenced when they became too uproarious by the officers. Jack found Smedley standing close to him, both having been appointed to the same gun. A handkerchief was bound round his head to keep his hair, which in the fashion of seamen in those days was worn long, away from his eyes. He was as cool and collected as the rest of his shipmates, but did not seem inclined to join in the jokes in which they were indulging.

"You seem somewhat out of spirits, Jem!" said John Deane. "What makes you so grave? we're sure to thrash the enemy, however big he may be."

"Just the thoughts of home, Jack," answered Smedley. "I was thinking just now whether I should not have been better off attending to my father's business, with the prospect of marrying pretty Mary Smithers, than out here, stripped to the waist, with a chance of having my head carried off before the day's over!"

"Nonsense, Jem!" answered Deane; "you should not let such thoughts trouble you. Your head is as firm on your shoulders as that of any other man on board."

"Ay, but how many other men will lose theirs?" said Smedley. "I cannot help thinking of home at all events, and though I may come out of this day's fight unscathed, I often wish I had remained quietly at home, without hankering after the sea. It all comes of that wild life we boys led in the forest. We did many things we ought not to have done, and it's to those I owe being out here. However, I will try to do my duty and bring no discredit on our native town."

"I am sure you will not do that," said Jack; "and I hope I shall see you throw up your cap with the rest of us, when the enemy strikes to our flag."

As the "Weymouth" drew near the stranger it was seen that she was a very large ship, considerably larger than the former, and probably carrying many more guns, with a more numerous crew. Still this in no way daunted the courage of the British seamen, but only made them the more eager for the attack. Most of them had already engaged in many a hard-fought battle with superior numbers, and come off victorious. They knew what British pluck and British muscle could do, and that if they could handle their guns twice as fast as the enemy could haul in and out theirs, that even should they have only half the number of their antagonist, they might still hope to beat her.

Jack had frequently spoken to the man whose countenance he thought he knew when he first came on board, but the latter denied ever having seen him before. Jack now saw him standing at a gun not far from the one where he was stationed. The man looked very pale, and, like Smedley, was not joining in the jokes of his shipmates. Jack watched his countenance, and now was more convinced than ever that he was Burdale.

As the "Weymouth" drew near, the stranger hoisted French colours, and finding that escape was impossible, hauled up her courses, and fired a gun in defiance, which was answered by one from the "Weymouth." Both of the shots, however, fell short of their aim. The combatants, without again firing, now rapidly drew near each other, with their flags and streamers flying and their trumpets loudly sounding. Men armed with muskets were stationed in the large heavy round-tops, each holding a dozen or more soldiers, while others were stationed in the topgallant forecastle, and others at the poop. Guns were also placed inside the forecastle, as also under the poop, with their muzzles turned in-board, so that should the enemy attempt to board, the decks might be swept by their fire. These guns, however, were not loaded with round-shot, but with langrage, which, by scattering around, might kill a number of persons at each discharge. The wind was moderate, the sea tolerably smooth. Captain Jumper stood in the mizen-rigging directing the movements of his ship, while the other officers were stationed in different parts in command of the guns, some on the upper and main-deck, others on the forecastle and poop. The surgeons were below in the cock-pit, getting ready their instruments, and lint, and bandages, and preparing the tables on which amputation when necessary might be performed. Here also were restoratives arranged, for those who might faint from loss of blood. They had taken a look at the enemy, and aware from her superior size that the fight would be a desperate one, were coolly talking over the amount of work in store for them. Not a word was now spoken along the decks, for all jokes were silenced by command of the officers. The captains of the guns stood ready with their slow-matches in their hands, prepared to fire at the signal being given. Already the two antagonists were within range of each other's artillery, but both waited to get still nearer that the greater effect might be produced by their fire. John Deane could not help holding his breath, as did many a brave man on board, not from any sensation of fear, but from intense eagerness for the moment when the combat was to begin. They had not long to delay. Captain Jumper had contrived to place his ship in the position which British officers of all ages have wished to hold with regard to the enemy—that is, broadside to broadside; and now he saw that the wished-for moment had arrived. "Fire!" he shouted. The word was echoed along the decks. The trumpets now brayed out their loudest sounds of defiance. The captains of the guns applied their matches, and the loud roar of artillery broke the silence which had hitherto reigned over the water. The Frenchmen were not slow to answer, and their shot came crashing on board with terrible effect. Many a fine fellow who had been laughing and joking with the rest was laid low. The white splinters were flying on either side, and ropes which had just before been trim and taut hung in festoons or flew out in the breeze, while many a shot-hole was seen through the sails. Without a moment's delay the guns were hauled in. The powder-boys sprang up from their tubs and handed out the powder, which being quickly rammed home, the shot was thrown into the muzzle. Again the guns were run out. No order was now required for firing, but as rapidly as the guns could be loaded they were discharged towards the enemy.

Thus for some time the English ship ran alongside her huge antagonist. Her name painted on her stern was the "Fougueux," and thirty ports were counted on each side. Jack Deane stood at his gun, hauling it in with right good will, and running it out still more eagerly as fast as his arms and those of his mates could work it, thinking of nothing else, and not looking round, even to see what had become of any of those near him. Now and then he heard a groan or a cry, and as he turned round to hand on the powder or the shot, he saw perchance a poor fellow amidst the smoke struggling on the deck. Next moment there was a loud crash close to him, and he found himself sprinkled over from head to foot with blood. He felt no pain, and scarcely knew whether it was his own or that of a shipmate. No sound was heard, but he saw that the man who had stood next to him the moment before was no longer there, but a few feet off a human being lay stretched on the deck. He was about to stoop down to help the man during the interval that the charge was being rammed home.

"Let him alone," said the captain of the gun; "he has drunk his last glass of grog. See, that's his blood which has turned you into a red Indian. Hurrah, lads! we'll revenge him, and all those who lose the number of their mess to-day!"

All this time the small-arm men were not idle. Showers of bullets were flying from the tops and forecastle, returned from those of the enemy.

Now an attempt was made by the "Fougueux," by bracing up her yards, to cross under the stern of the "Weymouth." This, however, was quickly prevented by Captain Jumper, by a similar manoeuvre, as he had no intention of giving up the advantageous position he held.

It was impossible to ascertain the effect which the fire of the British ship was producing among the French crew, but Jack could not help fearing that a considerable number of his shipmates were either killed or wounded. Those who were wounded were immediately carried below, while the killed were borne to the other side of the deck, and slipped overboard through the ports, in order to avoid discouraging the survivors. Still the fight continued with unabated fury.

"Fire away, my lads!" cried Captain Jumper; and his words were echoed by the officers in all directions. "We will sink the enemy or go down with our own colours flying. Never let it be said that the 'Weymouth' had to strike to a Frenchman!"

The speech was a very short one, but it had its effect in encouraging the crew. Scarcely a minute afterwards a fearful sound was heard. It was that of an explosion. And the ship trembled from stem to stern, while those on the quarter-deck saw the poop lifting up into the air, sending some of those on it overboard, and killing several others.

"Fire, fire!" was shouted; "the ship's on fire!"

"We have water enough alongside, my lads, to extinguish it!" cried the captain, in an undaunted tone; and in an instant those of the crew not actually working the guns were hurried up with buckets, with which they soon put out the flames. The Frenchmen shouted, thinking that they were about to gain the victory, but they were answered by a loud cheer of defiance from the British seamen.

It became now absolutely necessary for the "Weymouth" to stand away from the enemy for a short time to repair damages. The only fear of the British sailors was that in the meantime the enemy might attempt to escape.

"No fear of that, lads!" cried the brave captain, who knew what they were speaking of. "See, we have made too many shot-holes between 'wind and water,' and in a few minutes the main-mast will go by the board, if the wind increases."

This was very evident, for while the "Weymouth" put her helm down, to stand away from the "Fougueux" for a short distance, the other immediately ceased firing. The survivors of her crew were probably engaged in attempting to repair the damages she had received. This gave the English leisure to perform their own work without interruption.

Jack as he was leaving his gun to go aloft, looked round him. Of those who had stood but lately by his side, several were missing. Smedley was nowhere to be seen. He inquired among the crew of his gun.

"Yes; a shot struck him and he was carried below, but whether mortally wounded or not, no one could tell."

As he passed up the hatchway, the man whom he took to be Burdale lay on the deck. A bullet which had found its way through a port had struck him down. He was bleeding also from a wound in his shoulder. Jack sprang forward to assist him, but just at that instant the men who were appointed to carry the wounded below, lifted him off the deck, and bore him from his sight.

The decks now presented a very different scene to that which they did a short hour ago. Fore and aft they were covered with blood, and in many places they were blackened and torn up by the shot which had ploughed its way across them. The beams and stanchions in every direction were shattered and broken, and the whole ship showed the severity of the action in which she had been engaged.

"We may be in a bad state enough," Jack heard an old seaman say, "but if you were to go on board the enemy, you would see matters ten times worse. Their decks, depend upon it, are slippery with gore all over, and for one man we have lost, they have lost five."

There was little time, however, for talking. The officers were shouting here and there, giving their directions, and the men were springing aloft to obey them, or running wherever they were summoned. In a short time the ropes were knotted, the yards braced up, the damage done to the poop partially repaired, and the "Weymouth" again stood towards her opponent. As she approached she was received with a hot fire, which she returned with interest, while the big guns once more with loud roars sent forth their shot. The soldiers and small-arm men rattled away with their musketry, and the swivels, culverins, and other small guns, in rapid succession added to the uproar by their sharper reports. Bullets, round-shot, and langrage were flying thickly around.

"Depress your guns and fire at her hull!" cried the captain, seeing the effect that had already been produced on the enemy.

As the Frenchmen's fire grew slacker, that of the English became more and more brisk. Scarcely had a gun been discharged when it was again hauled in and once more sent forth its deadly missile into the hull of the enemy. Just as the action re-commenced, the enemy's main-mast went by the board. A loud shout burst from the throats of the British seamen. Scarcely had it died away when the mizen-mast followed; and now the stout ship was seen to be heeling over. A cry ran along the decks, "She's sinking, she's sinking!" Still her guns continued to send forth her shot, though with far less frequency than at first. Another and another broadside was fired into her; and now it became evident that there was truth in the belief that she was about to go down.

"Cease firing!" cried the English captain. "Not another shot will she discharge at us."

As he spoke the bow of the "Fougueux" was seen to rise out of the water. Loud shrieks and cries rose from her decks. Her stern gradually sank.

"Lower the boats!" cried the English captain. "Be smart, my lads: we must save the poor fellows' lives."

Unhappily, several of the English boats had been almost knocked to pieces. Those which could yet swim were immediately lowered. John Deane jumped into one of the first that reached the water. Ere, however, they could get up to the foundering ship, the sea had washed over her deck. Down—down she went, carrying with her all her wounded and a large number of those who had escaped unhurt. The rest had thrown themselves into the water, some to swim, some holding on to planks or broken spars: but of these, many who had delayed leaving to the last, were drawn down in the vortex of the sinking ship. As the first English boat reached the spot, the streamer at her fore-royal-mast-head was alone to be seen fluttering for a moment above the eddying waters, and then downwards it was drawn after the mast to which it had been attached. Some were still striking out bravely towards their late antagonists. The boats were soon among them, taking up all they met. Many, however, sunk before the very eyes of the English sailors, as they pulled towards them. The boats were soon loaded, and returned to the "Weymouth," fearing lest they should be swamped should they take on board any more of the struggling wretches. Having handed up those they had saved, they once more returned; but, in the meantime, many of those they desired to help had sunk beneath the waves: and out of a crew of six or seven hundred who had lately manned that tall ship, scarcely threescore remained alive. They confessed that upwards of a hundred had been killed and wounded since the commencement of the action, owing, as they acknowledged, to the rapidity with which the English fired at them. Thus the hard-won prize was lost.

Chapter Twenty Three
After the Battle

The brave crew of the "Weymouth" had enough to do to repair their own damages to escape a similar fate. As it was, the "Weymouth" was in a perilous condition from the number of shot-holes she had received in her hull, and probably had a gale sprung up, she also would have gone to the bottom of the ocean. Exhausted by the action as the men were, they still laboured away, as British seamen are ever ready to do, to repair damages, and to keep the ship afloat. A course was then shaped for Plymouth Sound.

As soon as Jack was able to go below, he inquired anxiously for Smedley. He had been carried to the cock-pit. Jack went there. It was the first time he had ever entered that place of horrors, and his heart sank, and he almost fainted at the sickly odour which reached him. As he approached it, cries and groans reached his ears. On the table lay a poor fellow stripped naked, looking already a corpse, on whose leg the surgeons had been operating. His leg, with several other limbs, lay in a basket of sawdust beneath the table. The blood had completely left his face, which still bore the marks of the agony he had suffered, which in those days there were few means of alleviating. One of the surgeons was pouring brandy-and-water down his throat, while another was applying burnt feathers and other restoratives to his nose.

"It's of little use, I'm afraid," said the elder surgeon: "he has slipped through our fingers after all!"

At first Jack did not recognise the countenance of the sufferer. He looked again: the features were those of Smedley! The surgeon spoke too truly; the previous loss of blood, and the agony he had suffered during amputation, had been more than his system could bear, and the lamp of life was already flickering in its socket. For an instant he returned to consciousness. Jack went up to him and took his hand, while the surgeons continued to apply their remedies.

"Shall I bear any message to your friends at Nottingham, poor Jem?" he asked.

A slight pressure of the hand was the only answer the sufferer could make. A sigh escaped his bosom. The surgeon put his hand upon his wrist.

"He has gone, poor fellow! there's no calling him back!" he observed. "Here, take the body away, and put Ned Jones in his place. His arm must come off, if I mistake not!"

Jack turned away with a sad heart. In the cots around were numerous forms. He was about to return on deck, when he recognised among them the countenance of Burdale. The man's eyes followed Jack, and seemed to ask him to return. He went up to him.

"Can I do any thing for you?" he asked. "We have met before, I think?"

"We have; but you cannot help me much, I suspect. Still, I thank you kindly for the offer. I knew you also when you came on board, and was glad to find that you had escaped the trouble into which I thought you would have fallen."

The ice was thus broken, and Jack, while wishing to be of use to the wounded man, whose time on earth he thought was likely to be short, determined to gain all the information he could from him respecting Pearson, and the circumstances which had brought them together. As soon as the ship had been put to rights, those who could be removed were carried to the main-deck, and placed in a part screened off, called the sick-bay. Here Jack had an opportunity of visiting his wounded acquaintance whenever he chose. The man grew weaker and weaker, and seemed indeed to suspect that his own end was approaching.

"Deane," he said, "there's nobody on board this ship I can trust but you; for though you know little about me, I know you to be an honest young gentleman, and very different from the greater number of wild blades on board. I have a wife and child living at Carlisle, and the poor girl does not know what has become of me, and never will, unless you will undertake, should you ever get on shore, to inform her. I had to leave the country in a hurry to save my life: for when they took to hanging a poor trumpeter for that affair of Sir George Barclay's, I felt very sure if I was caught hold of they would not spare me."

"What! were you engaged in that fearful plot?" asked Jack.

"Ay, lad, was I: you may well call it fearful!" answered Burdale. "And I should think you were too, Master Deane, whether you knew it or not."

"I am afraid that I was, though I did not know it," said Jack. "Still no man could have hated the thoughts of what was proposed to be done more than I did. But how were you mixed up with it, Burdale?"

"Why, just in this way," was the answer. "The man whom you know as Master Pearson, though he has as many different names as there are days in the week, was once one of the most noted smugglers on the coast, and I for several years served under him. We also took two or three trips to the Spanish Main, where we had varied fortune; Master Pearson on all occasions got the lion's share. I was a youngster, and could not look after my own interests in those days. We came back with a couple of chests of gold, and plate, and jewels. Somehow or other my master seemed to think that he had had enough of the sea. He met a lady, a real lady she was too, though I don't know her name, and he married her, and for the sake of her company he determined to remain on shore. He knew better how to make money than to keep it; and so did I for that matter, and in a short time the greater part of it was gone. However, he promised his wife not to go to sea, or we should soon have replenished our coffers. He set up, therefore, as a farmer and drover, though he did other turns of business as occasion offered. He understood as much about horses as he did about ships; and, as he had been accustomed to levy taxes on all merchantmen he met, with very little regard for the flag they carried, he now took to levying black-mail on shore. I, of course, joined him. What else could I do? Pearson also hoped to make friends at court; and as he fully believed that King James would come back to rule over the land, he heartily entered into the Jacobite plot, which has so signally failed."

"Then was it he who stopped our cattle as we were bound for Stourbridge Fair?" exclaimed Jack, suddenly.

"There's no doubt about it!" answered Burdale. "He made old Will pay pretty dear for his protection."

"Then were you the horseman I met, who advised me to offer payment?"

"Ay, my lad, that I was," was the answer. "I wonder you did not know me again when I came to you as a guide to conduct you to Pearson's farm in the fens."

"I thought it was you, and I was right."

"Yes; but I had good reason for not telling you so," said Burdale.

"Then who is Master Pearson?" asked Jack.

"Did you ever hear of the famous northern cateran, Ben Nevis?" asked Burdale.

"Indeed have I!" answered Jack.

"Ay, and you know him well," said Burdale; "your friend and he are the same. I would not tell you this, even though it would not matter to me, but I feel sure that you and he are not likely to meet again. In the fens he is known as Master Pearson, but he has gone by a dozen different names at various times, and taken up almost as many different characters. Both sea and land are much the same to him, though I think the sea was most to his taste. If it had not have been for his wife, he would have stuck to that probably. Next to Captain Kyd, I don't suppose there has been a more successful man out on the Spanish Main than he was; and I should not be surprised but what he will take to the same calling again, if England once becomes too hot for him. I think differently now that I see death coming on to gripe hold of me, to what I did when I was in health and strength, and I tell you, John Deane, you are fortunate in getting clear of him. When he first met you, he wished to get you to join his gang, thinking that you would be ready enough to do so from the way in which you were engaged. He would have invited Smedley and the others, but he saw at a glance that they were not lads to suit him, and so he kept his eye upon you. When he saw that you were not likely to be drawn in for that sort of work, he found employment for you in Sir John Fenwick's plot, and if it had not been for that, I can tell you that Mr Strelley and Will Brinsmead would never have seen the cattle he had undertaken to send south. As it was, it answered his purpose to send them safe. You were thus still further deceived about him. He was employed, as you know, by Squire Harwood and other Jacobite gentlemen—not that he cared for one side more than the other, and if King William's party had paid him better, he would have served them just as willingly. I say this because it's the truth, which you wish me to tell you; and I forgive him for all the harm he did me, for it was he who first led me away from an honest course when I was a mere lad, and tempted me to take to smuggling, and in the end to turn pirate and land-robber. I am thankful that I at last got free of him. If it was not for my wife and child in my quiet little cottage in the north, I would not complain of dying now, shot down for my brave king and country. But when I think of them, it's hard and bitter to go out of the world, and leave them to suffer the neglect and poverty which too likely will be their lot!"

The speaker's voice grew fainter and fainter as he went on with his narrative, till Jack could with difficulty hear what he said.

"I promise you, Ned, I will act the part of an honest shipmate, and try and find out those you love, and look after them. Besides, you know, your widow will be entitled to a pension, and I will put down her address and write to her as soon as we get into port, that she may apply for it."

"Ah, that's a comfort; are you sure you are right, Jack?"

"I have heard several of the men talking about it, and I'm confident I am not wrong," answered Deane. "The wives of seamen killed in action are always provided for, and a proper thing it should be so. It's one of the reasons, I have an idea, that our brave fellows fight so well. God looks after the fatherless and widows, and as long as our country professes to be a God-fearing nation, she must obey His commands."

Burdale put out his hand. Jack pressed it, and promised him again that he would not forget his wishes. Before another sun shone over the world of waters, poor Ned's spirit had winged its flight away from his once sturdy form; and before the ship entered Plymouth Sound, several others who had been wounded in the action breathed their last.

Chapter Twenty Four
Cutting-out Expedition—John Deane is Promoted—Capture of two Galleys

It was no easy matter to find a place in which to write a letter on board. Jack, however, got a board for a desk, and, sitting down near a port on the deck, wrote to Ned Burdale's widow, according to the address given him, telling her of her husband's death, and directing her how at once to apply for her pension. He promised also to go and see her if he could possibly manage the journey, and bring a few things which Ned had left to her and her boy, begging her, if she ever moved away, to write to him at Nottingham, that he might know how to find her.

So busily were all hands employed in refitting the ship, aided by extra carpenters and riggers, that Jack was unable to obtain even an hour's leave on shore. Immediately the ship was ready for sea, Blue Peter was hoisted, the anchor was run up to the bows, and under all sail she stood down the Sound.

Captain Jumper was worthy of his name. A more active officer was not to be found; and he soon made himself as much feared by the French as were Admiral Benbow, Sir Cloudesley Shovel, Sir George Rooke, and Captain Dilkes, who was soon to become an Admiral. Under such a commander John Deane had many opportunities of distinguishing himself. A squadron, of which the "Weymouth" formed a part, was sent in to attack the Island of Rhé and Belleisle, accompanied by several bomb-vessels. Saint Martin's was bombarded, and several small towns and villages were burned and plundered. The loss the French suffered on this occasion induced them to go to great expense in defending their coast, the cost to them being far greater than was that to the English in attacking it. Jack volunteered on all occasions of this sort, and on all cutting-out expeditions, and had thus an opportunity of bringing himself before the notice of his captain. As the "Weymouth" was standing off and on the French coast, several vessels, supposed by their size to be privateers, were seen at anchor within a small harbour, guarded by a fort. As these vessels, if allowed to get out, would probably commit great havoc among the English merchant shipping, it was very important to destroy them. An expedition was accordingly planned by Captain Jumper for that purpose. It was likely, however, to be a dangerous one, as the boats could not get in without passing under the fire of the fort, while the privateers themselves were likely to be prepared with springs on their cables, and guns ready to receive their assailants. Captain Jumper therefore resolved, as is usual on such occasions, to send in only those who would volunteer for the expedition. He had no lack, however, of men ready to undertake it. The more daring and desperate, the more it suited the taste of his brave crew. He had himself proposed to go in command of it; but his second lieutenant begged that he might have that honour. Among the first who volunteered was John Deane. The captain ordered four boats to be prepared, carrying in all fifty men. John Deane was in the boat with the first lieutenant, Mr Cammock, the leader of the expedition. The third lieutenant and two master's mates commanded the other boats. To mislead the French, the frigate stood off shore as evening approached, so that they might be led to believe that she had gone altogether. The night being very dark, her return could not be discovered. Jack and his shipmates, in the meantime, were busily employed in re-sharpening their hangers, and looking to their pistols and ammunition, putting in fresh flints, and seeing that they were not likely to miss fire. By midnight the ship came off the mouth of the harbour. The wind was off shore, so that she could lay to, and, at the same time, no noise which might be made in lowering the boats would be heard on shore. The boats were quickly lowered and manned, and with muffled oars their brave leader, Lieutenant Cammock, pulled with steady strokes towards the harbour. The outermost vessels were to be first attacked. While two of the boats boarded one, the other two were to attack the next. Their aim was to pass the fort without being discovered. If they were seen, they were to pull rapidly by, in the hopes that in the darkness the shot might not hit them.

Desperate as the work in which they were engaged was likely to prove, John Deane felt a strange pleasure in the undertaking.

The dim outline of the shore was seen before them, and on one side the straight line of the fort appeared up against the sky, though as yet the masts of the vessels could not be discerned. There was no doubt, however, of their being on the right course. Not a word was spoken. The men scarcely dared to breathe as they pulled on, so anxious were they to avoid discovery. Like a snake coiling its way among the grass, the line of boats advanced steadily up the harbour. The fort was passed. Deane thought he could hear the footsteps of the sentry as he passed up and down; but as yet they were not seen or heard. Probably not dreaming of an enemy approaching the harbour, he had neglected to turn his eyes down towards the entrance. Now he burst forth in a song about his distant home and its vine-clad hills. Jack could almost hear the words as they came floating over the still water. The boats had got some way up the harbour, and now the vessels which were to be attacked appeared before them. Suddenly a sharp report of a musket was heard. It was fired from the fort. The sounds of the oars borne from the harbour must have reached the sentry's ears. Another shot succeeded it from the same direction. The boats glided rapidly on. Lights were seen on board the vessels, and several sharp reports of muskets told them they were discovered. Not a moment was to be lost. The first vessel was a large ship, probably mounting between twenty and thirty guns. Mr Cammock ordered the boat next to him to board her along with him, while the two latter boats were to attack the vessel astern of her, which was not much inferior in size. The Frenchmen, roused from their sleep, started up on deck to meet the English climbing up the sides with their cutlasses in their teeth. Jack, following Mr Cammock, was among the first on board. They were met by a party of the French, led by one of their officers. On every side pistols were flashing and steel was clashing furiously.

"Clear the decks of them, my lads!" cried Mr Cammock, as with his hanger he rushed towards those who opposed him.

The Frenchmen gave way, so furious and sudden was the attack. Some leaped overboard, others jumped down below, and others cried for quarter. The lieutenant ordering the crew of the other boat to cut the cable and make sail, cried out to Jack and his own boat's crew to follow him, that they might take the next vessel. All obeyed with alacrity; but the work was far more serious than that which had just been performed, for the Frenchmen were on the alert and prepared to receive the borders. In spite, however, of the pikes thrust at them, and the pistols fired in their faces, the English climbed up the sides and made good their footing on deck. Jack, with his trusty hanger in his hand, kept close to the side of the brave lieutenant. The Frenchmen gathered thickly before them, and a tall figure, whom by his dress Jack saw was an officer, led them on, assailing Mr Cammock with great fury. His sword was about to descend on the head of the English lieutenant, when Jack, rushing between them, received the blow on his own blade, returning it with such interest that the French officer stretched his length on the deck. The fall of their leader discouraged the rest of the crew. Although they once or twice rallied, they were driven forward. Many were cut down, and others cried out for quarter. There was no time to be lost in getting the vessels out, for it was very evident that a greater number of the crew was on shore; and from the lights which appeared on every side, and the shouts which reached them, it was probable that they were coming off to the assistance of their shipmates. The next vessel appeared to have still fewer people on board.

"We cannot get her off," observed Mr Cammock, "but we can burn her, perhaps."

"I will do it!" cried Jack. "Who will follow me?"

Several men instantly volunteered, and Jack, jumping into the boat, led the way on board. The Frenchmen, perhaps, were not expecting an attack, for they made no resistance. Jack had snatched a slow-match as he left the other vessel. With this, light was set to different parts of the ship on board which he now found himself. The astonished crew were either drunk or frightened, and did nothing to put out the flames, but were seen to lower a boat and jump into her. The work accomplished, Jack returned to the last vessel which had been taken just as the cable was cut and sail was made on her to carry her out of the harbour. So rapidly did the flames of the vessel which had been set on fire burst forth, that even she with difficulty escaped from them, while, as they glided down the harbour, they were seen to extend to several other vessels near.

"Deane, you have rendered an important service to-night," said Mr Cammock, as Jack returned on board.

"I can make a favourable report of you to the captain, if we get safe out of this, as I hope we may."

Scarcely a quarter of an hour had passed since the first vessel was attacked, and four prizes, the reward of British valour, were now being carried off down the harbour with a considerable number of prisoners on board. They were not, however, to escape without molestation. The other vessels which had hitherto escaped the flames, opened their fire upon them, as did the fort; but the number of vessels, which kept some little way apart from each other, prevented the French gunners from taking very good aim. Several shots, however, struck the prizes. The French prisoners on board were the chief sufferers. They, poor fellows! shrieked out to their countrymen, entreating them not to fire, as nothing they could do would stop the desperate Englishmen from carrying off the vessels. Their voices, however, were probably not heard, and their entreaties were certainly not attended to. The breeze, blowing directly down the harbour, carried the prizes quickly clear of the fort, and in a short time they were alongside the "Weymouth," which made sail, and stood off with them towards the English coast.

Jack's heart beat high when the next morning he was summoned on the quarter-deck, where the captain and several of his officers were standing together. Jack stood hat in hand before the captain.

"Mr Cammock has spoken highly of your coolness and courage last night, John Deane," he said. "He tells me also that you saved his life by coming between him and an officer who would have cut him down. From what has been told me, I believe you will do honour to the quarter-deck, and I will therefore from this day rate you as a master's mate. It is the first step in the ratlines, and I have no doubt, if you go on as you have begun, that you will in time reach the top."

Jack's heart beat high at these words. He had hoped some day to become an officer, but he had not expected so soon to attain his wishes, and he was determined the captain's words should be verified, and that he would lose no opportunity of distinguishing himself. He had already a fair store of prize-money, so that he was able, without writing home, to fit himself out as became an officer, not so difficult in those days as in later years. He had no great fancy for gold lace suits, but a good serviceable coat and cocked hat was more according to his taste. He could now, however, write home with some degree of satisfaction, to say that he had become an officer, and that he hoped by sticking to the service to rise in the profession he had chosen. He certainly had a longing at times to go home and see those he loved so dearly. Often a vision of Alethea rose up before him, but still not without some doubts as to the position he held with her.

It would be impossible to describe all the exploits performed by Captain Jumper and his brave crew during the time the "Weymouth" was in commission. Few ships remained a shorter time in harbour than she did, and the crew might with a show of reason have complained of the hard work they had to go through. They were, however, well satisfied with the amount of prize-money which fell to their lot. Jack, in his new position, got a good share of it, and found himself better supplied with cash than he had ever before been in his life.

Some time passed away, when one day the "Weymouth" was standing towards the French coast in the direction the wind blew to Saint Martin's, the scene of some of her former exploits, when two vessels were seen to leeward. From the cut of their sails and general appearance they were known to be French.

Every stratagem is considered lawful in warfare. Captain Jumper therefore hoisted the French ensign, and as he was running down before the wind, the cut of his own sails could not so clearly be discerned, by which the character of the "Weymouth" would have been discovered. The two vessels for some time made no attempt to escape, believing probably that the stranger in sight was really French, and wishing for some reason or other to speak her. By yawing occasionally—that is moving the ship's head from one side to the other—the French ensign was visible to the two vessels to leeward. Thus the "Weymouth" was able to get within gunshot of them before her character was discovered. Quickly bracing up her yards, she poured a broadside into her two opponents, which were close together. They were found to be two large galleys, which carried some twenty guns on the upper-deck, and several on the quarter-deck, while between-decks were small ports, out of which their oars projected. They now began to work their oars, in the hopes of placing themselves on the quarters of the "Weymouth," but before one of them could do so, so tremendous a fire was poured into her that she was rendered unmanageable, many of the unhappy galley-slaves having apparently been killed, and her rudder shot away. The other galley attempted to make her escape, but the "Weymouth," following her, treated her in the same way that she had done her consort, and she was compelled to strike her colours.

Boats were now lowered to take possession of the prizes. Deane was sent on board the first, which lay almost a wreck on the waters. As he clambered up the sides he gazed with horror on the scene of slaughter which the decks presented. Numbers of the unhappy galley-slaves, chained to their benches, lay cut in two, with limbs shot off, and fearfully mangled in every possible way. Groans and cries ascended from the survivors, though many had already, more fortunate than them, ceased to breathe. A number of the crew had also been killed and wounded, and the galley herself appeared to be in a sinking state. Deane made a signal to the "Weymouth" to this effect, and begged that other boats might be sent to rescue the crew. Calling on those who had charge of the slaves, he ordered them immediately to knock off their shackles, he and his men holding pistols to their heads, as they seemed rather disinclined to obey the order. As soon as the poor fellows were released, he had them at once placed in the boats, greatly to the anger of the French crew, who considered that they ought first to have been carried off. It is true that many of the slaves were ruffians of the lowest order, sent to the galleys for their crimes; but Jack knew well, also, that many were Huguenots, whose only crime was adhering to the Protestant faith. At that moment it was difficult to discriminate between them, and he therefore determined to carry off all at once. The first cargo were quickly conveyed on board the "Weymouth," when the boats returned for the survivors of the crew, with whom Deane and his men had remained. He could not help looking anxiously for the return of the boats, for every moment the water was rising higher and higher in the hold of the prize. Again and again he urged the crew to man the pumps, and endeavour to keep their vessel afloat, but they were in no way disposed to do this, probably fearing that if the English returned in time, they might save her altogether from sinking, and carry her off as a prize. This the Frenchmen were anxious that their conquerors should not do.

Once more, as the boats were seen approaching the galley for the remainder of the crew, Deane went round the between-decks to ascertain if any of the wounded slaves still remained alive. A low groan reached his ears from a man who lay stretched out under one of the benches. The chain was still round his leg. Deane raised up the man's head. Though wounded, he was still perfectly conscious, and had become aware of the dreadful fate awaiting him had he been overlooked. Deane shouted to those on deck to come to his assistance. By the sound which the water made rushing into the hold of the vessel, he was very sure she would not float many minutes longer. To leave the poor man was contrary to his nature, and yet to release him without knocking off the shackle was impossible. The glance he had of the countenance of the wounded man convinced him that he was not one of the low class of criminals which formed a portion of the gang of galley-slaves, but that he was probably a Huguenot. Deane heard those on deck shouting to the boats to make haste as the galley was about to sink. At that moment one of his own men, finding that he was not on deck, sprung down below to look for him. Deane at once ordered him to bring the French master-at-arms with his keys or chisel to emancipate the unfortunate prisoner. The Frenchman pretended not to understand him, but a pistol placed at his head quickly made him come below and take off the shackle which held the slave to the bench. Jack in a moment, bearing the rescued man in his arms, leaped up on deck just as the boats came alongside. The French crew made a spring into them, for already they felt the galley sinking beneath their feet. Jack had only just time to lower the man down and spring in after him before the galley, rolling heavily, settled down under the water. The boats rapidly pulled away from her, and in another minute she and the mangled remains of humanity with which her decks were covered were hid beneath the waves.

The rescued galley-slave warmly expressed his thanks to Deane for having preserved his life. He had been struck on the head by a piece of one of the oars shattered by a shot, and stunned. Little blood having flowed from the wound, his strength was unimpaired.

"You have saved my life by your activity, young sir," he said, in broken English, "and I am grateful to you; but, alas! when too probably all I once loved on earth, my property, and my friends, will never again be restored to me, I have, I own, but little to live for!"

"Cheer up, sir," answered Jack; "your Huguenot countrymen are always welcome in England, and I doubt not that you will find many friends among them; and at all events the English will receive you as one, if you are, as I conclude, also a Huguenot."

"Yes, indeed I am!" was the answer. "The faith of the Gospel has sustained me under all the trials and hardships I have gone through. Though at times I have been cast down and fainted, I have once more gained courage and determination to await calmly whatever Providence has had in store for me."

On getting on board, Deane took the Huguenot to the captain, and explained who he was. He, therefore, and others whom he named, were separated from the rest of the prisoners, and treated as friends rather than as captured enemies. Some of the slaves were, however, ruffians, whom it was evident it would not be safe to leave at large. They therefore were treated as the rest of the prisoners.

As the other galley was taken possession of, a ship was seen standing out from under the land towards the "Weymouth," attracted probably by the firing, and the English seamen exultingly hoped that they should have another action to fight, and gain another prize. The Frenchman, however, on discerning the fate of the two galleys, again kept away, and ran back towards the land, taking shelter under the guns of the fort, from which it would have been difficult to cut him out. The "Weymouth," with her prize, now stood up Channel. As she had now been several years in commission, great hopes were entertained that she would be paid off. Her crew were not disappointed; and, being ordered into Portsmouth, those who had lived and fought for so long together were once again separated and scattered in all directions.

Chapter Twenty Five
The Galley-slave, and who he was

Jack took an especial interest in the unfortunate man whose life he had saved on board the galley. From his manners and language he guessed at once that he was a gentleman, although his hair was long and matted, and his countenance had that sickly hue which long confinement and hard labour had given to it. He visited him in his hammock, where he lay alongside other wounded men. The stranger recognised him at once.

"Ah, my brave friend," he said, "this is indeed kind in you, to come and see me! I know not whether my days on earth are already numbered, but as long as I remain here, my heart will never cease to beat with gratitude to you!"

Jack replied that he should have done the same for any human being, but that he was very thankful he had been of service in saving the life of one who appeared to be a gentleman and a man of feeling; especially one who had gone through so many hardships as he had.

"Ah, indeed I have!" he answered. "Because I loved Protestant truth, and desired to worship God according to the dictates of my conscience, I was cruelly deprived of my property, and my wife and child snatched from me—while I was carried off, and after undergoing numberless hardships, was sent on board a galley, associated with many of the greatest villains and most hardened wretches in the country! I was not entirely alone with them, however, for many other Huguenots were suffering with me, and we were thus enabled to support and console each other. But, alas! I might have borne the loss of my liberty, and my property, and the sufferings and hardships I had to go through, but I could not bear the thought of being separated from my beloved wife and our sweet daughter, and never being able to gain tidings of them. Even now I know not whether they escaped from France, or whether they suffered as did many who were attempting to fly from the country. Sometimes I fancy that they are alive, but whether the child and mother are still together I know not, or whether they have been separated by our cruel enemies. The fate of our little girl often presses heavily on me. I think sometimes she may have been seized by the Romanists and brought up in their faith, as have many children who have been taken from Huguenots."

Jack did his best to console his new friend, and assured him, as he had done before, that he would be kindly treated in England, and that perhaps his Protestant countrymen could give him some tidings of his wife.

"My only hope is that she may have returned to Holland," he said, "to which country she belonged, though she had resided many years in France. It was also my father's country, but by right of my mother I inherited a property in France—though little did I think at the time when I went to take possession of it, that it would have cost me all the suffering I have endured! As I had become a naturalised Frenchman, so as a Frenchman I was treated; but I love the country of my ancestors and my wife's country, and would gladly return to that. Indeed, could I effect my escape, I would do so, as I have some property there which the French have not been able to take from me."

Jack listened with great interest to this account.

"I was acquainted a few years ago with an English merchant at Norwich, one Mr Gournay, who has been very kind to the Huguenots; and as he has correspondents in all parts of the country, and throughout Holland also, and many other places on the Continent, if you will tell me your name, and describe your wife and child, I will write to him, and I have no doubt that he will make inquiries in that direction for you," he said.

"Thank you, thank you, my kind friend!" said the wounded man. "Your promise gives me hopes which I dared not before entertain. My name is De Mertens. My dear wife was tall and graceful, and noted for her beauty, and our little girl was called Elise, or, as you would call her in England, Elizabeth."

"This is indeed very strange!" exclaimed Jack; "for I met a lady at the house of the very gentleman I spoke of—Mr Gournay—who told me that her name was De Mertens, and that her husband had been carried off to the galleys, while, I grieve to tell you, for it will pain you much to hear it, the little girl had been snatched away from her just as she was embarking, and since then she has been unable to gather any tidings of her. She begged me to make inquiries, which I did as far as I was able, but circumstances compelled me to leave the country soon afterwards, and I was not able to gather any clue to her lost child."

"My wife still alive! and under the charge of kind friends!" exclaimed the wounded man, sitting up. "This is indeed joyful news! though alas that it should not be without its alloy! Yet the kind Providence which has preserved my wife, may have preserved our child to be restored to us. But what do I see, young man?" he exclaimed, seizing Jack's hand. "Let me look at that ring on your finger. It is strange that it should be there. Did my wife give it you?"

"No," replied Jack, somewhat astonished; "I did not receive it till some time after I last saw Madame de Mertens. It was given to me by a young girl, the daughter of a farmer and his wife, at whose house I was residing for some time. She was a sweet, dear little girl; and when I came away she told me that she had nothing else to give, and she insisted on placing that ring on my finger. She said she had worn it round her own neck since she was a child, and though she valued it greatly, she should be unhappy if I would not take it. Directly after I received it I purposed restoring it to her, as I did not think it right to deprive her of it, but was unable again to return to the farm before I came away to sea."

"This is indeed wonderful!" exclaimed Monsieur de Mertens. "Oh, let me entreat you to describe the little girl to me!"

Jack did so, and did not draw an unfavourable picture.

"The description is indeed like what I should suppose my sweet little girl to be by this time. Fair, with bright blue eyes, light hair, and gentle, winning manners; but you tell me that she was the daughter of a farmer and his wife?"

"For such she always passed," answered Jack; "but often I thought so rough a man as the farmer could not have so sweet and gentle a child; and from what I have since heard, I am inclined to believe that she was not really their child."

"Oh, no, no, I am sure she was not!" exclaimed Monsieur de Mertens, clasping his hands. "She must be my own dear little daughter! Oh, what joy and happiness it will be to see her again with her dear mother."

"If I can possibly get leave when we go into port, I will promise to accompany you to Norwich, where you will, I trust, find Madame de Mertens; and after that we will pay a visit to the fens and ascertain if little Elizabeth Pearson is really or not your child," said Deane.

"Thank you, thank you!" answered De Mertens. "But let me look at that ring again. I cannot be mistaken about it!"

Jack took off the ring, which De Mertens eagerly examined.

"Yes, yes!" he exclaimed; "it is one I myself gave her mother, telling her that it was an heirloom, and that she should bestow it upon her daughter. I doubt not that she fastened it round her neck before she fled from home, that should she and the child be separated, she might again recognise her by it. And you say the little girl you met was called Elizabeth? That would be the name of my dear child in English, and as she could speak quite clearly at the time of our separation, she would certainly have told those into whose hands she fell her Christian name, though it is possible that she might not have known the name of her parents."

As may be supposed, after this interesting conversation, Jack and Monsieur de Mertens constantly discussed the subject as they sailed up the Channel. At length the Isle of Wight hove in sight. Each well-known point and headland, village and town, was welcomed, as the frigate ran round the back of that lovely island, and at length anchored at Spithead.

Chapter Twenty Six
Visit to Norwich and to the Farm at the Fens—A bitter Disappointment

As soon as the ship was paid off, Jack took his new friend on shore, and procured for him a proper costume and other necessaries. He had himself a considerable amount of prize-money to receive, and instead of spending it as did many of his shipmates, throwing it away lavishly on every side, he visited the nearest horse dealer's in order to purchase a couple of stout animals to carry him and Monsieur de Mertens on their way. The horse dealer was rather astonished when the naval officer, whom he naturally supposed knew as much about horse-flesh as he himself did about the management of a ship, indignantly refused a couple of spavined animals which he offered for sale. Several others were brought forward, which Jack in like manner rejected. At length he fixed upon two beasts which, after passing his hands over their shoulders and down their legs, he thought might suit for the purpose of carrying them safe to Norwich, and from thence on to Master Pearson's farm.

"The finest animals in my stud!" exclaimed the horse dealer, as Jack ordered them to be led out. "Fit for chargers for the Duke of Marlborough himself, or suited to carry any noblemen as hunters across the country."

"I have not so long ploughed salt water as not to know something about ploughing the land," answered Jack; "don't you see the hay-seed still in my hair? Come, come, Mr Crupper, the horses will carry us along the roads without coming down on their knees at a decent pace, and if you like to take the sum I offer, we'll have them, if not, we will soon go and seek another dealer who is not so ready to pass off his broken-kneed beasts on poor ignorant 'Jack-tars.'"

The dealer, seeing that Jack was not to be taken in, at length agreed to the price offered.

In a short time, with their valises strapped to their saddles, their pistols in their holsters, with serviceable swords by their sides, the travellers took their way towards London. In those days not a few highwaymen beset the roads, especially those leading from the chief naval ports to London, as they were pretty certain of finding seamen and officers travelling up and down—those travelling towards the metropolis, generally with an ample supply of cash in their pockets. Hounslow Heath, over which they had to pass, was one of the spots most frequented by those knights of the highway. It did not matter much that the horses possessed but little speed, as De Mertens, not having ridden for so many years, was unable to proceed at a fast rate; and even Jack found that it was far pleasanter not to attempt going as fast as he would once have wished to have gone over the road. They were therefore obliged to sleep at an inn about half-way between Portsmouth and London, hoping to get into the big city at an early hour the next day. Jack's chief puzzle was to know where to find a lodging. As may be supposed, he had no fancy to go back to the only one he knew of at Hammersmith, although on their way they should pass not far from it. He felt very sure, however, that he might do so without any risk of being discovered, for instead of the rosy-cheeked lad he then was, he now wore a full black beard, while his countenance was thoroughly well bronzed, and there was a bold, dashing look about him which often marked the naval officer of those days who had seen hard service. As De Mertens had no wish to remain in London, they agreed to pass through the city, and to stop for the night at Hertford, or some other town to the north of it. On passing across Hounslow Heath they encountered more than one suspicious-looking gentleman, armed to the teeth, and mounted on a strong active horse. But probably Jack's appearance made the highwayman, if such he was, think it more prudent to allow the travellers to pass unquestioned. That sort of gentry, even in those days, in spite of all their boasting, were generally cowards at heart, and took good care not to attack those whom they did not feel sure they could intimidate or overcome without difficulty.

Jack did his best to keep up the spirits of poor Monsieur de Mertens, who as he approached Norwich became more and more nervous, dreading to hear that some accident had happened to his wife—that she was ill, or perhaps had died. Then he dreaded the effect which his sudden return might have on her; and more than all he pictured to himself her sorrow, when at their meeting she would be unable to present to him their beloved child.

On reaching Norwich Jack took his companion to the inn at which he had put up with Will Brinsmead, and begged him to remain there while he himself went on to the house of Mr Gournay, that he might prepare Madame de Mertens for his appearance.

Jack now began to feel very nervous himself. He would ten times rather have boarded a French ship, with pistols flashing and cold steel flourishing round his head, than go through the necessary interview with the wife of his friend. He first made his way to Mr Gournay's counting-house, that he might inquire for his intended brother-in-law Giles Dainsforth. Mr Gournay himself had returned home, but the clerks were still there. Giles Dainsforth was not among them.

"Oh, did you not know that he left us last year to go to Nottingham, to be married to Mr Deane's daughter? They sailed some time since for Mr Penn's new colony in America, which they call Pennsylvania," was the answer. "Several friends have gone out there from thence, and it's one of the most flourishing settlements in the New World."

Jack accordingly hastened to Mr Gournay's residence, and first asked to see Mrs Gournay. She received Jack very kindly, though she expressed her regret at finding that he was following a profession in which he was likely to shed the blood of his fellow-creatures.

"Young man, thou hadst better have taken a quill in thine hand, to labour as a clerk in a counting-house, or have remained a drover to conduct cattle up and down the country, than used a sword to deface God's image, as I fear too often thou must have done."

Jack did not wish to argue the point, but he assured her that he had no pleasure in killing his fellow-creatures, and that he had the consolation of believing that the navy had been the means of preventing a Popish King from coming over and re-establishing papacy in the country; and that he also in his humble way had been of some benefit to his fellow-creatures. "For instance," he said, "I was the means not long since of saving the life of a gentleman, a French Protestant, whom I have brought with me to see you."

Jack then explained who his companion was. Good Mrs Gournay was overjoyed.

"Mr Deane," she said, "we must break it gently to dear Madame de Mertens. She has been, especially lately, in delicate health, and any sudden surprise might be injurious to her. I will go and gradually tell her of what has occurred, and do you return to the inn and bring Monsieur de Mertens here. By the time that he arrives, it may probably be safe to allow them to meet."

It was very long since Jack had trod the ground with the elastic step with which he hastened back to bring his friend to Mr Gournay's house. He felt, indeed, very proud at the thought that he should thus have been the means of restoring two loving hearts to each other, and still more proud he felt he should be if he could discover their long-lost child. This he had great hopes of doing. And as he thought of Elizabeth Pearson's manner, her way of speaking, and many other little circumstances, he recollected that her accent was somewhat that of a foreigner. There was an intelligence and refinement, too, which he should not have expected to find in a young girl in her position in life, except, however, that Dame Pearson was herself very superior to any farmer's wife he had ever met, and was evidently a person who had belonged to a higher rank of society. He was also sacrificing himself for the good of others, for had he been left to his own disposal, he would, in the first place, have hastened on to Nottingham to enjoy the society of his own family, and, more than all, as he thought, to renew his acquaintance with Alethea Harwood. Often and often had her lovely countenance risen up before him, and he had enjoyed the hope that she would one day become his. At the same time it must be owned that another sweet face frequently presented itself before him, and though he had never associated it with the thought of love, yet surely it was one which must of necessity be very dear to him. It was that of little Elizabeth Pearson, so gentle, so bright and intelligent, and so confiding! He had now arranged to go and visit her, not for his own satisfaction, but for that of the friends who had hopes of discovering in her their long-lost daughter.

Leaving Mistress Gournay, Jack hurried back through the narrow streets of Norwich to the Bear Inn, where he found Monsieur de Mertens anxiously waiting for him. His friend trembled as he took his arm and led him out of the house.

"A kind friend will inform your wife of your arrival, and by the time we reach her house Madame de Mertens will, I trust, be prepared to receive you," said Jack.

"But she will, I fear, scarcely know me," said the poor man. "You cannot tell how anxiety of mind and physical hardships have changed me. When we parted I was young, and full of life and spirits, and now my hair is grey, the colour has left my cheeks, and I tremble in every limb!"

Jack tried to console him by assuring him that he had greatly improved in his appearance since he had been freed from the galley, and that he was sure his wife would know him by the expression of his countenance and the tone of his voice, even should she discover the change of which he spoke.

"Alas!" he said, "our joyful meeting must, however, be tinged with sorrow when she cannot present to me our dear child. May Heaven grant that through your assistance, my kind friend, that dear one may still be restored to us!"

"I have little doubt about it, my dear sir," answered Jack, who was not apt to indulge in what he called the "sentimental mood."

"I am sure that if little Elizabeth Pearson turns out to be your daughter, you will have reason to be thankful, even though she may not be the polished young lady she would have been had she remained under the charge of her mother."

Thus conversing they reached the door of Mr Gournay's mansion, and Jack had almost to drag in his poor friend, who appeared totally overcome by the agitation of the expected meeting. Mrs Gournay had kindly stationed a servant at the door to open it as soon as they were seen coming up the steps. She herself then came down, and taking Monsieur de Mertens by the hand, led him forward to the room where she said his wife was waiting to receive him.

The meeting need not be described, nor does it matter much whether the affectionate husband and wife thought each other greatly changed. It was not until they had been some time together that Madame de Mertens ventured to speak of their long-lost daughter; and then she heard with grateful joy that her husband entertained a hope of her recovery, with the aid of John Deane. When her husband showed her the ring which Jack had given him, and which she herself had fastened round her child's neck, all doubt as to the fact of Elizabeth Pearson being their child, vanished. Both she and her husband were eager at once to set out to the farm in the fens; but good mistress Gournay would not hear of her commencing so fatiguing a journey, nor was her husband indeed at all fit to undertake it at that time. Jack offered to go alone, but of that Monsieur de Mertens would not hear. It was finally settled that they should start together after a day's rest.

The two horses which had brought them to Norwich not being well suited for the continuance of the journey, Mr Gournay placed at their disposal two of the strongest animals he could procure. He also prepared a palfrey, and directed a groom to accompany it, that Elizabeth might be able to return without delay to the arms of her mother. When the hour arrived for their departure, Monsieur de Mertens declared himself fully able to undertake the journey, and urged Jack to push on over the roads as fast as their horses could go, so eager was he naturally to solve any remaining doubts with regard to the existence of his long-lost child. Jack had been so thoroughly acquainted with all the country round the farm, that as he approached the neighbourhood of it, where the high-road ceased and the devious tracks across the marshy land commenced, he had no difficulty in finding his way. He heard, however, that since he had been there engineers had come over from Holland, and were engaged with large gangs of workmen in draining the fen-country. He was able to traverse, therefore, many places which had before been impassable, and deep canals had been cut through others, which could only be passed by means of wooden bridges at considerable distances from each other. Still he felt sure that he could not mistake his way to the farm. The nearer, however, he approached the spot where he expected to find it, the greater difficulty did he experience in making his way. Several times he had to pull up his horse, and look around him to consider which direction he should take. Whenever he thought he was right, he pushed on across the country. Although there were many hard places, there were still many wide districts of fen-land, in no way changed in appearance to what it had been when he left it, and often with difficulty he avoided riding into bogs, out of which it would have been almost impossible to extricate the horses. At length, to his great satisfaction, he reached a group of willows which he remembered well. He was now sure that he could not be mistaken. His own heart beat quick. He saw by the working of Monsieur de Merten's countenance the agitation with which he suffered, as at length he pointed out to him in the far distance the trees which grew round the farm-house to which they were bound. Jack took the lead, his companion following close behind him. Already he could distinguish the windows of the house, and he expected every moment to see the old dogs, which once knew him so well, come out barking loudly, and then when they should recognise him, leap up, as they had been accustomed to do, and lick his hands. He hoped to see Dame Pearson or Elizabeth appear at the door, attracted by the noise, to observe the approaching horsemen. In vain he waited however. Not a sound was heard. No barking of dogs, either in anger or in welcome, reached his ears. As he advanced his heart began to sink. There was an air of desolation about the place which it had never been accustomed to wear. No cattle were to be seen in the neighbouring meadow. Many of the fences were thrown down. There were no fowls in the farm-yard. No pigeons circled around the barn. An ominous silence reigned over the place. Still he went on. He felt that he must speak to his friend. Yet it seemed to him almost cruel to utter the words which he had to say.

"You must be prepared for a disappointment, my dear sir. I fear that the former inhabitants of the place have left it. We may, however, be able to learn where they have gone."

The ground was now sufficiently hard to enable them to gallop on. On reaching the front door he threw himself from his horse and struck loudly against it. A hollow sound was the only answer returned. He lifted the latch, for the door was unlocked. He gazed round the room where the dame and Elizabeth had been accustomed to sit, after the chief labours of the day were over, with their distaffs or spinning-wheels—that very room where he had last parted from the young girl! The lighter articles of value had been removed, though the heavy pieces of furniture still remained in their places, thickly covered with dust. It was evident that for many months no one had entered the house. Green mildew was on the walls. The very floors were covered with damp.

Poor Monsieur de Mertens sank down on a seat, overcome by the bitter disappointment which he experienced. Jack endeavoured to re-assure him, by telling him that he knew several persons in the neighbourhood, and that he should probably be able to ascertain from them where Master Pearson and his family had gone. Before leaving the house, however, he would go over every part of it, to try and discover any thing which might give them the desired information.

The examination of the house was a very melancholy one, for not a sign could he discover to afford the wished-for clue. One of the rooms was locked. He hesitated about attempting to break it open. At length, on searching around, he found a bunch of keys. They had evidently been dropped by accident, and unintentionally left behind. Among them he discovered the key which opened the door of the closed room. He at first almost dreaded to enter, though he could scarcely tell why. At length he mustered courage. He breathed more freely when he found that the room was simply filled with bedding and bed-clothes and household implements. They had been placed there probably for the purpose of being afterwards sent for and brought away, and if such was the intention of the occupants of the house it had by some reason been frustrated. There were many signs, however, of a hasty departure, though why Master Pearson had suddenly gone away with his wife and reputed daughter Jack could not determine.

He feared, however, from the contents of the room which he had examined, that they must have gone to some distance, or otherwise these articles would probably have been sent for and brought away. Not a particle of food was to be found in the house, and it was therefore impossible for them to remain for the night, and Jack believed that there was time to return to the nearest village where accommodation could be obtained. He there also hoped to gain some information regarding Master Pearson's movements.

With heavy hearts the two horsemen mounted their steeds and took their way across the marsh. Night however closed in upon them before they were clear of it. At length a light appeared before them. It seemed to come from a cottage window close down to the ground. Jack was on the point of riding towards it, when he knew by the hesitation shown by his horse that he was approaching treacherous ground. At that instant the light vanished—again to appear, however, at a little distance farther off.

"Ah, how foolish I was to be tempted by such a 'will o' the wisp' as that!" he exclaimed. "We must keep away, my dear sir, to the left, and I hope ere long that we shall escape from this treacherous neighbourhood." He had been through a good many trying scenes, but he had never felt more perplexed than he did at this moment. He was grieved too, and sick at heart. Somewhat surprised also, perhaps, to find how much he felt the absence of Elizabeth, though he soon persuaded himself that it was more on his friend's account than his own. After riding some way, Jack did what under such circumstances is the only course to pursue. Going first himself, he allowed his horse to follow the path which his own instinct dictated; and by so doing, in the course of an hour the hoofs of his animal once more trod hard ground. In a short time afterwards a twinkling light appeared, far brighter, however, than the "will o' the wisp" which had before deceived them, and they rode up to the very inn which Jack had hoped to reach. The landlord was well pleased to see two well-equipped cavaliers arrive at his humble hostel, and under took to supply them with every thing they required. Jack's first inquiry, however, after Master Pearson, made him look more suspiciously at them.

"Master Pearson?" he said, "the farmer who lived out there in the fens? Ah, curious things have been told about him since he went away. I cannot exactly make out what to say about it."

"But where has he gone?" asked Jack eagerly; "can you tell me that?"

"No; nor no one either, master," he answered. "It's the better part of six months gone, when Bill Green, who was riding across the fen, made his way to the farm and found not a human soul there. Why they had gone, or how they had gone, or where they had gone, no one from that day to this can tell. The only thing we know is, that they did not come by this road, and so it is supposed that they made for the sea-coast. There was Master Pearson, and Mistress Pearson, who all said was a very good woman, and their young daughter; but not a servant or a follower of any sort did they take with them, that we know of. None of the farm-servants belonged to this part of the country, and they had all gone away some time before. Altogether the matter was a mystery, and is a mystery still to my belief."

This information given by Master Bowleggs, the landlord of the Goose and Goslings, was very unsatisfactory to Jack and his friend. They feared from the circumstantial way in which it was given them that it was too likely to be true. Jack had therefore great difficulty in keeping up the spirits of his companion. He undertook to make further inquiries in the neighbourhood, and to devote himself to the search for Elizabeth.

Leaving the anxious father at the little inn, Jack the next day rode off to call on the different people with whom he had been acquainted during his stay at the farm. Several days were employed in this manner, but none of those on whom he called could give him the slightest information. They all believed that Master Pearson had left the country, and some supposed that he had gone to one of the plantations in America, but that was only a surmise, as he had for some reason or other left no trace of the direction he had taken. Very unwillingly, therefore, Jack and his companion returned to Norwich.

Poor Madame de Mertens suffered greatly from the disappointment she felt at the account which her husband and John Deane brought. Her kind friends, however, entreated her to keep up her spirits, pointing out to her how thankful she should be at having her husband restored to her, and that the same kind Providence which had given her that blessing might yet further increase it by sending back to her her long-lost daughter.

Jack's mission at Norwich having been accomplished, though not in the satisfactory way he had hoped, he set forward to Nottingham. The greater part of his journey was speedily accomplished, and wishing to learn how matters were going on in that town, and also to arrive at home at an early hour of the day, he put up at his old friend the miller's, where he had stopped on his last visit to Harwood Grange. He had some difficulty in making the miller believe who he was, for from his dress and the arms he carried, the good man at first took him to be a highwayman, and even his dame would not believe for some time that he was the same lad she had known but a few years back. As far as he could learn, all his family at home were well, though the miller told him of the death of several people he knew. He inquired, not without some hesitation, about Harwood Grange and its owner.

"Ah! the Squire. He had to go abroad some years ago, about the matter, it was supposed, of Sir John Fenwick, whose head was cut off, you mind. Well, the poor gentleman never came back again, and it is believed that he took on so, about leaving his native land and horses and hounds, that he at last died. Certain it is that his daughter came into the property, and is now mistress of the Grange. Not that she lives there though, for I heard that she was going to marry some young gentleman in Nottingham, and she has taken up her abode there. Well, it is as well that she should give the Grange a master, for it is a pretty property, and it requires a gentleman to look after it."

This news was not over pleasant to Jack. He was sorry, certainly, to hear of the death of Mr Harwood, but the account of Alethea's intended marriage made his heart sink somewhat lower than it had ever sunk before. His only hope was that the miller's story might not be true. He could not believe that all his bright dreams should prove to be cruel unrealities just as he was returning home. He therefore answered the miller with as indifferent an air as he could, but the effort was somewhat vain, and the good dame, observing that he must be tired after his long journey, recommended him as soon as supper was over to seek his bed.

Chapter Twenty Seven
Returns Home

Next morning John Deane set out to Nottingham, mounted on his strong horse, with a hanger slung to a sash over his shoulder, a laced coat, having an undoubted nautical cut about it, with a cocked hat, his waistcoat with long flaps, also richly embroidered. Altogether, with his hat cocked rakishly on one side, though he was unaware of the fact, he presented a gallant and bold appearance. He was just crossing the bridge over the Trent, into the town, when he saw a party of ladies and gentlemen on horseback approaching him. First came a gentleman in a laced riding-suit, wearing a fair peruke with a buckle, as the mode then was, engaged in low conversation with a young lady in a cherry-coloured riding-habit, her long hair hanging in loose curls over her shoulders. In the first he recognised his brother Jasper, and in the lady, the fair Alethea. She glanced slightly at Jack's bronzed countenance, surrounded by a bushy beard and whiskers, and well-knit figure. He drew his horse on one side to let the party pass. But though she looked up a second time, she evidently did not recognise him, nor did his brother.

Following them came another young gentleman with his merry sister Polly by his side. She was laughing loudly, as was her wont, either at her own jokes or at something her companion had said. Jack fully thought that she at all events would find him out, but she was possibly too much engaged in her own pleasant thoughts to do so, for though she gave a look at the naval gallant whom she was passing, she took no further notice of him.

"I won't stop them," thought Jack, "but go home and have a talk with father and mother first; and if Jasper is the gentleman who it is said is going to marry Alethea, the sooner I'm off to sea again the better! It looked something like it, for it's certain he never used to dress so bravely; and, by the way he was looking at her, I cannot help thinking it's too true. Well, I wish him every happiness. There's no use repining; and I don't see how I could have expected it to be otherwise. Of course he would fall in love with her; and she certainly never gave me any reason to suppose that she cared especially for me."

Such were the thoughts which occupied his mind as he rode up to the well-known door of his father's house in the market-place. The servant who opened the door bowed respectfully to the gallant stranger who was inquiring for Mistress Deane, and Jack had actually entered the parlour, where his mother was sitting with her knitting in hand, and been desired to take a seat, when he wonderfully astonished the old lady by springing up and throwing his arms round her neck. She knew him then well enough; and after giving him a maternal embrace in return, holding him by both hands, she looked again and again into his honest countenance, as if to trace his well-known features.

"Yes, Jack," she exclaimed, "you are my boy! I would not believe any one who told me otherwise, though the sun and the sea air have given you a more brazen face than I ever expected you would wear, and you have grown into a big, sturdy young man, well able to fight the king's enemies."

Old Mr Deane soon afterwards entered, hearing that a stranger had been inquiring for him. He confessed that if Mistress Deane had not been there to swear to him he should scarcely have known his own son.

Jack did not allow any thoughts which would mar his happiness to intrude while he sat between his kind parents, each of them holding one of his hands in theirs, while he gave them an account of his various proceedings since he had last written, among which he described his rescue of the Dutch gentleman, and his visit to Mr Gournay. His mother told him of Mr Harwood's supposed death abroad.

"Yes, dame. It was not so unfortunate, however," observed Mr Deane; "the poor gentleman was so deeply implicated in the Jacobite plots, that he would have lost his property if he had come back; but through the interest of many friends, and I may say I was one of them, we contrived to preserve his estates for Alethea. Poor man! his last days were very sad. He went to James's court at Saint Germain's, where he expected to be received with respect, as having suffered in the cause of the king. He wrote me an account of his visit. The palace in which James resided was magnificent. A handsome pension was allowed him by the French king, and he had guards, and a large establishment of hounds and huntsmen, and every means of amusing himself. He was, however, surrounded by ecclesiastics who ruled every thing, including the king himself. Nothing indeed could be more dull than the life spent by the courtiers, their sole employment appearing to be backbiting each other. Mr Harwood soon found also that he himself had committed a great crime in the eyes of those by whom he was surrounded. He was a Protestant. He, with all the other Protestant Jacobites who appeared at the court, were treated with the greatest indignity by the

Roman Catholics. In every instance the Roman Catholic was preferred to the Protestant, and in every quarrel the Roman Catholic was supposed to be right. Several Protestant clergy who had given up their livings, and sacrificed every thing in the cause of James, were grossly insulted by the Romish priests. When they requested to be allowed to hold a service for their Protestant countrymen, their prayers were refused. The Protestant ministers were kept away from the death-beds of the Protestants, who were allowed to be beset by the Romish priests; these men endeavouring by all the arts they possessed, and often by force, to win them over to their church. Several Royalists, indeed, who died, were denied a Christian burial, and were thrown into holes dug in the fields at the dead of night, without any form or ceremony. The unfortunate Earl of Dunfermline, who had lost every thing for James, and had fought bravely for him at the battle of Killiecrankie, was treated in this way. While alive, he had been grossly insulted on several occasions. A number of Scotch officers who had served under him, requested that they might be formed into a company, and that he might be placed at their head; but this was refused on the plea that he was a Protestant, and therefore unfit to command men serving a Catholic prince. Those only who at the last gasp, scarcely conscious what was being done, were turned into Catholics, by having the consecrated wafer thrust into their mouths, were buried with all the pomp of the Romish Church. Poor Mr Harwood expressed his fears that he should be treated in the same way. He died at last of a broken heart, though he was able a short time before his death to remove from the court. His account shows us how James would have acted had he recovered the English throne, and we may be truly thankful to heaven that he was prevented from obtaining his wishes."

Mrs Deane and Jack heartily responded to this sentiment.

"You know Alethea, Jack? a pretty, sweet girl she is, I can assure you; though you saw so little of her, that you might not have discovered her good qualities," continued the old gentleman.

Jack's heart sank somewhat. He expected to hear his father give an account of the intended marriage of Alethea to Jasper. The old gentleman went on for some time enlarging on her beauty and accomplishments, and other attractive qualities.

"Your father means to say, Jack, that it has not been her fortune which has captivated your brother Jasper, for you must know that he has won her heart, and in the course of another week is to possess her hand. You have just come in time for the wedding. I am sure it will be a great pleasure to you to see Jasper made happy, as it adds greatly to our pleasure to have you back again amongst us."

Poor Jack's heart sank down to zero. His worst anticipations were thus realised. For some moments his head was in a whirl, and he knew not what to say. He speedily, however, recovered himself.

"I am thankful to hear of Jasper's expected happiness," he forced himself to say at last. He said it sincerely in one sense, for he loved his brother, and he felt that if Alethea was not to be his, he was glad that she should become Jasper's wife.

The time passed so rapidly, that he was surprised when at length the riding-party returned just in time to get ready for dinner. His brother and sister were truly glad to see him. Alethea received him with some little embarrassment, not that she was conscious of having given him any encouragement; but she recollected how she had endeavoured to draw him into the Jacobite plot, and she fancied that she was the principal cause of separating him from his family and sending him away to sea. Polly and her intended husband, who was something in her own style, soon, by the racket they made, and the shouts of laughter in which they indulged, drove away any thing like sentiment, and set every body at their ease. Kind cousin Nat shortly made his appearance, and holding Jack at arm's length, scanned him all over.

"I was not quite certain when I first saw you whether you were a buccaneer from the Spanish Main, or some other cavalier of fortune; but I now see that you are my own honest, good Jack, in spite of your somewhat ferocious appearance!" he exclaimed, shaking him by both hands. "You should get yourself, however, trimmed and docked, Jack, and you will be much more presentable in polite society."

Jack had not come without a few curiosities and trinkets which had been collected on board the prizes, or taken on shore. He was thus able to bestow some acceptable presents upon the intended brides.

Again the old house in the market-place was the scene of festivity. Two couples were to pledge their faith to each other, and guests from far and near assembled to do honour to the occasion. Jack wrung Jasper's hand.

"I wish you every happiness the world can give you!" he exclaimed, though as he spoke his voice trembled and the tears stood in his eyes.

Alethea looked more beautiful and attractive than she had ever done before, and Polly was more merry and full of life, not a bit abashed by the ceremony through which she then had to go. Jack performed his part well throughout the whole of it, and in the evening no one danced more lightly and merrily, or laughed louder than did he. At supper he sang some of his best sea-songs; and every one declared that Jack Deane was one of the finest young fellows who had appeared at Nottingham for many a long day.

Nottingham at that time could boast of some of the most agreeable society to be met out of London. It had been assigned as the residence of Marshall Tallard, the opponent of the great Duke of Marlborough at the battle of Blenheim, who was now a prisoner of war with a number of other gallant and polished French officers, who bore their captivity with resignation and cheerfulness, making themselves perfectly at home, and doing their best to amuse those among whom they lived.

Several curious traditions of their stay in the town still linger there. It was a French prisoner who first observed celery growing wild on the rock on which Nottingham Castle stands, Alainon Franchise, and having cultivated it successfully in his own little garden, he made that pleasant addition to English tables, from that time forth common every where throughout the kingdom. French rolls were also introduced from a receipt sent by the Marshall himself to a baker in Bridlesmith-gate.

It had been arranged that cousin Nat should reside with Jasper Deane, to whom he purposed giving up his practice when he should retire, which he expected to do in the course of a few years.

Jack was received in a friendly way wherever he went. The errors and wild pranks of the boy were entirely forgotten, when it was known that he had been fighting bravely for his king and country, and that he had by his own good conduct gained the rank he already held in the navy.

Jack, however, very soon got tired of leading an idle life. Routs and card-parties were not at all to his taste, and although Nottingham was not destitute of damsels possessed of a fair amount of beauty, he did not find himself attracted by any of them. He had speedily taught himself to think no more of Alethea, but in her stead another young and pretty form often rose up before him. He met with no one indeed, in his opinion, to be compared with sweet little Elizabeth Pearson, or rather, as he believed she should be called, Elise de Mertens. He made up his mind, therefore, to leave home at a short notice and hasten down to Portsmouth, where he saw in the columns of the *Post-boy* that a fleet was fitting out, under the brave Admiral Benbow, for the West Indies.

Chapter Twenty Eight
Serves under Benbow in the West Indies

It was early in March in the year 1702. As Jack Deane was approaching London, he heard a postman shouting, "Sad news! sad news!"

"What is it?" asked Jack.

"The king is dead!" was the answer. "Our good King William is no more!"

Jack, on making further inquiry, learned that the king had, on Saturday, 21st, gone out to hunt, as was his custom, near Hampton Court, when his horse fell, and he fractured his collar-bone. The injury was not considered serious, and he was conveyed to his palace at Kensington. Having been, however, in a very weak state, he did not rally, and it was evident to those around him that he was near his end. On the 8th of March one of the best and most sagacious of English monarchs breathed his last, holding the hand of the faithful Duke of Portland. His voice had gone ere that; but his reason and all his senses were entire to the last. He died with a clear and full presence of mind, and with a wonderful tranquillity.

On the accession of Queen Anne, the Jacobites remained quiet, under the belief that she would leave the crown to the son of James the Second, now known as the Chevalier Saint George. They were not aware of the sound Protestant principles of the great mass of Englishmen, and that any attempt to bring back a Romanist member of the hated House of Stuart, so often tried and found utterly unfit for ruling, would have produced another civil war. Those infatuated men, the Jacobites, did not conceal their joy at the death of the Protestant monarch. Banquets were held among them to celebrate the event, and some had the audacity and wickedness, it may be said, to toast the health of the horse which had thrown William. Another toast they drank was to the health of the little gentleman dressed in velvet, in other words, the mole that raised the hill over which Sorel (the king's favourite horse) stumbled.

Jack Deane on hearing these things felt as if, had he been present, he should have been very much inclined to challenge those who showed this disrespect to a sovereign whom he had learned to honour and love.

The fleet had taken its departure some time before John Deane reached Portsmouth, but he found a fast frigate on the point of sailing to carry despatches to the admiral, the "Venus." Admiral Benbow's object in going out to the West Indies had been to detain the Spanish galleons. When war was declared on the accession of Queen Anne, a French admiral had also sailed from Brest for the same station, with fourteen sail of the line and sixteen frigates, to meet the galleons and convoy them to Cadiz. Although the brave Benbow's squadron was far smaller than that of the French, he kept a sharp look-out for the enemy. He had performed many services in the West Indies to the merchants by capturing privateers and protecting their settlements from the attacks of the enemy.

Admiral Benbow's ship was the "Breda," of seventy guns, and her youngest lieutenant having died of fever, Jack Deane, greatly to his satisfaction, found himself appointed to that ship. Early in July, the admiral sailed from Jamaica, with seven sail of men-of-war, in the hope of joining Admiral Whitstone, who had been sent from England with a reinforcement to endeavour to intercept the French squadron which had sailed under Monsieur Du Casse. The admiral on the 10th of August, being off Donna Maria Bay, received advice that Du Casse had sailed for Carthagena and Portobello. He instantly went in quest of him, and in the evening of the 19th, discovered off Santa Martha ten sail of ships. On his nearer approach he found the greatest number of them to be French men-of-war. Four ships of from sixty to seventy guns, one great Dutch ship of about thirty or forty guns, and another full of soldiers, the rest being of a smaller size. They were steering along shore under their topsails. The admiral made a signal to form a line of battle ahead, and bore away under an easy sail, that those to leeward might the more readily get into their station. It was the admiral's intention not to make the signal of battle but only of defiance, when he had got abreast of the enemy's headmost ship. Before he reached his station, however, the "Falmouth," which was in the rear, began to fire, as did also the "Windsor" and "Advance," and soon after the Vice-Admiral was engaged; and now an act was performed which has rarely happened in the British Navy. After exchanging two or three broadsides, the "Windsor" and "Advance" luffed to windward out of gunshot, and left the admiral exposed to the fire of the two sternmost ships of the enemy, by whom he was very much galled. Neither did the ships in the rear come up to his assistance with the alacrity he expected. In spite of this, the brave Benbow continued to engage the enemy from four o'clock until night, and although the latter then ceased firing, yet he kept sight of them, intending to renew the action in the morning. On the following day at daybreak he found himself close to the enemy, with the "Ruby" only near enough to support him. Unintimidated by the misconduct of those who had so shamefully deserted him, he pursued the enemy, who were using every effort to escape. The "Ruby" in a short time was so dreadfully knocked about that he was obliged to order her to return to Port Royal. Two more days passed away, and still the brave old admiral kept up the pursuit. On the morning of the 24th, he got up with the sternmost ships of the French, and although receiving but little assistance from the rest of the squadron he brought them to close action. Round-shot, and chain-shot, and langrage came flying on board the "Breda," the British seamen sending back much the same sort of missiles as those with which they were complimented. Volumes of smoke from the guns rolled out of the ports. Still undaunted, and excited by the example of their brave admiral, the British sailors fought on. At length a shot swept across the quarter-deck, on which the admiral was standing. He was seen to fall. His right leg was shattered by it. Immediately he was carried below. He urged the surgeons to dress the wound as rapidly as they could, and then being placed in his cradle, he directed himself to be brought once more on the deck. There, in spite of the agony he was suffering, he continued to give his orders. One of the last he issued was to direct the other captains to "keep the line and behave like men." Great was his grief, vexation, and rage, when the recreant captains came on board and declared that enough had been done, and that it would be dangerous to follow the enemy. In vain the old admiral pleaded with them. They persisted that by so doing they would ensure the destruction of their ships and crews. Wounded and sick at heart he had at length to yield to them, and he issued the order for the squadron to return to Jamaica. Here the brave old admiral was carried on shore, and shortly afterwards died of the wound he had received. The captains who had refused to support him were tried by a court-martial, and two of them were carried home and shot on the decks of their ships, as soon as they arrived in an English port.

To return to John Deane. Soon after the "Breda" reached Port Royal, as she was likely to remain there for some time, and he was anxious for active employment, he got re-appointed to the "Venus," which was sent to cruise for the protection of British commerce.

As soon as the frigate was clear of the island, a bright look-out was kept for the French privateers or any other of the enemy's vessels. The frigate had been cruising for a week or more, and had already got some distance from Jamaica, having during the time captured several small vessels, some of which had been destroyed and others sent to Port Royal, when one forenoon a large ship was descried to leeward. All sail was crowded in chase, and as the frigate had the advantage of the wind, the stranger being almost becalmed, she soon came up with her.

As soon as the breeze reached the stranger, without hoisting her colours, she made all sail in an attempt to escape. Various opinions were offered as to her character. Some thought she was a Spanish galleon, though how she should have come thus far north was a question not easily answered. Others believed she was a large French merchantman, and some pronounced her to be a privateer. She was a fast craft, at all events, for as soon as she felt the breeze she slipped through the water at a rate which made it doubtful whether the "Venus" would come up with her. This made the English still more anxious for her capture, as, in the first place, if a merchantman, she was likely to have a rich cargo on board, and at all events she might be converted into a useful cruiser.

It was a general opinion in those days that the French vessels were faster sailers than the English, and certain it is that many of the best models of men-of-war were taken from the French. The Genoese, however, were reputed to be better ship-builders than either. A stern chase is a long chase always. The stranger persevered in her flight, in the hope that some accident might secure her escape. The English pursued in the hope that an accident to the chase might enable them to capture her.

The day wore on, and fears were entertained that the chase would escape during the darkness of the night. Every stitch of canvas which the frigate could carry was set on her, while the sails which could be reached were kept constantly wet, that no wind might pass through them. The crew cheered with glee when they found that their efforts were not without good effect, and that the frigate at last was overhauling the chase. At length she got near enough to fire a bow-chaser. The shot took effect, and cut away several of her braces. This allowed the sails to fly wildly in the air. In consequence, the frigate now came up more rapidly, and, as she did so, continued firing with good effect. The chase at length let fly all her sheets, and hauled down the French flag, which had just before been run up. As soon as the frigate hove to, Lieutenant Deane was ordered to board the prize with a boat's crew. She proved to be a rich merchant vessel outward-bound to the French colonies on the Main, with a large and valuable assorted cargo, and was evidently a prize worth taking.

The captain of the "Venus" was ordered to send in his prizes, as he should take them, to Port Royal, but as long as he had sufficient men to fight his ship not to return himself. It was important, however, that so rich a prize should be carefully navigated, and he accordingly ordered his junior lieutenant—John Deane—to take charge of her with a crew of fifteen men, to carry her into Port Royal. Ten of her former crew volunteered to assist in navigating her, and they were allowed to remain, while the rest, with the captain and officers, were carried on board the "Venus."

Jack now found himself for the first time in his life in command of a large ship. As may be supposed, he had not been asleep all the time he had been at sea, and he already possessed a very good knowledge of seamanship, as well as of navigation. He had no doubt, therefore, that he should be able safely to carry his prize to her destined port.

Two midshipmen were sent with him to act as lieutenants, and an old quarter-master to do the duty of boatswain. Jack was a great favourite among all with whom he had served, both with his superiors and with those beneath him. His two young midshipmen—Dick Lovatt and Ned Hawke— had become particularly-attached to him, while Will Burridge, the old quarter-master, would have gone through fire and water to serve him.

On one occasion, Burridge, whether he had had too much Jamaica rum on board or not it was difficult to say, managed to fall overboard into the harbour swarming with sharks. As the tide was running strong at the time, Burridge had already been swept some distance from the ship before he was perceived. Jack, regardless of the sharks, leaped overboard, and swimming towards the sinking seaman, kept him up, splashing about so as to make the monsters of the deep keep at a respectful distance till a boat arrived to take them both on board. Jack declared it was not a thing to be talked about, any body might have done the same, and therefore it was not mentioned at the time of its occurrence. It however raised Deane's character among the crew, and made them all ready to volunteer in any expedition where he was to lead.

As soon as the damages which the prize had received were repaired, the frigate stood on her course, and Jack made sail for Port Royal. The prize was called the "Coquille," and carried twelve guns, so that Jack hoped, should he be attacked by one of the enemy's privateers, or any small man-of-war, he might make a good fight of it, and beat off his opponent if he could not take her.

The first day the weather was very fine; the wind then fell, and there was a dead calm. The sun struck down with intense heat on the deck of the vessel, making the very pitch in her seams bubble up. The crew began to feel the effects of the heat, and moved languidly about the decks, exhibiting a listlessness very different to their usual activity. Jack with one of his officers was sitting below at dinner, when Hawke, the other, who had the watch on deck, entered the cabin.

"I thought it as well to tell you, sir," he said, "that I don't quite like the way the Frenchmen are carrying on. I have observed them for some time past whispering together, and I cannot help thinking that they expect to find us napping, and to set on us and try to retake the vessel."

"It's as well to be prepared," answered Jack. "Thank you for your forethought. But it will scarcely be right to put them in irons, unless we have evidence of their intention. I will tell Burridge, and hint to the men to be on the look-out, so that we shall be even with the Monsieurs if they make the attempt which you fancy they purpose."

Burridge soon made his appearance in the cabin, hat in hand, and receiving his directions hurried back to speak to the English crew. Jack and his two young officers, having loaded their pistols and stuck them in their belts, and fastened on their swords, made their appearance also on deck. The Frenchmen seemed to be watching them; but if they had any sinister intentions, the preparations which Jack had made to oppose them compelled them for the moment to keep quiet.

Chapter Twenty Nine
Hurricane—Captured by Pirates

Jack had not had much experience with the West India climate; but he had heard enough of the signs preceding a hurricane to make him somewhat anxious about the state of the weather. Gradually a thick mist seemed to be overspreading the sky, while there was not a breath of wind sufficient to move a feather in the rigging.

"We shall have the wind down upon us presently," he observed to Hawke. "We will clue up every thing, and strike the topgallant-masts. If the wind does not come it will be no great harm, as it will only give the Frenchmen something more to do; and if it does come, and we have all this gear aloft, it will be carried away to a certainty."

The order was immediately issued, and the hands flew aloft to carry it out. Before, however, the canvas was all secured, a white line of foam was seen rushing towards the ship, extending on either side as far as the eye could reach. On it came, rising in height, while a loud roar burst on the ears of the crew.

"Down for your lives, men, down!" shouted Jack, as the ship, struck by the furious blast, heeled over.

Some obeyed the summons and slid down on deck in time; but others, who did not hear the order, remained aloft, many in their terror clinging to spars and shrouds, unable to move. Over heeled the stout ship. The masts like willow-wands bent, and then, snapping in two, were carried away to leeward. The lower yards dipped in the water, and most of those upon them were torn away from their grasp, while others were hurled to a distance from the ship. For a few minutes she lay helplessly on her beam-ends, then happily feeling the power of her helm, which was put up, the canvas at the same time being blown away, her head paid off, and righting herself she flew before the gale. In vain the poor wretches who had been hurled into the water shrieked for help. No human help could reach them! In a few minutes they were left far behind, while the ship, lately so trim and gallant, was hurried on, too likely to meet that destruction which overtook many other stout vessels at that time. More than half the English crew had been lost, and only one of the Frenchmen, so that their numbers were now more equal.

On flew the ship. The sea torn and thrown up by the force of the hurricane, loud-roaring billows foamed and hissed on either side, while darkness soon came on to add to the horrors of the scene.

Undaunted, Jack and his crew exerted themselves to clear away the wreck of the masts and spars. The fearful working of the ship, however, made it too probable that if not very strongly-built, she would spring a leak and go down. Every instant the seas grew higher and higher, and it was with difficulty that she could be kept before the wind. Her boats were washed away by the seas which broke on board, and though often she was in danger of being pooped by those which dashed against her stern, still she floated on.

When morning at length dawned, the hurricane began to abate. The wind ceased almost as rapidly as it had commenced; but the once stout ship, now almost a wreck, rolled heavily in the still tumbling seas. As yet little could be done to get her put to rights. She was still at a considerable distance from Jamaica, and with his diminished crew, Jack saw that it would take some time to rig jury-masts, and thus enable him to shape a proper course for Port Royal. As soon, however, as the sea went sufficiently down, and the ship became steadier, he ordered the crew to commence the work. His own men willingly obeyed; but the Frenchmen walked forward sullenly, declaring that there would be no use in exerting themselves, and positively refusing to work. While they were acting thus, Burridge brought him word that several had, by some means or other, got hold of fire-arms and hangers, and were evidently prepared for mischief.

"We must watch our opportunity, and try to disarm them," observed John Deane. "Work they must, by some means or other, or else they must be put in irons."

To do this, however, was no easy task, considering that there were as many Frenchmen as Englishmen, and the former were evidently desperate fellows. Hawke was fortunately able to speak French very well, and Jack directed him therefore to address the mutineers, and ask them again whether they would assist in putting the ship into order. A flat refusal was the answer, and thus the whole day was occupied. The following night was one of great anxiety, as it became necessary to keep a constant watch over the Frenchmen, lest they should suddenly attack the English and attempt to regain the ship. Jack did not allow himself a moment's rest, but continued, with arms by his side, pacing the deck, while a constant watch was kept on the movements of the mutineers.

Dawn at length broke; and soon after the sun rose above the horizon its bright rays struck on the sails of a large vessel which was seen standing towards the "Coquille," with a light breeze then blowing. Jack anxiously watched her through his glass, hoping, from the cut of her sails, that she might prove an English man-of-war. As she came on, he hoisted on the stump of the main-mast the English ensign reversed, the signal of distress. On the nearer approach of the stranger, however, Deane observed that the English flag was not hoisted in return, which would have been the case had she been a friend. If she had been at sea during the hurricane, she had escaped wonderfully well, for her masts and yards were as trim as if she had just come out of port. Her decks, too, seemed crowded with men. In a short time, running under the stern of the "Coquille," she "hove to," and a man with a speaking-trumpet hailed from her deck, demanding the name of the vessel, and where she was bound to.

"A prize to Her Majesty's ship 'Venus,' and bound for Port Royal," answered Jack.

"And very little chance you'll have of getting there," replied the man with the speaking-trumpet, "We will send a boat aboard you and see about the matter."

In another minute two well-armed boats were lowered from the stranger, and soon came alongside the "Coquille." Their crews jumped on board.

"You have been caught in the hurricane, I see," said the man who seemed to act as the officer. "What is your cargo?"

Jack told him.

"Lucky for us, then, that you did not go down," was the answer. "And now set to work and get the ship in order. You must understand that you are a prize to the 'Black Hawk,' belonging to a company of gentlemen adventurers. There's no use grumbling: it's the fortune of war. And now bear a hand and get your ship to rights as fast as you can. We will help you, and carry you safely into port, though not the port maybe you were bound for."

Jack's heart sank within him when he heard this. Resistance would be utterly useless. Even had the Frenchmen remained faithful, the pirates, for such he had little doubt they were, numbered ten to one of his own diminished crew. At first he and his young officers felt disposed to refuse to work, but Burridge, an experienced old seaman, strongly advised them to obey.

"There's no use whatsomever, sir, to quarrel with these sort of gentry," he observed. "They would as likely as not make a man walk the plank if they're angry with him, and if we don't try to please them they will probably send every one of us to be food for the sharks before another day passes over our heads."

Jack saw the wisdom of this advice, so, putting the best face on the matter he could, he ordered his own people to commence the work he had been about to carry out when the pirate appeared. The Frenchmen were quickly made to change their tone, and the pirates, observing that they did not work with as good a will as the English, kept pricking them on, every now and then, with the points of their swords, amusing themselves greatly at the sight of the grimaces which were made in consequence of this treatment.

Poor Jack! this was the greatest trial he had ever gone through in his life. After having fully expected to enter Port Royal in triumph with a fine prize, thus to have it snatched from him by a band of rascally pirates! Still he did the best to keep up his spirits, hoping that some opportunity might occur to enable him ere long to make his escape.

"It cannot be helped," observed Burridge, "and 'what cannot be cured, must be endured,' as my old woman used to say when she allowed the porridge to burn on the fire. It's a long lane too, you know, sir, which has no turning, and though maybe these gentry will make us do a few things we shall not like, still, as long as they don't cut our throats, we will manage some day or other to get clear of them."

The pirates, to do them justice, were not idle themselves. A considerable number more now came on board to help get the ship into order, as it was very evident to them that she was a valuable prize. As soon as sail could be made on the ship, Jack and his officers were ordered to keep to their cabins, as he supposed, to prevent them ascertaining the direction which the ship was steering. This, so far, proved satisfactory, as it proved that the pirates had no immediate intention of taking their lives. Three days thus passed away, when from the perfectly smooth way in which the vessel glided on, Deane suspected that they were entering some harbour. The midshipmen were of the same opinion, and Hawke volunteered to try to reach the deck, to ascertain where they had got to. On going out, however, he found a sentry at the door, who ordered him back, telling him, that without the captain's leave they would not be allowed to leave their cabin. In a short time longer, the sound of the anchor let go, and the perfect stillness of the ship, convinced Jack that he was right in his conjectures. Soon after this a person they had not before seen came to the cabin.

"Now, friends," he said, "if you are wise men, you will enter with us and cut the service to which you have belonged. We don't serve either king or queen, and have only ourselves to obey, while instead of handing over the profits of our labours to others we keep them for ourselves. We have a jovial life of it. No lack of adventure and excitement, and as much gold and silver as we can pick up, though, to be sure, we now and then have a little fighting for it, but that only adds to its value. What say you, lads? Will you join us?"

"Thank you for your polite offer," answered Deane, "but we are well content with the service in which we're engaged, and have no fancy for changing it. We, too, have plenty of fighting, and can generally scrape up as much gold as we want."

"Enough is as good as a feast," observed Burridge; "and I'll tell you what, sir, with due respect to you, we would rather serve Queen Anne than King Mobb Sogg, or any other king in or out of Christendom; and though you gentlemen buccaneers are very fine fellows, we have no fancy just at present of becoming one of your number."

"It would have been better for you if you had made up your minds to follow my advice," answered the pirate officer; "I should have been able to set you at liberty at once and let you wander all over our island. As it is, you must be content to remain shut up on board, or maybe on shore, where we have a sort of prison which is sometimes useful."

Jack and his companions were in no way ill-treated, except in being confined to the cabin, while an abundance of provisions were brought to them. From the noises they heard they judged that the cargo of the vessel was being taken out of her, and they hoped when that was done that some change or other might take place in their condition. They had no fancy to remain prisoners for ever, and they determined that if not released by their captors, they would endeavour if possible to escape by themselves. Burridge had been allowed to join them in the cabin. He told them he was afraid that the rest of the crew had joined the pirates, as they had all left the vessel shouting and singing, and apparently in very good-humour. He alone had refused to do so, in spite of the threats of punishment which the pirates uttered.

"I have sworn to fight for our country and for our new queen, and I intend to do so as long as there is life in me," he observed.

In those days the bands of buccaneers which had made themselves a terror to the Spaniards had been dispersed. At the peace of Ryswick, finding that their occupation was gone, and that they would not long receive the support of the English government, many of them accepted offers of land in the plantations and became settlers. Those who were unwilling to lead a quiet life turned regular pirates, mostly hoisting black flags, with some hideous device, such as skulls and crossbones, and attacked all nations indiscriminately. Deane fully believed that he had fallen into the hands of characters of this sort, though he was surprised that they had hitherto treated him and his companions with so much leniency.

At length an officer visited them. He was a fierce-looking fellow, with his broad-brimmed hat and leather cocked on one side. A huge belt was slung across his shoulders, in which two or three brace of pistols were stuck. A hanger was by his side, with a silk coat covered with gold lace, while his face was adorned with a large moustache and a long black beard.

"Well, my hearties," he exclaimed as he entered, "I hope you like being shut up here like dogs in a kennel! It's a strange fancy if you do; to my mind, it would be better to have your freedom and enjoy yourselves on shore. What would you say, now, if I was to offer it you?"

"We should be obliged to you, master," answered Jack; "for we should like to stretch our legs on shore amazingly."

"Ah, that's sensible!" answered the visitor; "but you must agree to my terms if you do."

"That may alter the case," said Jack. "Let us hear your terms though, and we may judge whether we can accept them."

"Ah, they're easy enough!" said their visitor. "All you have to do, is to swear to be faithful to our fraternity, and if you're ordered to draw your sword and fight on our side, you will do it, even though our enemies should be your former friends."

"This is only mockery!" exclaimed Jack. "If you tell us to draw our swords against our countrymen, we tell you at once, we would die rather than do so!"

"Then you must remain prisoners, and be treated as such," answered their visitor. "However, as this craft will prove a fine cruiser, we are going to fit her out for sea, and if you don't choose to go in her, you will have to come on shore."

The pirate continued talking much in this way for some time, but without producing any effect upon his hearers. At last he got angry, and, slamming the door after him, went on deck. He soon returned, however, with a dozen men, whom he ordered to take charge of the four prisoners and to convey them on shore. They were accordingly marched up on deck, where for the first time Jack was enabled to examine the place into which the ship had been carried. It was a large lagoon, the entrance from the sea being so narrow that he could with difficulty make it out. Cocoanut and palm-trees thickly lined the shore, between which a few huts were seen, but no rising ground was visible, and Deane conjectured that they were on one of the quays which are to be found in the neighbourhood of Saint Domingo, and which had been the resort for many ages of pirates. The boat in which they were placed proceeded up the lagoon for some distance, when they were landed on one side of it, and surrounded by their guards and marched up away from the water. In a short time some huts of considerably larger dimensions than those they had already seen were reached, and one of them was pointed out as their future prison. It was close to the other houses, and was one of the largest in the village. Being ordered to go in, the door was closed behind them. It had, however, the advantage of a window, which, though strongly grated, gave them light and air, and enabled them to look out. It was, in other respects, a very undesirable residence, the furniture consisting of merely a couple of rough stools and a bench, with a rickety table.

"I am afraid, sir, we've fallen out of the frying-pan into the fire," observed Burridge, as he surveyed the apartment. "On board we had our beds to sleep on, and decent furniture, but here we have nothing to boast of, of that sort, while I'm afraid it will be more than ever difficult for us to get away."

It seemed but too likely that they were to be starved into compliance with the pirates' wishes, for hour after hour passed away and no provisions were brought them. At length Burridge, who had been examining the place, expressed his belief that they might be able to work their way through the roof, and so get out.

"If they attempt to starve us, it's a thing we must do," he observed; "and it will be hard if we go foraging about the island and cannot find any food; and then if it's impossible to get off, we must e'en before morning get back into our present prison, and maybe it will not be discovered that we have ever left it."

The two midshipmen were delighted with this proposal, though Deane doubted somewhat that it would be carried out. Their only amusement was looking out of the window, which there was room for two of them to do at a time; but it was too small to allow more than that number to look out of it together. Now and then people were seen moving about, and passing at a distance from the prison; but no one came near enough for the prisoners to speak to them. Jack determined to do so if he could, however, that he might try to ascertain something more of the character of the people among whom they had fallen. He had been looking out for some time when he saw a person approaching, whom, by his dress and gay sash full of pistols, his hat with a feather, and the rich, jewelled hilt to his sword, he concluded was an officer. The man turned his face for an instant up to the window. Although his hair was somewhat grizzled and his beard bushy and long, partly concealing his face, the conviction flashed across Jack's mind that he was no other than Master Pearson, as he called himself, with whom he had parted in the fens of Lincolnshire! The man turned away and passed on; but from his gait and manner, Deane felt still more convinced that he was not mistaken. Instantly a number of thoughts crowded into his mind. Was he there alone, or had he brought with him his wife and reputed daughter? Robber and outlaw as he might be in England, Deane still thought he was not debased enough to place them in so dangerous a position; and yet if they were not with him, where could he have left them? The one redeeming quality of the man was his devotion to his wife and the affection with which he seemed to regard the little Elizabeth.

Jack felt more than ever anxious that he might get out of prison that he might solve this question. Still, if it was Pearson, he had no wish to make himself known to him. He felt also a disinclination to mention the circumstances by which he had become acquainted with the man to his companions. He thought over and over again how he should act; but at the end of the time had arrived at no conclusion.

Chapter Thirty
Imprisonment in the Pirates'
Island—The Lovers' Meeting

Notwithstanding the fears of the prisoners, the pirates seemed to have no intention of starving them, for in a short time a man came to the hut with an ample supply of cooked meat and a basket containing several bottles of wine.

"There, mates," he said, "our captain sent you these things, and advises you to think over the matter our chief mate spoke to you about the other day. You will judge how we fare ourselves by the way we treat you."

As there was food enough to last for some time they naturally expected they should not receive another visit during the day. As soon, therefore, as they had satisfied their hunger, Burridge continued his examination of the roof, and found, by removing the bamboo rafters, he could without difficulty force his way out through it. He proposed, therefore, as soon as it was dark, to get out and find his way down to the shore, as, in all probability, the island being but small, he could do so without difficulty. He thought then that if a boat or a small vessel could be found, they might all manage to get on board and make their escape without being discovered.

"You see," he observed, "all is fish which comes to the nets of these gentlemen, and they will take small craft as well as large vessels. They are very likely to have captured a small schooner or sloop, and to have brought her into the harbour. They're certain also, if they have done so, not to keep any strict watch over her, and if we 'bide our time we shall find a way of getting on board without interruption. I have heard of the doings of these gentry, and, depend upon it, some night they will be having a carouse when no one will be on the look-out."

These remarks of the honest boatswain raised the spirits of his companions, and they determined, at all risks, to take advantage of the opportunity should it occur. The midshipmen proposed that the whole party should go together; but this Jack over-ruled, considering that should any body come to the hut and find it empty, search would be made for them, whereas by only one being absent, discovery was less likely. As soon, therefore, as it was dark Burridge made his way through the roof, and they heard him drop gently to the ground on the other side of the hut. He immediately afterwards came round to the window.

"All right, sir," he said; "I saw the glimmer of the water when I was on the top of the hut, and I shall easily find my way to it. The pirates are carousing down by the huts on the shore, for I heard their voices singing and shouting, so I shall have a good chance of not being found out."

Saying this Burridge glided away through the cocoanut grove by which the village was surrounded.

His companions waited anxiously for his return.

"If he is taken, I have a fancy they would not hesitate to send a pistol-bullet through his head," said Hawke. "I wish that I could have gone with him, Mr Deane."

"You would only have shared his fate, and so have gained nothing, and done him no good," answered Jack. "Let us wait patiently: he has his wits about him, and he will take good care not to be caught."

Two or three hours passed by and still Burridge did not make his appearance. His companions grew more and more anxious, both on his account and on their own. If he was taken their prospect of escape would be much lessened. In Jack's mind also a new difficulty had arisen. Even supposing that the opportunity should occur of escaping, he could not bring himself to leave the island without ascertaining whether Dame Pearson and Elizabeth were residing on it. Before therefore he could go he must settle this point, one almost as difficult as that of escaping.

At length a voice was heard under the window.

"All right," said Burridge, in a whisper; "I'll tell you all about it as soon as I'm safe inside again."

He soon made his way up to the top of the hut, and getting through the hole replaced the thatch and bamboo rafters before he jumped down to the ground.

"I was right," he said, "and made my way down to the harbour. It is farther off though than I supposed; and I heard people moving about, so I had to be cautious; and more than all, they have two or three of those Spanish bloodhounds with them, and it's a wonder the beasts did not find me out, and if they had come across my track they would have done so to a certainty. However I got down to the shore safe. I counted six or seven vessels in the harbour, besides two or three small ones, and several boats hauled up on the beach. So far as a craft is concerned, we have only to pick and choose. Then comes the difficulty of getting on board and finding our way out of the harbour. If we had been on deck when we came in we might have done that more easily, but to get out at night without knowing the passage will be a hard job indeed. However, it must be done by some means or other."

It was agreed at last that they must wait for a moonlight night, when by sounding with a boat they might hope to get the vessel, in which they finally expected to make their escape, safe through the passage. It would also be necessary that the pirates should be indulging in a carouse and be off the watch, and that the wind should blow down the harbour. Every time the men who brought them their provisions came Jack sent a message to the captain, begging that they might be released, and allowed to wander at their will throughout the island. Several days had passed, however, and no answer had been returned.

Deane possessed an iron frame, but the anxiety which he endured began to tell greatly upon him, and for the first time in his life, he felt that he was becoming seriously ill. The thought occurred to him that it might be the yellow fever. Every day he grew worse and worse. His head ached, his limbs were full of pains, still he kept up his spirits as well as he could, and he and his companions continued to entertain hopes of escaping. One night Burridge returned from his usual expedition in high spirits. He had important information to give. While wandering along the shore he came suddenly upon a person seated on a rock, apparently watching the harbour as he had been. At first he felt very nervous about approaching the man, doubting who he could be. Still it struck him that it was not likely to be one of the pirates. He therefore cautiously approached him and, in a low voice, asked him who he was.

"You may suppose, sir," said Burridge, "when he gave me the account my heart did leap with joy, when I found that he was an old shipmate—the pilot of a vessel I once sailed in! And what was more curious, he has been thinking of the same thing that we have, and hoping to make his escape in the same manner. He tells me that he has two companions on the island who are kept at work by the pirates as slaves; but that he has had an opportunity of speaking to them, and that they're ready to help him make off with a vessel. If I had not known him, I should have been afraid of treachery; but he is a true man, and we need have no fear on that score. There will be moon enough for our purpose about five days hence, and I've arranged that we should all meet him at the spot where I found him at midnight at that time."

This information raised Jack's spirits, which had become very low in consequence of his illness. The effect, however, was only temporary, for the following day he became worse, and his companions began to fear that he would be taken from them. Their daily visitor, as it happened, remained in the hut longer than usual, and had thus an opportunity of observing how ill Deane looked. The midshipmen and Burridge also told him that they were afraid their officer would die if he had not some help.

"True enough, master," said the man. "I will tell our captain, and perhaps he will do something for him. We have no objection to killing men in fair fight; but it is not our way to put them out of the world by clapping them into prisons, as they do in some countries."

Saying this the man took his departure, promising to inform his captain of Deane's state of health.

"Whatever happens to me," said Deane to his companions, "you must endeavour to make your escape, according to the present arrangement. If you can find your way to Jamaica, you will be able to tell the authorities whereabouts this island is situated, and they will then probably send a man-of-war to bargain with the pirates for my release, or if they will not do that, to get me off by force."

About an hour after their first visitor had left them, footsteps were heard approaching the door. It opened, and Jack, as he lifted his head from the bed of straw on which he lay in one corner, saw standing before him his old acquaintance—Pearson!

"They tell me you have fallen sick," he said, "and want a doctor. Now I'm none myself, and there's no one I can send here to cure you; but, as I don't want you to suppose that we are entire barbarians, if you wish it, I will have you taken to my house, and there are some there who, maybe, will look after you and help cure you better than any doctor we can find in these parts."

Under other circumstances, Deane would certainly have declined the offer, which would have made his escape impossible; but from the remarks made by the pirate captain, he could not help hoping that the persons he spoke of might prove to be Dame Pearson and Elizabeth. He felt, too, that even should he wish to attempt escaping, from his weakness he would be a great burden to his companions, while he would run the risk of losing his own life. He therefore replied that he was thankful for the offer made to him, and gladly accepted it. At this the captain summoned a couple of men who were waiting outside with a litter, and lifting Jack upon it, without allowing him much time to bid farewell to his companions, they carried him off. The midshipmen were greatly afraid that he would exact a promise from them not to attempt to escape. They were therefore greatly relieved when they saw him take his departure, leaving them at liberty to act as they thought best. They immediately consulted what should be done, and agreed, for his sake as well as their own, that they should endeavour to make their way to Port Royal as soon as possible, and despatch an expedition to destroy the nest of pirates.

Deane's bearers carried him along through the cocoanut grove for some distance, when they came before a cottage far superior in appearance to any of those he had before passed. A garden in front bloomed with flowers, and a wide verandah afforded shade to the rooms within. Deane's heart beat somewhat quicker than usual as he saw these and other signs of the presence of females.

"Here, dame, is a man who wants looking after. It will be to your and fair Bessy's taste, and he will be grateful I doubt not. He was brought in here some time since on board a prize, and if it had not been for me, he and his companions would have been food for sharks by this time."

Jack heard these words spoken as his bearers reached the door of the cottage. He had little difficulty in recognising the voice of Master Pearson, though perhaps had he not previously seen that individual he might not have done so. Pearson, for some reason or other, kept out of sight, and Deane found himself carried into a room and placed on a couch formed out of bamboos. The room was, however, in other respects richly furnished, with silk hangings, and gold and silver ornaments of all descriptions, quite out of character with the general appearance of the building.

"Dare, massa, you will do well," said one of the negro bearers, with a good-natured expression of countenance. "Soon lily-white lady come look after you. I is 'Tello, you remember me, massa; I love Englishmen."

Jack was not left long alone. Scarcely had the negroes taken their departure when he heard footsteps approaching the door. His heart beat quickly, for he fully expected to see Elizabeth Pearson, who he could not help persuading himself was an inhabitant of the island. Instead of Elizabeth, however, an old lady entered the room, followed by a black damsel. He turned his eyes towards the former, expecting to recognise the features of Dame Pearson. At first he could scarcely believe that a few years could have made so great an alteration in her, and he had to look twice before he was certain that she was the good dame who had treated him so kindly in the fens, sickness and anxiety having already worked a great change in her; yet Dame Pearson was the person who had just entered the room, of that he was sure.

"I was told that an English officer is ill, and requires aid," she said. "I therefore desired that he might be brought here. I will feel your pulse, sir, that I may judge what remedies to apply."

Jack was not surprised that she did not recognise him, and he thought it better not to make himself known to her at first. He felt however great disappointment at the non-appearance of Elizabeth; still, till he had told Dame Pearson who he was, he could not ask after her. From what the negro said, however, he still hoped that she might be in the house. The dame, after consulting with her attendant, retired again, saying that she would prepare such remedies as were most likely to benefit him. He thanked her, begging that they might be applied soon, for he felt so ill that, stout of heart as he was, he could not help at times believing that he should not recover.

"We will do our best for you, but the issue is in the hands of God," answered the dame calmly. "However, in the meantime I will send my daughter that she may read to you from His Word. Thence you will obtain more comfort than man can bestow."

Saying this she left the room. Jack's eyes kept continually turned towards the door, and in another minute it opened, and a fair girl entered the room. She was taller, however, and of larger proportions than the little Elizabeth he had so often thought of. She carried a Bible in her hand, and taking a seat at a short distance from him, scarcely giving him more than a slight glance, opened the Book.

"You will undoubtedly draw comfort, as we have done, sir, from God's blessed Word. I will therefore read to you from the Psalms of David, who was a man tried and afflicted."

She commenced reading in a low, gentle voice. Jack could with difficulty refrain from making himself known, for he at once recognised that sweet voice which he had known so well. She read on for some short time, and then turned to passages in other parts of the Book which she thought calculated to bring comfort to one in sickness and distress.

Jack at length could restrain himself no longer.

"Elizabeth," he exclaimed, "Elizabeth de Mertens! do you not know me?"

She flew to his side, and trembling took his hand which he stretched out towards her.

"Who are you?" she exclaimed. "Yes, yes, I know you, I know your voice! Jack Deane you are—yes, you must be! But oh, how did you come here? How do you know me, and that name by which you call me? I remember it well. It was my own name, though I had well-nigh forgotten it. Have you come to take me away from this dreadful place? and oh, from that dreadful man too?"

"Yes, indeed I am Jack Deane—and often have I thought of you, Elizabeth!" he answered; "and it was in consequence of the ring you gave me that I discovered your name. But sit down, and I will tell you by degrees what has occurred. If I was to give the history all at once, I have so many things to say that I should bewilder you. But I also want to learn about you—how you came here, and your adventures; for it seems strange that you have been brought out to this lonely island, to live among pirates and outlaws!"

"I am afraid you give them but their true name," answered Elizabeth; "but let me hear about yourself, and those from whom you learnt my name."

Jack could not speak without difficulty, but he managed, however, to give Elizabeth a brief account of himself, entering more particularly into the way in which he had discovered her parents. They were interrupted by the return of Dame Pearson and her black attendant.

"Hush!" said Elizabeth; "say nothing now: I will tell my mother when the girl is not present. I fear she is not to be trusted."

The discovery Jack had made, instead of increasing his fever, had a beneficial effect, so it seemed, as it restored his spirits in a way that nothing else would have done. All his thoughts were now occupied in devising a scheme for carrying off Elizabeth from the island.

So completely had the fever deprived Jack of strength, that for several days he was unable to rise from his couch, although, thanks to the kind and constant attention he received, he was gradually recovering. He was especially anxious all this time to hear from his companions; but Dame Pearson could give him no information, nor could Elizabeth, although they believed that they still remained shut up in their prison.

Chapter Thirty One
Dame Pearson's History—Engagement between the Pirate and Queen's Ship

Pearson all this time had never appeared, though Elizabeth told Jack that he was still on the island. One day, however, he heard his voice raised to a high and angry pitch, very unlike the calm tone in which he used generally to speak.

"This is the sort of watch you fellows keep over your prisoners!" Pearson was exclaiming. "While you are in your drunken fits the whole island might be attacked and taken, and all our vessels cut out. You say you do not know when they got off? Then why did you not, the instant you made the discovery, put to sea in the first vessel you could get ready, and make chase after them? Go! hasten now, villains! they can scarcely be many leagues away, and are sure to be steering a course for Port Royal."

Some grumbling remonstrances were heard in return to this address.

"Well, knaves, well, you shall sail in the sloop, and I'll follow in the ship as soon as she can be got ready for sea," exclaimed the pirate chief. "If you are afraid of being caught by a queen's ship, we shall be in time to save you from hanging; why, and if not, you will only meet the fate which is certain to be yours one of these days!"

"And yours too, captain!" shouted one of the men. "Why do you bring that up before us?"

"Marry, indeed! because I have a fancy to please you. There's this difference between us, however: you are afraid of it, and would do any sneaking thing to avoid the noose! I have no fear of that or any thing else, and so would not step out of my way to escape it. And now delay no longer, but be off with you all. I'll be down at the harbour anon, and we'll see how quickly we gentlemen rovers can get a ship ready for sea."

From the conversation he had overheard, Jack thus knew that his friends had escaped. At the same time he dreaded the consequences of their being overtaken, well knowing from the temper of the pirate and his followers that, should they be captured, they would have but little chance of preserving their lives. He earnestly hoped, therefore, that they might escape safely to Port Royal. Two days after this he heard from Elizabeth that Pearson and his followers had left the island in their big ship.

"Now you may, without risk, tell my kind second-mother who you are. It will make her more ready, I doubt not, to plead for you with her husband, should such become necessary. If your friends escape him, he will probably return in a very bad humour, and be much disposed to wreak his vengeance on your head," said Elizabeth.

Elizabeth, very naturally, took every opportunity of being with Jack alone, that she might hear more about her parents, of whom he had so much to tell, as also of his own adventures. The more he saw of her, the more he was struck by her natural refinement and intelligence, and the amount of information which she had been able to obtain. At length the secret was told to Dame Pearson. At first she would scarcely believe that Jack was the same youth she had formerly known, and she had to examine his countenance very narrowly before she would believe his and Elizabeth's assertions. At length, however, she was convinced.

"I see no more reason to doubt," she observed, "after all, that you should have changed from a drover to a naval officer, than that we, after living quiet lives as farmers in old England, should have become outcasts and wanderers on the earth."

Jack had almost recovered even before Pearson left the island, but he did not wish to appear so, lest it should be the signal for his being dismissed from the cottage. Now, however, being able to leave the house, he rapidly regained his strength, and was able to walk about the island in company with Elizabeth. Those were happy days! He no longer concealed from himself that he had given her his heart, and he had good reason to suspect that he possessed hers in return. They took care in their walks to keep at a good distance from the huts; the permanent residents in the island consisting chiefly of old buccaneers and the wives and families of others away in the ships. These latter were, however, chiefly mulattoes or negresses, and it any of them caught sight of him and Elizabeth, they merely staved, taking him probably for one of the buccaneers. He passed his evenings in company with Dame Pearson and Elizabeth, reading and talking while they sat at their work. The poor lady was at first somewhat reserved, but as her confidence in Jack was established, she described to him her grief and sorrow when she discovered the course her husband purposed to pursue.

"On the discovery of the Jacobite plot, believing that he himself would be betrayed, he suddenly determined to quit England," said the dame, continuing a narrative she had begun. "Going to a sea-port, he at first took out a licence as a privateer. That was bad enough, for his crew were bold and daring, and were constantly chasing or being chased; now and then fighting, but generally only attacking unarmed traders. Not knowing what to do with Elizabeth, and finding she was not averse to accompanying us, I had at first consented to bring her to sea, not at all aware of the life we were to lead."

Although several prizes were thus taken, this slow mode of gaining wealth did not suit the captain or the majority of his men, and they therefore resolved to go out to the West Indies and to hoist the black flag. The plan had been kept from Dame Pearson and her daughter, but they heard of it, though they in vain urged Pearson to abandon the undertaking. He laughed at their scruples, and promised that in a few years they would make enough to enable them to retire to Virginia, or to some other plantation, and there settle down and enjoy the fruits of their enterprise.

"Why should not I do as well as Sir Henry Morgan, and fifty other fine fellows have done?" he exclaimed. "To be sure, some have lost their lives, but they were either drunkards or too audacious—but I am much too careful to be caught as they were."

He only laughed at his wife when she pointed out to him the sinfulness of this proposed occupation, and at length told her that he had been a robber all his life, and that he had no intention of turning an honest man till he had made his fortune. This was the first intimation the poor woman had had of his career on shore, whatever might have been her suspicions on the subject. She was anxious on her own account, and still more unhappy on that of Elizabeth, when she found that nothing would turn her husband from his resolution. Still he had not lost all his former respect for her, and at length he consented to fix his abode on the island where Jack had found her. She had therefore only to wait patiently, hoping that he would soon put in execution the plan he had proposed, of finally settling down in one of the plantations. She had kept Elizabeth as much as possible in ignorance of Pearson's character, but she had, however, at length found it out; and though looking at him with a feeling somewhat akin to horror, still she had determined not to desert, even should she have the opportunity, the kind woman who had adopted her and ever treated her as a daughter. Elizabeth herself, however, was not free from annoyances, for her youth and beauty had attracted the attention of several of the buccaneers, or, as they called themselves, "gentlemen of fortune," and two or three of the officers, who looked upon their qualifications as superior to those of their companions, had made overtures to their chief for the hand of his supposed daughter. She, however, had rejected them with scorn, and Pearson still entertained so much respect and regard for her, that he had sworn that no man should have her against her will.

"Ah, Master Deane, you little know what quarrels have taken place about her!" said the dame, one day when Elizabeth was absent. "Three or four duels have been fought to my certain knowledge, and one young man among the gang was run through the body and killed, because he had sworn that no other than himself should be her husband. At last the captain had to declare that he would shoot the first man who killed another in any duel about her, and that, for a time, put a stop to the quarrels among them. I always thought myself that she was of gentle blood, from the account my husband gave me of the lady who placed her in his arms, and I am thankful therefore that she should not have been thrown away on any one beneath the rank of a gentleman, still more on any of these ruffian buccaneers, who, in spite of all their boasting, would very soon have broken her heart. The only wife fit for one of them, is a girl who is pleased with being covered with gold chains, and rings, and jewels, and cares nothing for her husband's love. I know by experience how sad a thing it is for a wife to be mated to a man below her in rank, however kind and generous he may be. Such my husband has always been to me since he saved my life, but I was born and educated as a gentlewoman, and I have frequently had cause to feel a difference between us. Since my marriage I have never met with any of my family. They were all dispersed in the Civil Wars. Many of my brothers were probably killed fighting on the king's side, and the youngest had set his heart on following the sea, which he probably did; but as our home was broken up, there was no place to which I could write to obtain tidings of them."

Jack felt that he should be very sorry when the pleasant life he was now leading should come to an end. He spent his days in greater ease and idleness than he had enjoyed since he left home, most of the time sitting by the side of Elizabeth, or taking walks with her along the sea-shore or through the woods.

One day as he was sitting on a rock by the sea-side with Elizabeth, holding her hand in his, and talking of that happy future of which lovers delight to discourse, a white speck appeared in the horizon, which they well knew to be a sail. Gradually it increased in size. Higher and higher it rose, till the white canvas of a tall ship appeared above the long, unbroken line in the distance. The hull next came in sight, and the ship glided on rapidly towards the island. While the lovers were watching her, wondering what she could be, whether the pirate vessel or some stranger, another appeared in the same spot where she had first been seen. Gradually the sails of that one also rose upward, till the whole ship came in sight. Both of them were nearly before the wind, carrying as much canvas as they were able to bear. The first came rapidly on.

"She is bound in for the harbour," observed Jack, "and from my recollection of the vessel which boarded us when I was made prisoner, I have no doubt that that is the same. If so, we must expect to have the pirate and his gang on shore again."

"But what can that other vessel be?" asked Elizabeth, pointing towards the stranger.

Jack stood up to examine her, shading his eyes with his hand.

"She looks to me wonderfully like a man-of-war. It is possible that she may be in chase of the pirate. And see, here comes another vessel, her topsails are already above the horizon—and a third also! The pirates have brought a whole host of their enemies down upon them. The authorities in Jamaica have, I know, long been on the look-out to discover the head-quarters of the buccaneers. They have come for the purpose of attacking the island, and will not let a pirate escape if they can help it. Ah, see, there flies out the black flag! A daring fellow commands that vessel, and, depend upon it, he is resolved to fight it out to the last. The queen's ship has hoisted her colours also. The object of the other is to disable her before her consorts can come up, and if he succeeds in that he hopes to get into the harbour, and there defend himself."

The lock on which Deane and Elizabeth had taken their seat commanded not only a view of the sea, and of the entrance of the harbour, but also of a considerable part of the harbour itself. They could thus from their position watch all that was taking place.

The royal cruiser under all sail had stood in shore, to intercept the piratical vessel, which it was naturally supposed would make for the harbour, and it was important therefore to prevent her doing this. It was only, indeed, when the wind blew right in, that a vessel could enter under sail. On other occasions, it was necessary to warp or tow her in—an operation which could not be performed under the fire of an enemy. The pirate, finding that he could not get into the harbour unmolested, hauled up his courses, and boldly stood back towards the British ship, receiving her fire and returning it with interest.

Elizabeth gazed with lips apart and pale cheeks at the combatants, which now, surrounded by clouds of smoke, were rapidly exchanging broadsides.

"Oh, how dreadful!" she exclaimed. "It seems as if they must destroy each other. How many souls will thus be launched into eternity! How fearful, too, if the pirate gains the victory! for I have heard tales of the horrible way they treat those they conquer, when their blood is up in such a fight as this."

"Little fear of that," remarked Deane. "Our brave countrymen are not likely to give in to a set of mongrel outlaws as are these buccaneers. But mongrels as they are, they fight well, I acknowledge that! See, there goes the mast of one of the ships!"

"I can scarcely distinguish one from the other through the smoke," said Elizabeth.

"It's the frigate's fore-mast, I fear," exclaimed Deane. "She is attempting to board the pirate. But no! she has not succeeded, the other sheers off, and continues firing at a distance."

As he spoke, the two vessels, which had for some short time been so close together as scarcely to be distinguished in the midst of the smoke, now separated, the pirate steering towards the land, while the frigate lay, with her fore-mast gone, and several spars shot away from the main-mast, while the rigging of the pirate seemed but little injured.

"How fearful!" exclaimed Elizabeth. "The pirates seem to have gained the victory."

"Not at all," answered Deane; "see, the red flag of England still flies triumphant, and probably, if we could see the decks of the two vessels, we should find that the pirate has been the greater sufferer. His object was to cripple his antagonist, and he has done so successfully, while the wish of the English captain has been to destroy the pirates."

Although the pirate was so standing that only her after-guns could be brought to bear on the frigate, she continued firing with them, in return for a shot which the latter sent after her. She now stood directly in for the mouth of the harbour, and as she approached close to it her sails were quickly furled, and several boats went out to her, to assist in getting her in, while her own boats were lowered for the same purpose.

Chapter Thirty Two
The Island Captured

"The game is not over yet," observed Deane, who with Elizabeth still stood on the rock watching the progress of the fight. "The crew of the frigate are busily employed in repairing damages. As soon as that is done, and the other two ships come up, depend upon it, they will attack the island, and, with the strong force the English will then have, the pirates will be utterly unable to resist them."

"Alas! alas! I wish we could have escaped from the island before this had occurred! I tremble for the fate of my poor mother, for such I must still call her—and what will become of Master Pearson? for, as far as I can judge, he seems to be the head of the whole community."

"For the kindness with which he has ever treated you, if he escapes with his life from the battle, I will use all my influence to protect him," answered Deane. "At the same time, I think it likely he will fight to the last. He seems a man who would not yield, as long as a hope of success remains."

"Let me go then and tell my poor mother of what has occurred, and prepare her for the worst," exclaimed Elizabeth.

"Oh, no! stay here, let me entreat you!" he answered. "You will be safer on this rock, and I may possibly be able to make some signal to the boats as they come in, and thus you will escape the desperate struggle which is likely to take place when the crews land and attack the pirates. Or stay! if you can persuade Mistress Pearson to come here, she will be safer than in her own house. But you must not go alone: I will accompany you, and try and bring her back."

To this plan Elizabeth willingly agreed, and she and Deane immediately hurried forward towards the village. The alarm of the poor lady was very great when she heard what was likely to occur, but she positively refused to quit the house.

"Go, go!" she replied to Elizabeth's entreaties. "Leave me to my fate: Mr Deane will protect you better than I can, and you are not bound either to that unhappy man my husband or to me."

Deane had now some difficulty in persuading Elizabeth to return with him, for she was unwilling to leave poor Mistress Pearson to the danger to which she would be exposed should the village be stormed, as it was too likely to be. At length, however, she yielded to her and Jack's united entreaties, and returned to the rock with Deane. By the time they reached it, the other English vessels had almost come up with their crippled consort, and a considerable flotilla of boats was seen collecting round them. The pirates meantime, having warped their vessel into the harbour, had placed her across its mouth, so that her guns pointed directly down towards an enemy approaching in that direction. A considerable number of the people were also engaged on shore in throwing up breastworks at various points likely to be assailed. Guns were being brought down from the stores and from the other vessels up the harbour, and every effort was being made which desperate men could think of to defend the place. The English seemed to guess what the pirates were about by the rapidity of their movements, for not a moment was lost after the vessels had met, before the boats began to pull at a rapid rate towards the mouth of the harbour. There were twelve boats in all, carrying a considerable body of men. The ships at the same time stood in as close as they could venture, to cover the attack with their guns.

Between the rock on which Deane and Elizabeth stood, was a sandy bay, affording tolerably safe landing. This spot the pirates seemed to have overlooked, though the English were evidently aware of it, for while one party of boats pulled towards the mouth of the harbour, another, suddenly leaving the main body, made a dash towards the bay, for the purpose of landing before the pirates discovered it and were prepared to resist them. On came five boats at a rapid rate, the water foaming at their bows, as their crews urged them through it. Deane could with difficulty resist the temptation of hurrying forward to meet them, but he could not leave Elizabeth, nor could he place her in the danger to which she would be exposed had he carried her with him. As soon as the ships came close enough they opened their fire at the hastily thrown up forts at the harbour's mouth, while the flotilla of boats dashed forward for the purpose of storming them before the enemy had recovered from the effects of the cannonading. The pirates, however, had been too long accustomed to desperate fighting of all sorts to be easily daunted, and the places of those who fell were quickly supplied by others who rushed forward to work their guns. Before, however, they could load and fire them, the boats' crews, springing on shore, rushed forward and attacked them, hanger in hand, and quickly mastered the fort.

The pirate ship now opened her fire upon the boats advancing up the harbour. This told with great effect, and again and again they were struck, but still undaunted, they pulled on. Meantime the other boats had reached the bay, and their crews also quickly threw themselves on shore. The pirates did not perceive their intention till it was too late to prevent them, and now in steady order they were soon advancing up from the shore towards the fort, which was also greatly annoying the boats in their advance. Taken in the rear, its defenders were quickly cut down, and now the party of English blue-jackets rushed up towards the pirate ship, but some of her guns being directed at them and others at the boats, no great loss was sustained by either. So quickly indeed did the party advance, that very few shot took effect among them. At length they got close up to the ship and opened a hot fire of musketry upon her killing and wounding the men at her guns. The boats were thus able to advance with much less molestation than before, and getting alongside, their crews with loud shouts dashed on board. The pirates fought desperately, but nothing could resist the courage of the English. The outlaws were seen jumping overboard on either side, and many were shot while attempting to swim on shore. No quarter was asked for by them. They had seldom given it themselves. Still, however, they exhibited great courage and hardihood, fighting desperately to the last. Meantime a party of them who had remained on shore, manning several boats, put off to the rescue of their comrades. Thus before the English could prevent them, a considerable number had managed to escape from the ship, taking their way to a point up the harbour where they could land without being molested.

The men-of-war's boats had been left with their boatkeepers in the bay. As soon as Deane saw that he could reach them without running the risk of encountering the pirates, he determined to place Elizabeth on board them.

"If we stay here, we shall very probably fall in with the buccaneers, who are likely to fly to this rock in the hope of defending themselves. Our way is now clear to the boats, and I will carry you there," he said, taking Elizabeth's arm.

"Whatever you think best I am ready to do," she answered; and they hurried towards the bay.

Fortunately, the officer in charge of the boats belonged to Deane's own ship, and recognising him, at once received Elizabeth on board.

"Now I have placed you in safety, I will go back and endeavour to protect our kind friend Mistress Pearson," he said.

Elizabeth thanked him warmly, though she evidently at the same time dreaded losing sight of him. Deane well knew there was no time to be lost, for the sound of the firing and the shouts and cries of the combatants told him that they were approaching the village. He hurried back therefore, taking a sheltered way among the trees. He had just reached the house, when he saw a number of buccaneers rushing towards the village, with the intention, he judged, of attempting to defend themselves behind the walls of the buildings. He found Mistress Pearson standing pale with terror at the sound of the guns which had reached her ears, not knowing which party had been successful. Deane once more entreated her to fly.

"If you remain, you will too probably lose your life in the struggle," he said.

Scarcely waiting for her answer, he had drawn her to the door, when he was seen by some of the pirates.

"Down with the villain! down with the traitor who has brought the enemy upon us!" they shouted.

They raised their muskets, but Mistress Pearson standing between them and Deane, prevented them from firing. Some of the fiercest were, however, rushing forward with the intention of cutting him down, when the cry arose, "The enemy are upon us! defend yourselves, lads!" and they had to face about to receive the charge of the British sailors, who dashed out from among the trees towards them. Several bullets whistled by Deane's and the poor dame's ears. The fighting was desperate. The pirates defended themselves, knowing that they should receive no quarter; but in spite of their bravery they were cut down on all sides. Deane had two or three times amid the clouds of smoke caught sight of Pearson, who was leading on the men, shouting to them to fight boldly. More seamen arriving, led on by a superior officer, the pirates at length began to retreat. As they reached the house of their chief, however, they made a stand, some threw themselves inside and began to fire through the windows, and others got behind the walls where they were sheltered from the fire of their enemies. Deane attempted to carry poor Dame Pearson to a place of shelter. Paralysed with fear, she could scarcely move. He found himself, therefore, surrounded by the combatants, and in great risk every instant of being shot.

The pirates here made a desperate stand; but the British seamen, again rushing on, cut down numbers with their hangers. Just then the house burst out into flames, and, surrounded by smoke, Deane could not be distinguished from the pirates who stood on the other side of him. Two or three seamen were on the point of cutting him down, when their officer interposed his sword.

"Hold, lads!" he shouted; "as I live, there is my friend John Deane, and protecting a lady too!"

This timely exclamation saved Deane's life. He had no time, however, to exchange greetings with the officer, whom he recognised as the captain of his own ship, as the latter had to lead on his men in pursuit of the flying pirates. The good dame now entreated him to look for her husband; but he remembered that after the commencement of the fight he had nowhere seen him. What had become of him he could not tell, and all he could do was to assure her he had not seen him fall. Jack was anxious to convey her to the boats that she might be carried on board and placed in safety; but just as he was leaving the village Captain Davis returned, saying that all the pirates to be found had been killed or made prisoners.

"I am thankful, indeed, to hear it, Captain Davis," said Deane. "And now I will ask you to assist me in conveying this lady on board."

"Captain Davis!" exclaimed Mistress Pearson. "Let me see you, sir. That was my maiden name; and I had a brother who went to sea, from whom I have been parted for many long years. Can you be Richard Davis, the youngest son of Colonel Davis of Knowle Park?"

"Yes, indeed, I am, madame," answered the Captain, coming up to her. "I was one of a numerous family, all of whom, to the best of my belief, have long since been dead."

"One of them is still alive," answered Mistress Pearson, "though a most unhappy woman. Do you not remember your sister Maria? Come, let me gaze on your countenance, for my heart tells me that in you I shall find one of my brothers. Yes, yes, I recognise your features! though I scarcely could expect you to know mine, so sadly changed as they must be."

She had taken the captain's hand, and gazed into his face as she spoke.

"No, I should not remember you," he answered; "but yet I remember the voice of the kind sister who was always ready to suffer for the sake of her wild brothers. Yes, Maria, I know that you are my sister, and I am thankful that I have been the means of rescuing you from this place. How you came here you must tell me by and by. And now I would wish you to go at once on board the frigate, under the charge of Mr Deane, while we make a further search round the island for any fugitives who may have concealed themselves."

Mistress Pearson trembled as her brother spoke these words.

"There is one for whom I would intercede," she said. "Mr Deane will tell you about him. He has ever been a kind husband to me, and never till lately did I suspect his occupations. If he has escaped death, let me entreat you not to hunt him down, and I feel sure that he will turn to some nobler course, where he will redeem the crimes he has committed."

Captain Davis very wisely made no answer to this appeal; but directed Deane, with a party of the seamen as a guard, to convey his new-found sister down to the boats, and to place her at once on board the frigate. He, meantime, having collected his men, commenced a further search for the pirates, some of whom, he was convinced, must have concealed themselves. The day was thus spent, though with no further success, and as night was coming on, a large party being placed on board the captured ships, the remainder returned in the boats to the vessels outside. The next day the search was continued; but no signs were discovered of the chief and other officers and men who were supposed to have escaped with him. The numerous prizes were carried out of the harbour, while all the huts, and storehouses, and other buildings were set on fire and destroyed, so that in a short time the whole island was reduced to that state of desolation in which the pirates had found it.

While the rest of the squadron returned to Jamaica, one vessel was left to cruise off the island, on the chance of Pearson and his followers, should they have been concealed on it, attempting to make their escape. When Jack arrived on board the "Venus," he found the two young midshipmen, Hawke and Lovatt, and the old quarter-master Burridge, who welcomed him warmly. They told him that they had managed to make their escape exactly as they had proposed while the buccaneers were carousing; and had, fortunately, fallen in with the squadron which had been despatched on purpose to try and discover their haunts.

Chapter Thirty Three
Sir George Hooke takes the Spanish Galleons in Vigo Bay

Elizabeth's joy at seeing Mistress Pearson was very great; and she did her utmost to comfort her in her affliction, aided by Captain Davis and Deane. As soon as they arrived at Port Royal, Captain Davis took a house for her on shore, where she and Elizabeth went to reside till a plan for their future proceedings could be arranged. Deane immediately wrote to Monsieur de Mertens, and told him of his recovery of his daughter, saying that she was still with her kind guardian, in whose company he hoped that he should, without delay, be able to escort her to England.

In those days the climate of the West Indies was as dangerous to Europeans as at the present, and ships seldom remained long on the station without losing many of their officers and men. The honest old Admiral Benbow was still alive, although rapidly sinking from the effects of his wounds and his annoyance at the conduct of his officers in the action with the French. Hearing of Jack's conduct, he appointed him second lieutenant of the "Ruby," in the place of an officer who had died. He was sorry to leave Captain Davis, especially as he expected now to have fewer opportunities of meeting Elizabeth. He had, however, the consolation to know that Captain Davis expected immediately to be sent home, and proposed taking his sister and Elizabeth with him. John Deane met with no adventures worth recording during his next cruise.

On the return of the "Ruby" to Port Royal, our hero found that the "Venus" had already sailed, and his ship was shortly afterwards also ordered home. On reaching England, he was immediately appointed to the "Lennox," of seventy guns, commanded by his old friend Captain Jumper. She formed one of the squadron under Admiral Sir George Rooke just on the point of sailing for the coast of Spain. Being unable to obtain leave of absence, he wrote to Nottingham and Norwich; but before he received answers to his letters his ship put to sea. Sir George Rooke had his flag flying on board the "Royal Sovereign."

On board the fleet were a large number of troops, under the command of the Duke of Ormond. On the 12th August they anchored before the harbour of Cadiz next day the Duke of Ormond sent in a trumpeter with a letter requiring the governor to surrender. The brave governor replied that as he had been appointed to the command of the place by his lawful sovereign, he would not yield it up as long as he could hold it. On the 15th the Duke of Ormond therefore landed with the troops, and in a few days took possession of the forts of Saint Katharine and Saint Mary. It being found difficult to approach Cadiz while the Spaniards were in possession of Matagorda Fort, an assault was ordered. The Spaniards defended the place bravely, and it was found that the English force was far too small to hope for success. The troops were therefore re-embarked with the intention of returning home. Soon after this, while the fleet was off the coast of Portugal, Captain Hardy of the "Pembroke" brought the intelligence that the galleons from the West Indies had put into Vigo Bay, under convoy of a French squadron. Sir George Rooke immediately called a council of war, and it was resolved to make an attack at once on the enemy in the port of Vigo. A strong gale of wind, however, drove the fleet to the north of Cape Finisterre, which prevented their getting off Vigo before the 11th of October. The passage into the harbour was extremely narrow, and well defended by batteries on both sides. Across the entrance a strong boom also was laid, at each end of which was moored with chains a seventy-four-gun ship. Nearer the boom were laid, also moored, five ships, each carrying sixty to seventy guns, with their broadsides to the sea to defend the passage. The shoals and sand-banks, and the shallowness of the water within the harbour, made it dangerous for ships of the first and second rates to enter without a leading wind.

Notwithstanding the strong force opposed to them and the batteries on either side of the harbour, the English admirals resolved to attempt the capture of the galleons, and it being considered impossible for the larger ships to get up the harbour, they shifted their flags on board smaller vessels. A boat was then despatched up the harbour to gain intelligence respecting the disposition of the French and Spanish ships. This being obtained, it was resolved that as the whole fleet could not together act upon the enemy's ships, but would from crowding the harbour impede each others' movements, fifteen English and ten Dutch men-of-war, with all the fire-ships, should proceed in to destroy the enemy's fleet. The frigates and the bomb-vessels were directed to follow this detachment, and the larger ships were to proceed in afterwards, should their assistance be found necessary. It was arranged that the troops should at the same time land and attack the forts on either side of the harbour. Vice-Admiral Hopson was ordered to lead the van, followed by Vice-Admiral Vandergoes, Sir George Rooke commanded the centre division, and Rear-Admiral Graydon brought up the rear. Sir George Rooke spent the greater part of the night going from ship to ship in his own boat to ascertain that each captain understood clearly the plan of the attack and the part he was to take in it.

The following morning, the 12th of October, the squadron got under weigh and stood in for the harbour. Great was the disappointment of all on board, when just as the van division had almost reached within gunshot of the batteries the wind died away, and it was necessary to anchor. A strong breeze, however, shortly afterwards sprang up, when Vice-Admiral Hopson, in the "Torbay," cutting his cable, crowded every sail his ship could carry and bore down upon the boom. The velocity gained by the ship gave her such power that the boom was snapped in two, and the "Torbay" was instantly placed between the two French line-of-battle ships, the "Bourbon" and "Espérance." These two ships immediately opened a desperate fire upon the "Torbay," which gallantly replied to them, though most of her men were falling, killed and wounded from the fierce fire to which she was exposed. Scarcely had the breeze carried her into this post of danger, than it again fell, and the other ships of the squadron had considerable difficulty in following her. While they were endeavouring to get up the harbour, a fire-ship was seen descending directly for the "Torbay." On it came. The destruction of the "Torbay" seemed inevitable. Now the flames burst out on either side from the fire-ship. The brave crew of the "Torbay" instantly lowered their boats for the purpose of towing her off, but two of the boats were struck and swamped, and many of those in them were drowned before help could be rendered by those on board. Just as the flames seemed about to catch the "Torbay" they suddenly decreased, and were deadened. It seemed almost like a miracle; but when the men afterwards examined the fire-ship, she was found to be loaded with snuff, which immediately the fire reached it completely deadened the flames.

While this event was taking place, Vice-Admiral Vandergoes and the rest of the squadron made their way through the passage which the brave Hopson had opened up, and directed their fire upon the "Bourbon," which in a short time was captured. The "Torbay," however, suffered very severely, losing a hundred and fifteen men killed and drowned, besides many wounded, including among the latter Captain Moody, her brave captain. While the troops were advancing, Captain Beckenham in the "Association," of ninety guns, laid his broadside against a battery of seventeen guns on the left side of the harbour, and Captain Wyvill in the "Barfleur" was sent to batter the fort on the other side, while there was a considerable firing from great guns and small-arms on both sides. The other ships defending the harbour were now attacked. They replied to the fire of the English with considerable vigour, though they in vain attempted to resist their advance. Meantime the Duke of Ormond had landed in a sandy bay about two leagues distant from Vigo. His Grace, meeting with no opposition, ordered the grenadiers, under Lord Shannon and Colonel Pierce, to march directly to the forts which guarded the entrance to the harbour where the boom lay. This they executed with much courage and alacrity, and so furious was their attack, that they soon made themselves masters of this important fort. The Duke himself, at the head of the rest of the forces, in the meantime marched on foot over craggy mountains to support the first detachment. As they advanced, they saw before them about eight thousand Spaniards prepared apparently to contest their advance between the fort and the hills. These, however, only engaged in a little skirmishing at a distance, and as the grenadiers advanced they retired. The batteries having been taken, the enemy retreated into an old tower, or stone castle. From thence, for some time, they fired briskly upon the English. It was said that there were nearly twenty thousand French and Spanish troops in and about Vigo at that time; but, undaunted by the superiority of the enemy, the British troops pushed on. They plied the defenders of the tower so warmly with their grenadoes, and pelted them so sharply with their fusees that they soon made the place too hot for them. Finding this, Monsieur de Sorel, the valiant captain of a French man-of-war, who commanded in the fort, having encouraged his men to make a daring push for their lives, opened the gates, intending to force his way through the English, sword in hand. The grenadiers, however, rushed immediately into the castle, made themselves masters of it, and took nearly three hundred French seamen and fifty Spaniards, with their officers, prisoners at discretion. A small party of the enemy endeavoured to make their escape through the water, but were stopped by a detachment of the Dutch. As soon as this was done, the boats of the squadron pushed up the harbour to take possession of the galleons. The French admiral, however, finding that all hope of defending the place was gone, gave orders for setting the shipping on fire. Before these orders could be executed, a considerable number of the ships were taken possession of by the boats. Besides seventeen ships, carrying between them nine hundred and sixty guns, destroyed or captured by the English and Dutch, three Spanish men-of-war, carrying a hundred and seventy-eight guns, were destroyed, and fifteen galleons were found there. Four of them were taken by the English, five by the Dutch, and four destroyed.

The brave Admirals Rooke, Hopson, and Vandergoes, were still furiously attacking the French ships placed across the harbour behind the boom. Suddenly flames were seen to burst forth from the French admiral's ship. This was soon discovered to be done on purpose, for immediately afterwards they burst forth from the other French ships, from which boats were at the same time seen putting off towards the shore. The French admiral, indeed, finding that the forts were in the hands of his victorious enemies, his fire-ship spent in vain, the "Bourbon" captured, the boom cut, and the confederate fleet pouring in upon him, so that the battle was lost, hoped by burning his ships to prevent their falling into their hands. The order he issued, however, was not punctually obeyed, in consequence of the haste of the French to get on shore. Immediately this was perceived, the boats of the squadron were ordered in to take possession of the galleons. John Deane found himself in one of the leading boats. Onward they dashed, amid the burning ships. On one side the "Torbay" lay with her fore-top-mast shot away, her sails burnt and scorched, her fore-yard burnt to a coal, and her larboard shrouds, fore and aft, burned to the deadeyes, so that indeed it appeared surprising that she had not been burned altogether. The leading boats dashed alongside some of the largest ships, which were so imperfectly set on fire that the confederates were enabled to extinguish the flames before they had spread far. They then pulled, as fast as they could bend to their oars, up the harbour towards the galleons which lay at the farther end. Every man had heard of the vast amount of wealth reputed to be on board these vessels, and all were eager to capture them, therefore, before they were destroyed by the enemy. Already flames were bursting out from some of them, and the French and Spanish boats were alongside, preparing for their destruction. The Dutch and English joined each other in the race. They rowed past the town, which the British troops, having captured the forts, were already entering. Now the boats got alongside the long-looked-for galleons. Already some were in flames, which had extended too far to allow of their being extinguished, but many others were saved. So rapid had been the movements of the allies, that the Spaniards had not had time to remove the cargoes of several of the galleons. These were in truth real prizes, and the wealth found on board them stimulated the crews of the boats to make desperate attempts to save the rest. Several, however, just as the flotilla approached them, went down at their anchors, but altogether the larger number were saved.

Great was the disappointment of the allies when they found that the Spaniards had landed the larger portion of the money with which the galleons had been freighted. Seldom, however, has a naval expedition been more judiciously planned and more completely carried out. This glorious and memorable victory, too, was obtained with a very inconsiderable loss on the side of the British; for, with the exception of the loss on board Vice-Admiral Hopson's ship, as already described, very few seamen were either killed or wounded, nor did the ships receive more than a slight damage. Of the land forces, two lieutenants and about forty rank and file were killed, and five officers and about thirty men wounded. Of the French, about four hundred officers and men were taken prisoners, among whom was the Spanish Admiral Don Joseph Checon, several French captains, and other officers of note.

The result of this victory was a vast booty, both of plate and other things, the value of which cannot well be computed. The fleet, indeed, was the richest that had ever come from the West Indies to Europe. The silver and gold was computed to amount to twenty millions of eight, of which fourteen millions had been taken out of the galleons and secured by the enemy before the attack. The rest was either taken or left in the galleons that were burned and sunk. The goods were valued also at twenty millions of pieces of eight, one fourth part of which was saved by the Spaniards, nearly two parts destroyed, and the other fourth taken by the confederates. Besides the property already mentioned, there was a great deal of plate and goods on board belonging to private persons, most of which was taken or lost.

The prize-money which thus fell to John Deane's share was very considerable, and it induced him to begin setting up a castle in the air, which he hoped to commence in a more substantial manner on his return to England, as he expected by the time he should get there to find Elizabeth restored to her parents, as he had left with her and Captain Davis full directions by which they could be found.

One thing most remarkable with regard to this victory, was not only the courage and sagacity of Sir George Rooke and the other admirals, but their readiness to sacrifice themselves and to risk their safety to ensure the success of the undertaking. This was shown by the way in which they left their large ships and placed themselves on board the smaller ones, as also by their leading the way into the midst of the enemy, strongly posted as they were. Great credit was also due to the land forces, for the mode in which they co-operated with the navy. Scarcely had the action concluded, when Sir Cloudesley Shovel with a large squadron hove in sight. The Duke of Ormond proposed to keep possession of Vigo for Don Carlos, considering it a safe place for the army to take up their quarters in, having a naval force to assist them. Sir George Rooke, however, thought that it was necessary to return home for want of stores and provisions. He left, therefore, Sir Cloudesley Shovel, to whom was entrusted the task of fitting out the prizes. He succeeded also in rescuing a large portion of treasure from the sunken galleons, and he recovered the "Dartmouth," an English fifty-gun ship which had been captured in the previous war. He also took out of some of the French ships lying aground partially destroyed, fifty brass guns and about sixty from the shore, and before sailing from the port he completed the destruction of every ship that he could not bring away.

The importance of this success was very great, as not only did the Spaniards suffer a heavy loss, but the naval power of France was considerably crippled by it, nor indeed did she during the war recover from its effects. Jack remained with the fleet under Sir Cloudesley Shovel. All hands were busily employed in fitting out the captured ships and preparing them for sea. At length, in a week, all those fit for sea were got ready, when the rest, amounting to a considerable number, were set on fire, and the squadron, as the flames bursting fiercely forth sent them to the bottom, sailed away down the harbour.

On the 25th of October Sir Cloudesley got clear of Vigo, but it proving calm, he anchored in the channel in the port of Bayonne, where, with a flag of truce, he sent several prisoners on shore, receiving some English who had been captured by the Spaniards. The next day he got under sail again, with the intention of going through the north channel, but the wind taking him short, he was obliged to drop anchor. Here a galleon, a prize to the "Monmouth," struck upon a sunken rock. Immediately the water rushed into her, and before it could be pumped out she foundered. Fortunately several frigates were on each side of her, and their boats putting off, all her crew were saved, with the exception of two who were below. The same day the fleet was joined by the "Dragon," a fifty-gun ship lately commanded by Captain Holyman. One of the officers came on board and gave an account of an engagement she had just had with a French man-of-war of seventy guns. In spite of the vast superiority of the enemy, Captain Holyman defended his ship with the greatest resolution. His crew worked their guns in a way British seamen have ever known how to do when alongside an enemy. At length the captain was killed, when his First Lieutenant, Fotherby, continued the defence, urging his men not to strike as long as they had a cartridge remaining and a shot in the locker. At length, although themselves greatly crippled, they had the satisfaction of seeing the enemy brace up her yards and stand away. Loud cheers burst from their throats, though they at first believed she had merely hauled off to repair damages. However she continued standing away, and ultimately her topsails disappeared below the horizon. Besides her brave captain, the "Dragon" lost twenty-five of her crew killed, and many more wounded. The fleet on their passage home encountered very bad weather. One of the ships, the "Nassau," had, in spite of the gale, the good fortune to make a rich prize. Standing in towards the fleet, however, the sea ran so high that the prize foundered. The gale continued to increase, and the whole squadron was thus separated, every ship shifting for herself. At length all got into the Downs.

Chapter Thirty Four
Hurricane in the British Channel—Sir George Rooke takes Gibraltar—Sea-fight off Malaga

On reaching England once more our hero had great hopes of being able to get on shore to visit his own family, as well as to make inquiries about Elizabeth, of whose arrival he had not yet heard. He had actually obtained leave to go on shore, and was proposing to set off the following day, when he experienced the truth of the old saying, "There is many a slip between the cup and the lip."

On the 26th of November, while his ship lay in the Downs—the weather having hitherto been fine—about eleven o'clock, the wind began to blow most violently from the West South West. John Deane was the officer on watch. He had been walking the deck for some time, looking out on either side—for those were days when it was necessary for seamen to have their eyes about them—when he observed in the quarter from whence the wind was coming, bright flashes of lightning. Soon the sea appeared through the gloom covered with a sheet of foam. Every instant the lightning increased in vividness, and now loud roars of thunder reverberated through the sky. Clouds came rushing on in vast masses.

"Call the captain!" said Deane to the midshipmen of the watch. "We are going to have a night of it, and he's not the man to remain in his bed at such a time. All hands on deck!" he shouted immediately afterwards.

The crew came rushing up from below with a speed which would have astonished any one not knowing how quickly sailors can put on their clothes, many of them, indeed, bringing them up in their hands and dressing on their way.

"Strike topgallant-masts!" he cried out. "Mr Grummit, range another cable for the best bower-anchor. We shall want every anchor out to-night."

Scarcely had these judicious orders been given, when the captain himself came on deck and took the command, next ordering the top-sail-yards to be lowered and the top-masts to be housed.

Now, with a loud roar, the gale burst upon the fleet, which lay at anchor in that exposed situation. The sea rising rapidly, torn up by the furious tempest, caused the ships to pitch and roll in a fearful manner, as if it would wrench them from their anchors and drive them against the dangerous Goodwin Sands. As Jack looked out he could see, indeed, some of the ships torn away from their anchors, apparently, and driven hopelessly before the gale. Over others the sea was breaking furiously, sending the spray high above them, and seeming every moment about to carry them to the bottom. Those who had been in many a battle, and gone through many a storm, felt their hearts, for the first time perhaps, sinking with fear, as the thunder crashed above their heads and the lightning flashed about the masts, while the foaming seas dashed up and round them on every side. The position of the "Lennox" was indeed perilous in the extreme, and little comfort could her crew gain by watching the fate of others. A large ship lay within sight—she was the "Mary"—with Rear-Admiral Beaumont's flag flying on board. Sea after sea came dashing and breaking over her. Now those whose eyes were turned in that direction saw that she began to move.

"She is driving! she is driving!" exclaimed several.

An instant afterwards she was seen carried before the gale, and ere many minutes had passed was thrown helplessly upon the Goodwins. Scarcely had she touched the fatal sands when her masts, bending like willow-wands, went by the board. The seas leaped triumphantly over her, and in the short time of one hour, scarce a timber of the stout ship hung together, while those who looked on knew well what must be the fate of all her brave crew. Not a man could be expected to live in that foaming sea. The same fate might any moment be the lot of those on board the "Lennox."

Thus the whole night was passed, no one knowing whether the next hour would not be their last. For a long time the gale gave no signs of abating. The thunder roared as loudly as ever, and the lightning flashed round their heads. Sometimes, as the vivid lightning enabled them to pierce the otherwise surrounding gloom, they saw far off some noble ship torn from her anchors, or the masts of another disappearing beneath the waves.

When morning broke at length, fearful was the scene of destruction which met their gaze. Here and there fragments of wreck could be distinguished on the Goodwins, while many other ships which had escaped the hurricane presented a shattered and forlorn appearance. By seven o'clock providentially the wind began to fall, and in a short time it ceased almost as rapidly as it had commenced. Sad was the number of ships which had foundered. Among those in the Downs was the "Northumberland," not one of her company having escaped. The "Stirling Castle" had also gone down, seventy of her men only having got on shore in their boats or on pieces of the wreck. Of Admiral Beaumont's ship, one man alone was saved on a piece of wreck, having been tossed about all night till at length he was cast on shore. The "Mortar" bomb-vessel had all her company lost. The number of sailors lost on the Goodwin Sands during that fatal night, and on all parts of the coast, many more being cast away in those few hours of the gale, amounted to fifteen hundred and nineteen. Thirteen men-of-war were totally wrecked, besides many others greatly injured. The newly-erected Eddystone Lighthouse was also blown down and entirely destroyed, the unfortunate men who had charge of it losing their lives. Several ships were forced from their anchors: among them was the "Revenge," which drove over to the coast of Holland, where she was nearly cast away. Happily, however, sail was got on her and she arrived safely in the river Medway. Another ship, the "Dorset," after striking three times, drove a fortnight to sea, where she was knocking about in an almost helpless state, till she was enabled to rig jury-masts and thus get safe back to the Nore.

In London the accidents which happened were numerous, and a large amount of property was destroyed. The gale blew down a multitude of chimneys, and even whole buildings; lifted the tops of houses, tore up a number of trees in Saint James's Park, in the Inns of Court, Moorfields, and at other places, by the roots, and broke off others in the middle. Several people were killed in their beds, among them Dr Kidder, Bishop of Bath and Wells, with his wife. A great number of vessels, barges, and boats were sunk in the river Thames, and the arches of London Bridge were stopped with the wrecks of them.

On the 12th of December the Queen published a proclamation for a general fast, which, on Wednesday, 19th January following, was kept with great strictness. The Order in Council also appeared in the *Gazette* for an advance of wages to the families of those officers and seamen who had perished in the storm, in the same manner as if they had been killed in battle. The House of Commons also addressed Her Majesty upon this melancholy occasion, desiring her to give directions for repairing this loss, and to build such capital ships as she should think fit, and promising to make good the expense at their next meeting. Thus, great as was the loss, the British Navy was restored to that state of efficiency which it is most important that it should ever maintain.

John Deane had a great disappointment in not being able, after all, to leave his ship. As soon as the damages she received in the storm were repaired, she was ordered to rejoin the fleet under Sir George Rooke. That admiral had been directed to convey the Arch-Duke Charles of Austria to Lisbon. Before the fleet had reached Finisterre another violent storm arose, which dispersed the ships and drove them back into the Channel. The tempestuous weather prevented the admiral from sailing before the 5th of February, and on the 15th of the same month he arrived at Lisbon.

A short historical account is now necessary, that the cause of the long war in which England was engaged may be understood. The King of Spain, who died in 1700, declared by his will, real or pretended, the Duke of Anjou, grandson to Louis the Fourteenth, King of the whole Spanish monarchy. The Spaniards, finding themselves threatened with war by the Emperor of Germany, and by England, in conjunction with the United Provinces, delivered themselves up into the hands of France. In consequence, both the Spanish Netherlands and the Duchy of Milan received French garrisons, and the French fleet came to Cadiz. A squadron was also sent to the West Indies, so that the whole Spanish Empire fell into the hands of the French. The Duke of Burgundy then having no children, the King of Spain was likely to succeed to the crown of France, and thus the world saw that a new universal monarchy might possibly arise out of this conjunction. Hence arose the War of Succession in Spain. With the object above mentioned of placing the Duke of Anjou on the throne of Spain, Louis had sacrificed his charming and clever niece, the granddaughter of our King Charles the First and Henrietta Maria to an imbecile husband, the thought of whom was hateful to her, and he also had engaged in a variety of other intrigues with the same object. The Spaniards in general gave the preference to the Arch-Duke Charles, or Don Carlos, who was the legitimate heir of the Spanish monarchy, second son of the Emperor of Austria. The object of Louis was first to secure his own authority over the Dutch; secondly, to injure the trade of England, and also of Holland; and, thirdly, to overthrow Protestantism in all the countries under his influence.

The object of William and the British government, on the other hand, was—first, to exclude Louis from the Netherlands and West Indies; secondly, to prevent the union of France and Spain in the person of the Duke of Anjou or his posterity; and, thirdly, to maintain the Protestant religion wherever it was established, including the Vaudois provinces. With these objects, William had exerted his utmost energies to form the grand alliance of England, Austria, and the States-general against France. To these were afterwards added some of the Italian states and Portugal.

The War of Succession lasted, from first to last, fifteen years. It ended by the accession of the Arch-Duke Don Carlos to the imperial throne of Germany, and Philip the Fifth, Duke of Anjou, was then acknowledged by all European sovereigns King of Spain, on the condition of renouncing all claim to the throne of France for himself and his descendants. The war had now continued for about two years. The chief exploit which had hitherto been performed was the capture of the galleons in the harbour of Vigo, which has already been described. The Arch-Duke, having landed at Lisbon, marched into Spain with a considerable body of troops, but was not able to make any progress for a considerable time. Sir George Rooke, with the fleet, proceeded into the Mediterranean and made an attack on the important, town of Barcelona. The fleet at length anchored in the roads of Tetuan, when, on the 17th of July, Sir George Rooke called a council of war, and placed before the members a plan he had devised for attacking the fortress of Gibraltar. Strong as it was, he believed that there was a prospect of capturing it, having received information that the garrison at that time was but small. It was a place, also, likely to prove of infinite importance during the war then going on, and it was hoped that the attacking this fortress would give a lustre to Queen Anne's armies, and possibly induce the Spaniards to favour the cause of King Charles.

As no time was to be lost, the fleet sailed in consequence of this resolution for Gibraltar, and, prepared for battle, took up a position in the bay on the 21st of July. As the British gazed up on the lofty rock surmounted by cannon, they might well have felt that it would require all their bravery and hardihood to conquer the place.

"It must be ours!" exclaimed John Deane, as he looked up at it while he walked the quarter-deck.

"It shall be!" observed Captain Jumper, who overheard him. "Deane, you shall accompany me on shore; and I hope before the world is much older, you and I shall find ourselves inside those walls."

"Or buried under them," said Deane. "For my part, however, I would as lief be on the top of them."

Meantime the marines, English and Dutch, to the number of eighteen hundred, were landed on the isthmus by which the rock is joined to the mainland, to cut off all communication between the town and the continent.

It was only of late that this fine body of men had been organised and received the name of marines, their duty being especially to serve on board ships. They were under command of the Prince of Hesse. His Highness, having taken post on the isthmus, summoned the governor to surrender, but that brave officer returned an answer, that he would defend the place to the last. On the 22nd, the admiral, at break of day, gave orders that the ships which had been appointed to cannonade the town, under the command of Rear-Admiral Byng and Rear-Admiral Vanderdosen, as also those which were to batter the South Mole Head, commanded by Captain Hicks of the "Weymouth," should arrange themselves accordingly. The wind, however, blowing contrary, they could not get into their places till the day was well-nigh spent. In the meantime, to amuse the enemy, Captain Whitaker was sent in with some boats, and a French privateer of twelve guns was burned at the Old Mole.

On the 23rd, soon after break of day, the ships being all placed in their stations, the admiral gave the signal for beginning the cannonade; and now the guns opened with a furious fire. The shot, like hail, flew against the Spanish batteries. The British seamen firing as fast as they could load, in five or six hours upwards of fifteen thousand shot were calculated to have been discharged against the town, and the enemy were driven from their guns, especially at the South Mole Head. Seeing this, the admiral sent an order to Captain Whitaker to attack the town with all the boats of the fleet. In the meantime, however, Captain Jumper, who saw what was necessary to be done, and Captain Hicks, who both lay next the Mole, had pushed on shore with their pinnaces and some other boats before the rest could come up. John Deane and two other lieutenants accompanied their captain. They, rushing forward as British seamen always will do when led by their officers, took possession of the fort with great bravery, but not without sustaining a considerable loss. As they, with swords and pistols in their hands, were rushing on, suddenly a fearful noise was heard. The earth seemed to lift up beneath their feet, and forty men and two lieutenants were carried up, fearfully burned and shattered. The survivors, among whom was John Deane, undaunted by this disaster, fought their way on and took possession of the grand platform, where they remained until reinforced by a body of seamen who had come in the boats under Captain Whitaker. The whole body then advanced and took a redoubt half-way between the Mole and the town, possessing themselves also of many of the enemy's cannon. The admiral then sent in a letter to the governor, and at the same time a message to the Prince of Hesse, directing him to send a peremptory summons, which His Highness accordingly did.

While this was taking place, John Deane, who had previously surveyed the rock, got leave from Captain Juniper to lead a body of men up a part of the cliff which the Spaniards had never thought it possible any human beings could climb. Deane, however, had often scrambled over the nearly perpendicular rock on which Nottingham Castle stands, and up its old rugged towers which yet remain. He had no lack of volunteers, with two or three midshipmen, ready to accompany him. Stealing away unperceived by the enemy, they got to the foot of the cliff. With their pistols in their belts and swords between their teeth they commenced the perilous ascent. Many who saw them thought they would never succeed, but they had resolved to persevere. Slowly but surely they proceeded up, hanging on by each craggy projection, aided by the shrubs which here and there grew from between the crevices of the rock. At length, when one after the other they reached the summit, they saw before them a chapel filled with women, with a vast number of others coming in and going out of it. These poor creatures had come out of the town, prompted by their superstitious notions, to implore the protection of the Virgin, to whom the chapel was dedicated. Jack and his followers, springing forward, threw themselves between the chapel and the road which led to the town. By gestures more than by words, he endeavoured to persuade the frightened matrons and damsels that he and his followers would do them no harm. With difficulty, however, he could make them understand this, though he signified by signs that they were all to get inside the chapel again. Their fears were somewhat overcome when they found that no insult was offered to any of them. He allowed, however, one of them to go back into the town to inform the governor that they had fallen into the hands of the English. The governor, finding that the forts were in possession of the English and that a large number of women had also fallen into their hands, consented to agree to the terms proposed by Admiral Rooke. Hostages were accordingly exchanged, and the capitulation being concluded, the Prince of Hesse marched into the town in the evening and took possession of the land and North Mole gates and the outworks. The Spanish troops were allowed to march out with all the honours of war, and provisions for a six days' march. Such inhabitants and soldiers who were willing to take an oath of fidelity to Don Carlos the Third were allowed to remain. The Spaniards were also to discover all their magazines of powder and other ammunition or provision and arms in the city. All subjects of the French King were, however, excluded from any part of the terms of this capitulation.

The town was found to be extremely strong, with a hundred guns mounted facing the sea and the narrow pass towards the land. It was well supplied with ammunition, but the garrison consisted of only a hundred and fifty men. However, in the opinion of officers who examined the works, fifty men might have defended them against thousands, so it was acknowledged that the attack made by the seamen was brave almost beyond example.

The British lost sixty men killed, including two lieutenants and one master, and two hundred and sixteen wounded, including one captain, seven lieutenants, and a boatswain. It is but justice to the naval part of the expedition to remark that as this design was contrived by the admiral, so it was executed entirely by the seamen, and therefore the whole honour of it was due to them. Nothing, indeed, could have enabled the seamen to take the place but the cannonading of it in a way which obliged the Spaniards to quit their posts.

After leaving as many men as could be spared to garrison the place, under the command of the Prince of Hesse, the fleet sailed for Tetuan, in order to take in wood and water. Immediately the fleet had watered, it stood out again towards Gibraltar, when on the lath of August about noon, the enemy's fleet and galleys were discovered to the westward, near Cape Malaga, going free. The allied fleet accordingly bore after them in a line of battle. On the morning of the 13th of August they were within three leagues of the French, and then brought to, with their heads to the south, the wind being east, and lay in a posture to receive them. In the English line, Sir George Rooke, with Rear-Admirals Byng and Dilkes, were in the centre. Sir Cloudesley Shovel and Sir John Leake led the van, and Vice-Admiral Calemburg and Rear-Admiral Vanderdosen commanded the ships in the rear.

The English fleet consisted of forty-five ships of the line, and eighteen smaller vessels. The Dutch had only twelve ships of the line, while the French fleet consisted of fifty ships of the line, eight frigates, and eleven smaller vessels, the line-of-battle ships alone carrying 3530 guns, while the English ships together only carried 3154 guns, and the Dutch ships about 1000 guns.

Though the French endeavoured at first to avoid the battle, yet they had the advantage over the combined fleet, as they were superior in force, and all their ships were clean and fully manned. They had also the advantage of fighting on the coast, and near a harbour of their ally, and had the benefit of a large number of galleys. The confederates, on the contrary, besides being away from any friendly port, were thinly manned, and had a great deficiency of stores and provisions, while the foulness of their ships was greatly to their prejudice in the day of battle. Notwithstanding this they were eager for the engagement.

The action which was about to commence was likely to prove of far more importance than any in which Deane had hitherto engaged, and his heart beat high as he saw the ships of England bear down upon the enemy. His own ship the "Lennox" was among those under the command of the brave Admiral Sir Cloudesley Shovel.

At about 10 o'clock, when nearly half-gunshot from the enemy, the French set all their sails at once, and seemed to intend to stretch ahead and weather the English fleet. Admiral Shovel, on discovering the enemy's intention, hauled his wind, and Sir George Rooke, seeing what would be the consequence if the van was intercepted, bore down upon the enemy with the rest of the confederate fleet, and put out the signal for a fight, which was immediately begun by Admiral Shovel. The battle raged with great fury on both sides till about two in the afternoon, when the enemy's van gave way. The Dutch engaged the enemy with the greatest courage and alacrity, and being provided with ammunition, continued firing something later than the rest, but night coming on put a stop to the engagement. Several of the French ships were compelled to quit the fight, long before it was over, to repair damages, some of them to stop leaks which would otherwise have caused them to founder. The French main body being very strong, and several ships of the admiral's and Rear-Admirals Byng and Dilke's divisions being also forced to go out of the line for want of shot, the battle fell very heavily on the admiral's own ship the "Saint George," as also on the "Shrewsbury." This being observed by Sir Cloudesley Shovel, he, like a good and valiant officer, immediately backed astern and endeavoured to reinforce the admiral. This act of valour and of good seamanship had two useful effects. First it drew several of the enemy's ships from the British centre, which was so hard pressed by a great superiority of strength and numbers, and secondly it drove them at length out of the line, for after they had felt the effects of the guns of others of the ships of Sir Cloudesley Shovel's division, which were astern of him, they considered it more prudent not to advance along his broadside. Being clean and better sailers, they set their split-sails, and with their boats ahead, towed away from him, without giving him the opportunity of exchanging a single broadside with them.

There can be no doubt that the British would have gained a complete victory had they not have been in want of shot. This had been expended by the vast number of guns fired at Gibraltar, though every ship had been furnished with twenty-five rounds the day before the battle, which would have been sufficient had they got as near the enemy as the admiral intended. As it was, every ship had expended her ammunition before night.

In the centre of the line a furious action was going on. The "Sérieux," a ship in the French admiral's division commanded by Monsieur Champmelin, however, boarded the "Monk," an English ship commanded by Captain Mills. He, with great activity and courage, every time cleared the deck of the enemy, and made them at last bear away. The same French commander had his ship afterwards so disabled that he was obliged with others to quit the line. Captain Jumper also added laurels to those he had already gained, by engaging with his single ship three of the enemy's; and on this occasion, as he had done at Gibraltar, John Deane especially distinguished himself. Captain Jumper shook him by the hand, and thanking him for the aid he had afforded, promised him that he would not rest till he had recommended him for promotion to the admiral.

About seven in the evening, one of the French admiral's seconds advanced out of the line, and began a closer engagement with the "Saint

George," commanded by Captain Jennings; but, although the "Saint George" had already suffered much, the French ship met with such rough treatment that she had great difficulty in rejoining the line, after the loss of both her captains and many of her men.

Among the actions of other brave commanders, that of the gallant Earl of Dursley, commander of the "Boyne," an eighty-gun ship, must be mentioned. He was but twenty-three years of age, yet he gave numerous instances of his undaunted courage, steady resolution, and prudent conduct.

The battle ended at the close of the day, when the enemy escaped with the help of their galleys to leeward. In the night the wind shifted to the north, and in the morning to the west, which placed the enemy on the weather side of the confederates. Their fleet lay by all day within three leagues of the French. At night the latter stood away to the northward. The English lost 687 men killed, and 1632 wounded. The loss of the French was a Rear-Admiral, five captains, and a number of other officers killed with 150 wounded, and upwards of 3000 men killed or wounded. Sir Cloudesley Shovel afterwards declared that this engagement was the most desperate that had ever taken place between two fleets in his time. Scarcely a ship escaped witshout being obliged to shift one of her masts, and many of them all.

Chapter Thirty Five
Home again—Another bitter Disappointment

Soon after the battle which has been described the fleet once more returned to England. The admirals and many of the captains were presented to Queen Anne, who complimented them on the actions in which they had been engaged. Among the officers who received promotion was John Deane, who was raised to the rank of captain. At length, as he was now without a ship, he was able to set forward to pay his long-promised visit to his home. In those days the post was very irregular on shore, and sailors often went many years without receiving letters from home. Such had been John Deane's case, and he still remained in ignorance of all the events which had taken place among those he loved since his departure. One thing had troubled him greatly; it was at not hearing of the arrival of Elizabeth and her faithful guardian, Mistress Pearson. He had gained a large amount of prize-money, which the agent at Portsmouth, where he landed, promised to remit to him at Nottingham. He took with him only a sum sufficient for his journey and to supply his wants while he expected to remain on shore. He met with no adventure during his journey. The number of loose characters who had infested the roads in the early days of King William's reign, had been drawn away to fight the battles of their country, either under Marlborough or at sea, and few highwaymen were to be met with in any part of the country. Deane would gladly have turned aside to go to Norwich; but it was greatly out of his way, and he felt that it was his duty in the first place to visit his own father and mother. He could scarcely restrain his eagerness as he passed over the Trent bridge once more, and took his way through the well-known streets which led to the market-place. It was early in the day, but no one knew him in his richly-laced coat, his countenance well bronzed by sun and wind, and his whiskers and beard of no mean growth. At length he stopped before the door of the old house and threw himself from his horse, calling to a boy passing at the moment to hold it. Not till then did it occur to him how long he had been absent, and what great changes might have taken place. His heart sank, for he expected almost to see his mother hurrying to the door, with his old father's fine countenance peering behind her; but the door remained closed, and he had to knock more than once before it was opened. His voice trembled as he inquired of the serving-damsel who opened the door whether Mr and Mistress Deane were at home.

"Ay," was the answer, "they are in the parlour at the back of the house."

He pushed past her and hurried on. The old gentleman and lady rose from their seats as he threw open the door, at first not knowing him.

"To what cause do we owe the honour of this visit, sir?" said old Mr Deane, taking Jack to be an intruder, or one of the officers quartered in the town engaged in a frolic.

"He is our son—our son Jack!" exclaimed Mistress Deane, who, knowing him at a second glance, threw her arms round his neck.

Old Mr Deane hurried forward, and grasping his hand, almost wrung it off. Then his mother bestowed her kisses on his bronzed cheeks.

"Yes, it's Jack—I know him now!" exclaimed the old gentleman, drawing back a pace, that he might look at him from head to foot. "Well, thou art grown into a brave lad, Jack," he said, looking at him affectionately.

And now Jack was seated between the two old people, who scarcely would allow him to ask any questions, so eager were they to hear his adventures. It was some time, therefore, before he could learn what had become of the rest of the family.

"And how is sister Polly and her husband, Tom Dovedale? It seems an age since the day they were spliced."

"They live six doors off, and are wonderfully flourishing, for from morning to night they do little else than 'laugh and grow fat,'" was the answer.

"And Jasper, where is he?" was the next question.

"The father of two fine cherubs, and Alethea as beautiful and cheerful as ever. He is a fortunate fellow, your brother Jasper. Cousin Nat now lives with him, and has given him up all his business, so that Jasper is the leading physician in the town, and, on my word, he bears his honours bravely, and is in no way behind cousin Nat in the estimation of the townspeople and neighbourhood. At first I feared that Jasper and Alethea would not have got on very smoothly together. She, as you remember, was a warm Jacobite, as was her poor father, but Jasper argued the matter so well with her, that he soon brought her over, and she became as loyal a subject of King William as any to be found within the realm. Had it not been, indeed, for her marriage to Jasper, it would have gone hard with her, for poor Harwood was so implicated in the plot against King William, that his property would have been confiscated. Cousin Nat and other friends, however, so earnestly petitioned the Government, that it was preserved for the sake of his daughter, and Jasper, after poor Harwood's death, became the Squire of Harwood Grange."

"And have you heard from Kate and Dainsforth, mother?" asked Jack. He had another question which he was eager to ask, but he wished first to inquire about his own family.

"Oh, yes! they're flourishing in their new plantation; and glowing are the accounts which they send us of the country. It must be a wonderful place, and although the free Government we now enjoy makes fewer people wish to go over there, yet many are tempted, from time to time, from the accounts they receive from their friends settled there."

Jack's next inquiry was about Mr Gournay at Norwich. He could only learn that a foreign lady and gentleman were residing at his house, but not a word about Elizabeth could they tell him. He concluded that they alluded to Monsieur and Madame de Mertens, but they were not aware even that they had a daughter, nor could they give him any account of the arrival of their supposed daughter.

Jack's visit to Jasper and Alethea and to cousin Nat must be briefly passed over.

Having spent a few days at Nottingham he became eager to visit Norwich. He found Will Brinsmead, who, in spite of his age, continued his journeys through the country, about to set off in that direction. Will begged that he would give him the honour of his company, but Jack laughingly assured him, that though he should have great delight in talking over old days, his eagerness to reach Norwich would not allow him to jog along behind the cattle. He, however, rode a few miles with him, when just as the old man was beginning one of his lectures on the "Pilgrim's Progress," Jack, shaking him warmly by the hand, pushed on his steed in advance of the herd.

On making himself known to Mr Gournay, he was received in the kindest way by him and his wife; but Jack's astonishment and disappointment was very great when he found that they had not received the accounts he had sent home of his discovery of Elizabeth, and of her proposed return with Mistress Pearson, under charge of Captain Davis, to England. Monsieur and Madame de Mertens were residing, he found, in a small house in Norwich, and they also had not received either his letter or one from Captain Davis. His heart sank within him. What was he now to do? The more he had of late thought of Elizabeth, the more completely he found that she had entwined herself round his heart, and he had anticipated the delight of meeting her again and receiving her as his bride from the hands of her parents. All these delightful visions had now vanished. Monsieur and Madame de Mertens received him with every expression of regard and affection.

"I can never forget the important service you rendered me in restoring to me my husband," said Madame de Mertens, "and I feel sure that, had it been in your power, you would have brought back to me my child. Even now I have a hope that you may possibly restore her to me."

Jack spent some time with his friends, and finally came to the resolution of returning to the West Indies, in order to make inquiries about Elizabeth and Dame Pearson.

"I will first go to the Admiralty and ascertain where the 'Venus' frigate now is, and then I will communicate with Captain Davis," said Deane. "Should he be unable to give me the information I desire, I will immediately set off on my projected voyage."

Captain Deane had been invited to return to Mr Gournay's to supper. On entering the house, the excellent quaker met him with a letter in his hand.

"I have just received this," he said, "from your brother-in-law Giles Dainsforth. He mentions a curious circumstance which occurred some time ago, which may tend to solve the mystery concerning the fate of Elizabeth de Mertens and her friend. He writes me word that information had been received in the plantation of the wreck of a ship on an island off the American coast, with several passengers, among whom were said to be some ladies. A small boat which had left the island, had, after a long voyage, the people undergoing great hardships, reached the mainland. They had come in the hopes of obtaining relief for those left behind. As soon as the information was received, a meeting of the inhabitants of Philadelphia was held, and it was resolved to send out a vessel for the rescue of the sufferers. Unfortunately, friend Giles does not mention the name of the vessel or the passengers, except casually he refers to the loss of a queen's ship."

This was indeed important information. It raised Captain Deane's hopes of the possibility of discovering Elizabeth; at the same time he was well aware that there were many probabilities of the wreck being that of some other vessel.

"Friend Dainsforth is very anxious that we should send out a vessel with a cargo of which he may dispose. It is a business in which I myself am not willing to enter," observed Mr Gournay; "but thou mayest find friends in Nottingham who will be more ready to engage in the speculation, and being thyself a seaman of experience, thou mightest take the command of it. It will be far better for thee than following the occupation of fighting, in which thou hast been engaged."

The plan thus suggested by Mr Gournay was much in accordance with Jack's taste. He, however, made up his mind in the first instance to go to London, that he might make inquiries as to the fate of the "Venus." If she had left the West Indies, and had not since been heard of, or if it was supposed that she had been cast away, he would then have very little doubt of her being the ship of which Giles Dainsforth spoke; but if, on the contrary, she had returned to England, or been sent to some other station, he would then only suppose that the wreck alluded to in the letter must be that of another ship, and thus proceeding to Pennsylvania would in no way forward the great object he had in view. Mr Gournay having fully agreed with him in the wisdom of his plans, after he had bidden farewell to Monsieur and Madame de Mertens, he set off on his visit to London.

Jack felt very differently from what he did before on his first visit to the metropolis in company with Long Sam. He was now a captain in the navy, with an honourable name, and money in his pocket. On going to the Admiralty, however, he could gain no satisfactory information regarding the "Venus" or Captain Davis. One of the clerks told him that he believed she was still in the West Indies. Another that she had been captured by the enemy. A third, of whom in his despair he made further inquiries, told him that she had been sunk; and another, that she was on her passage home. He had just left the office, and was taking his way disconsolately along the street, when he met an old shipmate.

"My dear fellow," he exclaimed, "you did not employ a golden key, I suspect, to unlock the mystery! Just go back with a doubloon in your band, and cross the palm of Master Dick Greedifist, and you will soon find that he knows more about the matter than you supposed."

Jack, though indignant that such a proceeding should be necessary, did as he was advised.

"Oh, certainly, Captain Deane!" answered Dick. "It was about the 'Venus' you were inquiring. Oh, ah, let me see! she was ordered home in 1702, and immediately afterwards the order was countermanded and she remained on the station for some time longer. Since then, she was sent to visit the plantations on the mainland of North America; and, in consequence of her not having been heard of for some time, it is feared that she must have met with some disaster. As soon as she had executed her mission she was to return home; and I know that some months ago she was expected."

This was all the information Jack required. He did not tell Master Greedifist the opinion he had formed of him, but, hastening out of the office, took his way to his inn. Jack as has been seen was a man of action. He took care of the minutes, well knowing that the hours would take care of themselves. As soon as he had sufficiently fortified the inner man, he again mounted his horse, and leaving all the wonders of London unvisited, spurred back northward towards Nottingham.

At the inn where he rested the first night of his journey, he wrote an account of the information he had gained to his friends at Norwich, saying that he proposed carrying out the plan suggested by Giles Dainsforth, and that as soon as he could make the arrangements he hoped to sail in a galley for Pennsylvania. On reaching home he found that Dainsforth had expressed the same opinion to his friends at Nottingham. He had, therefore, little difficulty in inducing them to join in a speculation for the purchase of a galley, to be freighted with goods suitable for the plantations, he himself having the command of her. Having made all the preliminary arrangements, he was about to start for London, when he received information from Mr Gournay that a galley admirably suited for his object was about to be launched at Lynn Regis. Scarcely had the letter been read, when Jack was on horseback, and spurring forward to that town. He was not disappointed in the appearance of the vessel. She was stoutly built, and roomy, capable of carrying a large cargo. As she reached the water she was named the "Nottingham Galley." John Deane, whose manners were such as to gain the confidence of his fellow-men, soon found a hardy crew to man her. By the time she was ready for sea, he had obtained a considerable share of his prize-money. His brother Jasper, his cousin Nat, and his father, with several other influential persons at Nottingham, took shares in the speculation. It would be impossible to follow Deane in his various journeys backwards and forwards to Norwich, Lynn, and Nottingham, while the galley was getting ready for sea. At length, having received a part of her cargo on board, sent from Norwich and Nottingham, and other places to the west, he made sail for the Thames, where he was to receive the remainder.

Chapter Thirty Six
Adventure in the "Nottingham Galley"—Shipwreck

Captain John Deane had now launched forth in a new character, that of a merchant adventurer, especially honoured in those days, as it deserved to be. The merchant adventurers a century and a half ago were the promoters of civilisation, the founders of kingdoms, while they were generally distinguished by their courage, perseverance, and honourable conduct. The "Nottingham Galley" had a crew of forty men, and she mounted twenty guns, with which her captain hoped to defend her against any enemies she might encounter. He had hitherto been a successful man, and he began to think that it would never be his lot to be otherwise.

The voyage was prosperous till the "Nottingham Galley" was within fifty leagues of the American coast. A furious gale then sprang up, and thick weather came on, so that no observations could be taken. Deane endeavoured to bring the ship to, that he might keep off the coast till the weather should moderate. In vain, however, did he make the attempt. The after-masts were carried away; and now the ship could only run before the gale, it being feared every moment that the seas which came roaring up astern would break on board. He hoped, however, that the weather might moderate before they reached the entrance of the Delaware river, up which the galley was bound. Vain hope! The darkness of night came on, and instead of moderating, the gale increased. The crew, hardy as they were, clung to the bulwarks and the shrouds, expecting that every moment would be their last. Still the fury of the tempest increased. The wind whistled through the shrouds, and the seas raged up alongside. A loud roar was heard ahead. "Breakers! breakers!" shouted the crew. The next instant there came a fearful crash. The helpless galley was driven forward amid the rocks. The seas swept over her. Many were washed away, or dashed furiously against the rocks. Deane felt himself lifted up by a sea which dashed against the devoted vessel. He suspected that the fate which had overtaken many of his crew would now be his. Onward the sea bore him. He struck out, struggling bravely for life. His feet touched the hard sand, and the next instant he was thrown high upon the beach. He staggered forward, and before the following sea had reached him he had escaped from its clutches. The despairing shrieks of his crew reached his ears. In vain he endeavoured to render them assistance. He rescued two, however, at the risk of being himself thrown back into the foaming surges. Three others had been thrown as he had been on shore.

When morning at length broke, they were the only survivors of the gallant band which had manned the "Nottingham Galley." Captain Deane's first thought was, that possibly this might be the very island on which the "Venus" had been cast away, supposing it to be an island, of which he was not yet sure. A vague feeling that even now Elizabeth and Mistress Pearson might be living on it, induced him immediately to set forth to explore the country. He had not gone far before in front of him he saw several huts, constructed evidently out of the wreck of a vessel. He hurried on, eager to communicate with the inhabitants whom he expected to find within them. As he reached the huts, however, he soon saw by the open doors and the silence which reigned on every side, that they were deserted. On searching around, however, he discovered signs that they had been inhabited by a considerable number of persons. One of the huts, built at a short distance from the others, was constructed in a better style. It was closed by a door placed on hinges, and there was a window which could be closed by a shutter. He lifted the latch. There were two neat bed-places within, and on the table some small shreds of silk, and a few other articles such as were used by females met his sight. This then might possibly have been the abode of Elizabeth. He looked eagerly around with tender interest, in the hope of finding some sign by which he might ascertain the truth. All the articles of value had been removed, but still it was evident that the hut had been abandoned somewhat suddenly. At length he found an object sticking between the crib and the wall, as if it had fallen down between them. It was a book. He opened it eagerly. On the blank page at the commencement were the letters "E.P." He had no longer any doubt that it was the property of Elizabeth. He placed it in his bosom and continued the search. There could be no doubt then, that the vessel which Giles Dainsforth had mentioned as being on the point of sailing in search of the shipwrecked crew had reached the place, and carried them off in safety. For this he was truly thankful, delighted as he would have been to have found Elizabeth still there, as he had almost expected to do.

On his return he told his companions what he had discovered. Their spirits revived as they began to hope that some vessel might pass that way, and carry them to the plantation. As they gazed, however, on the ocean, covered with foaming billows, their condition seemed perilous indeed. Of the ship herself, not a plank clung together, though the beach was strewed with various articles which had formed her cargo. One of her boats too had been cast ashore, without receiving any material damage. Deane immediately summoned his men around him, and pointed out to them the necessity of saving whatever provisions were washed on shore. By this time the gale had considerably abated, and they were enabled to drag up several casks and cases containing food, which they so much required. In the same way, numerous bales and other articles which had formed the cargo of the ship were saved. They found themselves on an uninhabited island of small extent, which seemed likely to afford them but scanty means of subsistence. In the far distance could be seen a long blue ridge of land, which Deane knew must be the continent. Their great requirement however was water, for without it their stores and flour would have availed them but little. They therefore immediately set about searching for it, and at length a slight moisture was found oozing out from beneath the roots of a large tree. After eagerly scraping away the earth with their hands for some time, the hole they had formed was filled with a small portion of the precious liquid. This encouraged them to hope that a sufficient supply might be obtained, and with better heart than they had hitherto possessed they took their first meal on the island.

On examining the boat, Captain Deane was of opinion that if repaired, she would carry them to the mainland: but as yet there were no tools found by which this could be accomplished. Thus were all their hopes of escaping frustrated. Their life on the island was that of most shipwrecked mariners. Even when partaking of their meals, they could not but feel that their store of provisions would in time come to an end, and that thus, unless relieved, famine would overtake them at last. Several days passed by, when as two of their number were wandering along the shore a chest was seen fixed between two rocks. Summoning their companions, not without difficulty they waded towards it. It was found to be a carpenter's chest. After considerable labour they contrived to break it open, when to their great joy they discovered within it a supply of tools and nails, with iron hoops and other necessary articles.

They now eagerly set to work to repair their boat, but as none of them were carpenters they found it a more difficult task than they had expected. Spars and oars and sails had also to be formed. No one, however, was idle, and they made up by diligence what they wanted in skill. The boat was at last launched and moored between the rocks. All the provisions they could collect, with a supply of water in such casks as would hold it were placed on board. They had left the island astern when a sail appeared in sight, rapidly approaching them from the east. Deane, supposing she was some vessel bound up the Delaware for Philadelphia, hove to, purposing if such was the case to take a passage in her, instead of risking the voyage in their open boat, still imperfectly repaired. As she drew nearer, she was seen to be a large ship carrying several guns, yet she wanted the trim appearance of a man-of-war. No colours were flying at her mast-head or peak, and altogether her appearance did not satisfy Captain Deane. It was now, however, too late to avoid her. Already the boat must have been seen by those on board. Still Deane thought it more prudent to fill his sails, and to stand away towards the opening which he took to be the mouth of the river of which he was in search. A shot from the ship told him that he had been discovered. It was the signal also for him again to heave to. In a short time the ship got up to the boat, and a voice from her decks hailed, ordering those in the boat to sheer alongside and to come on board. There was no use attempting to disobey this order, as they were already under the ship's guns. Having secured the boat alongside, Deane and his men stepped on deck. From the appearance of the officers and the number of men composing the mongrel-looking crew on board, who seemed to be of all countries and of all shades of colour, the thought at once occurred to Captain Deane that the vessel was a pirate.

"What have you been about, and where are you going?" asked a man who stepped forward from among the people on board. Though considerably older, and knocked about by climate and hardship, Deane had little difficulty in recognising his former acquaintance Pearson. The pirate captain looked at him two or three times, but if he had recognised him for a moment, he soon seemed to have altered his opinion. Jack felt that the best plan, whether he was right or wrong in his conjectures, was to tell the whole truth of himself. Pearson seemed interested in hearing Nottingham spoken of, and it made him give another glance at Deane.

"Ah well, my man," he said, "we wish you no harm, but we can allow no vessel to proceed to the new plantations."

"That's a hard rule, sir," answered Jack, "as we are likely enough to starve on the island we have just left, and if we remain at sea we shall perish in the next gale that comes on."

"You have your remedy," said the pirate captain. "You may join our brave crew. You shall be an officer on board, and your men shall share with the rest."

"We cannot accept your offer," answered Deane; "and perhaps for old acquaintance' sake, Master Pearson, you will grant my request?"

The pirate captain started on hearing himself thus addressed.

"Who are you?" he asked, looking again hard at Deane.

"One you knew in his youth, and who has never ceased to wish you well," answered Jack. "You have served one sovereign—I have fought under the flag of another. Do you know me now?"

"Yes, indeed I do; though you are greatly changed from the stripling you were when I knew you," answered Pearson, stretching out his hand. "I wish you well, for I thought you a brave and honest youth, and I am thankful to find you took your own course. Now, as I believe you to be unchanged, the promise I ask you to make, if I allow you to proceed, is— that you will not give information of my vessel being off the coast."

Deane was rather perplexed what answer to make.

"No," he answered at last; "I wish you no harm; at the same time, I cannot allow any honest trader to fall into your hands. Now hear me, Master Pearson. My object in coming out here is to carry home two persons in whom you were once greatly interested: the little Elizabeth whom you protected in her youth, and your own wife, whom I am sure you once loved. I throw myself, therefore, on your generosity."

Pearson seemed greatly agitated for some minutes.

"I will not interfere with you," he answered. "I cannot force that poor lady to undergo the hardships into which I once led her, and I will therefore leave her to your kindness and charity. I would that I could accompany you, but I cannot desert my comrades. But the time may come ere long, that I may enable them to secure their own safety, and I will then, if I still have the means, endeavour to visit Pennsylvania."

Much on the same subject passed between the two former acquaintances. The pirates' ship towed the boat to the mouth of the Delaware, when the latter cast off and stood up the river, while the pirate proceeded again towards the ocean.

Chapter Thirty Seven
Pennsylvania—Return Home—Last
Adventures and Conclusion

Captain Deane and his companions had a prosperous voyage up the Delaware, and in two days the buildings of the new city appeared in sight, standing at the junction of the Delaware and the Schuylkill. The Delaware is a noble stream, and the Schuylkill is as broad at its mouth as the Thames is at Woolwich. The banks of the great river above which the town was laid out were bold and high, the air pure and wholesome, while the neighbouring lands were free from swamps. Altogether the site was one admirably fitted for the purpose of a great city. Clay for making bricks was found on the spot, and quarries of good stone abounded within a few miles. Already the city was laid out according to the design of its sagacious founder, but as yet, although a considerable number of houses had been erected near to each other, forming streets, many were only scattered about here and there, according as the owners had purchased their town lots. Two streets, one of them facing a magnificent row of red pines, were planned to front the rivers. The great public thoroughfare alone separated the houses from the banks. It was arranged that these streets were to be connected by the High Street, a magnificent avenue perfectly straight and a hundred feet in width, to be adorned with trees and gardens. At a right angle with the High Street a broad street of equal width was to cut the city in two from north to south. It was thus divided into four sections. In the exact centre of the city, a large square of ten acres was reserved for the advantage of the public, and in the middle of each quarter a smaller square of eight acres was set apart for the same purpose. Eight streets, each fifty feet wide, were to be built parallel to the High Street, and twenty of the same width parallel to the rivers. Mr Penn's great object was to give a rural appearance to the houses of his new city. The boat reached the shore before a large building, which from the sign-board swinging in front of it, on which a large blue anchor was painted, was known to be a house of entertainment Deane and his companions, hauling up their boat, hastened towards it, as he hoped there to obtain the information as to where Giles Dainsforth and his sister were to be found. This building was then one of the most important in the province. It was not only a beer-house, but an exchange, a corn-market, and a post-office. It was formed of large rafters of wood, the interstices being filled with bricks, which had been brought in the vessels from England, in the same manner as houses to be found in Cheshire, and some built in the Tudor and Stuart periods. Already a magnificent quay of three hundred feet in length had been formed by the side of the river, and there were also stone houses with pointed roofs, and balconies, and porches, in different parts. Although in some portions of the city pine-trees and pine-stumps still remained, altogether upwards of a thousand houses had been erected. Among them was a large building devoted to the purposes of a public school or college. A printing-press had long been established in the city by William Bradford, a native of Leicester, who had accompanied Mr Penn in the "Welcome." Deane had, however, but little inclination to view the city until he had found his way to the house of his sister and brother-in-law. He had no great difficulty in discovering it, for Giles Dainsforth was already well-known as a man of mark, as sagacious, steady, and industrious men are sure to be in a new settlement.

"There is friend Dainsforth's house," said a worthy citizen to whom Deane addressed himself; and he saw before him a fine and substantial stone building, with a broad verandah surrounded by trees and flowering shrubs. A gentle voice reached his ears, singing an air he knew well. The door stood open and he entered. Passing through the house, he saw seated on a lawn, beneath the shade of the building, three ladies, while the same number of young children played about them. The nearest he recognised as his sister Kate, though grown into more matronly proportions than when he last had seen her. Near her was a fair girl. He required not a second glance to convince him that she was Elizabeth. He hurried forward, forgetting how he might startle them. A cry of delight escaped Elizabeth as she advanced to meet him. In another minute he found himself in the arms of his sister, while a sob of joy escaped from her companion's bosom.

"He's come! he's come!" she exclaimed; "I knew he would find us out."

The third lady was Mistress Pearson. She looked careworn and aged, as if her life had well-nigh come to an end.

Their history was soon told. When at length Captain Davis was ordered to visit the plantations, previous to returning to England, he obtained permission to receive them on board and to convey them home. When the ship was cast away, they, with a few only of the crew, had been rescued. The captain, however, although he was the last to leave the ship, had also been saved. Deane had fortunately told Elizabeth of the marriage of Giles Dainsforth to his sister, and of their intention of settling in Pennsylvania.

On their arrival, therefore, at Philadelphia, hearing his name, she made herself known to him, and it was thus that she and Mistress Pearson became inmates of his house.

In a short time Giles Dainsforth himself, accompanied by Captain Davis, arrived at the house, and a happy party were soon assembled round the supper-table. Deane heard a great deal of the flourishing condition of the plantation, and of its vast internal resources. He heard, too, from Dainsforth, that the settlers had resolved not to allow the importation of slaves into the colony. They had established it because they themselves loved freedom, and they were resolved to employ free men alone in the cultivation of their lands. He also heard that the whole territory had been purchased from the native tribes, and that not the life of a single red man had been taken away by the settlers since their arrival in the country. From the first, they had lived on the most friendly terms with the native tribes. This was indeed glorious news, especially in those days, when the traffic in negroes was looked upon as lawful, and when in most instances might made right in all parts of the world. Altogether the account which Deane received of the colony was so favourable that he could not help longing to come and settle in it. He had, however, promised to bring Elizabeth back to her parents, and poor Mistress Pearson also was very anxious to lay her bones in her native land. Captain Davis likewise desired to return home on the first opportunity, that he might stand his trial for the loss of his ship, which he considered himself in honour bound to do. Deane, however, resolved not to run the risk of again being separated from Elizabeth. She having no legal guardian, he instituted himself as such, and then gave himself permission to marry her, which she, nothing loath, consented to do forthwith. The marriage was celebrated with such religious and legal ceremonies as were then considered sufficient in Philadelphia. Colonel Markham, the acting governor, being one of the witnesses. Jack and his bride, accompanied by Captain Davis and his sister, soon afterwards embarked on board a stout ship sailing for England. They arrived safely in London, whence Jack wrote to Norwich to announce his safe return.

A few days were spent in the great city, that Elizabeth might recruit her strength after her voyage. During his stay there, he met with an old brother officer, Captain Bertrand, who, hailing him with pleasure, told him that he was the very man he was looking out for.

"I have taken service," he said, "with the permission of the British Government, under the Czar of Russia, the Great Peter, for such he is indeed. You will remember his labouring as a shipwright in England not many years since, to gain a knowledge of ship-building He is now constructing a large fleet, and he is anxious to secure the services of a number of active and intelligent officers like yourself. What do you say? I can promise you handsome pay, and the command of a line-of-battle ship."

Deane replied that he must think about it, as he had only lately married a wife, and had no inclination to leave her.

"Oh, you must bring her with you!" was the answer. "You can establish her in the new city the Czar is building on the Neva; and, depend upon it, you will have no long cruises to make. Foreign officers can be found; but he will have a difficulty in making seamen out of his serfs. Free men only are fit to become seamen, in my opinion."

Captain Deane begged that his friend would give him his address, and should he determine to accept his offer, after he had visited his friends, he would communicate with him. Leaving the unhappy Mistress Pearson with her brother, Deane set forward in a coach with his bride for Norwich. He had fortunately been able to procure the balance of prize-money due to him while he was in London, which amounted to a considerable sum, and he was thus, in spite of his heavy loss in the "Nottingham Galley," no longer crippled by want of means.

Words can scarcely describe the joy with which Madame de Mertens and her husband received their long-lost daughter. Though she had grown from a young child into a woman, they immediately recognised her, while the trinkets she had preserved prevented them having any doubt about the matter. After spending some time at Norwich, and receiving great kindness from the excellent Mr Gournay and his lady, the young couple repaired to Nottingham.

The loss of the "Nottingham Galley," however, caused Jack to be more coolly received by his friends than he had anticipated. In vain he tried to explain to them that they should find fault with the elements more than with him for the ill-success of their speculation. He undertook, if it was their wish, to command another galley, and to embark all his property in the enterprise. To this, however, none of them would agree. Yet there were two of his friends who received him in a different manner to the rest—his sister Polly and his sister-in-law Alethea. Prosperity had not improved his brother Jasper, and he appeared to be more bitter than any of the family who suffered from the wreck of the galley. A reconciliation was however at last brought about by cousin Nat and Polly. Jack had been dining at the house of his sister and her husband, where he met Jasper, to whose house in Fletcher-gate he agreed to walk in the evening. On their way, some remarks made by Dr Jasper irritated John Deane, as he considered them unfair and unjust, and angry words were heard by some of the passers-by, uttered by him to his brother. They reached the door together. A flight of stone steps led to it from the street. Unhappily, at this moment the doctor repeated the expressions which had justly offended the captain, who declared that he would not allow himself to be addressed in so injurious a manner. As he spoke he pushed impatiently past his brother, who at that moment stumbled down the steps. The doctor fell; and as Captain Deane stooped to lift him up, to his horror, he found that he was dead! Rumour, with her hundred tongues, forthwith spread the report that the fire-eating captain had killed his brother. The verdict however of the jury who sat to decide the case was, that Dr Jasper Deane had died by the visitation of God. Still Captain Deane was conscious of the angry feelings which had excited his bosom at the moment, and he felt that the mark of Cain was upon his forehead. He could no longer remain at home, and though those who loved him best knew of his innocence, and did their utmost to console him, he determined to leave the country. He accordingly wrote to Captain Bertrand, accepting his offer of a naval command under the Czar of Russia; and in a short time he and Elizabeth sailed for the Baltic. He rendered great assistance in organising the navy of that wonderful man Peter the Great, and after serving with much credit for a few years, he returned to England.

Captain Deane had during this time found a number of friends, and by their means he was soon afterwards appointed English consul at Ostend, where he lived with his wife Elizabeth till they were both advanced in life. As an elderly couple they came back to Nottingham once more, and went to live in the sweet village of Wilford, on the opposite side of the silvery Trent. It was the peaceful green retreat that had beckoned him back to England from many a scene of foreign grandeur, and smiled across many a time of tumult and of battle. He and his wife both loved the Dutch home where they had so long lived, and when he built a house for himself in a thorough English village, he constructed it in the Dutch style, which indeed in his early youth had been the very height of fashion. Next to his own, behind the same trim garden and row of silvery poplars, he built one also for his sister Polly, who was then a widow. Alethea, after the death of her husband, had returned to Harwood Grange with her children, and devoted herself to them, endeavouring so to bring them up that they might love and serve God. She by this time had also gone to her rest; so also had most of those who have been mentioned in the previous history. Mistress Pearson did not live long after her return to England, and she was saved the misery of hearing the tragical death of her husband, who, with all his faults, had at all events loved her. In a desperate action with a Queen's ship, he with all his crew had been blown up, shortly after Deane had encountered him at the mouth of the Delaware.

The tomb of John Deane, Captain R.N., and of Elizabeth his wife, is to be seen on a little green promontory above the sparkling Trent and near the chancel of the parish church, where sweet strains of music, accompanying the sound of human voices and the murmurs of the river, are wont to mingle in harmonious hymns of prayer and praise. A more fitting spot in which to await in readiness for the last hour of life than Wilford can scarcely be imagined, nor a sweeter place than its church-yard in which the mortal may lie down to rest from toil till summoned by the last trump to rise and put on immortality.